THE
STERADIAN
GATE

A Novel By

NATHANIEL BLEVENS

FIRST EDITION

Book Cover Design by 100 Covers

Identifiers:
Library of Congress Control Number: 2024902304
ISBN 9798990033702 (Hardcover)
ISBN 9798990033719 (Paperback)
ISBN 9798990033726 (eBook)

For my children.

May you find the thrill of adventure
even in the darkest of times.

LUNARIA
NATION OF MARALDI
Northern Grasslands
Roris
Lake Aestatis
Veris River
Mincer
Kinsford
Brexel
Barlow Sea

Mt. Hadley
Fresnel Woods
Bonitatis River
Heraldrin
Lake Thera
Devon Falls
Berwyn Mountains
N
Bonitatis Farmlands
Capella

CONTENTS

Prologue

A thick fog hung in the air as the sun set over the horizon. It was a typical cold autumn evening, but the cold had never bothered Jerran Burke. He didn't think his brother Mason minded the cold either, but ever since they'd arrived at the edge of the woods, he'd been complaining about it. He even used his young son, Ethan, as an excuse to head home after only a half hour of metal detecting. Jerran knew better than to believe Mason was worried about Ethan catching a cold—chalking it up to Mason simply not wanting to be there. Watching them drive away, Jerran was glad they'd taken separate cars, allowing him more time to search.

He hated how Mason had taken Ethan home so quickly, making his nephew miss the thrill of the search. He shook his head, frustrated given how long they'd been planning this trip. The ability to see his nephew was becoming more rare, and he'd been looking forward to just spending time with them. While disappointed, he refused to be deterred. As a relic hunter, he'd been alone many times before and wasn't about to let his brother or some chilly weather ruin the day. It was time to refocus. He'd been hoping to unearth something, anything, from the Civil War era; an old cannon ball, part of a musket—maybe even gold.

Jerran continued through the forest, the smells of autumn surrounding him while the fallen leaves crunched with each footstep as he swept the metal detector back and forth. He enjoyed these metal detecting sessions as it not only got him away from the monotony of the day to day, but he found the sweeping motion to be therapeutic, something Mason never seemed to catch onto, always wanting to see artifacts which had already been discovered instead of making discoveries of his own.

It'd been a couple hours since they'd left and his fingers had numbed from the cold. There had been no squeaks or even a peep from the metal detector, proving this to be a stingy site, but the promise of finding any artifacts from the mid 1800s was a lure that kept him going.

Having already explored a couple older castles in Europe and searched for lost pirate treasure in Florida with Mason, his nephew, and nieces, it was now time to discover something new, something he could put the name Burke on. He hoped to be seen as a peer to great explorers and treasure seekers of the past that had found something of historical significance. If he could reignite the sense of adventure in Mason, all the better, as he'd need a trustworthy partner if the find was something big enough.

A branch snapped in the distance to his right and he stopped in his tracks to hear more clearly. Only silence greeted him and with as thick as the fog was, he couldn't make out anything beyond a few feet. Then the sound came again. He took a couple of steps towards whatever it was and a thick tree trunk come into view. He stopped again to listen, suddenly feeling as though he were being watched.

A light breeze swept past him, picking up fallen leaves, scattering them, and he squinted at the cold fog stinging his face. Then, in front of him, a shadow appeared, emerging from behind the thick tree trunk. Fear took over, and he turned, bolting the opposite direction. He had only made it a few dozen feet before turning back to see if he was being followed, only to find nothing. Whatever it was had disappeared back into the fog.

Not watching where he was going, his foot caught the edge of something, knocking him off balance. The metal detector went flying, and he tumbled, rolling, and smacked his back into something hard. He winced, taking a moment to catch his breath, and slowly sat up. His back throbbed, and he cursed at himself for not being in better shape; not able to tell if his chest pounded from the short sprint or the adrenaline.

He pushed himself to his feet and the sound of leaves crunching moved towards him. He froze, fixing his gaze on the noise; his heart pounding in his ears. Squinting into the fog, the same shadow appeared again. He considered running, but as the figure came closer, its shape took form. He exhaled, unaware he'd been holding his breath, and realized the shadow was just a deer. A chuckle escaped him. He couldn't believe a deer had him running like a fool through the woods.

The animal just stood a few feet off, staring at him, occasionally taking bites of grass and leaves. It chewed slowly, making him feel like it was judging him.

Annoyance flared, and he waved his hands at the animal. "Get out of here!"

Its head jerked up, trying to determine if the man was a threat.

Jerran reached over, grabbing his metal detector, turning it off and back on at full volume, causing a loud squelch. The startled animal jumped backwards, unsure what to make of the noise, and ran off.

"That'll teach you," he said, leaning back against a tree to help slow his breathing.

He took a deep breath of cool air and noticed he was standing in the middle of some old ruins. A brick wall stood just beyond where the deer had been grazing, standing about five to six bricks high, with a portion missing. It seemed he'd tripped over a brick protruding from the ground; presumably having tumbled from the wall many years prior. Moss had overtaken most of the construction and a large tree root had grown upwards through it, having caused the collapse. He followed the wall, not having to go far before it tapered off.

Who had built this place, and how long ago? How has no one discovered it yet? The odds of him getting any answers were slim, given how old the ruins looked; at least until he could get Mason to help him investigate. Just beyond the wall lay a pile of stones between what could have once been two pillars. They had long since fallen over; their remains stretching twenty or more feet.

It was apparent, whatever he had stumbled over was far older than anything Civil War era. He adjusted the settings on the metal detector, excited at the possibility of the find. He started sweeping it back and forth, walking towards the pile of stones, continuing to sweep the detector, hearing a squeaker come from below the pile when he neared. A rush of excitement hit him and he swept the detector a few more times, getting a repeatable signal.

Satisfied to its location, he knelt, putting the detector down and began moving stones aside. A couple proved heavy, but it was worth it when a glint of silver and blue caught his eye. He shoved a last stone to the side, leaning closer to the half-buried artifact and began digging it out with his hands, prying it from the dirt. He brushed away years of sediment, bringing it closer to take in the details and determine what it was.

Odd markings he'd never seen before were spread out evenly around the circular parameter. At its center was a blue stone with what looked like eight compass directions pointing away from it, and he could make out gears below a portion of glass. Regardless of the patina, much of the detail was still clearly visible, which could help him identify what it was with some research.

The blue stone at the center looked like a sapphire, but he was no geologist. He grazed the stone with his thumb, and a glow came from under it, flashing a moment, making him almost drop it in surprise. He suddenly felt heavy. Maybe the running was a bit much for him, he thought. He struggled to keep his eyes open, and his world went dark before he felt the pull of gravity, falling backwards into the leaves.

Inheritance

Ethan Burke looked up at an enlarged photo of his Uncle Jerran prominently displayed in the center of a table filled with different foods his uncle had enjoyed. He looked around, not recognizing most of the people paying their respects at the reception.

His Aunt Michelle sat in the living room on the couch; the look of shock still on her face that her husband was gone. Throughout the evening Ethan thought she looked out of place, as though she were trying to host a party, making sure everyone was enjoying themselves while the rest of the time she just stared off into nothing, wrestling internally with her new reality.

Ethan's mother, Ellena, had sat next to her for support since she'd arrived. They would sit quietly until a guest came up to greet them. An awkward silence would hang before the guest built up the courage to give their condolences. Some would share a story of how they knew Jerran or one of their favorite stories they had heard him talk about.

Ethan wasn't sitting very far away and could hear most of what was being said. It seemed the story of Jerran waking up alone in the middle of the forest ten years ago was the favorite for most. They would laugh and wonder why he was out there or how he even fell asleep in the middle of a forest at all. Everyone knew he wasn't one for drugs or drinking, so it was always a mystery.

Ethan had once asked his uncle why he never told anyone what had happened, but Jerran would simply grin, saying he never planned to say because he wanted their imaginations to run wild. Some of his friends used to joke that it was aliens who had abducted him, dropping him off at the wrong place.

Ethan smirked at the thought before feeling his phone vibrate in his pocket. He checked, seeing a text from the girl he'd taken to dinner a few days back. She had ghosted him until now, which piqued his curiosity.

In case it's not obvious, I don't think it's going to work between us,
but sorry to hear about your uncle.

Ethan rolled his eyes, putting the phone away as his father, Mason, took a seat next to him. "I saw that eye roll from across the room. Anything I should worry about, kiddo?" he asked, ruffling Ethan's short hair. His dad had always called him that, and he found it annoying. Even tried telling him to stop, but his dad continued anyway.

Ethan shook his head. "No, just the girl I took on a date last week breaking up with me during a funeral. Not sure if she meant to do that, but it seems like it."

"Dodged a bullet if she's trying to make that kind of statement."

Ethan sighed, looking over at the portrait of Jerran again. "It's weird having a funeral for him when they never found his body." He looked over at his aunt, who continued staring off into space. "It's also hard watching Aunt Michelle with all of this. She looks lost."

"I know, kiddo. I know." He paused, trying to find the right words. "It's going to take her time to get back a sense of normalcy. As for your uncle, I suppose we should consider ourselves lucky they found his phone and a shoe, of all things," the last couple words coming out in stutters. Ethan looked over, seeing his dad tearing up. He wasn't used to seeing him cry often, but understood the importance every time. He reached over, squeezing his dad's shoulder. Mason wrapped an arm around him, squeezing back. "Thanks, kiddo. I'm ok."

They sat in silence for a few more minutes, watching more guests leave. Only family remained as friends and colleagues had slowly left over the last hour. His dad had told him during his grandfather's passing that there really weren't words to help anyone during a time like this. People can feel awkward coming up with what to say, which is often why some will leave as quickly as they can. It wasn't to disrespect anyone. Many just didn't know how to deal with it.

Ethan's stomach growled, pulling him from his thoughts. He stood up. "I haven't had anything to eat today. I'm going to go grab a couple of biscuits. Maybe they'll cheer me up like they did for Uncle Jerran." He did his best to fake a smile.

Mason smiled back. "Your aunt wants us in the living room in a few minutes. Said something about wanting to give you and your sisters something from your uncle he wanted to pass on. We'll call you over shortly."

Ethan nodded, walking over to the table of food. He picked up a biscuit, taking a bite. Even when in mourning, his aunt made some of the best biscuits. Still, it didn't taste as good as it would under different circumstances. Someone hit his shoulder from behind, making him almost drop his food. He turned to glare, hearing his sister's voice.

"Hey bud!" said Lilly, wiping a tear from her eye. He noticed she wasn't exactly dressed the part, wearing a white sun hat, maroon knee length dress and a short white cardigan. She always had her own style, though.

"Did that make you feel better?" he asked, unamused.

She smiled. "Punching my brother? Yeah, it always makes me feel better. Thank you for asking." Her smile faded as she looked down at all the food. "I guess most people aren't hungry in these situations." Ethan nodded, taking another bite, and she raised an eyebrow at him. "Except for you, I see."

"I haven't eaten all day," he said, shrugging. "What do you expect?"

She sighed, not really having an answer. "Did you hear Aunt Michelle is considering staying with you guys at mom and dads for a few days?" He shook his head before she continued. "I think it's good. It'll keep her from being alone while she adjusts. I'll also get to see their dogs more often as she'll be bringing them."

"I'm sure Patches will enjoy having some other dogs to run around with."

"Yeah. He's getting up there in age. If he gets hurt playing with the puppies, you won't have to call a random vet. Just call me," she said, grinning.

"Yes. We're all very proud of you for finishing up your veterinary degree. You're just far more proud than the rest of us."

Ethan felt a smack on his other shoulder. "You two need to remember we're at a funeral reception. Not some happy party," said Aiza, his eldest sister. Ethan turned, looking at her with a mouth full of biscuit. "Show some respect for the deceased by showing some respect to each other." She shot a glare at each of them. Ethan shrugged, pointing a thumb towards Lilly, causing Aiza to roll her eyes. "I don't want to hear it with your mouth full. Come on. Mom sent me to get you two into the living room. They're starting." Aiza grabbed Lilly, pulling her away.

Ethan finished his bite before putting the remaining bit of biscuit back on the table and headed into the living room where his parents sat on the couch. Lilly and Aiza sat in chairs across from them. He headed towards the couch to sit next to his mom, but she stopped him.

"Your Aunt Michelle will be back in a moment. She went to get a couple of things and will need her spot back." Ethan knew it wasn't the time or place to argue, opting to take a seat on the floor between his sisters.

A few moments later, Michelle came from the hallway carrying a box and sat next to Ellena. "Your Uncle Jerran always said that if he were to pass before me, he would want me to give these items to the three of you." A tear rolled down her cheek as she picked up a book from the box. "Now, I don't understand everything that's in these, but he wanted to make sure you each got a specific one." She read the spine. "Ah. This one is for Aiza." Getting up from the couch, she handed Aiza the book.

"Thank you," Aiza said. She looked at the spine, reading the word *Research* that was handwritten. She opened the cover and started flipping through the pages.

Michelle picked up the second book, reading the spine. "This one is for Lilly." Grabbing a third book from the box, she walked over to Lilly and Ethan, handing Lilly one of them.

Lilly took it, "Thank you." She opened to the first page, seeing the words *Animal Compendium,* and her eyes lit up. She flipped through pages, seeing sketches of various animals with information about each of them. "Did he draw these himself?"

Michelle smiled. "Oh yes. He was always doodling something in these journals. We would go—" she stopped herself, thinking for a moment about the right words to use. "We would go on trips and see amazing things, doodling and documenting as we went. He wanted each of you to have a part of his work."

"Are these the journals I think they are?" Mason asked. Michelle nodded and smiled, making him shake his head with disapproval. "I'm not sure giving the kids this information is a great idea."

Ellena elbowed him in the side lightly. "They're all adults now. I think it's information they can handle." Ethan, Lilly and Aiza all looked up, curious about what their parents had known and never told them.

Mason sighed. "You're right." He looked over at them, still frowning slightly.

Michelle handed the last book to Ethan. There was a key tied to the bookmark dangling out of the bottom. He reached up and took it. "Thank you," he said, looking at the spine. Nothing was written but the leather cover had an embossed shape of an eight directional compass. He ran his hand over the cover, feeling the texture.

"Now," Michelle began, "You'll notice the key. It goes to a lock-box at the bank over at First and Madrona Way." Ethan lifted the key, examining it; the number ninety-one etched into it. She continued, "While Jerran may be giving the key to you, Ethan, he wanted to divide up his work among all three of you. He wanted to make sure you worked together on this and continued with it if you found the time."

Aiza was the first to speak. "What was his work? What are these journals?"

Michelle shook her head. "All I will say is that Jerran and I had many adventures over the last ten years. We both hoped these journals would bring you some as well." The three of them looked up at her questioningly. "After you've read them, you'll better understand."

Ethan looked over at his sisters and down at the journal he'd received. He stood up, walked over to his aunt, and gave her a hug. "Thank you."

She smiled, and another tear rolled down her cheek. "You're quite welcome." She saw him look down at the journal again and could tell he wanted to see what was in the lockbox. "Jerran would have loved to see your enthusiasm. Why don't you run off to the bank and see what's in the box. It closes in an hour." She saw the hesitation in his eyes. "Go on. I won't be offended."

Ethan looked over at his parents, making sure they gave their approval and was happy to see them both nod, regardless of his dad's apprehension.

Aiza stood up. "Why don't I give you a ride over to the bank?"

"Thanks," he said, looking at Lilly to see if she was coming as well.

She shook her head. "I'll stay here to talk with Aunt Michelle a bit longer and grab a ride with mom and dad."

Aiza walked over, giving Michelle a hug. "I'll drop by and see you at mom and dads in a couple days." Michelle nodded, her eyes still watering.

As they left, their dad called after them, "Drive safe! No one else does."

Aiza looked back at him. "I always do."

***

Neither Ethan nor Aiza spoke much on the way to the bank. Aiza had gone into autopilot while Ethan flipped through the pages of his new journal. It was a short drive and before he knew it, Aiza had pulled up to the bank, parking. "Anything interesting in there?" she asked.

He shook his head. "Nothing that I understand. There are some sketches of animals, some odd symbols, and a lot of information that I really don't know what it means."

"Well, we're here. Let's go in and see what he left you."

Ethan closed the journal and got out of the car. He waited for Aiza to join him before heading towards the entrance.

As they walked into the lobby, a clerk was waiting and greeted them. "Welcome. What can I do for you?"

Ethan pulled out the key, holding it up. "I'm hoping to get to the safe deposit boxes."

The clerk nodded. "Ah. Right this way." She pointed the two of them off to the right, walking around the desk.

"Follow me," she said, heading down the hall. She led them to a door, opening it for them. "Can I see the key, please?" Ethan handed it to her. "Ninety-one," she read out loud, walking over to the box. She pulled out her master key, inserting it into one of two keyholes before doing the same with Ethan's. The two keys were twisted to the right simultaneously, and she pulled open the small metal door. She removed a metal box from within, bringing it over to a table in the center of the room. "If you wish, you can lock the door behind me after I leave. There are complimentary bags here on the table if you need to take anything with you. You're welcome to stay as long as you need, but please come see me at the desk before leaving, so I can help put the box back and return your key."

"Thank you," Ethan said. She nodded, pocketing the master key, and left the room, closing the door behind her. He looked over at Aiza. "Well, that was official sounding. I wonder how many times she has to say that in a day?" Aiza shrugged.

He looked at the box and opened the metal lid, revealing a clear plastic case laying inside, holding what looked like a rounded compass with eight directional points. He pulled the case out and looked closer at the object. "What...is...this?" He picked it up, examining it.

The object was circular, with a four and a half inch diameter, having a slightly raised silver outer ring with strange symbols etched into it he didn't recognize. At the very center of the compass, a dark blue sapphire about the size of a thumbprint had obsidian creeping up around its sides, as though it had been dipped into a liquid version of the volcanic glass before being attached. Under the compass, connecting the directional points, was a circle of frosted glass. Then, along the southern points, was a thicker glass with internal gears showing from underneath.

Just inside the outer ring along the top were five emblems etched at the mid to northern compass points. The emblem at the western point looked to be a sword. The one at the northwest was a tree overlooking the water, with some land in the distance. At the north was a compass. The northeastern point had a wolf creature with spikes protruding out of the back of its head. The last emblem was a helmet.

He flipped it over to see if there was anything on the back, but other than some patina, there was nothing noticeable. He flipped it back over and looked at Aiza. "Ever seen anything like this before?"

She shook her head, "Never have, but it's beautiful. Looks old too, but could be a replica made to look old. Hard to say without examining it further."

"Do you recognize any of these symbols?" he asked, pointing.

"No. None of these looks familiar, but I'm no expert."

He squinted, trying to make out the detail of the emblems. "I mean, it looks like a compass, but it doesn't work like one. There's no needle." He tilted and turned the object in an attempt to see if there was a gyroscopic mechanism, but nothing moved.

Aiza peered down at it. "Might be helpful to take it out of that case and do a scan on it at my lab in the morning. We'd get a much better view of those symbols. Then I can copy them over and do a search. See if I can find anything about them. Maybe figure out if they're part of a language."

"Yeah. That sounds good," he said, reaching for one of the bags on the table. He put the object in and closed it, using the rope at the top to cinch it shut.

"I've got work in the morning. You good to head out?" she asked.

"Yeah, I'm all done." He closed the lid to the deposit box.

After the clerk had returned their key, Aiza dropped Ethan off at their parent's home as he was still living with them while he figured out what he wanted to do with his life. As he got out of the car, he leaned back down, looking at his sister. "Thanks for the ride. I'll come by your lab to see you in the morning."

She smiled. "See ya, bud."

He closed the door and waved as she backed out of the driveway and went inside. Their blue merle mini–Australian Shepherd came hobbling around the corner with his entire rear end wagging. He crouched, giving the dog a pat on the side. "Hey Patches! How has your night been?" The dog jumped up at him, licking his face. He realized quickly he was the first one home and opened the back door to let Patches out. He stood at the door, letting the cool breeze of the night air out the room.

Ethan left the door cracked so Patches could get back in and headed upstairs. It was getting late, and he was tired after the emotional drain of the day's events. Opening his bedroom door, he flipped on the light and tossed the bag with the object onto his bed before taking a seat on its edge. He glanced over to his nightstand at a picture of him with his dad and uncle, and leaned over, grabbing it. He looked at the photo, remembering the night.

The photo had been taken three years prior, after completing one of the many escape rooms they used to do together. His dad always told him the puzzles helped create critical thinking skills. His uncle would usually laugh and add that those with critical thinking capabilities were an endangered species. Ethan never knew if he was joking or not, but the memory made him smirk. He let out a sigh and looked over at the bag next to him.

He grabbed it, loosening the rope and pulled out the case with the object in it. He studied it for a second, but the glare from the bedroom light made it difficult to see any of the detail. Pulling the case's lid off, he picked up the object. His sister was right. It was a beautiful piece. He traced his thumb along the side of the outer ring, moving it slightly. He raised an eyebrow, wondering if it could go full circle, and began turning it clockwise. Other than a satisfying clicking noise, nothing happened.

He held it up closer, looking at the embedded stone. The blue gem was smooth until it got to the obsidian surrounding it, where it became bumpy, like the waves of a choppy ocean. He slid his finger across the top of it and saw a flash of light for a second, making him nearly drop it in surprise.

He brought the object closer, squinting to see if he'd actually seen what he thought he had. The frosted glass under the compass lit up again, but this time brighter. He backed his face up and the light pulsed, intensifying in brightness. Then suddenly, he felt heavy, as though all his remaining energy had been drained. He fell backwards on his bed, no longer able to keep his eyes open and the object fell from his hand, hitting the floor with a thud.

Summer

Ethan woke to the sound of knocking at his bedroom door. He stretched and slowly sat up, seeing Lilly standing from the hallway, judging him with one of her hands resting on her hip. "Really?" she asked. "You slept in your nice clothes?" He shrugged. It was too early for him to deal with his sister's judgmental stares. She rolled her eyes. "Get yourself ready. Dad's already making some coffee. Looks like you could use some." She headed downstairs, leaving him to his thoughts.

Ethan was still groggy, but remembered a flash before passing out. He quickly looked around himself for the object, unable to find it until he leaned forward, seeing it peek out from under his bed. Reaching down, he picked it up, but it wasn't glowing or flashing. He pressed his thumb against the sapphire, holding it in place for a few seconds. There was still no reaction from it, making him wonder if he'd dreamt it.

He got up, tossing the object onto his bed and changed clothes, putting on a clean collared shirt and some deodorant. He grabbed the journal and headed downstairs. His parents and Lilly were sitting around the table. Patches happily ate his breakfast nearby, displaying his odd habit of taking a mouth full of food from his bowl and chewing it a few feet away before returning for more.

Ethan's dad, Mason, looked up, seeing he had joined them. "How'd you sleep, kiddo? You looked pretty zonked when we came home last night."

Ethan smiled, "Yeah. Everything from yesterday must have just wiped me out." He grabbed a mug from the cabinet, filling it with coffee and took a seat next to Lilly. He noticed she was on her phone shopping for shoes. "You're needing another new pair, huh?"

She gave a grunt of annoyance before answering. "There were a few nervous pets the other day that messed all over my last pair. I'm taking mom's advice and getting some water-resistant ones this time."

Their mom, Ellena, sat across from her and smiled. "You should have listened to me sooner. Then you wouldn't be in the position of having to buy another pair so soon."

Ethan took a long sip of coffee, getting a look from Lilly, "You're lucky Aiza's not here. She'd have punched you in the shoulder for that noisy slurp."

He smirked, "Well, she's not, so I don't have to worry about being loud."

Ellena stared at him for a second, clearing her throat to get his attention. "There're limits on what the rest of humanity is willing to listen to. I realize you're an adult now, but you need to start acting like one too. Use your manners," she reminded, giving him a hard stare.

"I know. I know," he said. His phone buzzed on the table and he glanced down, seeing it was a text from Aiza, scowling after reading it.

Can't meet up today. Plan for tomorrow.

"Who was that?" Lilly asked.

"Aiza. We were supposed to meet up today to scan that thing Uncle Jerran left me, but she's apparently too busy now."

Lilly raised an eyebrow, "Something he gave you that's scannable? Do show."

Ethan shook his head. "I honestly don't know what it is. The thing looks like a compass but isn't used like one. Hopefully, when I take it to Aiza's lab tomorrow, we'll get some answers. In the meantime, I've been looking through this," he said, holding up his journal, flipping through the pages. "What all was in yours?"

Lilly put her phone down and leaned over the table excitedly. "I was looking through it last night and it's basically an encyclopedia of animals. Some of which shouldn't exist, but he documents them like they do—even has drawings of them. I've never seen reports or photos of them before. One even looked cute enough that I kind of want one as a pet. It was a zem...zemp?" she shook her head. "I can't remember, but it looks like a kangaroo mixed with a fox. I'd buy one in a heartbeat if they existed."

"Sounds right up your alley," he said, flipping through more pages. Sketches of animals, a map of an area he didn't recognize, different symbols and lots of documentation flipped by. A loose piece of paper fell onto the table. He stopped and picked it up, unfolding it. It looked to be written by his uncle.

To whomever has found this journal,

Inside you will find detailed notes on another dimension called Lunaria. The people of Lunaria are technologically at least a century behind us. A few years ago, a group calling themselves the Kriva Rasturna started invading from another dimension called Primula. They are a malevolent group, and I fear their goal is the destruction and enslavement of the Lunarians. Should you find the set of symbols to visit the other dimensions, avoid Primula at all costs.

Jerran

Suddenly finding himself concerned, questions swirled in his mind. Different dimensions seemed a bit of a stretch. He shook his head, dismissing the note as his uncle trying to come up with some kind of fictional story. He folded the paper and put it back in the journal, glancing over at the clock on the microwave. It was just past nine. "I'm going to head over to the library and see if I can dig up anything on the object I got from Uncle Jerran." He got up, rinsing out his mug and put it in the dishwasher.

His mom looked up. "What time are you planning to be home?"

"Not sure. I'm just wanting to see if the library has any information." He grabbed the journal, stuffing it into his backpack. "See you guys later," he said, heading out the door. The library was only a couple of blocks away, and it was a pleasant morning. The cool breeze felt good and the view of the trees changing colors during autumn was a great start to his day.

Regardless of the beautiful scenery, his mind kept going back to the night before. Had the object actually lit up? Did he pass out because of it, or was he just tired after the day? If he had passed out from the object, how did it do that? He didn't feel any different this morning. Then that weird note. The thoughts kept racing in his mind and he could only hope to find some of his answers at the library.

He took a deep breath of fresh air to calm himself a bit. He had never been a fan of research; especially online. "Behind you," a voice shot out at him. He turned, seeing a jogger out with their dog. Ethan moved to the side as they went by. There weren't as many people out today as there usually were. A drop of water hit him on the head; rain clouds had quickly taken over the sky. He picked up the pace to beat the rain, happy the library was just across the street.

Jogging across the road, he reached the awning over the front doors as the downpour began. He went inside and the rain was hitting the windows hard enough to sound as though the glass would break. He noticed a couple of figures running to their cars outside; his view, blurred by the deluge hitting the glass.

"Welcome!" a middle-aged receptionist called to him. His head jerked towards her, not expecting the greeting. "Good timing on getting here when you did. Let me know if you need any help finding anything."

"Actually," he said, "I was wondering if you had any books on old artifacts."

"Are you in a college class writing a report?" she asked. "I'm not used to getting requests like that and I've gotten two in one day."

"No, I was just curious—wait. Who else is looking for ancient artifacts?"

"Not artifacts per se," she said. "There was a girl about your age looking for books on magic portals a few minutes ago. I pointed her to the science fiction section, but she didn't seem happy with that. Best I could do is point her to the historical section, considering we don't have a section on magic. As for you, your best bet is the archeological section. It's around the side here, down about halfway on your right," she said, pointing her thumb behind her.

Ethan nodded. "Thanks for the help." The receptionist smiled, going back to checking in returns. He found the library nearly empty as he walked to his section, only seeing a couple people on the computers and a kid sitting up against the wall watching something on a tablet. When he reached the archeology section, he found a pile of books on the ground with a couple opened. He heard someone on the other side of the aisle rummaging through books on the shelf.

He started scanning the titles of shelved books, looking for something that would pop out at him. It took a couple minutes before one caught his attention. *Ancient Artifacts and Relics.* He pulled the heavy book from the shelf, feeling its weight. It was too heavy to read where he was, so he took it to one of the tables, taking a seat. The book was old, giving off an almost earthy smell with a bit of must. The decorative light brown cover had significant wear on the corners.

He opened it, turning to the contents page. The book divided the artifacts up by the location where they'd been found. He didn't have any idea when or where his object had been located, and this book was written well before his uncle would have come across it. He turned to the first chapter and started flipping through the pages, happy to find each artifact had a quick sketch and description. There were notes of where, who, and how each had been found, giving him a tinge of optimism.

Ethan continued to flip through hundreds of pages, occasionally stopping at one that caught his eye. Growing up, he'd watched many adventure movies and played various video games with adventure narratives. The thought of going on a quest to find some artifact had always been something he had hoped to do one day. It was also a dream of his father's, which is why some of the family vacations ended up being fun treasure hunts where, of course, nothing had been discovered. This would be different, though, as Ethan already had the artifact. Now the problem was finding out what it was and where it came from.

He was so lost in his thoughts that he nearly missed a sketch that made him stop. It displayed a front view of a circular object with an interior ring that had markings around the parameter. In the center was an oval with compass directions protruding outward from it. While it wasn't exactly what his artifact looked like, it was close enough that it could be it. He scanned the page for any information finding *The Key* written above it. Ethan's eyebrows furrowed. It certainly didn't look like any key he had seen before. There was a brief passage under the name.

Originally found in 1842 by Cairbre O'Farrells. It was discovered just west of Binghamstown, Ireland, near Cross Lake. Cairbre O'Farrells' descendants provided a sketch of the artifact to the Irish Constabulary in 1843, after he had gone missing. Their report to the authorities simply stated, Cairbre had been holding what they called 'the key', when it glowed. They were frightened, leaving Cairbre alone with it as they ran from the home. When they returned minutes later, both he and the key were missing. The only thing found was a circle burned into their wooden flooring—

Books slammed down on the table in front of him, jolting him from the reading. He jerked his head up, seeing a girl about his age wearing a teal sweater and jeans taking a seat across from him. He froze, finding her attractive with beautiful green eyes and naturally red hair pulled back into a ponytail. Time almost stood still, as he was unsure what to do or say for a moment before she finally spoke.

"Sorry," she said. "I didn't mean to drop them like that. They were heavier than I thought. Do you mind if I join you?"

Still coming back to his senses, he couldn't help but stare into her eyes. She looked at him, waiting for a reply until eventually raising her eyebrow, "Are you...ok?"

He finally snapped out of it, having stared longer than he'd wanted. "Yes, of course. Feel free," he said with an awkward smile.

He half raised himself out of his chair, extending his hand out to shake. "I'm Ethan."

Her eyebrow stayed raised as she sized him up. "A handshake, huh?"

His smile faded a bit as he looked at his hand and back at her. "Yeah…" he said, slowly sitting back down.

She quickly leaned forward, grabbing his hand and shook it. "I was only teasing," she said smiling, "I'm Summer. Good to meet you."

He grinned. "A bit old school, I know." He sat, glancing at the pile of books in front of her. "What are you researching?"

"I…uh—try not to judge."

"What? An old school guy like me judging what you're researching? Unlikely," he said, still displaying a goofy smile.

"You have a point." She took in a deep breath. "I'm researching…magic…portals." She squinted her eyes, pausing for a second, waiting for his reaction. He seemed unfazed, allowing her to relax a bit. "About a month ago, I saw a flash of light near Fox Run Lake. I'm trying to figure out what caused it, but I seem to only find what it wasn't. It wasn't lightning, as there wasn't a storm. It wasn't a lamppost lining the path. Every time I look online for answers, I always seem to end up on sites saying the only thing it could have been was a UAP. Which, that's not it as it wasn't flying. It was just a flash of light."

"Fox Run Lake?" His smile finally faded. "Did you see anything other than a flash of light? Were there any people? Any sounds that went with it?"

She sat up in her chair, tilting her head slightly. "Did you see the light near the lake too?"

He looked down, letting out a long sigh. "My uncle died last month near that lake. Police have no idea what happened to him. They haven't even found his body."

"I'm so sorry for your loss," she said empathetically. "Thinking back. I don't recall hearing anything odd at the time. No gunshots or anything like that."

He looked up at her and gave a half smile. "Thanks." He glanced down at the book, then back to her. "Actually, his passing is why I'm here. He gave me something and I'm trying to figure out what it is. I was just reading up on a relic that looks similar. I'm not sure if it's the same one as mine, but there's not much information here on it either. Just that a person who found it disappeared with it back in the 1800s."

Her eyes lit up seeing the sketch in front of him. "Looks promising. Is it possible a magical object may have created the light?"

He shrugged, "It's possible."

"You know, we seem to have some overlap in our research," she said. "We could team up our efforts. You can research artifacts and I can research magic. We might speed up finding our answers if we work together. What do you think?"

He smiled, pulling out his phone and took a photo of the page he was on. "I'm up for that."

"Great, let's get to it," she said, opening one of the books in front of her.

Over the next few hours, the two of them searched various books in the library, copying down any leads or bits of helpful information to move forward. They even tried finding answers online but only found posts from those with questionable reliability. Ethan plopped himself down in a chair next to her and began rubbing his temples. "You weren't kidding about everyone thinking your light revolves around aliens."

She smirked, "Told ya. It's exhausting. Not every unknown light is an alien."

"I didn't get much further regarding my artifact, either. I switched topics, researching the O'Farrells more, but they aren't tied to it beyond what's listed in that first book. There were thousands of stories of people disappearing but again, got pointed to aliens." He rolled his eyes. "I'm sure you can imagine what my search results looked like when I searched 'the key'. None of them were the one I was hoping to see. Plenty of locksmiths, though."

She let out a laugh. "I'll bet." She flipped around a book she was reading and pointed to a paragraph halfway down the page. "You'll be happy to know I think I may have found something. It says here there are legends of an ancient magic that open a door between worlds. When opened, the door looks like a ball of light that flashes before disappearing."

He lowered his hands. "You think there was someone in the park using magic to go between worlds?"

"I think it's the best lead I've gotten over the last few hours."

He pulled his phone out, looking at the time. It was nearing four in the afternoon, and they had skipped lunch. His stomach growled. "I can't believe how long we've been here," he said, pausing, trying to put together the next sentence carefully in his head. "I know I'm hungry and I'm willing to bet you are, too. Want to join me for an early dinner? My treat."

Summer pulled out her phone, snapping a photo of the paragraph she had found. "Are you asking me out on a date?" she asked, looking up at him with a smile.

He grinned, "Yeah, I guess I am."

She closed the book in front of her. "Good. I'm starving. What did you have in mind?" she asked, walking the book back to the shelf, replacing it.

Ethan had followed her. "There's a nice café across the street that has a variety."

"Perfect," she said, looking out the windows as they crossed the lobby. "Even looks like the rain stopped."

"Good. I didn't bring a coat today," he said, reaching the entry and opening the door for her. The air was still cool, and the smell of ozone hung in the air from the storm. They crossed the street, and he opened the door of the café for her.

A bell chimed and the smell of freshly baked bread greeted them before the hostess did. "Party of two?"

Ethan nodded, "Yes, please."

The hostess smiled and waved her hand off to her right to seat them. She placed two menus down on their table. "Your waiter will be with you shortly." She smiled, walking back to the front as they took their seats across from each other.

"So...when you're not researching strange artifacts, what do you do with your free time?" she asked.

"Oh, I'm working on a three-year plan. Trying to figure out what I want to do with my life. Working part-time, but you know how places have been cutting hours."

"Try not to judge, but I'm still living with my mom. Feels like you need three jobs just to afford a studio apartment anymore, even in our small town."

"I can't judge. I'm still living with mine, too." He watched her grin and found it infectious. "You've got an incredible smile."

She blushed. "Anything other than work and research?"

"Uh huh. Well, other than those, I enjoy learning about history. I sketch sometimes. I always had fun hanging out with friends, but we've had less time to hang out recently with most of them moving out of town. Makes it difficult. What about you?"

"I like music, specifically orchestral with violin solos. I never really had a group of friends I could depend on. Girls can be pretty mean sometimes, and I generally find it hard to talk to people. Except with you, it seems."

"Must be my PhD in public speaking," he said with a goofy grin.

She cracked a smile. "That must be it."

They looked over the menu a moment before Ethan broke the silence. "What makes you so interested in that light at the park?" Summer put her menu down, becoming more somber. She was about to say something when the waiter arrived.

"Hello. My name is Tom and I'll be your waiter for today," he said, placing glasses of water in front of them. "What can I get for you?" Ethan motioned to Summer to have her go first.

She quickly scanned the menu one more time before deciding, "I'll go with the turkey and ham sandwich, please."

"And for you?" the waiter asked.

"I'll go with the club. Thanks," Ethan said, handing the waiter his menu. The waiter nodded with a smile, heading off to put the order in.

Ethan looked over at her, concerned. "You seem a bit down. Not exactly the reaction I was hoping for on a date."

She nervously adjusted herself in her seat. "Now that we've gotten a chance to know each other a bit...there's more to my search than just finding out what a light was." She tried to figure out where to best start her explanation. "It's my brother, Alex," she finally said. "He's been missing since I saw that light."

"Missing? Have you gone to the police?" he asked.

She nodded, "My mom did, yes, but they haven't been able to find anything which pushed me to start my own investigation." She took a sip of water, taking the time to recall the details. "I'm sure you remember the constant drama of high school. Well, Alex had had a bad day. Something about his friend circle," she said, trying to recall. "I had taken him to the park to relax, thinking maybe just getting him away from things and being able to talk would help most."

Ethan hung on every word as she continued, "While we were there, I saw this flash of light and the next thing I know he's gone. There are more details I'm not ready to get into just yet, but the light is the only clue I have as to what's happened to him."

"You believe the light was some kind of portal then?" he asked, processing the new information she'd provided.

"Yeessss..." she said slowly, waiting for him to laugh at her.

"That makes our work a bit more difficult. We're not getting very far simply researching lights and portals. We keep getting pointed to science fiction when we need science fact."

"You believe me?" she asked, shocked as she realized he was taking her seriously.

"I believe you believe what you saw. I think our next move should be to search the park. It's been a month, but maybe there's still something there. Something the police may have missed. I doubt they'd be looking for any signs of portals, though."

"Our...next move?" she questioned. "You're still willing to help me find some answers?"

Ethan sat up straight in his chair. "Of course. You believe you saw something enough to cause you to start your research. Your brother's missing. Police aren't finding any clues about what happened to him. Sounds to me like you're needing help. So yeah, I'm going to help you find some answers. Maybe I'll get some answers about my uncle as well."

She smiled warmly at him. "Thank you. It means a lot."

He smiled back, "Least I could do, but we'll probably need to exchange contact info. What's your number?"

"Oh, so that's your ploy," she teased. "Might need my full name, too. It's Summer McKeown." She gave him her phone number, watching him enter the information into his phone.

"Alright, I think I got it," he said, texting her his name. "There. Now you have my number too." Her phone buzzed. "I've already got plans to meet up with my sister in the morning. She's a bit of a science geek. Works at a lab. We're going to scan the relic and hopefully get some answers. Are you good with meeting at the park in the afternoon? Say around one o'clock?" The waiter returned, putting their food in front of them with a nod before leaving.

"That works great," she said, resting her elbow on the table to hold up her chin. She stared at her food for a moment. "All this talk, I'm not even that hungry anymore. I know the whole portal thing sounds crazy. Not even my mom believes me about it. She doesn't know what else to do other than wait for the police to find something." She looked up at him. "I have to ask. Why are you willing to help me with as crazy as it all sounds?"

"Oh, you know...a beautiful girl, lost in research, needing help. Seems straightforward," he said with a shrug.

She shook her head, blushing, "That can't possibly be the only reason."

His smile faded. "You're right. No, my parents always taught that if you see someone needing help and you're able, then you should help them. Doing a bit of research when I'm already researching? Seems like the least I can do."

"Your parents sound nice," she said.

He smirked, "Oh, they can get on your nerves like any other parents."

She leaned forward slightly. "Not to get more serious, but as annoying as parents can be, appreciate them while you still have them around. I lost my biological parents when I was a kid."

"I thought you said your mom didn't know what to do about your brother?"

"That's my adoptive mother," she replied. "Alex and I were taken into the foster system when we were kids. We got bounced around from house to house for about a year until we landed with them." She sat back in her seat, reflecting on the memory. "We got lucky. Many kids in the foster system never find their 'forever home'. Our adoptive parents couldn't have kids of their own and they loved us enough to adopt." She took a sip from her water, watching his reaction. "Didn't mean to hit you with my life story." She wanted to switch topics to lighten the mood. "You said you enjoyed learning about history. What started that for you?"

She had caught him with the question while his mouth was full of sandwich. He swallowed the bite in a rush and took a sip of water. "Where do I start?" he said, clearing his throat. "My dad and uncle, the one who recently passed...they would always take me on mini adventures. It started with camping and eventually evolved into archeological searches and treasure hunts. We would go to beaches along the east coast and forests all over the country doing metal detecting. We would go two to three times a year, but the most we ever found were some old iron nails. Never treasure, but it didn't stop the sense of adventure. When I got older, they would take me to escape rooms. Have you ever done one?"

She shook her head. "No, but I've heard about them."

He nodded. "Most are fun, but I wish we could have had a bit more time to figure things out. There's no treasure at the end, so the fun is figuring out the puzzles."

Summer's phone buzzed on the table. She glanced down, seeing it was a call. "It's my mom. Give me just a sec," she said, answering it. "Hi mom...I've been at the library all day...well I'm...yeah...yeah...I'll be home in a few minutes...ok...love you mom. Bye." She hung up, putting the phone down with a sigh. "I'm sorry. My mom is—well...with my brother missing, she's wanting me—"

He held up his hand. "Don't worry about it. I understand."

"Thank you," she said, getting up.

Ethan pulled out his wallet, putting cash on the table for their meal. He looked out the window at the sunset. "At least it's not raining like it was this morning." They left the café feeling a chill in the evening air.

She looked over at him. "Thank you for everything today."

He smiled at her, "Of course. I'm looking forward to seeing you tomorrow."

She smiled back. "I'll give you a call when I'm at the lake. Night."

"Night."

She was still smiling as she turned and started walking the opposite direction he needed to. She pulled out her phone, putting it up to her ear. "Hi mom. I'm on my way."

He turned to head home but could still hear her in the distance, "I met a guy today...yes...I like him."

He smiled.

S.E.A.L.

Ethan rolled over in his bed, hitting the top of his alarm clock as it blared at him. His hand lazily dropped to the side of the bed, knocking something off the nightstand, causing a muffled thud as it hit the carpet. He cracked his eyes open; everything remaining blurry for a few seconds. As his vision cleared, he found himself peering down at the relic his uncle had given him. His eyes shot open, suddenly excited to take the object to his sister's lab but also at getting to see Summer again.

He grabbed his phone, seeing if maybe Summer had texted him this morning already, but his hopes quickly faded when no new messages were waiting. He considered texting her a good morning message, but thought better of it. They had only been on a single date, and he didn't want to come off the wrong way. Besides, there were other things he needed to focus on.

Swinging his feet out from under the covers, he sat up and brought up the photo he had taken of the sketch from the library. He hopped off his bed and grabbed the relic off the floor to compare it. He shook his head in disbelief, finding that aside from detail work, they looked practically identical.

He sat on his bed, grabbing the journal from his nightstand, hoping maybe there were answers he may have missed. He flipped to where he had left off yesterday, seeing a sketch of a small creature that looked similar to what Lilly had described to him yesterday; the word *Zemper* written above it. This must have been his uncle's main field journal, with the others being written later to categorize the different types of information.

He turned the page, finding a set of seven symbols sketched at the top he recognized from the relic. The word *Lunaria* had been scribbled above them with some notes below.

Will need one of the keys to open The
Steradian Gate between worlds / dimensions.
We live in the Delphinium dimension.
Dimension glyph combinations on back page.

He immediately flipped to the last page to see how many dimensions his uncle had visited, only to find it had been torn out; uneven bits of paper jutted out from the binding where it used to be. "Well crap," he said, looking annoyed. He flipped back to the glyph combination for Lunaria and took a photo with his phone. "One of the keys," he read out loud.

Picking up the relic, he took notice of the outer ring, rotating it clockwise, and hearing the satisfying clicking as it moved with little resistance. He held his breath, expecting something as it came full circle, but only found disappointment when nothing happened. He sighed, grabbing his nearby backpack and put both the relic and journal in it before glancing at his clock. It was near ten in the morning already. He chastised himself for sleeping in and texted his sister. Hopefully, she was still ok with having him come over to her lab today. He got ready for the day, putting on a dark grey t-shirt and pulling on some jeans. His phone buzzed with her response, confirming she was still expecting him.

He hurried down the stairs, tossing his backpack onto a chair at the table. "He lives!" his mom joked from the table. A plate of freshly baked muffins sat on the counter. Without hesitating, he took one and started inhaling it. "Hey! Slow down on that," she said. "I don't need to be doing the Heimlich on my son today." He quickly poured a glass of milk, chugging it before returning the gallon back to the fridge. She looked at him curiously. "Why are you in such a hurry this morning?"

"I'm heading over to Aiza's lab. We're going to scan that thing Uncle Jerran gave me. After that, I'm going over to Fox Run Lake to meet up with Summer. We're going to look for clues to what might have happened to her brother."

"Who's Summer?" she asked. "I haven't heard of Summer before."

"I met her yesterday at the library. Then...I took her on a date," he said, smiling.

"A date!?" she asked, grinning from ear to ear. "When am I going to meet this girl?"

Ethan groaned. "I honestly don't know. Right now, I'm focusing on helping her find her brother. From what she's told me, the police haven't found any clues. I figure I could help her look around the park where he went missing. Which brings me too—"

His mom cut him off. "You need to borrow the car. Don't you—wait. Did you say missing brother?"

"Yes," he said. "Police already know. Can I please borrow the car?"

"I'm not working today, so that's fine. But—" she paused.

He looked at her, pleading, "But?"

She smiled. "I want you to bring that girl over. I'll make a nice dinner and we won't harass her...too much." He didn't look amused as she continued, "I'll leave the baby photo scrapbooks on the shelf. I promise."

He rinsed out his glass, not willing to make any promises. "I'm not sure about tonight, but I'll bring her by when I can. We literally just met yesterday."

"We'll set a day so you can formally invite her," she pressed.

He grabbed his backpack off the chair and walked over to his mom, giving her a kiss on the cheek, "Love ya, mom. Thanks."

"Love you, Ethan. Be safe," she yelled after him as he took the car keys and headed out the door.

***

Ethan pulled up to Aiza's research laboratory. The sun glared off the large windows of the second floor, but it was the radio satellite dish extending from the roof that caught his attention. He parked the car and grabbed his bag, heading in. The words Science, Engineering, Astronomy Laboratories were above the main entrance with a S.E.A.L. logo plastered on the double doors that slid open. No matter how many times he visited, he never expected the cold air from inside the lab that greeted him. It didn't matter what time of year it was. It was always cold inside.

Walking up to the security checkpoint, the guard sitting behind the desk looked up at him. "How can I help you?"

"I'm here to see my sister, Aiza Burke."

The guard nodded. "Let me check your backpack. Just need to make sure there aren't any weapons." Ethan handed him his pack, and the guard opened it, rummaging for a second before zipping it back up and handing it back. "I'll give Aiza a call letting her know you're here. You can take a seat if you want."

"Thanks," Ethan said. He looked around the main lobby of the lab as he waited. One wall displayed a timeline showing various photos with information on S.E.A.L's first robotics creation from over a decade ago to what they were currently working on with early concept designs from their engineering department. Then in the middle of the main walkway was a scale model of the radio dish on the roof with the Drake Equation printed on the front of the stand.

Aiza came around the corner in a hurried walk, wearing her usual white lab coat and black slacks. "Thanks Mike! I've got him from here," she said with a wave. The security guard waved Ethan through. "I just took lunch," she said, "so I have a little under an hour to scan this thing and it's going to take at least half that. Let's get moving."

"Alright," he said, following her down the corridor. He almost had to jog to keep up as they took a hallway off to the left. There were many rooms they passed where he could see groups working together on various projects. He had slowed for a second as they passed a window where a robotic arm moved to grip a handle off a table.

Aiza noticed the sound of his footsteps had stopped and looked back, seeing her brother distracted. She rolled her eyes. "No time for sightseeing. We've got work to do," she said, tugging at his arm.

"What was that?" he asked.

"It's a project that's a long way off. It probably won't be ready to show for at least another year," she said. They took a short offshoot to the right that quickly dead ended into double doors. She pulled her badge from her lanyard, holding it up to the card reader, which unlocked the door with a click as the indicator light turned green. She pulled the door open, walking past offices on either side of them.

The room widened, having large windows with daylight pouring in. Off to his left sat a large laser scanner with two computer monitors.

Aiza pulled out a chair, taking a seat. "Alright, just logging in. Go ahead and put the device on the table here next to me. Ethan put his backpack on the table, unzipping it, and produced the relic, doing as she asked. She picked it up, looking at it closely. "This doesn't look very old. Maybe it's a piece of art handmade by someone? The scan should get us some answers." The scanner's main compartment door lifted, allowing her to put the relic inside. She returned to the keyboard, typing a name for the project scan before clicking "ok" on the monitor. The compartment door closed, and a low hum came from the machine.

"This scan will probably take a few minutes to finish up, but it's looking for more than just what it looks like. It will detect any invisible anomalies coming from it, such as radiation or frequencies. It also uses XRF spectrometer and microtomography technology. When it's done, it will tell us what elements this thing is made of while having completely rebuilt it digitally from the inside out. This is about as top-of-the-line as it gets," she said proudly.

Ethan flatly looked at her, "I heard, 'rebuilt digitally'."

She let out an exasperated sigh. "You just don't get how cool this thing is."

He shrugged. "As long as it can get me some answers on if this thing can do what I think it can, then I'll be happy."

"Oh? And just what do you think it can do?"

"Ok. Hear me out before making any snap judgement, but from what I've been reading, this thing may be able to transport people to other worlds." The look on her face told him she didn't believe him. "Look, even if it can't do that, it flashed the other night and I'm pretty sure it made me pass out." She still didn't look to be taking him seriously, which annoyed him. "I didn't make that up," he said, shooting her a look.

She suddenly looked concerned. "Hey. I'm not saying you're making anything up. It's just...it's more likely you passed out from being exhausted from everything that's happened. Stress takes on different forms for different people."

His shoulders sagged a bit. "Maybe," he said, "but yesterday, while I was at the library researching, I found an old book with a sketch of it. Looked nearly identical. There was a blurb saying some guy had found it before, back in, like, the 1800s, and he had disappeared."

She shook her head, "How did Uncle Jerran get it then? It looks more modern than anything because I'm not seeing the pitting or patina buildup one would expect from an object that's a hundred and fifty years old or more." She sat back in her chair. "I'll bet it's a reproduction." They heard a beep from the scanner and the hum stopped. The door to the compartment slid open, and she grabbed the relic from the machine, handing it to Ethan. "It's going to take a few hours for the computer to analyze everything. Are you heading back to the library while we wait for the results?"

"Actually, I'm meeting a friend at the park."

She stared at him flatly, "Ethan...aren't you a little old for a playground?"

"Not a playground. I'm meeting up with a girl I met yesterday."

Her eyes widened, and a mischievous grin crossed her face. "It's about time you got yourself a girlfriend. What's her name?" she prodded with an inquisitive tone.

"Her name's Summer and she's not my girlfriend. We've only been on one date and today doesn't count as the second," he said, cutting off her line of questioning.

"Oh, I think a stroll in the park can count as a second date," she said with a smirk.

He rolled his eyes. "I'm meeting her there to help look for any clues leading to her brother. He went missing. Not exactly a date topic."

Aiza glanced at the floor for a moment. "Ok, I get it. Not a date." She grabbed her thermos, taking a sip. "You're a good guy, Ethan. Hopefully she sees that too."

His phone buzzed in his pocket. He checked, seeing it was a text from Summer. He smiled. "Looks like she just got there."

She looked over at the clock. "Good. If I'm going to get to eat anything during my lunch, it'd better be now. I'll walk you out."

Ethan put the relic back in his backpack, zipping it closed. As they started walking, Ethan remembered he had taken a photo of the symbols from the journal. He pulled out his phone, bringing it up and handed it to Aiza. "I came across these symbols in my journal in a specific order. The same ones on the relic. If it's a doorway between worlds, it might be worth looking into them."

Aiza looked down at his screen. "Is there just the one world we can go to with this thing?" she said sarcastically. He didn't look amused. "Fine, I'll look closer at it once the scanner is done. I don't expect much from it, but I'll let you know the details."

He texted her a copy of the image as they reached the security desk. "Appreciate it."

Aiza reached over, giving him a hug. "Love you, little brother. Go help your girlfriend," she poked at him one more time.

He let out a sigh. "You're not going to stop with that. Are you?"

Fox Run Lake

Summer had texted that she'd be at the southern end of the lake. Luckily for Ethan, there was plenty of parking due to the morning joggers already having left for the day. Even so, there was still a bit of a walk to where she had told him to meet her. He grabbed his backpack and headed down the path, following the water.

It was a cloudy afternoon with a light breeze creating small ripples across the lake; the autumn leaves reflecting reds and yellows off the water's surface. Up ahead was a small, arched bridge where the lake sectioned off into a small inlet. It still amazed him how massive the lake was, as he could barely make out large sailboats docked at a private pier across from him.

He passed an older male walking their golden retriever, who was busy sniffing everything in sight, occasionally looking up when a squirrel ran by. Ethan smirked, knowing Patches wouldn't have any self-control and would run after them in a heartbeat, following the small creature half up a tree before falling to the ground in a vain effort.

Ahead of him, a large old oak tree stood in the distance; its branches jutting off in all directions, with a couple nearly touching the ground. It sat on a small hill surround by thick grass and there, under its branches, stood Summer, looking out over the water.

Her red hair almost matched the leaves above as it gently moved with the wind. He nearly called out to her to say hi when she pulled her phone out, touching the screen and put it to her ear. His phone buzzed in his pocket, and he checked, seeing she was calling him. He answered, "Hey Summer."

"How close are you?" she asked.

"Just a few seconds," he replied. "Look to your right."

She turned seeing him and disconnected the call. "Hey! Glad you made it," she said, walking over to him.

"Nice day," he said, jogging to meet up with her. He noticed she was wearing the same dark teal sweater from before. "You look warm."

"It's a favorite sweater." She chuckled nervously. "To be honest, I thought I had scared you off with the whole...'my brother's gone missing' spiel from yesterday. Most people wouldn't get involved at that point. So, thank you," she said, brushing her hair over her ear.

"Here to help," he said, looking around the area. "Is this where he disappeared?"

She nodded, pointing at a couple of oak trees behind them. "We weren't far from over there and were running towards where you just came from. There was a bright flash of light behind us right about here, and by the time I got to the parking lot, he was gone."

"Why were you running? I thought you two were here to relax from a bad day."

She looked away for a moment. "Not to sound more crazy, but remember when I said there were details I would go into later?" She turned back to him, deciding to trust him. "I...I thought I saw something that night. I'm not sure what it was...a shadow or a...a...creature. It freaked me out." She reflected on the memory. "I grabbed Alex's arm and told him to run. He must have seen it too, because he was running with me for a bit." She looked down, letting out a sigh, "I…just don't know what I saw. Then there was the light behind us and the next thing I knew, I was alone."

"Why not tell me this before?" he asked. "That's a pretty big detail."

"It's a lot to take in before the creature," she said. "Missing brother. Strange light. Possible portals. I didn't think you'd believe me, thinking I was some nut job."

"Fair, I guess," he said, pacing while he pieced the new information together. "Did you see any people or what caused the light? That could be helpful."

She shook her head. "My brother and I were running away from it and never saw what caused it. I know it was real. I just haven't found any proof yet."

"Alright, let's start looking. There must be something. Show me where you were at when the flash of light occurred."

She led him to a small bend that headed to the bridge and pointed to the ground. "I was about here when I saw my shadow. The light was intense enough that it was like a car's headlights right behind me."

He looked around the area, seeing some leaves blowing across the ground. "I'm still not sure where my uncle went missing from this park. The police found ones of his shoes and his phone the next day. My dad believes he was murdered."

"Alex isn't dead!" she snapped.

He shook his head. "Not what I meant. I'm simply saying I bet we find something of your brother's…assuming it didn't already get picked up by someone since." He looked down the path, thinking out loud, "It's too small of a path for a regular sized car. Maybe a golf cart? No…headlights from a golf cart wouldn't be bright enough."

"Sounds like you watch a lot of mystery shows," she said, regretting her tone earlier.

He chuckled. "I've seen a few."

"Hey...I'm sorry for biting your head off. I'm just—"

"You're worried. I get it," he interjected. "Nothing to apologize for."

"Thanks."

The path ahead of them forked, eventually rejoining in a large circle. To the left, the path led to some playground equipment surrounded by bushes and trees, while the path to the right led to the arched bridge going around the inlet.

He took in a deep breath of fresh air, letting it out. "That light could have been anywhere behind you, and it looks like we've got a decent amount of ground to cover. Should we start toward at the playground?"

"Sounds good to me."

As their investigation began, the two of them spread out, searching around and under playground equipment, bushes and trees. They found an occasional lost toy or piece of trash, quickly dismissing them from being relevant. When they moved along the path, a thick grouping of trees and bushes split the playground off from where Summer had stated she saw the light behind her, making the search beyond a certain point unnecessary as the foliage would have blocked any light from coming through. They regrouped where they initially met up and began combing the grass and nearby bushes for anything out of the ordinary, continuing along the main path. Hours passed with Ethan occasionally coming across something and calling Summer over to see if she recognized it, but it never turned out to be something she could tie back to her brother.

Eventually, they reached the bridge. Ethan walked up the concrete slope and leaned on the railing, looking out over the water. A steady breeze came off the lake, with the clouds turning pink and orange from the sun setting. Summer joined him frustrated, "We've been out here for hours and haven't found anything." She rested her arms on the railing, burying her face in her hands. It had gotten dark enough the lights along the path and bridge had turned on.

Ethan let out a sigh, looking over at her. "We still have to check the other side of the bridge there."

She looked over at him as he gestured his thumb to the grass on the other side. Her gaze focused on the trees and bushes waiting to be searched and didn't feel she had the patience to continue, feeling as though she had looked at a hundred trees since starting the search and was getting sick of them. Then, with the help of the added lights along the path, she noticed the grass in front of one of the trees looked to have a dark spot. She raised her head, squinting. "What is that?"

She pushed off from the railing, jogging over to the spot in the grass with Ethan right behind. The spot was inside a ten-foot circle burned into the grass. She knelt, touching the burned area. Pieces of charred grass broke away, crumbling between her fingers.

Ethan followed the circular area with his eyes. "This wasn't made by hand. No way someone could go around with a hand torch and make a perfect circle like this." He crouched, touching a larger burned spot within the circle. "Think this has anything to do with your brother?"

"I don't know. It's the only thing we've found so far."

He stood up, pulling his phone out and took a picture of the spot. "Honestly, this looks familiar," he said, bringing up his phone gallery. He enlarged a photo he'd taken of the relic sketch and held it up to show her. "It's not a perfect match, but it's similar. A circle with something near the outer edge. Granted, there's only one spot showing here in the grass and five in the sketch, but the placement is spot on."

She looked at the photo and back at the grass. "Didn't that book say that the key glowed, making the others run, and then the guy holding it was gone?"

"Yeah...I think you're right." He checked the burned circle again. "Did the key have something to do with your brother's disappearance? Maybe my uncle's writings are more than just fiction?" Rustling came from the bushes up ahead, grabbing his attention. He was sure the breeze wasn't strong enough to cause that kind of impact on the branches.

Summer slowly got back to her feet. "Are you seeing this too?"

A dark figure slowly stepped out from behind the bushes, and the details came into focus; a four-legged creature nearly the size of a Great Dane stood before them. It wasn't like any dog Ethan had seen before, looking sickly, hairless, and almost skeletal, but still walking with a powerful stride. It stared at the two of them with eyes flickering green when the light caught them right.

"What the hell is that!?" he asked through his teeth. He looked at the ground, finding a baseball bat sized tree branch, and quickly picked it up. Summer was frozen in fear. Her gaze never left the creature as she remembered the night her brother had disappeared. Ethan grabbed her arm lightly, getting her attention. "We need to get out of here," he said, not daring to talk louder than a whisper. She still hadn't moved. "Now." He pulled on her arm to guide her backwards.

The creature bared its teeth and growled, stepping in a circular motion as though deciding how best to attack. Ethan kept the branch ready while using his free hand to guide her behind him as they continued to back away, keeping their eyes on the beast. "We need to get back to the car. White SUV," he said, pulling the keys from his pocket, and handing them to her.

She took the keys, never taking her eyes off the creature. "How are we going to get to the car? That thing can outrun us easily."

Ethan glanced, seeing they were near the end of the bridge. "You run and unlock it. I'll deal with this." Suddenly, the creature rushed towards them. "Go!" he yelled. Summer started to run, and the creature leapt at Ethan with its claws, nearly slicing his stomach as he dodged. He swung the tree branch, hitting the creature square in the face, but it was unfazed by the strike.

It lunged towards his leg with its jaws while swiping at him at the same time. While he managed to dodge being bitten, the beast's claws sliced his forearm. He recoiled at the fresh wound but still held the branch, swinging it again. The creature lunged, pushing him onto his back; the wind nearly knocked out of him. He gripped the branch tighter with both hands, pushing it up against the creature's jaws. It snarled just inches from his face, with drool dripping onto his forehead. It was stronger than Ethan thought it would be, and it pressed harder against the branch. His arms strained, and the creature jerked its head, trying to rip the branch out of his hands. Ethan kicked hard, striking it in the rib cage, but it only enraged the creature. Its eyes narrowed, and it tried to rip the branch from his hands again. The branch cracked, giving Ethan a sense of dread. It was the only thing keeping him from getting ripped apart. The beast pressed the branch down further with the wood continuing to snap.

An almost sickening crack sounded, but not from the branch. The creature yelped simultaneously and its eyes rolled up. It went limp, falling over to its side with a thud. Ethan looked up to see Summer holding a rock in both hands with a look of shock and disgust in her eyes. He pushed himself out from under the creature's weight, noticing its chest rise, and quickly got to his feet. "Appreciate that." She remained motionless, continuing to take in the sight in front of her. "Are you ok? It didn't get you, did it?" he asked.

She didn't respond initially, still shocked by its appearance. "I...I'm not crazy. This thing is real. It's real..."

He looked back down at it, and one of its legs twitched. Ethan had seen enough horror movies to know if the creature was still breathing, it would get back up. "This thing is going to wake up at any moment. We've got to get out of here before that happens. Come on," he said, pointing down the path towards the parking lot. They started running as quickly as they could. The sounds of their shoes hitting pavement and the rustling of the car keys in Summer's hand were the only noises heard as they bolted towards the car, not chancing to look back.

The car was up ahead and Summer pressed the unlock button. The headlights blinked, and it let out a double beep echoing across the lake. A howl came from behind them. "Keep going!" he yelled as they neared the car. Summer reached it first, getting in the passenger seat and slammed her door shut while Ethan ran around to the driver's side. He slammed his door, pressing his foot on the brake, and pushed the startup button. Nothing happened. The car had disconnected from the key fob. "Not now, dammit!" He looked over at Summer, holding out his hand. "Keys please."

Summer continued to look out the window. "It's coming!" She handed him the keys. He grabbed them, putting the key fob next to the startup button to reconnect them, tapping his foot impatiently while it took a couple of agonizing seconds before finally connect-ing. "It's almost here!" He pressed the startup button hard, and the SUV's engine finally roared to life. He hit the gas and Summer screamed. The creature leapt at the passenger side window just as the car moved forward, making the creature miss its mark, smashing into the rear passenger door instead, shattering the window; bits of glass flew into the back seat and the car lurched from the impact.

Ethan kept his foot on the gas, navigating to the exit. He sped through the parking lot, pulling a U-turn out onto the main road. The tires squealed as he picked up speed and the creature jumped over the sidewalk into their path, baring its teeth. "Ah crap! Hold on!" The creature lunged at the vehicle and Ethan gripped the steering wheel, bracing for impact. Summer watched in disbelief, holding her arms up to shield herself as the creature smashed into the glass, flipping over the roof with a yelp. A shattered indent appeared where the creature's body had impacted; cracks splintering throughout the windshield. Ethan could barely see, but continued speeding down the street, refusing to stop.

After a couple of blocks, his heart still pounded, but he could finally catch his breath. "Are you alright? Any cuts from that thing or from glass?"

She shook her head, "No. No, I'm good. Having a small heart attack, but I'm good." She looked over, seeing blood drip from his right forearm, "Oh my God. You're bleeding."

He glanced down at his arm, feeling the pain more now that the adrenaline was wearing off. "I'll worry about it more when we get to my house. We aren't far. My mom has a medical background, and this doesn't look too deep."

She found a roll of paper towels on the floor in front of her and picked them up. "We need to get the bleeding stopped." She held her hand out. "Arm. No arguments."

He held it out, feeling the warmth of her hand before wincing as she applied pressure to the wound. His other arm jerked slightly, causing the car to swerve a bit before he got used to the pain and straightened the wheel.

"Try not to kill us, please," she said, only half joking.

"Working on it." He was glad most people were off the roads for the evening. They sat in silence for the next few minutes while she continued to hold pressure on his arm. "We're nearly there." He turned the car up his street and came to a stop in front of his parent's house. "Great," he said, seeing Lilly's car in the driveway, "My parents are going to be pissed when they see the car and my sister is going to pile it on."

"I'm sure your parents will understand when we tell them what happened."

"A massive skeleton dog tried to kill us at the lake," he said sarcastically. "I'm not sure I'd believe us if I hadn't seen it myself." He reached over to the back seat for his backpack, wincing again, having temporarily forgotten about the laceration on his arm. Shaking off shards of glass covering his pack, he brought it forward.

"If they don't believe the story, they'll believe your injury." She got out of the car, closing her door lightly, causing shards of glass to break free from the window's frame, falling to the street with a smattering of tinks. Even more fell when Ethan got out.

He frowned, looking at the state of the vehicle. "This looks worse from the outside. Yeah. Dad's definitely going to kill me." While walking to the front door, he thought it best to prepare her. "Meeting the family is usually a big step. As a heads up, you may end up getting asked a thousand questions. My family knows we went on a date yesterday, so..."

She smiled. "Should I be worried about what questions they ask?"

"I guess we'll find out." He smirked, opening the door for her. He followed her in, putting his backpack on the bench at the entry-way and walked into the living room. His parents were on the couch watching TV and Lilly could be heard in the kitchen singing along to a song.

Ellena noticed them first, standing up with a smile. "Glad you're home finally. Who is this?" she asked, knowing full well what the answer was. Mason sat forward and Lilly came around the corner, peering into the living room at them after hearing the question.

"This is Summer," he said, motioning to her. "The girl I told you about."

Summer wore an awkward smile and waved to everyone, "Hi, it's great to meet you. Ethan has been helping me with some research."

Still smiling, his mom continued with introductions, "I'm Ellena." She pointed over to Ethan's dad. "This is my husband, Mason." She turned her head, seeing Lilly peering in, "And the curious one in the kitchen is Lilly."

"Please come in and have a seat," Mason said, standing.

"Actually," Ethan said, "We had a bit of a problem at the lake. Needing some of your help with this one, mom." He moved his arm forward, showing the makeshift bandage Summer had applied. The wound must have been deeper than he thought as blood started seeping through.

"Oh, my God!" Ellena said, rushing forward. "Go have a seat at the table." She rushed to grab medical supplies. "Don't bleed on my carpet!" she said from the hall.

"What happened?" Mason asked, following them into the kitchen.

"I'm not really sure where to start," Ethan said, taking a seat.

Ellena jogged back down the hall with an arm full of medical supplies, taking a seat near him. Summer and Lilly joined them. Ellena put her hand out for Ethan's arm, and he held it out for her. She pulled the bloodied paper towels off, revealing the wound. Ethan grimaced, looking down at his torn flesh.

"Needing some details," Mason pressed. "What happened?"

"We were at the lake and got attacked by some kind of big dog. I've never seen anything like it. The thing looked like it was sick, or at least hadn't eaten in days. We were lucky to get out of there." He winced as his mom cleaned his arm. "Summer saved my rear when she knocked it out. Gave us time to get back to the car. She helped control the bleeding, too."

Ellena looked up at her. "Thank you for helping him."

"Of course, but Ethan protected me first, putting himself between me and that thing. You should be proud of him."

She smiled, looking up at him, "We are."

"I actually have more bad news," he said. "The dog-thing—it did a lot of damage to the car. A window is completely busted out. The windshield is destroyed. I haven't seen all the damage, but I wouldn't be surprised if the passenger side of the frame is dented, given how hard it hit us." The look on Mason's face said enough. "Sorry."

Mason sighed. "I'll go look at the car. From the sounds of it, I'm just glad you made it out of there alive." He grabbed a flashlight from the counter and headed out.

"Hold on a sec," Lilly said, getting up from the table. She ran into the living room, returning after a moment, and flipped through the pages of her journal before taking her seat again. She continued to flip a couple more pages, stopping to examine a sketch before turning the book around for the others. "Is this what attacked you?" she asked, pointing at the sketch.

Summer reached her hand out. "Can I see that closer, please?" Lilly nodded, pushing the journal to her. The sketch was hand drawn with the words *DANGEROUS* and *AVOID* in bold capital letters written above it. "This definitely looks like it," she said, holding it up for Ethan.

He nodded. "Yeah, that would be it. Seems Uncle Jerran has seen them before." Below the sketch was an acronym he read out loud. "T.A.K. What does that stand for?"

Ellena began wrapping his arm in gauze. "We'll keep it wrapped overnight and check it in the morning. Any deeper and you'd have needed stitches."

Ethan handed Lilly her journal back. "What is that thing? A dog? Some kind of wolf? You're the animal expert."

"How big did you say this was?"

"I don't know," he said with a shrug, "About here with me standing." He flattened his hand, putting it just to the top of his stomach.

Her eyes widened, looking over at Summer, who nodded in agreement with his measurement. Lilly shook her head. "There aren't many dogs or wolves that get that big," she said, looking down at the sketch again. "If I had to guess, I'd say it was a malnourished Great Dane, but they're usually very gentile dogs."

Ellena was just finishing wrapping up Ethan's arm when Mason came back in, "Hey Hon! Does our insurance cover animal attacks?"

"Just call them in the morning," she said.

Mason walked into the kitchen and slumped in the chair. "Car is totaled. We can't drive it until the windshield is fixed at a minimum. Did you run over the thing or what?"

"It was attacking us. Ran straight at the car, trying to jump through the windshield," Ethan said. "I didn't really have time to swerve out of the way."

Lilly handed Mason the journal, pointing to the sketch. "This is what they're saying attacked them."

Mason had a flash of recognition. "This? This is what you saw?" He put the journal down, glancing back and forth between the two of them.

Summer nodded, "Yes. Have you seen one before?"

His eyes narrowed as he took another look at the sketch. "Where exactly did you see this thing? It's important."

"We saw it over near the short bridge at Fox Run Lake," she said.

"Dammit," he said, sliding the journal away from him. He brought his hand up, rubbing his eyes. "That idiot. I told him not to go there anymore. I knew something like this would happen and he just wouldn't listen."

Ellena's eyes narrowed. "What haven't you told me?"

He let out a sigh, "Jerran and I used that compass he'd found to visit some place called Lunaria. I only went twice."

"When did you go?" she asked angrily. "You told me you heard about these places from Jerran. Not that you had gone there!"

He shook his head. "I had told you that before I had gone. I went after he had been there many times, about eight or so years ago, but that's not important. What's important is what we saw when we were there. For the most part, the people were nice, but there was a lot of fear surrounding a tyrannical group that started taking everything over. The people tried to push back, and that's when this group began using these wolf-things against them. Whatever this group was, they had a police force that used these to control the people through fear. They were very much like the collectivist groups we've seen in our own history. It only took a couple of demonstrations of these creatures, ripping people up for the rest to back down. I can't say I blame them."

He paused a moment, looking down at the table, remembering the panic in the streets as people ran for their lives, the screaming and atrocities he'd witnessed. He looked up, realizing everyone was watching him, and shook it off. "We were there when they let these things attack. It was horrible." He looked over at Ellena. "We came back right after that, and I told him we can never return. We couldn't chance them finding us and bringing those things here."

"You've been to another dimension?" Ethan asked.

"Yeah, and I'll never go back."

Ethan looked over at Summer. "We didn't see any blood when we looked in the area. Is it possible this group took your brother?"

"He's only sixteen," Summer said, looking at everyone around the table. "I have to get him back, especially if people like that have him." She looked back at Ethan, worried. "If this relic of yours can get me to him, I need to borrow it. I need to get to him."

Mason shook his head. "I'm sorry about your brother. I really am, but using the relic is impossible now. The day after we got back, I went to Jerran's, and he had already begun planning a return. He had the notion of teaching the people how to fight back as though they didn't know how to. I grabbed his journal and ripped the page out that had the travel codes, tossing them in the fireplace. I couldn't take the chance of that cult endangering the kids." He sat back in his chair. "Jerran was pissed at me for a good long while after that."

Ellena glared at him. "When the hell were you going to tell me about your adventures!? You didn't take the kids, did you!?"

He shook his head, "Of course not! We didn't know what we'd be walking into. The kids going wasn't on the table until we knew they'd be safe."

"Glad to hear you had some intelligence." She got up from the table, getting a glass from the cupboard. "You have a lot to explain to me later tonight."

He sighed, glancing down at the table and back to Summer. "I'm sorry, but the relic is useless without that page. There are literally thousands of combinations you could try before finding the right one. Even then, you'd have to be able to activate it. Most people can't, including me. The only one I knew who could activate the thing is Jerran, and he died."

"What do you mean, most people can't activate it?" Ethan asked.

"I honestly don't know. Not sure why or how it works. I only know your uncle told me when he first found it, the thing glowed for a second and then he passed out. That's why he was sleeping in the woods the next day."

Lilly broke in, "Why does everyone say he was drunk, then?"

He shrugged. "People say that because it's the easiest way to explain an event, they otherwise couldn't. Besides," he said, "you know we aren't much for drinking. That includes him." He shook his head, looking over at Ethan. "Where's the device at now?"

"I'll get it," he said, getting up from the table. A moment later, he returned, unzipping the bag, and pulling it out. The stone in the middle glinted in the light as he handed it over to his dad.

"I didn't think I'd ever see this thing again," he said, staring at it. He put it down, sliding it back to Ethan. "Glad it's nothing but a paperweight now."

Ellena glanced over at the clock on the microwave. It was nearing ten in the evening. "It's getting pretty late," she said, looking at Summer. "You're welcome to stay the night given everything you've been through."

Summer pulled out her phone. She hadn't updated her mother in a while. "Let me call my mom and let her know. She's been worried about losing me as well since my brother went missing. Thanks for letting me stay." She got up from the table, walking into the other room to make the call.

Ellena looked at Ethan smiling, "She seems like a nice girl."

"Yeah, way to show a girl a good time," Lilly mocked. "Second date and you get her attacked by a rabid dog thing. Maybe tone it down a bit, Romeo."

"Ha ha," he replied sarcastically.

THE STERADIAN GATE

Ellena came down the stairs the next morning, pausing at the bottom when she spotted Ethan and Summer passed out on the couch. Summer was using the couch's arm as a pillow with a thin blanket draped over. Her feet were stretched out over Ethan's legs as he slept sitting up. On the coffee table in front of them were clues of a long night of research with two opened laptops, opened books, and notes scribbled down on a pad. She smiled, looking at the two of them, and headed into the kitchen to start some coffee.

Ethan awoke to the sound of water running in the kitchen, followed by ceramic mugs clinking. He stretched out his arms, yawning, and felt a weight on his lap. It took a moment for him to register his surroundings and saw Summer still asleep. Not wanting to wake her, he lightly lifted her feet off to the side and stood up. Not realizing one of his legs had gone to sleep, he nearly fell over, knocking his shin into the coffee table; the blood rushing back in, causing pins and needles. He stretched his leg, rubbing the muscle, and headed into the kitchen to see who else was up.

Ellena was sitting at the table listening to the latest news story as she scrolled through the rest of the articles. She smiled, noticing him come in, "Morning. Looks like you two had a long night. Were you able to find anything that can help her?"

Pulling out a chair, he sat next to her. "Yeah. We're working to find the right set of glyphs to activate the relic." He had already found the correct glyph combination needed to get to Lunaria in his journal, but didn't want his mom to worry. "We also talked about needing to find the right combination to get back. We can't launch a rescue mission if we can't return home," he said, seeing a look of concern cross her face. "It's her brother, mom. If it were Aiza or Lilly, none of us would stop until they were back. You and dad have always said family is important. Can you blame her?"

"Family is important," she agreed, "Which is why your father and I are worried about what happens to you if you go to this...this other world and can't get back. Especially one with some hostile cult that's taken over."

Summer's eyes slowly opened to the sound of the conversation in the kitchen. She could make out Ethan's voice and felt a little guilty for eavesdropping, but was curious about what he had to say. Regardless that they'd only known each other a couple of days, last night's encounter with the creature made it feel like she knew him better than most. She stretched on the couch and sat up quietly to listen better.

"Look mom," Ethan continued, "I'm an adult now. I love that you guys still worry about me, but this is something I've decided to do."

"You really like this girl, huh?"

"We just met, but yeah. I like her."

Ellena got up from the table and poured coffee for the two of them. "You know, your dad saved me when we first met, too. It wasn't to the level of hopping over to another world, but it was welcome just the same. He worked at a movie theater, and I was visiting a friend who worked there too. My friend needed his work schedule and told me to wait in the lobby for him. Some weirdo from the concession stand was trying to flirt with me by showing me pictures of his exes he kept in his wallet." She cringed at the memory as she stirred in the creamer. She brought Ethan one of the mugs, taking her seat. "Your dad was a lead and saw what this guy was doing. He intervened, telling the guy to go do something to get him away from me."

Summer smirked at the story, still listening in. She decided she needed to stop snooping and join them. She got off the couch and walked into the kitchen. "Morning. Thanks again for letting me stay last night."

"Good morning," both Ethan and Ellena said in unison.

"Do you want some coffee?" Ellena asked.

Summer nodded with a smile. "That would be great. Thank you."

Ethan was taking a sip of his coffee when he realized his mom wasn't getting up. Glancing over at her, she was staring at him for a second before motioning her eyes to the cupboard. He put his mug down, finally getting the message, "Let me get that for you." He stood up awkwardly. "Do you like creamer? We have French Vanilla."

"Yes, please," she said, taking a seat.

"How are your parents doing with all of this? Do they know you're investigating?" Ellena asked, while Ethan got the coffee ready.

"My mom cries a lot," she said, looking down at the table. "Ethan knows, but my brother and I were adopted. My foster parents had always treated us like we were their own, but my foster father passed away a couple years ago from cancer. My mom really misses him." She sighed. "He and Alex were really close, too. If he were alive today, he'd be spearheading the search." Ethan put the mug in front of her and she took a sip.

"It sounds like you and your brother have been through a lot," Ellena said.

"We were lucky to get adopted by our foster parents. Even though they gave us a family, a home, we were still kind of trapped in the mindset of being on our own. The feeling had faded over time, but when he passed away, it hit Alex hard. He's been a bit of a problem lately; constantly running off to hang out with the wrong friends and worrying mom. They had gotten into an argument about it right before he disappeared, and she blames herself." She looked down at her mug. "I'm...I'm sorry. You don't want to hear all of that."

Ellena shook her head. "Don't ever be sorry for trying to help your family. Kids go through these rebellious phases. I'm sure he'll come around."

"We have to find him first," she said.

"I think what we found at the park before getting attacked tells us at least one important thing," Ethan said, pulling out his phone. He brought up the photo of the burned circle in the grass and placed it in the middle of the table pointing to it, "If this circle is caused by a portal opening, and the so called 'key' that Uncle Jerran left me was locked up, then there's more than one of these relics able to open portals."

"We don't even know how to use it or if it can still open portals," Summer said.

"Actually, I think I found some answers flipping through the journal last night," he said, getting up and heading to the living room. He returned shortly with the journal in hand, flipping through the pages. He placed it in front of her, pointing at the top of one of the pages.

At the top were scribbled notes, difficult to read due to the poor penmanship. She squinted, trying to decipher some of the words while she read.

Rotate outer ring clockwise to first glyph. Then counterclockwise to the second. Clockwise for the third. So on and so forth for all seven glyphs entered. When one of the glyphs on the key light up, touch the stone in the center to activate.

"We could have gone to get my brother last night?" Summer asked, suddenly angry. "Why did you keep this from me?"

Ethan looked perplexed. "I didn't keep it from you. We were both tired and after getting attacked, I thought we could use some sleep first. Not to mention, we don't know the set of glyphs needed to get back. We agreed we needed that before we go."

Summer took a deep breath. "I know. I know. I just...I need to get him back." She lifted her mug, taking another sip. "We need to go back to the library and see if we can find anything else now that we know what we're searching for. We should get ready and head over." She took another sip, feeling her unkept hair against her neck. She looked over at Ellena. "I hate to ask, but do you have a spare hairbrush and toothbrush I could use?"

"Of course," she said, "Follow me. We have spares of everything." The two got up from the table walking into the other room.

Ethan sat, flipping through more pages. He had gone through almost the entire journal last night and didn't see any other glyph combinations. The thought crossed his mind that maybe his uncle kept the combinations in the other journals. He texted both of his sisters, asking if they had seen any symbols while flipping through theirs, and sent them a photo of the set of glyphs he had taken as an example. He didn't expect a response from them quickly, as they were both more than likely at work already.

Ellena walked back into the room, putting her hands on the top rail of a chair, leaning against it. "She's a nice girl. I don't blame her for being frustrated at the situation." She reached down, grabbing her mug from the table and took a drink. "You should really eat something before you head back to the library."

"I'm not hungry yet and honestly, I don't know what else we'll find at the library. We're running out of ideas on where to research. Today, I think we should go visit Aiza and see if the scan we did will give us any answers. We'll also have to go back to the lake. Might do that first while it's still light out, though. I don't want to run into that thing again, but we don't have much choice.

She raised her eyebrows. "I'm not sure your dad is too happy with how borrowing the car turned out yesterday. You may not have a ride to get there."

"We can take the bus."

She walked over to the counter, grabbing a small plate from above. "I'll make you guys a couple of sandwiches to take with you. How about you get ready for the day?"

He nodded, "Thanks mom." He got up from the table and headed upstairs.

"Thanks for the brushes," Summer said, entering the kitchen.

"Anytime," Ellena said. "Ethan thought it would be smart to go back to the lake today and look for more clues. Do you feel comfortable doing that after last night?"

"Sure. Going back to the place where we were attacked by a monster and barely escaped with our lives. That sounds great," she said with a hint of sarcasm.

Ellena chuckled, "You could tell him you don't want to go."

"He's right though. We were chased out of there right when we found something."

"I'm making the two of you sandwiches to go. Would you mind grabbing his backpack from the living room and putting a couple bottles of water in there as well? They're in the pantry on the floor."

"Thank you," Summer said, retrieving the backpack and placing it on the table. Sensing that Summer didn't know where the pantry was, Ellena pointed to the correct door. Summer grabbed the waters, putting them in the pack, and felt something cold. She looked in, finding the relic nestled in the bottom, and realized she could borrow it to get to her brother. If she succeeded, she wouldn't have to worry about Ethan or his family getting into anymore danger. She grabbed it, tucking it under her sweater. "Is it ok if I go to your backyard to call my mom? I wanted to let her know I'm ok and what our plans for the day are."

"Of course," Ellena said, continuing to make the sandwiches.

Summer grabbed the journal from the table while Ellena was distracted and headed to the living room. She sat, taking a moment to write down her mom's name and phone number on the notepad on the coffee table, glancing back at the stairs occasionally to make sure she wasn't seen. She wanted to say goodbye to Ethan, but couldn't chance him getting involved more than he already was. Seeing her opportunity, she got up and went outside to the backyard.

***

Ethan pulled a clean shirt over his head and looked at himself in the mirror. He wasn't sure if they were going to find anything at the park, but he needed to be ready if they were attacked again. Did he even want to put Summer in danger, knowing the creature could still be there? Remembering how strong the thing was and the sound of the branch cracking sent a chill up his spine.

He brushed off the feeling, but knew he needed some advice on what to do next, and remembered his dad worked from home today. He walked down the hall to his dad's office and knocked on the door.

"Come on in," he heard his dad say.

He opened the door, seeing his dad staring at the computer monitor sipping coffee, "Hey dad. Do you have a sec?"

"Yeah." Mason put his coffee down, pushed away from the desk, and swiveled his chair around. "Just trying to get an idea of what the next scene will look like in the book. What's up?"

"First off, I wanted to say sorry about what happened to the car last night. I was just trying to get us out of there."

His dad shook his head. "Not your fault, considering the situation. What I'm more concerned with is your tendency to take on the world by yourself. I hope you realize, you were lucky Summer was there to help. You're not as invincible as you think and need to learn to rely on others a bit more."

"I know," he said, "but there's another thing. We need to go back to the lake to check some things out, and I was hoping you'd have something I could take with me for protection?"

His dad got up from his chair and walked over to a dresser, pulling open the top drawer. He shuffled items around inside before pulling out a knife in a belt holster. "Your uncle got me this as a gift many years ago. It's still sharp and should give you a chance." He handed it to Ethan, who pulled the eight-inch blade from its sheath, examining it. "That said, if you see one of those things again—get out of there. Don't try to fight it to impress the girl. You'll only get the both of you killed."

"Oh, I'm not planning on a rematch." He attached the knife to his belt. "We'll run if we see it."

Mason stared at him for a second. "Remember, that knife is a last resort. Sometimes protecting those you care about means not putting them in dangerous situations to begin with."

"I'll try not to get us into any..." he trailed off with something catching his attention from the corner of his eye. He took a step closer to the office window, looking out over the backyard. Below, Summer was pacing back and forth, and in her hands, he saw both the journal and the relic. "Crap. She's going to activate it!"

***

Summer rotated the outer ring of the relic to the final glyph in the Lunaria combination. The wolf emblem lit up in purple at the northeastern point of the relic while a chime sounded, signaling a correct combination had been entered. The instructions were clear enough. All she had to do now was touch the stone at the center, but she hesitated with what-ifs entering her mind. She paced back and forth, deciding if she should go now or wait.

Ethan's idea of having a way back was smart, but any delay could end up being too late for her brother. Going alone would be stupid. She could easily get killed by something or someone without help, but if Ethan came, he could also be killed, or they could both die. She didn't want to be responsible for that, especially with how kind he and his family had been. Not to mention she liked him. She sighed and looked down at the shimmering stone embedded in the relic. Ethan would most likely try to stop her from going if she didn't go now, and she needed to get her brother back quickly. She'd decided, pressing her thumb down on the stone and hoped she was making the right choice.

A chime sounded from it, and the frosted glass at the center lit up in blue. Immediately, a bright blue dot appeared on the ground a few feet in front of her. It was small, maybe two inches in diameter, glowing brightly as it started moving quickly in a clockwise circle around her. She followed it with her eyes, watching until it eventually came back around to its starting point, creating a glowing blue circle. The glow pulsed as a wolf emblem made of purple light appeared on the grass in front of her, matching the one on the relic. The glow from the circle intensified, erupting upward to become a transparent dome of light closing just a couple of feet above her.

Wind started swirling around her, but strangely, none of the trees or bushes outside of the dome appeared affected, giving her second thoughts about her decision. The wind continued to swirl, growing stronger and forming a funnel that pressed against the inside of the dome. Then it began to extend towards her like a small tornado. She felt the funnel pull her forward, filling her with regret, and she took a step back, dropping the journal, but the journal never hit the ground, floating in place instead.

"Summer!" yelled a voice from behind. She turned, watching as Ethan leapt from the back porch with his backpack in hand, running towards her. Her feet lifted off the ground and she struggled to move, only managing to twist her body. She did her best to lean away from the funnel, reaching her hand out towards him, but the pull from the funnel made it difficult.

He stopped short of the dome, seeing her floating a couple of inches off the ground with her hair flipping around as though she were in the midst of a storm; her eyes welling up in fear. He reached in, grabbing her hand and pulled, but she wouldn't budge.

"I'm sorry," she yelled over the wind; a tear flying off her cheek.

Ellena looked out the back door, wondering why Ethan had run through the house the way he had. She couldn't believe what she saw in front of her. "What the hell!?" She sprinted towards him, hoping to get to him in time. "Hold on!"

Ethan tossed his backpack into the dome, amazed that it slowed and floated, turning inside the dome like he'd tossed it into a pool. He planted both his feet and reached in with his other hand, gripping Summer's arm tightly. The light from the dome felt as though it were burning his arms, making him clench his teeth. He squeezed his eyes shut and pulled on her arm harder, putting his entire weight into it, but she seemed stuck.

Ellena was nearly to him, reaching to grab his shirt, when she watched him get pulled in. An impossibly bright flash lit up the backyard. She held her arm up, covering her eyes, when a powerful gust of wind pushed against her, flinging her backwards. She slammed into the ground, not able to breathe for a moment before she rolled to her side. Still trying to catch her breath, she pushed herself up to a sitting position. She looked back at where the dome used to be, but the yard was empty. No dome and no Ethan.

She quickly got to her feet, running to where they had been just moments earlier, only seeing a circular burn mark in the grass. "Ethan!?" Panic set in. She looked around the yard frantically, finding herself alone. "Ethan!"

Mason ran out the back door, seeing Ellena checking behind a large bush. "Where did they go?"

"They're gone," she said, tearing up. "There was a flash of light and they're gone!" She fell to her knees, watching the smoke rise from the circle of smoldering grass.

Lunaria

E than hit the ground hard, rolling a few feet. Fresh scratches from the twigs of bushes began to burn. He laid on his back a moment, letting the dizziness wear off before opening his eyes. High above was a thick forest canopy with bits of sky peering through. There had never been trees this tall in his backyard. At least, not since he had lived there. A cool breeze touched his cheek, carrying the sweet smell of a forest. His body hurt all over. He rolled onto his side, groaning. "That felt great," he said sarcastically, pushing himself up.

He heard footsteps running towards him. "Ethan!? Are you ok?" Summer asked. He looked up, seeing her concern; her hand extended out to help him up.

Annoyance flared up within him. He ignored her hand, getting himself back to his feet, and dusted off his pants. "I'm fine. Are you hurt?"

She shook her head, "I'm ok. I...I tried to get out of that bubble, but—"

"I can't believe you did that," he interrupted angrily. "We needed to find a way home before coming here and now I don't know if we can get home!"

She was taken aback by the anger in his voice. "I'm sorry," she said defensively. "I know I should have waited, but I needed to go after Alex. Now. Not later! He could already be dead and there was no guarantee we'd ever find the combination to get back."

He took a deep breath to calm himself. "I understand, but you should have come to me and asked. We had a solid plan of researching a way back before we left."

"I know. I know!" She threw her hands up, flustered. "Are you done being mad?"

He flattened his shirt, stopping to take in their surroundings. They were in the middle of an ancient forest. Impossibly tall redwood trees surrounded them with moss growing halfway up the thick trunks. The trees were numerous and lush green grass, ferns, saplings, and other underbrush covered the landscape.

Sunlight beamed through the canopy in a stunning display, highlighting a nearby fallen trunk covered in moss that looked to have been laying there for decades. A squirrel popped out of one of the downed trunk's knotholes, eyeing them before it took off running. The sounds of wildlife slowly returned after their loud entry into the area.

"So, this is Lunaria," he said, looking around for any clues on which way to go. Unfortunately for them, there was no visible path. "Now the question is, which way?"

"Our stuff is over here," she said, pointing to a nearby tree. She walked over to it, crouching down to pick up both the journal and the relic. He followed her to a singed circular area, finding his backpack. He picked it up, unzipping it as she stood, turning to face him.

"May as well keep our way home safe." He held the pack open for her.

She placed the items in, seeing food and water had been packed. Then she noticed a red stripe across Ethan's forearms. "You're burned." She reached over, touching his arm lightly.

He looked down at the bright red marks across his arms, seeing small blisters already forming. "Looks like it."

"Is that from the bubble of light?" she asked.

"That's my guess. Makes sense when you see how it affects the grass and the leaves," he said, pointing to the still smoldering ground around them. "I'm probably lucky the burn wasn't worse." He zipped up the pack, slinging it over his shoulder, ignoring the burns. "Alright. Being lost 101. My dad taught me that if I ever get lost in the woods—stay where you're at so you can be found. That's not an option here, so, step two, find a water source and follow it downstream. That might lead to a town or a road or something."

"What happens if we can't find a stream?" she asked, swatting away a swarm of flying insects. "Stupid bugs." Frustrated at the situation, she flailed at them till they flew off. He held up his finger in the air, motioning her to stay silent for a moment. "Don't shush me."

"I need quiet so I can listen for water." He tilted his head, occasionally turning to hear in different directions. It took a few moments before he smiled. "That way," he said, pointing behind her. "Pretty sure I hear a stream or a creek."

She looked at him suspiciously. "I didn't hear anything."

"We don't have a lot of choice. Would you rather pick a different direction?" he asked, crossing his arms. "We can do that, but our best odds of getting out of here are to head towards the water."

"Fine. We'll try your water idea." She turned, walking off before he could reply. The two of them continued in silence for the next few minutes to let their frustrations cool off. It wasn't long before the sound of flowing water became louder, sounding as though they were coming up to a small waterfall.

The uneven landscape eventually revealed a creek with a small cavern off to their left. A waterfall careened down towards them from thirty feet up. The water had been a part of the landscape for eons, having eroded the cavern over time. Thick moss grew up the rock cliff, making it unscalable, while across the shallow creek, a game trail showed a favorite drinking spot of the local wildlife. Slick rocks peeked out of the crest of the water, creating a path they could work their way across if they were careful.

Ethan hadn't noticed the small creature nearby until it moved, hopping away as they neared the water. It looked very similar to one of his uncle's sketches. "I think I've seen a picture of that thing before," he said, pointing at it. "What was it called?" He shook his head, not caring for the moment. It was more important to find some form of civilization before it got dark, or they'd be in serious trouble.

He leapt onto the first rock, feeling the sturdiness before moving to the second. So far, each had held his weight without budging, boosting his confidence in getting across dry. Then he landed on the third rock and it tilted. He tried to catch himself futilely before flailing backwards into the frigid water with it splashing up his shirt, making him freeze instantly. He held his arms out to his sides, regaining his composure. The water was only a few inches deep, but it was enough to completely soak his clothing. His expression had Summer doubled over, laughing. As he stood, water dripped off of him. He glared at her and stomped the remaining few feet across to the other side, making her laugh harder still.

"You're all heart," he said, taking his shoes off to pour the water out.

The laughing subsided, and she showed a hint of compassion. "Let's see if I do better," she said with a smirk. She looked across the path of stones, sizing up what she needed to do to not end up in a similar situation. She gracefully hopped from one stone to the next without falling until she was safely on the other side with him.

"How did you do that so easily?" he asked, getting back to his feet, catching up to her as she walked down the makeshift trail; his jeans sloshing with every step.

She smiled, trying to stop herself from bursting out laughing again at the sound of his pants. "My foster parents put me in gymnastics for a few years. I used to enjoy it but stopped after my third year. It taught me balance, but I honestly didn't think I'd ever really use it."

"What made you quit?" he asked as her smile faded.

She shrugged. "The team I was a part of was more competitive with each other than the other teams. Instead of cheering each other on like I've seen most other teams do, the girls on my team were always tearing each other down to make themselves feel better. It was toxic, and I didn't want to be around it anymore."

Ethan nodded. "I get it."

As they continued down the path, the sloshing of his jeans had finally subsided. "Did you know you'd be able to activate that portal? I mean, my dad said most people can't."

"It never really crossed my mind. I was just following the instructions your uncle had written." Something across the water stopped her in her tracks. "Wait," she said in a hushed voice, pointing to something moving. A two-foot-tall burnt orange furry animal had been drinking from the water when its head jerked up, hearing them approach. They stayed motionless for a couple minutes before it tilted its head back down to continue drinking.

Ethan knelt, removing his backpack, and unzipped it quietly. He removed the journal, flipping a few pages before standing again and holding it open for her. She glanced down seeing the sketch of the same creature, a furry kangaroo with a fox tail; the word *Zemper* written above it. She looked across at the animal and he closed the journal, replacing it into the pack. The zemper's head jerked up again, hearing him zip up the pack, and it bounded away from them. Her eyes widened in amazement when a half dozen others they hadn't seen jumped out of hiding, following the first.

"Those things are so cute."

"Seems I'll have to add some notes to my uncle's sketch." He pulled out his journal, adding details to the sketch and adding notes about how the animal behaved.

Over the course of the next couple of hours, Ethan continued to sketch different animals they saw while also making a simplistic map in case they needed to get back to where they first entered their new surroundings. The creek they followed wound around the thick forest, over sometimes difficult terrain, and their legs had become heavy with each step; their pace slowing. Eventually, the trees became fewer and the foliage less dense, with the forest opening to a clearing. The creek snaked down and around to the right with a grassy hill straight ahead. The change in scenery was welcome as he needed to let his legs rest, expecting Summer could use a break too.

"Let's take a quick detour," he said, pointing to the hill. "We can see if we're close to getting somewhere and take a lunch break." The sun was nearly overhead when they neared the crest of the hill. The valley below came into view. At the bottom of the hill, a dirt road curved around and off in the distance lay a small village.

"Thank God," Summer said. "We can reach that in less than an hour."

Ethan took a seat and removed his pack, pulling out a couple of sandwiches and waters his mother had packed them. "Here," he said, handing her one of the bottles.

"Thanks." She took it and sat across from him, opening the bottle, downing half the water. He handed her a sandwich. She nodded in appreciation, and they sat in silence for a few minutes, eating and regaining their energy.

He reached into the pack, pulling out his uncle's journal and started flipping through more of the pages, reading some notes. "According to my uncle, the water and food here are fine for us to eat. The people should be friendly enough too. He notes many people speak what they call 'Common' here, but we'll probably need a translator," he read, raising an eyebrow. "Whatever that is."

"It makes sense. Think of all the countries that have multiple languages," she said, looking over to the village in the distance. "Who knows what languages they speak and what 'Common' is?"

"There's a note that Lunaria is a hundred years behind us in technology. That would put them early to mid-nineteen hundreds. I expect a translator may be a person, meaning we're going to need money to—" He stopped mid-sentence, continuing to scan the notes.

"Money to what?"

"This can't be right," he said, scrunching his forehead. "It says the translator has hundreds of languages programmed on it. If they're a hundred years behind us, how would they have that kind of technology?"

Summer shrugged, not sharing Ethan's curiosity. She pulled out a photo of her brother from her back pocket and stared at it, hugging her knees.

Ethan looked up from the journal, seeing she looked distant. "You have an actual printed photo of him…impressive. I thought I was the only one who kept printed photos. Can I see it?"

She nodded, handing it to him. "Printed photos don't rely on a battery." She smiled. "Who do you have a photo of?"

"My family. It's about a year or so old." He looked at the picture seeing a teenage boy with short red hair, green eyes and freckles. The smile on his face was awkward, as though forced by whoever the photographer was. "Is this what Alex looks like now?"

She nodded, "Basically. His hair's longer, but not much." Ethan handed it back to her. "He hated having his picture taken. Said he never looked good in them. Most of the time, he would go out of his way to make weird faces for them."

"I was thinking maybe we can show his photo around that village." He gestured towards the homes in the distance. "Maybe someone will recognize him. The quicker we find him, the quicker we can look for a way home."

He pulled his phone from his pocket. "Still at ninety-five percent battery. Looks like we're roaming, though." He allowed himself a laugh and opened the camera app, holding it up at Summer. "Photo for our first day in Lunaria?"

"Sure." He angled the phone, so she was off center with the village showing in the distance. She tucked a strand of hair behind her ear and posed with a smile. He snapped the photo and checked to make sure it wasn't blurry.

He looked up and saw she was still smiling. "You really do have an incredible smile."

She felt her cheeks go red a moment before standing and brushing the dirt off her jeans. "How about a selfie with the two of us?"

Ethan got to his feet and stood next to her. She wrapped her arms around him, putting her chin on his shoulder, and smiled at the phone. He smiled from ear to ear, wrapping his free arm around her back and framed the picture to have the village behind them before snapping the shot.

"Let's see it," she said, untangling her arms from him.

He brought the photo up on the screen, showing it to her while he covered the sun's glare with his other hand.

She smiled. "We look good together. Send that to me when you can."

"I will." He turned the phone off to preserve the battery and put it back in his pocket. "Ready to head out?"

They moved on, following the creek down the hill, and found a road at the bottom. It was a mix of dirt and gravel that came from their right and curved ahead towards the village. Getting to the outskirts of the village took another hour of walking. Their feet ached and Ethan wished they had a car, or at least a bicycle. He found it strange they hadn't seen any cars or other vehicles travel by since they'd been on the road. "They had cars a hundred years ago, didn't they?" He looked behind him on the path for any sign of one.

"I thought so. I haven't seen any bicycles either, and they've had those around much longer."

They had finally made it to the edge of the village when a two-story tall church made of stone stood to greet them. The bell tower in front jutted upwards, an extra story coming to a point where a large cross was on display. The rest of the buildings on the road were bland in comparison with most being made of wooden slats with roofing coming to a point at the center in a common front gable design.

Getting further into town, they felt something was off. The few people that were out stared at them. Some looked to be afraid, crossing the road just to get away from them. Occasionally, Ethan would hear someone whispering to another in a language he didn't understand, but he could tell it was about them.

Summer noticed everyone wearing tan or dark brown colored cloaks over their clothing. The women all wore bland colored shin length dresses looking well worn. Only some of the men had cloaks on, but all had on what appeared to be work clothing, a tan long-sleeved shirt and dark-colored pants; most of which were becoming tattered at the bottom.

She looked down at her own clothing, seeing both she and Ethan wearing a t-shirt or sweater and jeans; a stark contrast to the local fashion being worn by everyone else. Her teal sweater looked especially bright in comparison. "We need to find something different to wear while we're here. We stick out like a sore thumb."

It took him a moment to catch on, inwardly shunning himself for being oblivious to his surroundings. A shop up ahead had a small sign above the door. He couldn't make out the words, but a painted carving of a beer stein below made it obvious it was a tavern. He pointed towards it. "Maybe we can get some answers in there. It might be the only place to eat in this town, so your brother may have stopped in. We can see if they saw him."

"It'll get us off the street, anyway. Just glad I didn't wear my jeans with the holes at the knee." They quickly made their way towards the tavern and entered. A bell rang, and they found the establishment mostly empty. Round wooden tables spread out across the room, each of them having a small vase with a flower sticking out at the center. On the opposite side of the room was a bar with the stools sitting upside down on top of it. Near a window to their right was a couple having breakfast, who had stopped eating to stare at the two of them.

A woman wearing an apron over her frayed dress came from behind a swinging door at the back. She picked up a couple of menus from the bar; the hinges continuing to squeak as the door swung back and forth. When the woman finally looked up, her pace slowed, and she looked hesitant as she neared the two of them. She greeted them in a language they didn't understand and paused, as though waiting for an answer.

The two of them looked at each other and shook their heads. "I'm sorry," Ethan said, "I didn't understand you."

The woman nodded in understanding. "Well, you have manners. That's more than I can say for other visitors we get through here." She gave them a once over, judging their attire. "Strange clothing you have, but welcome to the Brexel Tavern. Have a seat wherever you like."

Summer pulled out the picture of her brother. "Actually," she said, holding it up for the woman to see, "I'm looking for my brother. I was hoping maybe you saw him come through here a few weeks ago?"

The woman leaned closer to get a better look, but shook her head. "No, I'm afraid I haven't seen him, but we don't really get many visitors here."

Summer's shoulders sagged. "Thanks for looking."

"He's gone missing?" the woman asked.

Summer nodded. "He went missing about a month ago."

"Well. You were smart to come here. Not everyone in town speaks Common. Knowing a couple of extra languages has helped me bring in customers that my competitor would lose." She looked the two of them up and down again. "First off, the two of you are going to want a change of clothes. No one wears clothing like that here. Second, you'll need a translator and those aren't cheap. Do you have funds?"

Ethan looked over at Summer and back at the woman. "I have a debit card."

"A what?" she asked. She shook her head with a wave of her arm. "Never mind. I don't know what that is, but it doesn't sound like coin. I've heard TerRan has been known to barter before. His shop is just across the way, and he speaks Common as well. He'll have what you need there, assuming you can find something he wants in trade."

The door to the tavern opened, the chime of the bell catching their attention. A tall middle-aged man dressed in a hooded black trench coat walked in. With the man's hood up, Ethan thought he saw a faint blue glow near the right ear. The glint of gold caught Ethan's eye, where a sword was strapped to the stranger's belt.

The man pulled the hood down, revealing dark, greasy, slicked back hair, orange eyes and unshaven stubble with a prominent goatee that came down a couple of inches from the chin. The woman they had been speaking to gasped and her body language immediately shifted.

"I need a table away from anyone else and some water to start," the man demanded in a dismissive tone. He looked at the woman trembling, seeing she had recognized him. "Well?!"

The woman stuttered as she bowed. "Pa...pa...pardon me, Czar Dwyll. Right this way." She walked him over to a table opposite from the couple that had already been eating. Seeing who was being seated, one of them pulled out some coin and put it on the table before getting up quickly to leave. Dwyll took the seat facing the front door.

Ethan and Summer stood silent, not sure if the woman would return to talk with them. They watched as she handed the man a menu and rushed to the back. "Okay," Ethan said slowly, "Let's head out." He opened the door for Summer before looking back at the man, who continued to stare right back at him.

Dwyll's eyes narrowed as he watched them leave.

Chance Encounter

A now familiar chime sounded as the two entered the shop the waitress had recommended. The space felt small and crowded regardless that they were the only customers. Trinkets of every design lined the wall to their left, with shelving just below equally stuffed full of knickknacks. Clothing racks in the center of the room were filled to the brim with different shapes and sizes of cloaks, dresses, slacks, and shirts. An "L" shaped counter with more expensive items encased within it started at the back of the shop, wrapping around to the right, and behind the counter were more shelving units filled with books, trinkets, and bladed weapons.

A short, pudgy man behind the counter looked up from a book and lowered his glasses. Ethan noticed archery bows and quivers hung on the wall behind him before the man started speaking in a language neither he nor Summer knew.

Ethan shook his head, looking at Summer and back at the shopkeeper, "Hello. We were told someone by the name of TerRan speaks Common here and might be able to help us?"

"Ah!" the shopkeeper said with excitement. "I'm TerRan. Welcome. I haven't seen clothing like that in many years. Come. Come," he said, motioning them forward.

The two walked up to the counter, getting a better look at him. The window light glinted off his mostly bald head, causing long shadows where tufts of hair stuck out at the sides above his ears. His dark purple eyes took in their appearance. "What can I do you for?" he asked, causing his bushy mustache to move like a small animal when he spoke. Summer couldn't help but chuckle to herself at the sight.

Ethan shot her a look, and she coughed to cover the laugh, regaining her composure before he spoke. "You've seen people dressed like us before?" he asked, turning back to TerRan.

"Oh Yes. Yes," he said, "but keep yer voices down. Judging by yer clothes and yer eyes, I'm guessing yer not with them and that you've inadvertently stepped in it." TerRan looked them over again, seeing the confusion on their faces. "Yer obviously not from here. How did you come to visit us in Brexel?"

Ethan cleared his throat. "I won't go into specifics, but I recently inherited something that dropped us into the forest a few miles away, and we walked here."

TerRan smiled mischievously. "Dropped you into the forest, you say? Then my suspicions may be true," he said, smacking his hand on the counter as though he'd won a bet. "Answer me this," he said, leaning in. "By chance, do you know a man named Jerran from Delphinium?"

Ethan was shocked to hear his uncle's name. "Delph...whatever-you-said sounds familiar, but I don't know what or where it is. My uncle's name was Jerran, though." He looked down at the top of the counter solemnly. "He recently passed away."

TerRan's smile faded at the news. "I see." He let out a slow sigh before continuing, "Then you've come into possession of his Steradian Key through sad means and without instruction."

"Steradian Key?" Ethan asked.

TerRan nodded, speaking in a hushed voice, "Yes. The device which brought you here is a Steradian Key. Specifically, the Delphinium Key." He leaned in closer to Ethan, "Keep quiet what I'm about to tell you. Even now, one of the Kriva Rasturna's Czars is here in Brexel looking for any leads to where—"

Summer interrupted, "A waitress across the street looked pretty scared of a guy she called 'Czar Dwyll' when he walked in. Was that him?"

The color in TerRan's face drained. "Yes...that'd be him. Did he see you?!"

"Yeah," Ethan nodded, "I don't see how he could have missed us."

"Then we haven't much time," TerRan continued, "Listen up. There are only five keys in existence which open the Steradian Gate. It's the passage between the dimensions and if you have one of them with you, then you had best keep it close and keep it secret. The Kriva Rasturna will happily kill to possess them all, and they only have three left to find. It's the single most important reason they invaded Lunaria a few years back, starting here in the once great nation of Maraldi. Since then, they've done what they can to destroy our way of life and remove freedoms to make us little more than slaves helping them in their search. It started with the corruption of our government, but people have died, and families torn apart. Whatever happens, they can't be allowed to find yer key."

"Why doesn't anyone fight back?" Summer asked.

TerRan let out a snort of offense. "We're trying," he started, "We have resistance cells spread throughout Lunaria, fighting against 'em." His gaze shifted to Ethan. "Yer uncle was one of the founders of our resistance. He helped us see what was happening, and that we had to fight back. Even started our training based on what he called history lessons from Delphinium."

Ethan couldn't believe it. "He did what?"

Looking down at the counter, TerRan spoke quietly, "It is sad to hear of his passing. He was a great man and Lunaria owes him a debt, but we still have a hard fight ahead." He looked back up at Ethan. "I'm happy to get the chance to return the favor as best I can, so no charge for getting the two of you supplies today. You'll need a change of clothes or at least a cloak to cover up what yer wearing now. What else can I get you?"

"We were told we'd need a translator," Ethan said.

"It would probably be helpful to get some local currency as well," Summer added.

TerRan nodded, thinking over options. "I don't have much coin I can just give away, but I do have some translators that just shipped in from Devon Falls yesterday. Let me see what I can do. In the meantime, go look at the clothing racks for something that fits." He walked to a back room where they could hear him shuffling things around.

Summer started looking through the racks. The most colorful of cloaks was a dark faded purple, with most being gray, tan, or dark brown. She pulled a purple one from the rack and draped it around her shoulders, pulling the strings to tie it up. She looked down, seeing it wrapped around her nicely, covering her clothing down to her knees.

"What do you think?" she asked, smiling and doing a half twirl.

Ethan looked over at her as he pulled a gray cloak from the rack. "You don't look like a tourist anymore," he said with a smirk. He put the cloak on, following her lead. He shrugged, holding out his arms to pose. "Well?"

She let out a laugh. "It looks like you have bat wings."

He looked at his outstretched arms, and his amusement faded. He put his arms down, checking his appearance as best he could. "Better?"

TerRan walked in smiling, "Ah, that's more like it. Now the two of you can pass as locals." He took a seat on a stool behind the counter, opening a box he had brought out from the back. "Found 'em," he said with enthusiasm. "This...technology—it's still new to us. They come from Primula or Helenium—Not sure which." He pulled out a silver object the size of a coin, examining it. "It's probably the only good thing to make its way here via the Kriva Rasturna," he said, thinking about it for a second. "Nevermind." He held it out to Ethan. "Here you go."

Ethan walked up to the counter looking at it, "Thanks," he said, looking at them unimpressed. The main body of the device had a very similar design to that of large earbuds with an ear hook. Its hexagonal shape was an inch wide and half as thick, with a cone shaped portion sticking out that went in the ear. He continued to examine it, seeing the side that faced away from the user's head had a reflective smooth surface that occasionally shimmered in the light and along its edge were a white and two black buttons. He squinted, seeing a small circle near the white button that had a line through it. "How does it work?" he asked as Summer joined him to look at the curious object in his palm.

"Hold down the white button to turn it on or off. The two black buttons are to make it louder or quieter," TerRan started. "Other than that, it does what it's supposed to. When someone speaks to you in a language you don't know, you understand them as though they were speaking yer native tongue." He picked another one up from the box, marveling at the device. "Truly an incredible technology."

Ethan held down the white button, seeing a blue light glow at the center of the device for a second, indicating it was on. He put it on his ear, adjusting it slightly until it was comfortable.

"We need to get you some food next," TerRan said.

Summer tapped Ethan on the shoulder with a confused look. "Did you understand him?"

"Yeah," he said, with a nod. "He was saying we need to get some food."

TerRan's bushy mustache shook when he let out a laugh. "Good! It's working."

It took Ethan a moment before he realized what had happened. "You weren't speaking Common?"

"I spoke to you in the local language—Nubium. That's why yer friend couldn't understand me," TerRan said, gesturing towards Summer. She turned on her translator, putting it on. "Food has been more scarce lately, but I have some bread you can take." He put a couple loaves on the countertop. "As for coin, I can part with some in trade if you have something of interest." Ethan took off his backpack, lifting it up on the table and began rummaging through it. He pulled out the empty water bottles, placing them in front of Summer.

She pulled out the photo of her brother, showing it to TerRan. "Have you seen this kid?" She pointed to the photo. "He's my brother and the reason we're here. His name is Alex, and he was taken. At least, I think he was taken," she said with uncertainty.

TerRan shook his head. "I'm afraid I haven't seen him in town."

"Please, if you know anything, it would be appreciated. We're just trying to get him back."

"I'm sorry, my dear," he said with an apologetic look. "The only thing I can offer is information. The Kriva Rasturna have been tracking down those they think can activate the Steradian Keys across all the dimensions. Those that have the ability are called Catalysts and they're very rare. If they think someone's a Catalyst, they'll take 'em to the capital—Heraldrin, which now acts as their headquarters." He paused a moment, remembering times before the invasion. "The people of Maraldi were once free, but they've been stripping us of our freedoms in the name of social justice since they got here. All a bunch of crap, of course."

Ethan hadn't found too many things to be considered of value in his pack. Aside from the journal and Delphinium Key, which he wouldn't part with, he had only found a flashlight, some coins and his smart phone. "Not much in here," he said, pulling out the phone and coins, placing them on the counter.

"You'd sell your phone?" Summer asked.

"I don't have a lot to trade. Besides, it won't do me any good here."

TerRan picked up a couple of the coins, turning them slowly in his hand. "I don't recognize these coins, but I suppose, to the right collector, they could be worth a good amount." He moved on to the phone. "What'd she say this was?"

"It's my phone—A way of talking with each other over long distances, but that function won't work without a network in place. It does other things, though—takes pictures, plays music and games." He swiped his finger across the screen, activating it. TerRan's jaw dropped when the screen lit up and a chime sounded.

"May I?" TerRan asked, holding his hand out.

"Let me show you some things it can do," Ethan said, starting a music app. He selected a song ensuring the volume wasn't up too loud and let the music play for a few seconds before pausing it. Then he selected a game to start up, summarizing how to play before handing it to TerRan. He played for a few minutes, getting frustrated at the controls.

"Here," Ethan said, pausing the game for him. He closed out of the game, getting back to the home screen and showed him a green battery symbol at the top. "Looks like there's ninety-three percent battery left, but once that's gone, you can't use this anymore. I expect it'll be good for another seven to ten hours depending on what you're doing with it, but there's no way to recharge it here that I know of."

"That is truly incredible and well worth some coin," TerRan said, stroking his chin, deciding how much to offer. "I'll give you a hundred and twenty coin for the...phone...and the coins. I cannot go more than that."

"How much will that get us?" Summer asked. "We'll need food and shelter."

"Spend it wisely, and it should be enough to stay at a nice hotel and stay fed for a week or more. It's a generous sum."

Ethan looked to Summer with a shrug, "Ok. I guess we'll take it."

TerRan nodded with a smile. "Good." He went to the back room and returned with a pouch that jingled when he placed it on the counter in front of them. "A bit of advice for yer travels. The closer you get to Heraldrin, the more guards you'll see on patrol. Keep yer hoods up and keep yer distance. Also, stay away from those with grey eyes. We call 'em the Greys. They're those that are with the Kriva Rasturna and likely don't even know it."

"Grey eyes?" Summer asked.

TerRan's face reddened, and he clenched his fist. "People across the land have been taken for speaking against the Kriva Rasturna. They kidnap 'em and inject 'em with something. It messes with their minds, stripping any sense of individuality and removing the ability to think critically. They aren't themselves anymore, becoming loyal only to the Kriva Rasturna." He let out a long sigh, relaxing more. "The injection affects people differently. Some still act normal for the most part, but hate anyone they believe is against the Kriva Rasturna. Those types are usually used as proselytizers. Others turn into little more than blithering idiots not able to do much more than scream incoherently." He looked down at the counter, "I...I lost a good friend too it. One day he was speaking publicly against 'em when he was arrested. Arrested for speaking his mind." He slammed his fist on the counter. "The next morning when I saw him, he sucker punched me cause I cursed the Kriva Rasturna for taking him. Said that if I ever spoke out against them again, he would report me to the guards and have me arrested. It was then I saw his eyes weren't even purple anymore."

"He punched you for standing up...for him?" Ethan asked.

TerRan nodded. "He wasn't himself. When their eyes have gone grey, they belong to the Kriva Rasturna. Most Greys will stay in groups with each other to shout down anyone that speaks against 'em. Some will just call you foul names and disrespect you at every turn, acting as a petulant child would. Some will go as far to beat you, saying yer words are the violence that justifies their blows. They refuse to believe anything said against the Kriva Rasturna, having been fully indoctrinated. It's as though they've died, and it's torn apart families and friends—a great chasm ripped across our community."

"I'm sorry you've all had to go through this. I wish we could help somehow," she said.

TerRan shook his head, "This isn't yer fight, lass, but maybe we can help get yer brother back. The resistance has members in every town. You should head to Kinsford and contact the cell there. The town is about an hour's walk northeast from here. They're better equipped to help you. More so than me, anyway. Best to contact them tomorrow. For tonight, I recommend you stay at the Inn near the market. When you're ready to contact them, find the fountain—It's hard to miss. Sit on the edge of the basin, placing three of yer coins in a triangle pointed towards the cathedral. Someone will contact you within the hour."

"Thank you for everything," Ethan said, putting out his hand.

TerRan gripped his hand tightly, giving a single shake. "I wish you two well." His gaze shifted to Summer, "and I hope you find yer brother."

Ethan grabbed the coin pouch, putting it in his backpack with the bread while Summer had put the two water bottles back, having refilled them when Ethan was showing off the phone.

TerRan escorted them to the shop's door, opening it a crack to peer out into the street. "I think yer good to go." He opened the door fully, stepped out and looked down the street both ways, seeing a handful of people walking down the road. He took a deep breath, returning inside. "I don't see Dwyll anywhere. Now's the time to leave."

"Thanks again," Summer said, raising her hood up before leaving.

TerRan nodded, patting Ethan on the shoulder as he walked by. "Good luck."

Ethan slung his pack over his shoulder, stepping out onto the street. He felt the cool breeze on his face, noticing the sunshine from this morning had been replaced with overcast. "Thanks for everything." He waved back at TerRan as they headed down the street. Out of caution, the two of them walked in silence until they were safely outside of the small town where they could see people working the fields in the distance, but were otherwise alone.

"That was a lot to take in," she said finally. "I mean. It seems almost worse than what your dad had described. Losing your individuality?"

"TerRan believed what he was saying and if what he said is true, we have a reason for why your brother was taken. Being able to access the Steradian Gate with the key is obviously something you can do. Your brother probably can, too." He shook his head. "That's assuming TerRan was right, with only a few being able to activate it."

"Did they mean to take me instead?"

"It's possible. What did TerRan call where we're from? I've seen it somewhere before." He tried to recall the word. "Del...Delf—"

"Delphinium," she answered.

"Right. Delphinium," he repeated, attempting to put it to memory. "According to him, that's where we're from. We need to look for a glyph combination with the word Delphinium next to it in order to get home. The question now is, where do we look for it?"

"They have way more information on the dimensions here than we do. There has to be someone who's written the different combinations somewhere."

"Agreed, but we have a lot of ground to cover." He smiled to himself. "Intentional or not, it seems my uncle had one more adventure for me to go on."

"I'm glad you're here. I don't know if I'd be able to do this alone."

"If I had to be pulled into an alternate dimension with someone on a quest to save her brother," he said sarcastically, "I'm glad it's with you."

She let out a laugh. "You've gone on quests before?"

"Not quests per se, but my family would take us on those mini adventures. Mostly camping. A few years ago, we camped near some old settlement. By old, I mean homes dug into the side of cliffs old. I can't remember where it was, but there were tour guides that would walk you around and explain what everything was."

"Was it an outside museum?"

He shrugged. "I guess, in a way. Given that most the homes were sectioned off, you couldn't go climbing around them. Anyway, we were hiking on a nearby trail when my dad told us all to stop. When I looked ahead to see what was going on, there was a bear about a hundred yards ahead of us. That was one of the scariest moments of my life."

"I would have run."

"My dad had us back away slowly while still facing it. He explained that you never turn your back on an animal or run. If you run, you give them a reason to chase you and they will catch you."

"Did it attack?" she asked.

"I thought it was going to kill us, but my dad said we were safer once we started backing away. It was off in the distance, and there were no cubs around it. That's when you really have to watch out. After we returned to camp, my dad told me if you ever see a bear cub, stay away from it because the mom is close and would have killed us just for being around it."

Summer became acutely aware of the thick forest on either side of the road. "Do you think they have bears here?" She looked at the tree line with unease.

"That dog creature came from here. Right?" he said.

She felt a chill at the thought of seeing another of those beasts. She moved a step closer to Ethan as they continued to walk. "We should have bought one of those swords from TerRan while we were there."

Ethan cocked an eyebrow. "Have you ever used a sword?"

"A little," she said. "My dad used to really be into them."

He smirked. "I'm trying to imagine you swinging a sword around."

"What is that?" she asked, looking ahead. "A bridge?"

"An old bridge from the looks of it."

The trees opened to a clearing meeting a cliff's edge. An old wooden bridge spanning forty feet had the appearance of not being repaired in years. The left side railing leaned heavily, looking to be held on by a couple nails, while half the railing on the right was completely gone. Ethan peered over the side of the cliff, seeing the rest of the railing on a rocky bank fifty feet below—the edge of the wood touching the rushing water of a river.

"Well, that doesn't look—" Summer gave a yell of surprise, causing Ethan to swivel. Standing next to the cliff's edge was the man from the tavern, holding her still with a knife to her throat. Ethan instinctively went for the dagger he had strapped to his belt, moving the cloak aside, but before he could pull it from its sheath, he heard the man speak in a low growl.

"Don't," he said, with a crooked smile, "unless you'd like to see her die. It'd be quick. Be a shame though. So...pretty..." He lightly traced the blade from her neck to her chest, making sure she wasn't cut. "Where are my manners?" he scoffed. "Name's Dwyll. What's yours?" His gaze lingering where the blade had stopped.

Ethan glared, watching the fear and revulsion on her face. "Ethan. My name's Ethan. What do you want?"

Dwyll shifted his gaze towards him, "You have something that belongs to me." He tapped the tip of the blade on Summer's chest. "You're not from here, meaning...one of you has a Steradian Key. So which key is it? It cannot be the Lunarian Key...leaving Alchemilla or...Delphinium," he said, his mouth contorting into a twisted grin.

Summer slammed the heel of her foot down hard, making Dwyll grunt. She pulled away from him, but his grip was too strong. He roughly pulled her back as Ethan lurched forward to get between them, grabbing his knife from his belt.

Dwyll expertly spun the dagger in his hand, jamming the handle hard into Summer's ribs. She doubled over, unable to yell, having the wind knocked out of her. He placed the tip of the dagger at the back of her neck, glaring at Ethan, who froze in place. "Stupid," he said. "Very stupid." He pulled her back to her feet, replacing the blade under her neck. "Do something like that again and I'll give you a new hole to breathe through. Come to think of it, maybe I should anyway and just search your corpses," he snarled. "Would be easier for me."

"Let her go," Ethan demanded.

Dwyll laughed, "You're not in any posit—"

Something whistled past Ethan's ear and Dwyll staggered backwards as an arrow pierced his shoulder. He howled in pain, dropping the dagger. But before he could regain his footing, he slipped on the gravel. His eyes widened, realizing his momentum was carrying him over the cliff. He gripped Summer's arm tighter to rebalance, but it was too late. He was going over the cliff and knew there was no stopping it.

Summer screamed as she was pulled towards the cliff's edge. She tried bracing herself against Dwyll's weight, but the gravel made it impossible and his grip around her arm was so tight it hurt. Ethan sprinted forward, watching in horror as she was yanked backwards—her free arm stretched out towards him with a look of panic on her face. He heard the two of them scream, losing sight of them over the edge.

He scrambled, hearing a splash before reaching the edge, and looked down. He was relieved to see Summer holding onto a thick root sticking out from the cliff, but Dwyll was nowhere to be seen. Ethan got to his stomach, reaching down to her. "Give me your hand!"

She looked up at him, appearing paralyzed with fear. "I'm slipping!" she said, panicked.

He inched forward as much as he dared, extending his reach. "I know you're scared," he said in a calm voice, "but I need you to take my hand. Get a good grip on that root, then reach up...and take my hand."

"Ok," she nodded, adjusting her grip. She hesitated a moment, taking a deep breath, and reached up, gripping his wrist tightly. She tested her weight before summoning the courage to reach up with her other hand, grabbing his.

Ethan started to pull her up when he heard footsteps running towards him. "Not now," he said, unable to see who was coming. He heard the shuffling of shoes on the dirt next to him as someone crouched nearby.

"Glad I followed you," TerRan said, reaching over the edge to help them. She reached over, gripping TerRan's wrist as well, and the two of them pulled her back over the edge to solid ground, making sure she wasn't in danger of falling back over.

Ethan quickly checked her neck, looking for any wounds. "Are you hurt?"

Summer was breathing hard. She shook her head, "He...he didn't cut me."

Ethan stood up. "Thank you. That could have ended a lot worse."

"I had a feeling Dwyll might try this, given he saw the two of you at the tavern." TerRan said, handing Ethan his dagger. "You dropped this running to catch her."

"Appreciate it," Ethan said, taking it. "My dad gave it to me."

"You'll need more formidable weapons than that if you're going to the capital," TerRan said. "When you contact the resistance cell in Kinsford, tell them TerRan sent you. They should get you what you need." Ethan helped Summer to her feet before turning to shake TerRan's hand again. TerRan smiled, "You two better get going if yer to make it to Kinsford before nightfall. Keep that dagger at the ready and don't be afraid to use it."

"Thank you for everything," Summer said, giving TerRan a hug. He looked down at her with a smile.

"Think nothing of it," he said, taking a step back. He waved them off and headed back to Brexel.

Ethan turned, looking at the rickety bridge with a frown, "Honestly forgot about this."

Summer took his hand, holding it tightly. "We'll get through this together."

Kinsford

Dwyll had been carried down the river a half mile before he managed to get to the riverbank—hauling himself out. He held himself up on his elbows and coughed up water, taking in deep breaths, savoring each until regaining some strength. Brexel was within walking distance, but he wasn't in any shape to get there yet. He rolled himself onto his back, wincing at the pain in his shoulder. Looking down at his wound, the arrow shaft was still embedded, having broken off, leaving only a few inches sticking out. His entire body ached after having been poked and prodded by sticks while being swept across boulders beneath the rapids.

He lay on the sand, catching his breath, trying to remember what happened before plummeting over the cliff. An image flashed in his mind of a man hiding in the trees with a bow a few dozen feet behind the boy. The only discernable feature he could recall was a large, bushy mustache.

He looked over at the broken arrow shaft again and gripped it tightly, gritting his teeth together. Bracing for the inevitable agony, he took a couple of deep breaths and yanked the arrow from his flesh. An uncontrolled scream escaped his mouth and his world spun as fresh blood oozed from the newly opened wound. He stayed still, taking deep breaths, regaining his senses through the throbbing.

"That son of a bitch is going to pay," he said under his breath. He pushed himself to his feet with his good arm, wincing, and started walking towards town. He applied pressure on his shoulder in an effort to stop the bleeding, but he really needed to take a Hemofib pill.

He was sure the two new arrivals were from Delphinium, but how did they get one of the keys? Jerran had had the Delphinium Key last he checked. He shook his head, wondering if he was wrong and they were actually from Alchemilla. They couldn't have the Lunarian Key, as it was still hidden somewhere, and they certainly didn't look like locals.

"No," he muttered to himself. They weren't from here. Their clothing gave it away. They also didn't seem to recognize him at the tavern and everyone in Maraldi knows a Czar of the Kriva Rasturna when they see them.

It didn't matter where they were from. He was sure they had one of the Steradian Keys with them. If he could get it and bring it to Sovereign Rusak, he would be rewarded handsomely. Maybe Rusak would even assign him as ruler of Lunaria once the takeover was complete. A smile crept across his face.

First, he needed answers. Whoever had attacked him would know where the two were headed. All he had to do is what he did best, apply pressure on the citizens to extract the information he needed. It wouldn't take long to identify his assailant.

His clothing had dried by the time he made it to the main road of Brexel and he knew exactly where he needed to go to get those answers. His arm ached from pressing on the wound. Blood had dripped down his arm, leaving volcanic lava-like trails. He was nearly at the tavern, knowing he'd need to medicate soon. He barged in, flinging the door open, and knocked someone out of the way.

"Hey!" a voice came, followed by a gasp of recognition.

He ignored the voice, becoming dizzy from blood loss. Ahead, he saw a man sitting at a table, enjoying his meal with a full glass of water. Dwyll walked forward, stumbling only slightly before slumping in the chair next to him. The man looked bewildered, and then Dwyll muttered a single word. "Leave." The man got up, giving a quick bow and rushed out of the tavern.

Dwyll grabbed a small pouch from his pocket, dumping the contents on the table. A small bottle rolled, hitting a plate, stopping it from falling to the ground. He grabbed it, flipping the top open, and poured out the Hemofib pills onto the table. Dizziness washed over him again, but he forced himself to focus, tossing two pills into his mouth and chugging the glass of water. He shut his eyes and leaned back, waiting for the pills to do their work.

The waitress from earlier came out from the back, hearing the commotion. "You're...you're back, and...bleeding," she said shakily. "Can I get you anything?"

"Information. Come. Sit." She stood motionless, considering the option of fleeing, before he kicked the chair out for her. It nearly fell over, slamming into her hip, causing her to cry out in surprise. "I said...sit," he growled.

She rubbed her hip, slowly taking the seat. "What kind of information?"

"The two you were speaking with this morning when I came in. Where were they going?"

She shook her head and spoke softly, "I...I had never seen them before. I don't know where they went after they left here. Just...just...please. I don't know."

The pill he had taken was already helping with the dizziness and pain in his shoulder. He glared at the woman, disgusted that she was so spineless to not even be able to carry a conversation without stuttering. "I don't have time for your crap." In a swift motion, he grabbed her arm, pulling her closer while also taking out a small syringe from the interior of his jacket. He pulled the cap off with his teeth.

Her eyes went wide, recognizing the glowing orange liquid within it. "No!" she yelled, pulling against him in a feeble attempt at escape, but it was too late. He plunged the syringe into her shoulder, injecting her with the orange substance. He removed the needle, releasing her arm, which caused her to topple backwards out of the chair. She hit the ground, backing away until her back was against a booth. She cradled her arm and lay down on her side, weeping. The remaining patrons quickly fled the tavern, leaving the two of them alone.

He rolled his eyes at her. "Pathetic." He got up from his seat, walking up to her. "Get up," he demanded, watching as she continued crying, having buried her face in her hands. Annoyed, he reached for her, roughly pulling her up. She gasped as he hauled her back to the table and shoved her into the chair.

"Get a hold of yourself. It won't kill you." He took a seat across from her, staring as her sobbing subsided to sniffles. She became calmer as the scopshade he'd injected took hold. He leaned closer, watching the color drain from her lavender eyes, turning them a grey color. Her breathing slowed, and she looked ahead blankly, as though nothing had happened.

"Good. Let's try this again. Where were those two from this morning headed?"

She shook her head, speaking in a calm, even voice, "They never told me."

He cursed under his breath, glaring at her. "Do you know anyone with a big, bushy mustache that lives around here?"

"Sounds like TerRan. He runs the shop across the street. I had told the two from this morning to visit him to get a translator."

Dwyll took in a deep breath. "That's something, anyway." She continued to stare blankly as though waiting for instruction. "Looks like you get a crash course. Go get me something to drink and I'll tell you about the greatness of Sovereign Rusak and the Kriva Rasturna."

***

The sun had nearly set, and storm clouds were threatening rain by the time Ethan and Summer reached Kinsford. Ethan noted almost everything here seemed decades ahead of what Brexel offered, even down to the electric streetlights illuminating the cobblestone road. Having not seen a road like this before, he decided it was like walking into the early nineteen-hundreds. Even many of the homes looked to be from that time, having bicycles out front within fenced yards.

A glaring difference from their own dimension was the lack of cars. Instead, the primary mode of transport appeared to be a three wheeled motorcycle. Ethan had seen nothing like them outside of comic conventions back home, looking to belong in a steampunk movie. Most had two wheels in the front and one in the back, with a large handlebar that connected to the front wheels curving up towards the driver. A large lever came up from the bottom connected to what looked to be part of the engine and behind the backing of the leather seat was a storage area with the exhaust below.

"I'm not going to lie," Ethan said with a grin on his face, seeing one speed by. "I really want to drive one of those." The vehicle's engine continued reverberating in his ears until it turned a corner in the distance.

"You'd look great in one of those hats with the goggles they're wearing," she teased as they entered the outskirts of the Kinsford market. Most of the shops had closed for the night, with merchant booths being packed away and the road nearly emptied of people.

A light highlighted a sign across the street from them. "Pine Street Inn," he read. "That must be the Inn that TerRan was talking about." He pointed to it and felt a raindrop hit his hand. "Let's get inside before we get drenched." They crossed the street, entering the inn just as the rain started.

The decorative display of the lobby left them awestruck. The center of the large room had a tan circular couch with a man leaning back, reading a newspaper. A chandelier hung directly above and at the other side of the lobby was a wide staircase with banisters widening at the bottom. A massive fireplace was lit along the left wall, giving off the crackling of a freshly fed fire and on each side were large tapestries with an unfamiliar symbol in front of a French-style couch. Plush chairs with a coffee table between them displaying hand carved detailing sat next to it.

"This is incredible," Summer said.

A woman from behind the counter to their right chimed in, "Checking in?"

Ethan nodded, "Yes. We'd like a room for the night, please."

"Very good. And good timing, as you got here just before curfew." She looked down at a paper marking it. "It's ten coins for the night or you can upgrade to one of our suites for fifteen coins per night. We just installed wash cubes from Helenium in all the suites."

"Wash cubes?" Summer asked.

The woman became excited. "They're little machines that can clean and dry a full set of clothes in minutes. We're the first inn of Kinsford to have them installed." It was obvious she was proud to advertise that. She leaned closer to Summer, speaking in a lower voice, "Between you and me, I wish I could afford one myself."

Summer looked over at Ethan with an almost pleading grin that made him crack a smile. "We'll take the suite." He took his pack off to get the money out.

"Great," the woman said.

"What did you mean by curfew?" Summer hadn't remembered ever dealing with one.

She glanced up at Summer from her paperwork, confused. "The Kriva Rasturna has a curfew in place." She put the pencil down for a second. "No citizens may be out past eight o'clock. You will get arrested if the guards catch you."

Summer didn't think that was right. "That seems...extreme. There must be some kind of exemption for people that aren't from here and don't know the rules yet."

"First let me welcome you to Maraldi. I loved this country growing up. Sadly, there is no exemption, even for travelers." The woman took on a more serious tone. "Let's just say I'm glad you got here when you did." She shook her head, wanting to change the subject. She picked up her pencil and her demeanor changed quickly as she put on a fake smile. "So, what brings you to Maraldi, and Kinsford, of all places? Honeymooning?"

Summer noticed the unease in her eyes, but shook it off. "Not quite."

Ethan put the coin on the counter. "We're just passing through."

"I understand," she said, taking the coins with a smile. "The suite only has one bed, but there's also a comfortable couch that's large enough to sleep on. There should be a couple of extra pillows and a blanket at the top of the armoire." She held out a brass key with a tag displaying the room number. "You're going to be in room 201, which is up the stairs to the left."

"Thank you," Summer said, taking the key.

"You're quite welcome. Oh, we have a complimentary breakfast starting at six and checkout is at ten. Have a good night."

The two of them made their way up the stairs finding their room. Upon entering, they found themselves in a high-end spacious room with everything they'd need. The king-sized bed sat centered against the wall opposite of the armoire, dresser and desk. The large couch the woman mentioned was positioned under the windows in front of them. A small coffee table was in front of it, with an extra lounge chair off to the side.

Summer went to check out the bathroom, finding a clawfoot tub with a shower head and curtain attachment. The vanity took up a majority of one of the walls, with a massive mirror and two sinks embedded in the countertop. Various small bottles of different shampoos lined up between the sinks, with three bars of soap stacked upon each other. She noted the toilet looked normal enough before turning and seeing a two-foot cube with rounded corners hiding behind the door. Just to the side of it was a small table that had a box of powdered laundry detergent and some written instructions for how to use it.

Eager to test the machine, she opened the top and took off her purple cloak, stuffing it inside. Following the instructions, she put some of the detergent in and closed the top. It was a simplistic design with only three buttons; power, start, and off. She turned it on and pressed the start button with a green indicator light. The little machine whirred to life. Pleased that she'd be able to have fully clean clothes, she left the bathroom to let the machine run.

Ethan had already begun making his bed on the couch when he heard Summer behind him. "Bed's all yours." He took off his cloak, putting it over the back of a chair.

"Oh, it wasn't up for debate," she teased, taking a seat at the end of the bed.

"After today, I'm pretty sure I would find the floor comfortable enough."

"It's been a day for sure." She looked around their new room, taking it all in. "I got that laundry cube thing working, too."

"There were two bathrobes in the armoire when I grabbed the sheets and pillows. We can wear those until our clothes are clean." He took a seat next to her. "Do you want dibs on the shower?"

"Dibs?" she asked.

He chuckled to himself, "Yeah, my dad says that all the time." He cleared his throat, rephrasing, "Do you want the first shower?"

"Umm, yes. Yes, I would." She'd noticed how empty the top of the dresser looked. "I think this is the first time I've been in a hotel without a TV."

"I don't think they've been invented here yet."

She shook her head. "That's so weird to think about." They sat in silence for a moment, giving Summer time to recall the day's events. Specifically, how the cold tip of the dagger felt against her throat. "How do you think that guy knew we had one of the keys with us?"

"Back at the tavern, he saw our clothes. Maybe that was enough," he said with a shrug before displaying a goofy smile.

"What could possibly have you smiling about that creep?"

"You should have seen the look on his face when you smashed his foot," he said. She snickered. Then a detail of the encounter entered his mind. "Did you ever get a look at his eyes?" he asked. "I don't know about you, but they looked orange to me. I've never seen orange eyes before."

"I didn't get the chance to see his face, but I've seen people with purple eyes around here," she said. "TerRan had purple eyes. So did the waitress at the tavern. Different shades, but they were both purple."

"What would cause orange or purple eyes?"

A muffled beeping sounded from the bathroom. "I'm too tired to think about it. I'm going to take my shower and get some sleep." She got up, walking over to the armoire and grabbed one of the bathrobes.

Ethan looked at his backpack leaning up against the desk as the bathroom door closed. He hadn't had time to do much sketching with everything that had happened over the last week. Drawing was often a way for him to relax when he'd had a lot on his mind. He walked to his pack, getting out the journal and a pencil, taking a seat at the desk. Flipping through the pages, he found a blank one and started sketching.

After some time, Summer stepped out of the bathroom wearing the robe with a towel wrapped around her hair. The long shower was needed and relaxing. She saw Ethan at the desk, sketching. "What are you drawing?"

He quickly closed the journal, putting the pencil down. "Nothing. Just doodling. Helps me relax."

"That wash cube thing had my clothes done before I was out of the shower. Please use it," she said, only half joking.

He smiled getting up from the desk. "I plan on it." He grabbed the remaining bathrobe and walked into the bathroom.

Summer looked from behind the curtains at the street below. The rain had subsided and the glow from the streetlamps reflected off the wet cobblestone street. There were a couple of people still walking around with umbrellas. She heard the water turn on from the shower and closed the curtains, curious as to what Ethan had been drawing.

She sat at the desk, opening the journal and flipped through its pages. A sketch of the creature that had attacked them back at the lake greeted her, giving her a chill as she remembered how ruthless the thing was. She quickly turned the page, seeing a sketch of a zemper remembering the creature from their walk earlier. She had been surprised how graceful the animal was as the group of them bounded away into the forest.

Turning the page again, she found herself shocked, staring at a sketch of herself. She smiled, impressed at the detail, when a noise from outside caught her attention. She closed the journal, returning to the window and peered out at the street below.

A man was in the middle of the street with his hands up and two guards were walking towards him—their guns drawn. A third guard was back a few feet holding a leash with one of the dog creatures on it that had attacked the two of them the day before. She could hear the growl reverberate through the glass.

She closed the curtains as much as possible while still being able to watch what was transpiring below. It wasn't clear what the man had done, and he didn't appear to have anything other than his clothes on him. One guard approached him, talking, but she couldn't make out the conversation.

The man got to his knees, placing his hands behind his head in an act of surrender. Then, suddenly, the other guard smacked the man in the face with the butt of his rifle, causing him to yell and crumple to the street. He held his face while the other guard kicked him in the stomach and pointed at him, yelling. A second kick landed on the man's jaw, and he lay motionless.

The guard that had initially struck the man started yelling at the other. Eventually the two of them picked up the man under his arms doing a crutch carry and took him away in the direction they had come—the man's feet dragging lifelessly behind him.

"What the hell is going on here?" she said to herself.

The Market

A vehicle with an overly loud engine passed on the street below, startling Ethan from a sound sleep. He stretched out on the couch, rubbing his eyes. Daylight peaked through the curtains, giving the illusion they were glowing. A noise he couldn't quite place came from across the room, making him quickly sit up. He scanned the room only to find the noise came from Summer. He smiled, realizing she was snoring but couldn't blame her for sleeping hard after the day they'd had.

Turning his attention back to the window, he moved the curtain aside, instantly regretting it when sunlight beamed into his eyes. He squinted, waiting for his vision to adjust. Down below, Kinsford was busy with people going about their day. Occasionally one of the three wheeled motorcycles would go by with its engine rumbling.

There was far more variation in clothing styles here than they had seen in Brexel. People still wore cloaks to keep them warm from the cool autumn morning, but underneath he saw many of the women wearing different styles of dresses while the men wore anything from suits to worker's clothing.

"Anything interesting out there?" Summer asked.

Ethan turned, startled and held back a laugh at the sight of her messy hair. "Sorry. I didn't mean to wake you."

"You didn't," she said, getting out of bed. "I'm going to get ready for the day. Get this rat's nest under control." She hopped out of bed, ensuring her robe was tightened, and grabbed her clean clothes, heading into the bathroom to get ready.

Having slept in his robe as well, Ethan changed into his freshly clean clothes that he had laid out over the back of a chair the night before. He stuffed his journal into his backpack, bringing the Delphinium Key out, looking at it for a moment before placing it back in.

Summer came out of the bathroom a few minutes later, ready to go. "I'm starving. They said something about breakfast when we were checking in. Want to see what they have?"

Ethan felt his stomach grumble and realized they hadn't eaten anything since lunch the day before. "Sounds like a plan."

The two put their cloaks on and headed downstairs to the lobby. A man was dropping off a new stack of the day's newspaper on the coffee table near a couple of women talking to each other. An older woman waved from behind the counter to someone she had just finished speaking with and turned, seeing the two of them nearing the counter. "Checking out?"

"Yes. Room 201." Ethan handed her the key.

"Is there anything else I can do for you?" she asked, putting a check mark on a paper she had in front of her.

"Actually," Summer said, pulling out the photo of her brother and showing it to the woman, "I was wondering if you've seen this boy come through town?"

The woman leaned in. "I'm afraid not. But if someone were coming through town, I'd expect they may have gone through the market. Maybe try asking some of the vendors there? The market is large, with its center being a couple of blocks to the left as you leave. When you see the cathedral, you'll have arrived. There will be lots of people. You can't miss it. Oh, and while we have some...dry...scones here, if you're in the mood for a good breakfast, there is a wonderful baker in the market that has all kinds of delicious pastries. Her name is Diana."

Summer pocketed the photo. "That sounds great. Thank you."

The woman bowed her head slightly. "I hope you consider staying with us again."

They waved, heading out the main doors and walked down the street. The morning air was cool and refreshing as they passed a small park. Children played, running around, chasing one another while the parents sat monitoring should anyone get hurt.

The steeple of the cathedral towered over everything around it, casting a long shadow over the central market. Even from a distance, the area was bustling and loud. Various stands were setup, getting more crowded as they neared the center. The street widened, becoming a large circle going around a decorative fountain. The statue of someone they didn't recognize stood at its center, with streams of water shooting out in arcs into the basin.

Ethan took Summer's arm in his to get her attention. "That must be the fountain TerRan was talking about," he said, nodding towards it. The vendors had set up their stands surrounding it, but left the area directly in front of the cathedral empty.

Three men dressed in different colored religious robes were talking with a guard at the base of the cathedral stairs. Another guard nearby held one of the dog creatures at bay. It snarled at the men as a warning to not come any closer. It was apparent to Ethan that the creatures were uglier in the daylight now that he was getting to see more detail.

"Please return God's house to us," said one of the religious men. "The Kriva Rasturna do not own God, nor his house." The guard ignored him, almost pretending he hadn't spoken at all, but the robed man refused to be treated in such a way. He stepped forward to be better heard. "Let us worship God in peace."

The guard brought his rifle up, pointing it at the man's face. "Leave. Now," he said coldly.

Before seeing the outcome of the situation, Ethan steered Summer away by the arm towards the vendors. They passed stands with homemade jams, handcrafted jewelry, and unique art pieces before they passed a large tent with different bladed weapons.

A dark-skinned merchant in front of the weapons stand held a short sword to show off the craftsmanship. A display table lay before him showcasing various swords and axes laying on top of display cloths. "With the Kriva Rasturna removing our rights to own pulser weapons, protect those you love with the edge of a blade," the merchant yelled out to the crowd. The merchant spotted Ethan arm in arm with Summer and pointed to him, "You, sir! You have a beautiful lady to protect. I guarantee...you will not find better made swords or axes anywhere in Kinsford."

Ethan nodded to the merchant, "We'll come by after we've had some breakfast."

"I look forward to it," the merchant said with a smile before continuing to announce his sales pitch to others walking by.

Nestled between stands were a grouping of tables, with people finishing their meals. A small bakery lay just beyond with a serving window—a small line formed in front of it. The smell of the freshly baked bread wafted towards them, demanding their attention. "It smells fantastic," Summer said, looking at the various fresh breads, muffins and pastries displayed. "Let's get something here."

A middle-aged woman stood at the window, wearing an apron and a plain white bonnet. She handed two loaves of bread to a man and thanked him for his business. The two of them stepped forward, reviewing what they wanted to order, almost missing the woman's greeting. "Hello. My name is Diana and welcome to my shop. What can I get the two of you this morning?" she asked cheerfully.

Before they could answer, a commotion between the men in front of the cathedral started. "You desecrate our place of worship!" one yelled at the guards. The ambient noise of the market dropped momentarily as the outburst caught the attention of most within earshot. The guard said something to the man Ethan couldn't make out, but the man continued his argument. "It's time for you and your friends to leave!"

The guard brought up the butt of his rifle, cracking the man across the face with it, felling him to the ground. Another guard spat at the man who lay holding his face where blood now poured from the fresh wound. "Where's your God now, you bigot!" the guard screamed. The others in religious robes looked on in horror as they scrambled to get their friend to his feet and lead him away. Onlookers shook their heads, shrugging the incident off, and the ambient noise of the market rose back to its previous level.

"What's going on with the guards over there?" Ethan asked Diana.

She sighed, leaning closer to inspect his eyes. She gave a quick nod. "The Kriva Rasturna have been taking over all the places of worship they can in an attempt to separate the people from their religious beliefs. They do this because they know God gives both freedom and hope and they know they'll have a harder time taking over the minds of those of us that are followers of God and his teachings," she said sternly. She took a breath to regain her composure. "Apologies. I just get so worked up."

"No need to apologize to us," he said with a reassuring smile.

"We'll take two of your scones with the—is it raspberry filling?" Summer asked.

She nodded, "It is, and thank you."

Summer pulled out the photo of her brother, showing it to her. "Have you seen this boy at all? He's gone missing."

Diana handed Ethan the scones in exchange for coin and looked at the photo. "Can I hold it? My eyes aren't what they used to be." Summer handed her the photo, and it took only a moment for a visible spark of recognition. "Yes, I believe I saw him a few weeks ago. He stood out because he was being escorted from the cathedral over there." She pointed across the way. "If my memory serves, the guards looked to be taking him towards the airfield. Makes sense as they've been taking quite a few to Heraldrin as of late. An airship is the quickest way to get there."

Summer turned to Ethan as he shoved half the scone in his mouth, biting it in two. "Were you able to even taste it?" she asked, making him freeze, knowing he had forgotten his manners. "I think we should consider the airfield. Might make our trip quicker."

He finished chewing and swallowed his food, grabbing a napkin, and wiping his mouth as Summer began eating. "Agreed. Thanks for the information," he said, turning to Diana, whose attention was focused down the street.

A group of people entered the market shoving others out of the way, daring any to do something about it. A dark-skinned woman in her early twenties led the group with an air of smugness, continuing their commotion before approaching a pale-skinned preteen girl who hadn't noticed them until it was too late. The woman leading the group shoved the young girl out of the way violently, letting out a laugh as she watched her topple backwards into the nearby stand—bits of jewelry spilling everywhere.

As the young girl held her arm and began to cry, the aggressive woman flashed a smile of smug elation, yelling at her, "Maybe that'll learn you to bow to your superiors, you trash!"

Disgusted at the display, Summer moved to intervene. Diana cautioned her, "Wait! You'll get yourself hurt, dear!"

The group started cheering when the young girl tried to get back to her feet, only to be pushed to the ground again by another in the group. They all reveled in the look of fear and confusion on the girl's face, not paying attention to Summer approaching.

"What the hell is wrong with you!?" Summer yelled. "She's a child!"

The lead woman's head spun so quickly that to Summer she almost appeared inhuman. "What did you say?" she snarled with a look of contempt. She faced Summer, snapping her fingers to have her followers surround the newcomer.

"Why would you push a child?" Summer asked angrily.

"Isn't it obvious?" the woman asked dismissively. She looked Summer up and down, giving a look of disgust. "You must be new here. Maybe the guards would like to ask you some questions." The group chuckled menacingly. "Or...maybe we can show you what we do to those that don't know their place," she said, grinning with anticipation. The mob slowly moved in towards Summer, but stopped short as Ethan approached.

He pulled out his dagger, fixing his gaze on the leader. "If any of you lay a finger on her, I won't hesitate to use force to protect her." Seeing an opportunity, the merchant at the bead stand stepped around the broken table, helping the young girl up and getting her to safety.

The leader held up her hand to keep the rest at bay. "Let her go..." she said, glancing down at Ethan's dagger smiling. "You two are obviously new here, so let me point this out. The Kriva Rasturna is the new order and those of you that aren't cleansed are at the bottom of that order. Your eye color tells us if you're truly one of us and only those of us with grey eyes are Cleansed. We are above you and all others and are perfectly justified in teaching the...child...that lesson."

"What does eye color have anything to do with how you treated her?" Summer asked, glaring. "Discriminating against her based on the color of her eyes or anything else is ridiculous!"

The woman laughed. "You can't discriminate against the non-Cleansed."

"Discrimination is discrimination," Ethan said.

"Whatever," the woman said, dismissing them. "I'll let you slide this once, but the next time we meet, if you haven't joined us, you had better be kneeling." She turned her attention back to the mob, motioning them to follow her. She shoulder-checked Summer as she strode by for good measure, appearing pleased with herself. Many people that had been out shopping left the area immediately following the incident, while those that remained gave a wide berth to the group.

Ethan sheathed his dagger, leaning closer to Summer. "Holy crap. That's about as psychotic as I've seen in a while. Come on. Let's get our breakfast." Summer was speechless from the encounter. She took Ethan's arm, heading back to the bakery and kept an eye on the malevolent group.

It didn't take them long to find another person to intimidate, stopping in front of the weapons stand. The merchant looked at them with unease but gave his spiel with a forced smile. "You won't find better made swords or axes anywhere in Kinsford." He began to pick up a short sword in its sheath. "Great self-defense starts with—"

The woman slapped the blade out of his hand snarling, "What do you think you're doing selling swords? Don't you know that swords kill hundreds of people every year?! Think of the innocents you're helping to kill by selling these to just anyone! Did you sell that dagger to the non-Cleansed back there?" She looked around at those remaining, ensuring they agreed and wouldn't stand up to her.

Ethan and Summer had returned to the bakery, confused as to why no one else was speaking up against them. Summer leaned in closer to Diana. "Why are they acting like that?"

Diana lowered her voice to a whisper, leaning towards Summer but never keeping her eyes off the mob, "They call themselves the Cleansed and view the Kriva Rasturna not as a religion but as their only sense of belonging and reason for existing. We call them the Greys because the purple of their eyes disappeared, erased by a narcotic called scopshade wielded by the Czars. Once injected, they are quick to snap and always angry. Not even their own families are safe. If you don't change your beliefs to match theirs, they will bully you into submission—or worse. You were lucky your friend had a blade, or they would have severely beaten or maybe even killed you."

"Why don't the people fight back against them?" Ethan asked in a hushed voice.

Diana's anger subsided more. "We try to reason with them, but they won't have it. You're either with them or you're their enemy and they mean to destroy you. They'll do it by discrediting you, making stuff up about you by spreading lies, and even physical violence." She looked saddened, saying it out loud. "We don't want to fight them. They were our friends and family. We can only hope they see what they've become and change their ways."

They turned their attention back to the confrontation as the woman feigned being offended. "You saying you're not responsible for what people do with the weapons shows your ignorance! Your denial kills people, you bigot!"

"What are you going on about?" the merchant asked. "I'm not a bigot. I sell these weapons to anyone who needs self-defense. Those without knowledge of how to use one should seek training. I'm a merchant, not a mentor in the art of wielding blades."

Suddenly, the others in the group started chanting loudly, "Bigot...Bigot...Bigot..." They raised their fists in the air, repeating their mantra. One of them reached over, grabbing a leg that held up the canopy covering the stand and pulled hard. Another in the group helped, causing the maroon cloth to come down.

"Stop that!" the merchant yelled.

The lead woman grabbed the edge of the table, flipping it towards him, causing blades of various kinds to spill. The merchant screamed in agony when an axe struck his shin, embedding itself in the bone. He crumpled to the ground and those in the group laughed at the pain they caused, pulling out the remaining posts holding the canopy up, bringing it to the ground. They continued to chant as one of them kicked at a lump under the canopy where the merchant was still howling in pain. Ethan took a step forward to intervene, but stopped himself seeing they now had access to the weapons.

The woman turned to the crowd that looked on with horror and bewilderment, smiling at her audience. "Let it be known," she yelled with a wild-eyed grin, "If you buy from this merchant, you will be deemed a bigot as well. Enemies of the Kriva Rasturna! And you should expect to be treated the same!" She raised a fist. "To Sovereign Rusak!" she professed before continuing down the road, with the others following. No one did anything but stare in silence for the next few moments. Some eventually returned to their shopping, thankful they weren't the targets today. Ethan rushed forward, pulling the canopy back, revealing the merchant. He had pulled the axe from his leg. Blood ran down to his foot and his lip was bloodied after the last kick had found its mark.

"We need to get you to a doctor," Ethan said, grabbing one of the display clothes from the ground, pushing it hard against the wound. "Hold this tight. It should help stop the bleeding."

The merchant looked at Ethan with surprise. "Why are you helping me?"

"I'm not with them."

Summer and Diana joined Ethan with others following shortly after seeing their example. "You really stepped in it today, Jon," Diana said. "Be glad it wasn't the guards with one of their TAKs, or this could have been far worse."

"TAKs?" Summer questioned.

She nodded towards the guard holding a leash with one of the skeletal creatures attached. "Those wolf creatures. My husband told me the Kriva Rasturna call them Tactical Attack K-9's, using an odd abbreviation for canine. They're called TAKs for short. He told me they're not natural and I believe it. Vicious things. It would have killed Jon in seconds."

Two bystanders picked up Jon, readying to walk him to a small hospital nearby. "My blades," Jon pleaded. "I can't just leave them here."

Diana put a hand on his shoulder. "I'll hold your weapons while you get fixed up." He nodded in agreement, thanking her before being led away.

"How did all this happen?" Ethan asked.

Diana pointed to a building at the far side of the market. "The old museum over there was converted to display the history of the Kriva Rasturna. Sadly, they twisted reality to shed themselves as a beacon of truth. That'll give you a sense, but know anything positive said about them is nothing more than propaganda."

"We'll check it out. Hopefully, we'll get some answers."

"Also, be mindful of who's around you before you speak. Not everyone can be trusted, even if their eyes aren't grey. I wish you both the best." She smiled before continuing to pick up the weapons scattered across the ground.

The two left the market heading to the museum, happy it was a short walk. Summer was still reeling from the encounter. "I can't believe anyone would treat someone the way those people did."

"There's obviously a lot of manipulation going on here. I think we should take Diana's advice and watch what we say around people. We may end up in a fight if we say something in front of the wrong person."

"You can hide if you want, but I'm not going to hold my opinion to appease these nut jobs."

"I get it, but you saw how they ganged up on you before I pulled my knife. They would have done to you what they did to Jon back there. They seem to get some sick pleasure from hurting others."

"They're bullies on a power trip. Nothing more."

"I know, but I can't let them hurt you. That means we need to be careful. Ok?"

Her edge softened, understanding what he was getting at. "Fine, but I don't have to like it."

THE STATE ARCHIVE

R ows of decorative cement steps greeted them at the museum with a single guard posted at the bottom having his rifle leaning against his leg while he ate a pastry. Draped above the museum entrance was a large black banner with the words *Kriva Rasturna State Archive* in large print. Smaller text was written just below that Ethan read out loud, "Peace through Compliance." He shuddered at the implications, but it was upon entering the building that his jaw dropped. Hanging in the entryway was a detailed painting of a Steradian Key.

Summer nudged him. "I think we're in the right place."

On the opposite side of the large room, various displays lined the outer rim, with the closest one catching his eye. Encased within looked to be five Steradian Keys lined up behind the glass. Upon nearing the display, he found the keys were replicas with one having a blue stone at the center like his. It looked similar enough to the one in his pack, but the details were slightly off. The word *Delphinium* was written just below it on a small card with an emblem for the dimension matching the one on the key.

The other replicas had intricate designs, and each a corresponding name and emblem displayed below it. The left most replica had a dark grey stone with the name *Primula*. Next to it was one baring a green stone, with the name *Alchemilla*. The third was the replica of his, with the fourth having a purple stone with the name *Lunaria*. The final had an orange stone at the center with the name *Helenium*.

Summer began to read a blurb sealed in the case with them.

The Kriva Rasturna have rightfully claimed the Primula and He-lenium Steradian Keys. If you have any information on the other three, it is your duty to help restore peace by telling the closest guard what you know. If no guards are present, report to the nearest Kriva Rasturna controlled cathedral. Failing to comply will be met with harsh punishment for both you and your loved ones.
You control their fates.

"They've been here for years and still haven't found the Lunaria Key," she said, moving to the next display. A painted portrait of a middle-aged man standing in a heroic pose holding the Primulan Key was displayed with bits of rubble at the bottom.

Ethan leaned in, reading the information.

Leader of the Kriva Rasturna, Sovereign Rusak, after the initial bat-tle to conquer injustice within Primula. Sovereign Rusak lead Kriva Rasturna forces against those responsible for social injustices that had been occurring for centuries. He tore the power from those with evil and hatred in their hearts, returning it to the people so they could be their true selves. He enlightened all the people of Primula that the self is the center of the universe, bringing equity to all.

A grim look crossed Ethan's face as he walked to the next display depicting a city in flame because of a riot occurring in the streets with hundreds of people fighting. Statues of people he didn't recognize were being pulled down with ropes while countless bodies lay dead.

The people of Helenium helped Sovereign Rusak conquer injustice in Helenium a decade after Primula. They saw the truth and knew they had to protest peacefully against the evils of their neighbors.

Another display had a painting depicting yet another riot, but was focused closer to the street. At the center, a child could be seen being ripped from their mother with a person behind her swinging a weapon towards the back of her head.

Those that turned away the helping hand of the Kriva Rasturna, soon had the evil in their hearts destroyed either through becoming one of the Cleansed or through death. The non-believers would no longer be allowed to hold sway in the markets and businesses. Children were removed from the non-believer's negligence and brought to education centers for cleansing and enlightenment.

They moved to the last display depicting Rusak having just entered Lunaria with legions of guards from the other two dimensions behind him.

Now Sovereign Rusak fights to conquer injustice in Lunaria, starting here in the now worthy nation of Maraldi. He wishes to bring you all into the fold with plans to expand to other Lunarian countries soon.

The ways of the Lunarian ancestors were wrong. You can fight against your bigotry by joining us in the fight against injustice. Report those who do not follow the path. Report any who oppose the Kriva Rasturna.

Ethan leaned towards Summer, speaking quietly, "Well, that got dark."

"Really? What part?" asked a voice from behind them.

The two of them turned, seeing a pale woman in a light grey, knee length business dress standing behind them. Her blonde hair was slicked back, and she had a look of condescending amusement behind her glasses.

Summer pointed to the image of the child being pulled away. "It's a bit much to take away someone's kid and bash her in the head. Isn't it?"

The woman stepped forward between them, pulling her glasses down slightly to look at the display. She smirked. "She could have easily avoided her fate had she only complied. Peace through Compliance, right?" she tilted her head, smiling.

"What did she need to comply with?" Ethan asked.

The woman's smile faded, and she pointed to the woman. "This part of Helenium history is after Sovereign Rusak mandated children report to their schools for corrective lessons. Kriva Rasturna corrective instruction is required for all, including children. Of course, you should know this already. This birthing person didn't comply, so she had the child removed as property of the state."

"It's the right of the parents to know what their children are being taught or if something should be taught to them at all," Summer said sternly. "The government shouldn't be mandating any ideologies to children." Ethan's eyes widened slightly as he slowly turned his gaze towards her, wondering what kind of trouble she'd gotten them into.

The woman's features twitched ever so slightly as her indifference changed to a harsh stare. "Interesting," she said, pushing her glasses back up. Summer only then noticed that the woman's eyes were grey before she turned, walking away from them casually. They watched as she picked up speed, weaving through museum goers before entering the next room and over to an armed guard. She leaned close to him, saying something they couldn't hear, and looked back in their direction, pointing at them. The guard locked eyes with Ethan.

Summer realized what she'd done, but it was too late. "I think we should leave."

"Yep," Ethan agreed, grabbing her hand and pulling her towards the entrance. They ignored the guard, yelling at them to stop, continuing to hurry. More people were funneling into the archive, forcing the two to push their way through the crowd. Many gave looks of bewilderment and shock as they were shoved out of the way until the two finally got outside and rushed down the stairs.

The guard from earlier still stood at the bottom with his back to them. Not wanting to get his attention, Ethan slowed to a walk, hoping to blend in as they neared, but the hope shattered at the sound of a shrill whistle being blown from the main doors. The guard turned, looking for the disturbance.

Summer looked back at a guard pointing directly at them from the entrance. "Stop those two!" he yelled. The guard at the bottom of the steps raised his pulser rifle, but Ethan was close. He grabbed the forestock, shoving it upward hard into the guard's face. They heard a sickening crunch, and the man yelled out, dropping to his knees. A woman screamed and passersby started running, causing a commotion that gave the two of them enough cover to cross the street and duck down an alley. Amidst the chaos behind them, they heard another whistle and the unmistakable sound of a growl.

Ethan glanced behind them as they ran where two guards entered the alley, following one of the TAKs. A knot formed in his stomach, seeing the menacing creature giving chase. "Keep running and don't look back," he said. Nearing a T junction in the alley, he pulled Summer to the left just as a pulser shot whizzed by her head, striking the brick building instead.

The TAK snarled directly behind them but lost its footing, slipping on the loose gravel of the alleyway and slammed into the building. Running at full speed from the alley, they entered the busy market, continuing past shoppers who gasped in shock as they ran by. Screams followed shortly after, with the TAK still in pursuit, knocking into one of the nearby stands.

People panicked, scrambling to get away from the beast as quickly as they could with one person knocking into Summer, almost causing her to fall, but Ethan still had a tight grip on her hand, helping her up quickly, getting them sprinting again. When they neared the fountain, they heard the rumble from one of the three wheeled motorcycles. Ethan saw it coming and pulled Summer hard across the roadway just when the TAK leapt to attack. It slammed hard into the vehicle, toppling it over with ease before it mindlessly tore into the unwitting driver.

The two ran past more stands and around the fountain. Pulser shots flew by them, striking the fountain, causing bits of marble shards to fly. They entered another alley, hearing more ear-piercing whistles from their pursuers. Shots flew past them into the nearby brick walls, and Ethan continued leading Summer away from the chaos. His breathing became labored and his side started aching, but he knew if they stopped, even for a second, it would be their end.

His focus to keep moving was so intense that he barely registered hands gripping his clothing and jerking him off his feet. While being pulled through a door, he had the odd sensation of weightlessness before Summer's hand was torn from his, hearing her shriek in surprise. He crashed hard onto a concrete floor, knocking the wind out of him. A figure loomed over, putting a hand on his chest, holding him down while putting a finger to their lips.

"Stay down and shut up or the guards will find us all," the figure said.

Ethan strained to see Summer but could make out that she was being held down as well with someone's hand over her mouth. Her wide eyes returned Ethan's stare. His vision began to adjust to the new lighting, allowing him to make out a third figure crouched near a dirty window next to the door they had been pulled through. Shadows flew by the window, coupled with the sound of running footsteps outside. The running came to a halt only a moment later.

"Where did they go!?" a frustrated voice demanded.

Another voice piped up, "They must have doubled back into the market. Come on!" The shadows moved, and the footfalls faded.

The figure near the window stayed completely still, listening for the next couple minutes, before peering up through the glass. The daylight revealed a tan-skinned woman in her early twenties with shoulder length black hair. She wore a dark turtleneck sweater and slacks with a thick belt showcasing a sheathed knife. When she was satisfied the guards weren't returning, she turned, looking at the two of them on the ground. "Check their eyes," she ordered.

"Green," reported one near Summer.

A large, dark-skinned man in his mid-twenties wearing a thick tan coat loomed over Ethan. "Blue," he reported.

"What?!" she said, surprised. She walked over to Ethan quickly with a flashlight, motioning for him to sit up. She shone the light in his eyes, blinding him temporarily. "Blue. This can't be right," she said, shaking her head. She walked over to Summer, double checking her eyes as well. "What the hell is going on?" she said, standing and flipping off the light. "Check them for weapons."

The guy over Ethan roughly brought him to his feet and grabbed the dagger from his belt, tossing it to the ground. He flipped Ethan around, taking his backpack. "I'm going to take that personal in a minute," Ethan said, half joking.

The man ignored him, kneeling and continuing to shuffle through the pack, when his expression quickly shifted to shock. He slowly pulled out the Delphinium Key, staring at it. "I don't think they're from here," he said, standing up, holding it out.

The woman grabbed the key, examining it for a moment before glancing up at Ethan. "Looks like we have a lot to discuss," she said, handing the key back. "Put that in his pack with the dagger. We need to get these two down to Fletcher." She walked over to Summer, extending an arm to help her up. "Caleb. You're on watch." She looked at Ethan and then back at Summer. "The big guy here is Liam," she said, gesturing towards him. "He'll be leading the way. You're coming with us."

"Who are you people?" Ethan asked.

"I know you probably have questions," she said, "but it'll have to wait until we're somewhere safe. For now, just know we're not going to hurt you."

Summer leaned closer to Ethan. "We're better off with these guys than those guards."

"Can't argue with that. Let's hear what they have to say," he said, still trying to figure the group out.

"This way," Liam said, waving them forward. He led them to a room at the back and silently pulled an old metal storage locker out from the wall. It swung open like a door, revealing it was on wheels and attached by a hinge. Embedded in the wall was a short, narrow passage with a hole in the floor at the back. Liam's broad shoulders barely fit when he turned to go down a ladder.

Ethan followed, looking down into the darkness where Liam was now barely visible, being at least two stories down when he heard him step off the ladder onto what sounded like concrete. He turned, looking at the woman, "Are you sure about this?"

She rolled her eyes at him. "What, are you afraid of the dark or something? We'll turn the lights on after I close this door behind us. Promise." She motioned her arm towards the ladder, growing impatient.

Ethan didn't look amused but opted to go down the ladder regardless, followed by Summer shortly after. Before he reached the bottom, the light faded, and they heard the fake door latch into place from above. They were lost in a sea of darkness until Liam flipped on a switch, filling the claustrophobic concrete passage in dim yellow lighting. The passage before them seemed even narrower than the one above, barely being shoulder length in width.

Ethan shuddered as the cold of the concrete enveloped him. "Where are we?"

"This is a left-over bunker from the Great War that happened about fifty years ago," Liam replied. "I doubt our grandparents thought they'd ever be used again, but they've turned out to be an asset."

As the group followed Liam through the passage, Ethan felt the temperature continue to drop the further they went. He had lost track of what direction they were headed, but estimated they were well outside of the market area. Eventually, they came to a dead end where Liam walked up to the wall, knocking in a pattern. A second later, they heard a latch and the wall in front of them slid open, revealing a large concrete room with a half-dozen people looking busy.

Liam waved to the person who opened the door for them. "We've got some visitors for Fletcher," he said, nodding back towards Ethan. Seeing the newcomers, another person guarding the entrance raised their rifle, giving them a reason to not cause problems.

Two others off to their right were busy listening to some large radio equipment scribbling information down. Others looked to be inventorying supplies that had just come in. There was a room to the left and at the far wall were hallways that jutted off to either side. Ethan heard the entrance shut behind them with a thud, catching him off guard.

Liam escorted the group into the room on the left, where a conversation was occurring. A tall, muscular man wearing a white-collared shirt and rough work slacks with a full utility belt stood hunched over a table with his back to the group. He was talking to a young woman opposite of him wearing glasses, a brown button up vest over a white-collared shirt and matching brown slacks tucked into her knee-high boots. "You're absolutely sure this is where it is? Because I need you to be a hundred percent confident about this, Elise. We don't have the resources for multiple attempts."

Elise had a determined look as she abruptly shut a notebook. "It's here just north of where the river splits at the base of Mount Hadley. I'm sure of it," she said, stabbing the map with her finger. "For three generations, my family has been researching Mystell and the keys. Everything points to the lost city being right around here. We just need to follow the river until we find a specific rock formation."

"Any way to narrow that down?"

"According to my grandfather's findings, the formation should look like an old musical pipe organ on the side of the mountain. I don't know details or exactly how big."

The young woman who had escorted them with Liam cleared her throat, walking up to the table to get the other's attention. The guy turned, excited to see her before noticing Ethan and Summer; his mood drastically shifting as he shot them glares.

"Who the hell are they!?" he demanded, gesturing towards Ethan. "Talia, are you crazy!? You can't just bring people down here! You've compromised our base of operations!"

Talia raised her hand. "Let me explain before you rip my head off." She looked over at Liam, motioning for him to give her the backpack. He tossed it to her, and she put it on the table, opening it and pulled out the Delphinium Key, placing it in front of the others. Elise's eyes went wide.

"They had this with them," Talia said. "We've checked their eyes. They aren't Greys and from what I can tell, they aren't with the Kriva Rasturna either."

Ethan piped up, "Just so we are clear, after what I've read at that museum, there's no way in hell I'm letting you give that to them. Plus," he said with a shrug, "we need it to get home."

Fletcher's glare faded. "Museum?"

Talia smirked. "They made quite the commotion when they bolted down the stairs at the state archive. Whatever they did caused a chase that almost got them shredded by a TAK. Unfortunately, some poor guy drove his revbolt by at the wrong time, getting the brunt of it becoming collateral damage."

Summer put her hand to her mouth, shocked. "Oh, my God. Are they going to be, ok?"

Talia and Fletcher stared blankly at her for a second before he responded, "Probably not. Those things were created to destroy."

Elise picked up the Steradian Key. "I've never been this close to one of the actual keys before." She turned it in her hand, examining it with reverence, holding it directly under the light while she took in the detail of the emblems, talking to herself, "Compass design. The five emblems of the dimensions, including the Guardian." She ran her finger around the edge, looking at the glyphs, turning the outer ring slightly before bringing it up closer to investigate the stone in the center.

"This isn't the Lunarian Key," she said finally. "The compass design and the stone being blue. Ours would be lavender or a deep purple. They're not from Lunaria," she said, looking up at them. "I think they're from Delphinium."

Fletcher glanced at Talia, then at Ethan. "Ok. If you're not with the Kriva Rasturna and you're not from Lunaria, then why are you here? Why come here if you're from a dimension free from Rusak?"

Summer pulled out the photo of her brother, handing it to Fletcher. "We're here looking for my brother. He was taken about a month ago. We just need to find him and get out of here. That's it. We're not here to cause trouble."

Fletcher shook his head, handing the photo to Talia. "I don't recognize him. Have you seen this kid?"

Talia nodded. "Caleb mentioned a kid matching this description taken from the cathedral a few weeks back. This is the one they made a deal about being some kind of terrorist the regime had been looking for." She looked to Summer, "Of course, no one in their right mind believes this kid is a terrorist."

"We were told he may have been taken to an airfield," Summer said.

Fletcher sighed. "That would make sense, given what we've seen the last few months. If they thought he was a Catalyst or could get them one of the keys, they'd have taken him to Heraldrin." He looked at Ethan. "Alright, I believe you're not a threat to us, but that only answers one question. How did you obtain this key in the first place?"

He hated the constant reminders of his uncle's death. "It was passed to me by my Uncle Jerran. He...passed away not long ago."

"Jerran Burke?" Fletcher asked, glancing at Talia, who also looked surprised.

"Yeah," Ethan nodded.

"Did you know your uncle had a hand in helping the resistance get its start?" he asked.

"TerRan told us a bit about that back in Brexel," Ethan confirmed.

"You two get around," Talia said.

Summer stepped forward. "TerRan helped us get away from someone named Dwyll. I'd be dead if he hadn't stopped him."

"Dwyll, the Czar?" Fletcher asked. "If he's coming after you, that means he thinks you have the key." Fletcher turned, seeing Elise still examining it. "Can I see it, Elise?" She nodded, handing it to him with a look of disappointment. "You'll get another look at it, I promise."

He studied the key for a moment. "We've been fighting the Kriva Rasturna since Rusak and his regime arrived a few years ago. They started converting people through blackmail or bribes where they could. Then they moved on to using scopshade; a drug that makes those injected with it more susceptible to manipulation and control."

"We've all lost loved ones too it," Elise interjected.

"They started with those in government," Fletcher continued, "Those trusted and elected by the people to keep our freedoms intact. Then they moved to control the flow of information, taking over the newspapers. Eventually, they took over businesses and even school boards and teachers with their indoctrination, corrupting them one by one to all bow to them. They spread hate and division, all while saying they're fighting injustice, but their end goal is clear. They want to control everything and enslave the people."

"We got some firsthand experience with some of the Greys in the market," Ethan said.

"We saw," Liam said. "We've been monitoring that group for a while now. They've become pretty bold knowing they won't be held responsible for their actions given they're ideologically aligned with the guards."

"Is there any way to reverse the drug for those infected?" Summer asked.

Talia shook her head. "Not that we know of. They don't listen to reason or logic and won't let us work with them to find a cure. From what we gather, they don't even believe their own memories, as they're taught that everything they learned as a child was a lie and a manipulation. It affects some more than others."

Summer grabbed Ethan's arm. "We need to get him out of there. They may have already drugged him."

Talia shook her head. "It's likely he was injected before being transferred."

Elise pipped up, "If he's actually a Catalyst, he might be immune to scopshade. We saw it with the Lunarian Catalyst last year. The Kriva Rasturna tested people for months using the Helenium Key and when they refused to help, they were injected. It had no effect on the Catalyst, so they were imprisoned before—" Elise stopped herself.

"Before what?" Summer asked.

"Before they were killed for not complying," Talia finished.

"The fight hasn't been going well against them," Fletcher said. "We've lost a lot of good people and it seems the regime has their hands in everything. But..." He looked down at the Delphinium Key, "I think we have an opportunity that will help us both."

Guinea Pig

Alex immediately regretted opening his eyes, squinting at a bright light above him. He attempted to move his arms, only to find they were tied down with straps crossing over his chest and legs as well, holding him tightly to a table sitting at an angle. Once his eyes adjusted, he looked around, finding himself in an operating room that looked straight out of a retro horror movie. Charts lined the walls and ahead of him was a large two-way mirror with a metallic door next to it. He looked down at a cart with vials of different colored liquids, cotton balls, and various metal utensils, including needles, that looked alarmingly large to him.

He struggled against the restraints, finding it a futile attempt just before the door opened. A lanky, middle-aged, balding man walked into the room wearing a white lab coat followed shortly by a dark-skinned woman wearing a formfitting black dress suit. The man looked up from his clipboard at Alex and shook his head, annoyed.

"Prevara. Why am I looking at some kid?" he asked.

"Come now, Haas," she said, "This is the brat we've had over in holding. You know...the one the TAKs cornered in Delphinium a few weeks back?"

Haas raised an eyebrow. "This is the one that's been immune to the scopshade?"

Prevara nodded, "That's right. I believe there's an opportunity here and Rusak agreed."

"Sovereign Rusak?!" Haas said, surprised. "What was so important that you had to bother the sovereign?"

"Rusak and I demanded you be here because we need you to take a blood sample. If he's immune, maybe you can use that fancy bioengineering degree we helped you get to find a way around the immunity. Do that, and the sovereign will be immensely appreciative."

Haas brought his hand up to his chin. "Interesting. It may be possible to isolate the gene responsible for the insusceptibility." His eyes narrowed. "Exactly how appreciative would the sovereign be? You've promised without delivering before. Why should I believe you this time?"

"I could always just inject you with scopshade if you decide to become uncooperative," she said with a smile. "Unlike our friend here, you're not immune, so do not...test me."

Haas furrowed his brow. "I'm not testing. Just wanting to be recognized for my accomplishments."

"And you will be. If...you're successful in removing his immunity. We wouldn't have had as much resistance here if the Lunarian Catalyst hadn't been killed when they were found to be immune. Maybe we can avoid that kind of push back in Delphinium with the boy here."

"Perhaps," Haas said, walking to where Alex was restrained. He tossed his clipboard onto the metal tray table, where it clattered loudly, knocking a vial over. "What's your name, kid?"

Alex glared at him. "You guys have had me locked up for weeks, injecting me with all kinds of crap. Why the hell am I here? Why did you take me!? Who are you people!?"

Haas shook his head. "I won't be answering your questions. The only thing you need to know is that you're here because we deem it necessary. You'd best get used to your new normal because it won't be changing anytime soon. Now...again. What's your name?" Alex remained silent, refusing to budge on any request. "Fine," Haas said. "How about I make up a name for you? Maybe...Fido or Chomper? How about calling you what you are...Guinea Pig."

"Screw you!" Alex yelled. "I'm not answering any of your questions!"

Seeing the conversation going nowhere, Prevara unbuttoned the top of her blouse and folded the collar of her shirt to the side, revealing her cleavage. She strutted past Haas, smiling innocently, and leaned close to Alex. "Perhaps we could take a different approach, hmm? What can I do to apologize for how we have treated you the last few weeks?" she asked, placing her hand on his chest. "Just answer his questions and maybe after...I'm sure we can think of something. We want you to be happy here. Make you feel you belong."

The perfume she wore was intoxicating, making Alex look her over and consider what she was implying. She was an attractive woman with burning orange eyes—the color initially catching him off guard. Her long black hair was brushed back, having a red streak with strands falling as she moved her lips close to his, teasing him, but he recognized the manipulation. He sighed. "You're too old for me, lady."

Prevara took a step back, annoyed as Haas let out a single loud laugh, as though he'd been bottling it up for a year. "Looks like you've lost your touch, Prevara."

Prevara grabbed a syringe. "Let's get this done. Shall we?" She stabbed the needle into Alex's neck.

"Hey!" Alex yelled, grimacing.

"What are you doing!?" Haas demanded. "That's not the proper way to take a blood sample."

She pulled the syringe out. "Oh, I know," she said, smiling. "I just wanted to do it." She jabbed the needle in Alex's leg, making him yell uncontrollably. Reveling in his pain, she watched his expression, twisting the needle around before releasing it. She scoffed at him, leaving the needle embedded before turning and walking out the door.

Haas removed the needle, placing it on the table. "You've got balls, kid. I'll give you that. She is not a woman that enjoys being rejected."

"No kidding," Alex said, still feeling the burning of the fresh wounds.

***

Dwyll had finally made it to Kinsford. He took a deep breath of fresh air, deciding it was a good day watching with delight as people recognized him and moved out of the way when he neared. He enjoyed the peasant's fear. It kept them in check and, even better, made it so he didn't have to interact with the lower life forms in this dimension.

He was also fortunate enough to have discovered the assailant who shot him with an arrow. It was quick work to discover where TerRan would be, and he hadn't minded waiting for him in his shop to return the next morning. He prided himself on being able to extract information from people, but took a special interest in

TerRan, inflicting as much pain as he could. After all, it was fair, given his shoulder was still sore.

Dwyll had to give him credit, though. He remained tight-lipped even after cutting his hand off. Others he had tortured usually gave up shortly after using a dagger to slice open one of their thighs. TerRan impressively withstood all the physical torture looking like he was willing to endure more. It was only after the threat to kill everyone in Brexel, starting with the children, that he finally relented.

Now he had his target's names, that they had the Delphinium Key, and that they should be here in Kinsford to join up with the resistance in a misguided effort to rescue the girl's brother. And as a thank you for the information, Dwyll found he was benevolent enough to end TerRan's suffering. He smiled, remembering the look of regret on TerRan's face before firing an arrow through his eye with a crossbow.

He snapped out of his thoughts as a TAK walked by him with a group of guards. He had reached the market, which was mostly deserted. One stand was disheveled, laying in a pile on the ground while the others looked abandoned. A shredded body lay next to an overturned revbolt near an alley. Groups of guards looked to be combing the area, tracking something or someone.

"What the hell happened here?" he asked a nearby captain of the guard.

The captain looked up, recognizing Dwyll, and snapped to attention. "We pursued two outsiders in the area about an hour ago. We're trying to pick up their trail as they seemed to just vanish during the chase. They have to be here somewhere, and we'll find 'em."

Dwyll wasn't amused, considering half the guards to be completely incompetent. "Take me to where they were first spotted."

The captain motioned him towards the state archive. "This way, Sir."

A dozen guards were still investigating the interior as they entered the building. Newspaper reporters trying to get the story harassed guards that had been on site at the time—the guards becoming visibly more agitated at them by the minute.

Dwyll was escorted through the crowd and pointed to a woman in a grey dress suit. "She's the one who first reported them," the captain said.

Dwyll noticed he was in the historical section explaining how the Kriva Rasturna arrived and why they were there. "Doing some research. Interesting." The woman the guard had pointed out was giving an interview to a reporter, and he snaked his way around the crowded room to her.

The reporter saw him approaching and bowed to him. "Czar, a pleasure to meet you. I'll return in a few minutes to conclude the interview," she said to the woman before leaving.

He looked down at the woman, seeing her eyes were grey. "You know who I am?"

"Yes, Czar," she started, "and I'd be happy to go over the incident."

"Good," he said. "Start at the beginning."

She smiled, bowing her head. "A boy and a girl in their early twenties were dressed in cloaks to blend in, but the clothing underneath betrayed their façade. I spotted it from across the room. That's when I went to talk with them."

Dwyll leaned against the wall, imagining the interaction. "Did they say anything out of the ordinary? Maybe what they were looking for here?"

"They seemed to be disturbed by the imagery of the child being taken from their birthing person," she continued. "They also seemed confused by the idea of 'Peace through Compliance'. The girl even went so far as to say that 'parents'," she gestured, "should have the right to know what their children are taught." She scoffed. "Birthing people don't have rights over children. All belong to the Kriva Rasturna, and we will take children as we see fit." She bowed again to Dwyll.

Dwyll chuckled in amusement. "Rights?"

The woman nodded. "Yes, I thought it strange as well. It was then that I went to report them so they could be taken into custody for re-education. But before the guard could react, they were running for the door." She pointed to the entrance Dwyll had come in.

Dwyll stood back up and lifted the woman's chin slightly with his finger. "You've done well, child, doing the Kriva Rasturna a great service in your quick thinking. Remain vigilant," he said, lowering his arm. "These two are more dangerous than you could imagine, having stolen one of the Steradian Keys that rightfully belong to Sovereign Rusak and the Kriva Rasturna as a whole. Feel lucky you weren't harmed. Just yesterday, they even had the audacity to attack me, a czar, which, as you know, is punishable by death."

The woman gasped. "Then they are beyond re-education. They are...enemies...of the Kriva Rasturna. They must be destroyed."

"Perhaps," he said. "Peace through Compliance." He gave a half bow.

The woman bowed in return. "Peace through Compliance." She left, retreating to another room, leaving Dwyll to mull over the new information. He glared across the room at the image of the child being taken. He hated having to deal with tearing people from their self-given rights with each of these dimensional take overs. If what the woman said was accurate, Delphinium was going to be another pain in the ass. He shook his head in disgust before a thought entered his mind. Perhaps if he got the Delphinium Key for Rusak—hand delivered it...perhaps Rusak would leave the incursion of Delphinium to Prevara. Maybe even give him the position of leading Lunaria. A grim smile crept across his face.

"Hey!" Dwyll yelled to a nearby guard walking by.

The guard jerked his head at the noise, standing at attention upon recognizing the czar. "Sir! How can I help you?"

"Find the two outsiders. That...is your priority," Dwyll spat.

The guard nodded. "We received good news only moments ago. Our informant in the Kinsford resistance has set up a meet for tonight. We believe they'll have information on the whereabouts of the fugitives."

"Good. Pay them handsomely if it leads to their capture."

The guard nodded, "Yes sir!"

"Second, I have business in the capital and will leave tonight. I want these two captured alive. Not dead. Do you understand?"

The guard nodded, "Yes."

"When you have them, you are to get them onto the first airship to Heraldrin. I don't want to be kept waiting. Inform your men this comes direct from me."

"Right away," the guard said, bowing before shuffling off.

Dwyll walked over to the display of Steradian Keys the woman had pointed to. He crouched, getting a better view, smiling at the replica of his objective.

THE PLAN

Ethan and Summer were escorted by Talia to the mess hall for further debriefing. They had walked past the radio equipment near where they entered, taking a corridor at the end of the hall to the right. Feeling the chill of the air, Ethan was impressed by how well the concrete walls kept the entire base cooled. They passed a room filled with bunks and took a right into the mess hall. Walking through the room, they noticed others that had been eating or conversing had stopped what they were doing and began staring. Whether it was from suspicion or fear, Ethan couldn't tell. They took a seat at an elongated metal table, where Fletcher brought them some food and water.

"So, you're the one that activated the key?" Elise asked.

Summer nodded. "Yes, but to be honest, I didn't know what to expect."

"If that's correct, it explains why the Kriva Rasturna took your brother," Fletcher said. "They apprehend anyone they think has the slightest chance of being a Catalyst, using specially trained TAKs when they can. If they control the Catalysts, they control travel between the dimensions. However, this time, it would seem they grabbed the wrong sibling."

"Wrong sibling?" Summer asked.

"Yeah," Elise said excitedly. "Being a Catalyst is so rare that not even those in the same bloodline always have the ability to activate the keys. Being related just makes it more likely. There are many stories written in Lunarian history where siblings would fight because one would have the ability and the other would not. A great example of this is the Procellarum War where two kingdoms, whose leaders were brothers, went to war to take the—"

Talia held up her hand. "We don't need a history lesson right now, Elise. We haven't even been properly introduced. I highly doubt they want to hear the history of a land they know nothing about."

Fletcher stood from the table. "Let's fix that then, shall we? Fletcher O'Connor," he said, holding out his hand to Ethan, who shook it. "I'm in charge of the resistance cell here in Kinsford."

"Ethan Burke," he replied. "Resident of...Delphinium, I guess?"

Fletcher smirked and pointed to Talia. "Over there's my second in command, Talia Mendoza." Talia waved and he pointed to the next. "Then we have Elise Fleming, our historical researcher and science division." Elise wore a big grin on her face, doing a quick wave. "Continuing," he pointed at Liam, "This big guy over here is Liam Gomez; our communications and technologist." Liam smiled, giving a nod. "I believe you met our recon, Caleb Parks, back when they pulled you off the streets. He should be in later tonight."

Summer stood up, reaching across the table to shake Fletcher's hand. "Summer McKeown," she said, smiling as she shook the hands of everyone around the table.

"Can I continue with the history lesson now?" Elise asked.

Talia rolled her eyes. "No...Elise. Not now." Elise sighed, leaning back in her seat, feeling dejected.

"Is it possible that my brother, Alex, would have the ability to activate the key if he tried?"

"It's possible." Elise said, sitting forward as though getting ready to speak to a riveted audience. "We also have stories of siblings that could both activate the keys, but I won't bother going into it," she said, shooting Talia a look.

"By chance, were you able to activate it too?" Fletcher asked Ethan.

Ethan shook his head. "I haven't tried, and I don't know the combination to get back. We're stuck here until we can discover what it is because my dad destroyed the page with all the combinations."

"Why would he do that!?" Elise asked, half offended.

"He said he was trying to protect me and my sisters."

"I've heard stories about your uncle," Liam said. "Never thought I'd get to meet any of his relatives, though. You really don't know how much he helped us. Do you?"

"I don't have the details. Just that he was here off and on for the last ten years. He never said anything to us about Lunaria. Only my dad knew. I didn't even know this place existed until I read about it a few days ago."

"We're in his debt," Fletcher said, "but going back to the topic, if Jerran could activate the keys, then there's a good chance you can. Both of you may be Catalysts, which means the Kriva Rasturna will stop at nothing to get you both once they figure that out." He paused a moment, glancing between Ethan and Summer. "You don't look like it, but are the two of you related?"

"Thank God, no," Summer said with an awkward laugh.

"Ok. Just keep in mind with at least one of you being a Delphinium Catalyst, if the regime gets their hands on either of you, we could lose this war tomorrow. I think it's best if you guys stick with us to make sure that doesn't happen."

"What if we hide the key and come back for it later when we're ready to go home?" Ethan asked. "Then he wouldn't have the key if he got us. No key, no traveling to other dimensions. Right?"

Elise shook her head. "If you can activate one of the keys, you can activate any of them. That's actually how Rusak discovered the Lunarian Catalyst last year. He had the czars testing people by the hundreds, using the Helenium Key. Once they found someone that could activate it, they arrested him. It wasn't long before they were publicly executed for refusing to join them. It's also how we discovered Catalysts are immune to their scopshade."

"That's their play, though," interjected Talia. "If they control all travel between dimensions, even if that means killing, then we don't have any hope of getting reinforcements from anywhere to help stop them. That's why you two are so important. Now that we have an actual Catalyst who's against them, maybe we can get the help that Rusak and his regime won't be expecting, and hopefully, before they expand to even more countries."

"Of course, for that to work, we'll need to help you find the Delphinium combination to get you back home," Fletcher added. "We can help each other out. Elise has been researching where the Lunarian Key is. If we can retrieve it, that gives us access to two keys and maybe two Catalysts, putting us neck and neck against the Kriva Rasturna—at least dimensional travel-wise."

"They had been sending expeditions into the Fresnel Woods for about a year and a half," Elise said. "We're not really sure why they stopped last year, but there have been some interesting stories coming from a few that went. Their expeditions line up near where I believe the lost city is, and that's where we'll find the key."

"How do you know they haven't found the Lunarian Key after all these years?" Ethan asked.

Liam shook his head. "There's been no chatter that they have. Besides, if they'd found it, they'd have had celebrations flaunting it."

"Agreed," Fletcher said, looking at Summer. "Here's my proposition. If we go after your brother, we need the two of you to vow that you'll help us recover the Lunarian Key. We need to keep it out of Rusak's hands at all costs, but it needs to be found before we can do that. Elise and I have been planning an expedition for a few months and with your arrival, now's as good as it gets for timing. What do you say?"

Summer nodded, "I'm in." She looked over at Ethan. "You're coming, right?"

"Of course I'm coming. I mean...I've been dreaming about an adventure like this since I was a kid. Ancient artifact in a lost city? You bet I'm in."

Talia smiled. "Alright then. Let's make a plan."

Elise reached under the table, grabbing a rolled-up map. "I was going over this with Fletcher when you guys walked in," she said excitedly, unrolling it across the table. "This is a map of the Fresnel Woods just north of Devon Falls."

Talia and Liam grabbed saltshakers to put at each corner of the map to prevent it from rolling up. Elise reached under the table, producing a transparent sheet, placing it over the map. Then she grabbed a marker, taking the cap off with her teeth, and drew a circle around the point where she had indicated Devon Falls was.

"My family's research leads me to believe that the lost city of Mystell is located right about here," she said, making another circle on the map. "Leaving from here, we would have to hike northeast through the woods for a few days, cutting through the airfield initially. We could also follow the Veris River until it intersects with the Bonitatis River. From there, we would follow it for a few miles until we see indicators. Mystell shouldn't be far from the river, as it was their water source. Then somewhere within the city...should be our key."

"I'm a bit new to all of this," Ethan said, "but these Steradian Keys look relatively newer to me. Not something that would be hidden in a city lost to time."

Elise was almost bubbling over with excitement. "There have been debates for decades on how old they are. Both archeologists and scholars alike have been studying them and eventually found mention of them from more than a thousand years ago. They may not look it, but the keys are ancient. We don't know who created them or how. It's been a mystery that many have tried to uncover, and that's just a couple of the reasons I've wanted to locate the Lunarian Key."

"A thousand years?" Summer questioned.

Elise had an enormous grin. "I know! It's insane to think about. Can I see your key again, please?" Ethan opened his backpack, grabbing the key and placed it on the table. She leaned over, tracing her finger around the edge. "See the detail work all around the edge? The different glyphs? The basic function and these glyphs will be the same on all the keys, but each key has differences outside of the color of their stone. You see how this one looks similar to a compass with the eight directional points? The Helenium Key looks vastly different, having what looks like a helmet similar to the emblem here, but with flames surrounding it. We don't know what the Lunarian Key looks like. The replicas in the state archive leave these details out because they don't know what they look like either."

Summer nodded. "Yeah, the replica of ours didn't have the compass points on it."

"Exactly!" Elise said, pointing at her. "They don't know."

Fletcher glanced at Ethan. "You're sure the guards never saw your key?"

"I never took it out. We were there simply looking at the displays and getting a quick history lesson."

"While my research has given us a good idea of where to look," Elise started, "we don't know exactly where the city is. No one does."

"We're going after my brother first, right?" Summer asked with a bit of tension. "Before we go find this lost city? It's clear he's not safe. He's only sixteen."

"Agreed," Ethan said. "People come before artifacts. We gave our word we'd help you find your key, but that has to come after we recover Alex."

Talia nodded in agreement. "Of course. We'll get your brother out and then move to locating the ruins."

"Elise," Fletcher said, pointing to where the lost city was indicated on the map, "How long of a hike is it from Heraldrin to this spot? Maybe we can do both without backtracking."

"It's a similar distance if we left from here. You can't see it here on the map, but Heraldrin is right about here." She pointed to a spot a couple of inches off the map.

"That's not bad," Fletcher said. "We'll go to Heraldrin to get your brother first. We can meet up with the resistance cell there for provisions and then head towards Mystell."

Summer nudged Ethan, getting his attention, mouthing 'thank you'.

"If we can get your brother out of there, he'll have to come with us," Talia said. "Sixteen or not, he's going to have to keep up. We can't expect the Heraldrin resistance to babysit or, worse yet, have their positions given up should he have been turned."

Fletcher looked grim. "It's a last resort, but if they have indoctrinated him into the Kriva Rasturna, we'll have to deal with him. We can't have him running off to alert guards at every turn."

Summer glared, "What do you mean, deal with him?"

Fletcher didn't like the idea of alienating their new friends, but he had to draw the line. "First offense, we'll detain him. Tie him up and take him with us. I'm hoping it doesn't go beyond that."

Seeing the tension grow in Summer's face, Talia opted to change the topic quickly. "Liam, we'll need you to send a message out to the Heraldrin resistance cell to expect us. We'll need to move quickly once there—meaning we need them to do some of the legwork for us and find where the kid is being held."

Liam nodded, getting up from the table. "I'll get that sent now."

"Even if Rusak doesn't have the key, how do you know it's still in Mystell?" Ethan asked. "How long has this city been lost? I mean, if it's been centuries, then the key could have been moved. Right?"

"It's been lost for nearly five hundred years," Elise confirmed. "That said, there's no documentation of the Lunarian Key being anywhere after it was last known to be at Mystell. Then, of course, even if we find Mystell, we won't know where it is in the city. Maybe an old temple or church would be a best guess."

"Just so we're clear," Talia said seriously, "There's another reason to keep the Steradian Keys away from the Kriva Rasturna than that of traveling between dimensions. Elise, why don't you fill them in?"

Elise cleared her throat. "There's a legend...that if someone has all the keys, they gain some kind of ability. Not sure what it is, but that's why the Lunarian Key was hidden away, and the city lost. It was purposefully hidden so that no one would gain whatever that power is." She looked at Summer and Ethan, seeing blank stares of disbelief. "It...It's just a legend though," she said, stumbling over the words, "It could be nothing."

"It's just a legend. A legend, the Kriva Rasturna take very seriously," Talia said flatly. "And if Rusak is taking it seriously, then we have to take it seriously. We can't chance him gaining power that could give him any edge. If we lose to him, we lose our freedoms forever."

"Switching gears," Fletcher said, "With going to Heraldrin, the quickest way to get there is going by airship. Those are heavily guarded and the two of you are fugitives now."

Talia looked at their clothing again. "Not to mention you're easily spotted with what you're wearing. You'll need a complete change of clothing to look like you belong. The guards are going to be looking for a guy and a girl together, so we need to split the team up into two groups. Let's not give them a reason to suspect us at all."

"Good thought," Fletcher said in agreement. "Elise, you'll team up with Summer. Liam and I will go with Ethan. We can give the girls a five to ten-minute head start so guards don't think we're together. If they recognize you, we won't be far behind to help."

Elise looked confused. "Talia, aren't you coming with us?"

"I'll be catching up with you in Heraldrin in a couple of days. In the meantime, I'll be training a temporary replacement to monitor things here while we're gone."

"Question," Ethan said, raising his hand for a moment. "What happens if I'm recognized after Summer and Elise are already on the airship? Wouldn't it go into heavy lockdown the second an alarm sounded?"

Fletcher sighed. "If that happens, then they'll have to take the airship to Heraldrin without us. Elise would contact the resistance when they arrived. As for us, we're going to have a team keeping an eye on us when we pass through the security gate. They'll have our backs."

Ethan looked over at Summer, concerned. "Can I carry a weapon of some kind to help defend ourselves?"

Fletcher shook his head. "No weapons allowed on airships unless you're a guard, but that brings us to the next topic. How much weapons training have you two had and what kind?"

Ethan shrugged. "I'm decent with a bow, I guess. But I haven't practiced in months."

"I also have some practice with a bow. Also, a little with swords," Summer said.

Ethan looked at her shocked, "You were serious?"

She smiled. "I told you my adoptive father was big into swords. He was obsessed with a TV show where they made them. Eventually, he took lessons and passed that down to me and Alex when we were growing up. I didn't think I'd ever use the skill. I guess I was wrong."

Fletcher nodded. "Ok people. We leave in the morning." He glanced at Talia. "Would you mind taking them to the training area? You're one of our best with the sword. Maybe you can take them under your wing for the afternoon?"

Talia stood up from the table. "Of course."

Fletcher looked over at Ethan. "I'll send Liam down after he's done sending the Heraldrin cell the message. He's great with a bow and can help fine-tune your technique. At the very least, knock some of that rust off ya."

"This way, guys," Talia said, heading to the door. Ethan and Summer got up from the table, following her past the radio equipment and down the hall to their right. Past the mess hall, at the end of the corridor, they walked through a doorway, finding themselves in a large room. Various weapons lined the wall to their left, including swords, axes and staffs, among others. Three damaged wooden practice dummies were lined up ten feet apart and sitting on racks just beyond them were bows of varying sizes and types with small arrow filled tubes lined up to practice with.

Talia looked at Summer first. "You said you had experience with the sword? Go grab one off the wall and let's see your form." Then, looking at Ethan, "Do you have any experience with swords?" He shook his head. "Well, you're going to learn today. Go grab one of the wooden practice swords and we'll start you on basics."

The next few hours were some of the most strenuous Ethan had undergone since being in high school sports. Once Talia upgraded him to a real sword, he had underestimated the weight of it, being used to the wooden one, but over time, he became familiar with it and wielding the sword became more natural. Glancing at Summer, he felt she wasn't having any trouble remembering her teachings, and was glad he wasn't at the receiving end of her blows.

Liam had joined them a couple of hours into their practice session, giving some refresher training on archery. While Ethan was a beginner with the sword, his accuracy with the bow didn't take long to recover; regularly hitting near the center.

"That's good for today," Fletcher said from the entry of the gym. "How about you two hit the showers? We have a change of clothes and a hot meal for you. I can show you where to get cleaned up and where your bunks are for the night."

Summer wiped the sweat from her forehead. "That sounds great. Thank you." She put the sword back on the wall. "Also, thanks for the lessons, Talia."

"You're doing well. Next time, we'll spar instead of you going after just the dummy."

Ethan put his bow away, happy to have a break. His arms ached after the extended practice, and he was dripping with sweat.

Liam cleared his throat. "I was considering waiting until tomorrow's briefing, but with a majority of the team here..."

Fletcher gave a nod. "Go ahead. Let them know."

"The Heraldrin cell were informed we're going to be arriving tomorrow and why," Liam said. "The news here is that the regime has decided to use your brother as a propaganda victory point, announcing they've captured a fugitive from Delphinium. We have reports the Kriva Rasturna have therapists working with him for..." he looked solemnly at Summer, "re-education purposes."

Summer glanced from person to person confused, "What does that mean exactly?"

"There's a silver lining here," Fletcher said in a reassuring tone. "It means they've more than likely tried using scopshade on him and it didn't work. By saying they are trying to re-educate him, that means they won't kill him. At least not anytime soon. It means they'll attempt to convince him to join them through manipulation, and that takes time. If your brother has a good foundation on reality, he'll be just fine. That also gives us the extra time needed to get him out of there."

Ethan could see the panic of losing her brother in her eyes and imagined how she felt. If it were one of his sisters, he would go to the ends of the earth to make sure they were safe. He walked over to her, gently placing his hand on her arm. "Hey," he said, looking her directly in the eyes. "We get him back tomorrow," he tried to reassure.

She was lost in her own imagination before eventually refocusing on him. "Ok," she said, nodding. "We'll get him back."

Recruitment

Dwyll opened the heavy door to the Kriva Rasturna head-quarters in Heraldrin. The two guards posted at the entrance nodded to him as he entered the three-story tall lobby. Decorative furniture surrounded a fireplace to his left and large Kriva Rasturna banners hung from the ceiling. He walked over to a couch where the morning's paper sat on a glass coffee table. Picking it up, he took a seat. The front page had a photo of a boy being escorted in handcuffs with the title *Delphinium Fugitive Captured*. He smirked, talking to himself, "So this is the kid she's been bragging about for the last month?" The sound of high heels walking on the marble floor came from behind, giving away who it was before she even spoke.

"Well, look who finally showed back up in the capital," Prevara said in a snarky tone. "Were you able to keep the peasants in Brexel under control?"

He chuckled as he stood. "Prevara!" he said, faking his enthusiasm. "So great to hear your shrill sarcastic voice again. It's been too long." He pointed at the front of the newspaper, holding it up. "I see you've begun parading around your trophy."

"No help from you. I captured a Catalyst from Delphinium." She grinned. "The TAKs made a better partner than you ever did."

"You wound me." He folded the paper, tossing it onto the coffee table. "As it just so happens, I had a run in with his sister and her boy toy. They've managed to make it to Lunaria and are looking for him—Getting help from the resistance as well. Do you know what that means?"

She didn't feel like dealing with his ridiculous questions. "Obviously, we'll have to kill her if she's working with the dissidents. You know that."

"Ah, true...but it also means we have to convince this kid to join us, or we may lose both the Delphinium Catalysts, as I believe his sister to be one. Rusak would agree we can't afford that. We'd lose preliminary knowledge of how Delphinium works, what weapons they have, what technologies and how resistant. We need this kid or his sister to be our ambassador. She's not expendable just yet. With that in mind and given we already have the boy, take me to him." He knew he'd touched a nerve, seeing the annoyance in her eyes.

"You've been talking with Rusak, hmm? He said the same when I gave a report on the problem the kid has been. I had Haas with the Biochem Division working on a more potent scopshade that may be able to turn Catalysts, but he isn't anywhere near completing it. Without scopshade and his imprisonment on top of that, you have no chance at convincing him to join us."

"Then you won't mind me succeeding where you've failed."

"Succeed?" she sneered. "Try if you must. He's down in the holding area—cell B. You know where it is." She flipped her hair over her shoulder and left the building, not wanting to continue the conversation.

Dwyll headed to the elevator, smiling to himself. He always knew how to get under her skin and relished every time he made her storm off in a huff. He entered the elevator, pressing the button for the holding cells and felt the floor sink below him. Once off the elevator, it was a short walk to cell B. He looked in the small window of the door, seeing the teenager laying on a cot pouting and held his thumb up to the scanner. The door opened with a hiss and he walked into the cell, leaning up against the wall. "Looks like you've had a hell of a time. Want to get out of here?"

Alex sat up. "You're supposed to be what? The good cop?"

Dwyll held up his hands. "Hey, if you'd rather, you can stay here. I'm just trying to fix a mistake we made."

"You kidnapped me and had me locked up here for a month. I've been injected with something, beaten by guards, and stabbed with a needle by some psycho!"

"I don't condone what the guards did, but...they go into every situation assuming anyone they arrest is with the dissidents—an extremist group. Then, one of our TAKs mistook you for a terrorist we've been after. I apologize for how you've been treated. Let me start by getting you out of here with a change of clothes and some food."

"TAKs? You mean those skeleton dogs?"

Dwyll nodded, "That's correct. They're genetically modified canines from Helenium—the dimension I'm from. We specially train them to assist our military. The skeletal look is an unfortunate side effect, but the benefits they provide make it more than worth it." Given the lingering look of hostility he was getting, he wasn't sure if the kid would join him just yet, and decided to sweeten the deal. "I do have some good news for you. We've received word there are a couple of people here in Lunaria looking for you. From the sounds of it, one of them is your sister."

"Summer's here!?" Alex said, excitedly standing up. "Where is she?"

"We lost track of them, but have guards on the lookout. If we can pick them up, they'd be brought here to reunite the two of you." Dwyll pushed off the wall to leave. "Name's Dwyll, by the way. The changing room is just around the corner."

Alex got up, following him. "Why let me out now?"

Dwyll grabbed a set of clothes from a cabinet, tossing them to Alex. "Go get changed. I'll explain more when you're done."

Alex entered the changing room with the door hissing shut behind him. He looked around for any means of escape, but found none. He sighed, not wanting to deal with this Dwyll guy, but knew he had little choice. Not if he wanted out of jail. He quickly got changed and opened the door, seeing something fly across the hall at him. He fumbled for a moment, barely catching it before recognizing his smart phone.

"Not sure what that is, but it was in your pocket when they brought you here. Walk with me." Dwyll headed towards the elevator.

Alex looked up in disbelief. "They don't have phones here?"

"That's a phone?" Dwyll asked, raising an eyebrow while pressing the elevator call button. "How do you use it to talk?"

Alex tried turning it on, but the battery no longer had a charge. "Dammit. It's useless without a charger." Dwyll grabbed something from his pocket handing it to him. Alex looked at the small device. "What's this?" The elevator doors opened.

Dwyll smiled getting on the elevator. "That's...our phone. Put it in your ear. It automatically detects other devices, connecting you to those around you while translating whatever someone says, regardless of the language they're speaking. Another great advancement we brought from Helenium. Actually, we brought a lot of technology here to Lunaria. These people were more than a hundred years behind technologically before we arrived. It's just one of the many things we're trying to fix." The elevator chimed, and the doors opened.

"How does it know who to call?"

"It detects when you're wanting to make a call and who you're thinking about, reaching out to that person via looking for their profile on the network and auto-connecting. It does all this using a scanning method that acts as a neural interface," he said, walking into the main lobby.

"That's pretty cool."

Dwyll smirked, "I can tell you're used to technology. You understand it without further explanation because you come from a dimension with technology. Those of us from the more technologically advanced dimensions are superior to those that aren't. Come, there's a restaurant close by that's a favorite."

As they left the building, Alex realized this was the first time he'd been outside for the last couple of weeks. The sun was setting, but there were still dozens of people out and about. Many of the buildings surrounding them looked to be under construction.

Dwyll put his arm in front of Alex, stopping him from crossing the street. "Watch out for revbolts. I've seen more than one person get run down who wasn't paying attention."

"Rev-what?" Alex asked, as two vehicles speed by with their engines roaring in his ears before he realized they were what Dwyll had been referencing. The exhaust left behind made him cough. He swatted the air to clear it and followed Dwyll down the street. He found it odd that people seemed to keep their distance from them, looking afraid.

A disheveled man with scraggly hair ran up to a couple of guards on patrol, demanding they look into his drugs being stolen. The guards laughed. "Here old man," one said, pulling some pills out, "Have your fix." The man went to grab the pills, only to be struck in the stomach with one of their batons.

"Keep walking," Dwyll said. "You'll get used to things around here pretty quickly." It was another block before they saw a small line formed outside of a nice restaurant. Dwyll walked past the line directly to the hostess. "Need a table for a meeting."

"Name please?" the hostess asked, not looking up as she marked her table chart. Dwyll said nothing, instead opting to just stand and wait for her to acknowledge his presence. "Name?" she asked again. Annoyed, she looked up, and her eyes went wide with alarm. "Cz—Czar..." she stammered. "Apologies. We've been very busy. Right this way." She escorted them through the busy restaurant to a table with two well off looking people reading menus. "Excuse me," she said, "but there's been a mistake. We meant to seat these two first."

"That's not my problem," the woman said behind her menu. Dwyll cleared his throat, getting their attention. She looked over, seeing who it was, and immediately got up from the table. She flinched, having knocked her knee into the table's leg. "Apologies, Czar. We'll wait for the next table," she said, grabbing the slack jawed man she was with and pulling him to his feet. Dwyll sat, inviting Alex to do the same. The hostess bowed quickly, leaving to inform the waiter of the change at their table.

"Why does everyone seem afraid of you?" asked Alex.

"I have a reputation for not taking anyone's crap. That, and I'm a Czar with the Kriva Rasturna. The title comes with a certain level of respect."

Alex looked out the nearby window and watched a group of people gathering on the opposite side of the street. A few of the gatherers were looking up and pointing. He couldn't see what they were looking at and turned his attention to his menu, finding he didn't recognize anything listed. "You said you weren't from here," Alex said. "That you were from someplace called Helenium? Why did you come here?"

"I came to Lunaria to pay it forward," Dwyll said, putting his menu down. Seeing the clueless expression on Alex's face, he figured he'd have to explain. "I guess some history is needed here." He paused, wondering where to begin. "Many years ago, Sovereign Rusak, from the Primula dimension, saved his world from ideas like bigotry, racism, and different religions. He taught his people how to be their true selves and that they're entitled to basic human rights like housing, food and a basic income. All the people had to do was follow him and he would provide. After he had brought peace to Primula, he moved on to do the same for Helenium. He brought his message of 'Peace through Compliance', and many didn't like the idea. They fought him, claiming they had freedoms and rights."

"Why not just leave them be if they didn't want to join up?" asked Alex.

"It's an all-or-nothing type deal," Dwyll said. "It takes everyone to make the system work. I and a few others were onboard from the beginning, but those that didn't want to join were misguided and usually hateful, refusing to acknowledge their bigotry. If they weren't with us, they were considered a threat to our democracy and were removed from power. Many were taken into custody to help them see the light and taken to our education centers. I joined up with the Kriva Rasturna to make Helenium a better place. Shortly after, it was discovered I'm one of the few referred to as a Catalyst. I can activate the keys, opening the Steradian Gate between dimensions and I believe you're a Catalyst as well. It's rare." He said, taking a sip of water. "As Rusak helped me to see the error of my ways, I hope to take you under my wing to help free the people of Lunaria and eventually your dimension, Delphinium, of social injustices."

Alex heard screams from across the street, ripping his attention from Dwyll. People scrambled to move as a streak fell from above, landing with a sickening crunch. Alex couldn't believe what he'd seen. "Was that..." he pushed his chair out to get up from the table, wanting to investigate.

Dwyll leaned across the table putting a hand on his arm, "There's nothing you can do for the mentally ill. Please. I'll explain. There have been a few, shall we say...extremists...that have decided to protest us in a very public way. They think tossing themselves off rooftops will turn them into martyrs and sway the Kriva Rasturna into abandoning our mission here to help bring peace. It's sad, but they don't like that their old ways are being torn down," he said in a solemn tone. "Some that have a hard time have made a scene as we...shine a light...on their hatred, racism and bigotry."

Alex knew those were all bad things, but something didn't seem quite right. Still, he was new here. Perhaps he just didn't understand. He needed more information. "Isn't there anything that can be done to help people...adjust?" he asked.

"You're young and probably haven't had much experience with death," Dwyll said, looking out the window at the masses as guards came running up to the scene. "Death happens. If these people can't accept they are part of a systemic hatred passed down through generations, then it's probably best that they stay out of our way permanently. After all, no one cares about another bigot dying." He took another sip from his water, going back to his menu with indifference at the chaotic scene outside.

Alex continued to look for a moment before turning back to Dwyll. "How can we know they were a bigot, and that's why they jumped? It sounds like you believe someone can hate someone else even if they don't know they hate them. How does that work?"

Dwyll sighed, "It's engrained in their person. They're born with hatred and raised to hate, regardless of if it's on a subconscious level. They often aren't even aware. We help those that have been victims of that hate rise to the top, giving them the advantage in the new order. Think of it like the scales of justice being righted. Fairness equals equity in all things, right?"

Alarms sounded in Alex's mind again at his answer. "Did those you help work for that advantage? I've been on school projects with groups where half the people don't do any work. That leaves the rest of us twice as much work to make sure our grades don't fall."

Dwyll smiles, "Good, then you understand."

Alex looked confused. "Understand what?"

"The need to build up those that can't do the actions needed to succeed."

"That makes no sense," Alex said, shaking his head. "I know if those people that didn't do any work, had done their fair share, the rest of us wouldn't have been as stressed out. It sucked, but I worked hard for my grade—I earned that A."

Dwyll's smile faded. "Hmm, perhaps you don't quite understand yet then...but we can work on that. In fact, I'm going to get you in touch with one of our proselytizers. They can show you around more tomorrow and go over what they do to help us and the people of Lunaria."

"You want me to help your group after you kidnapped me?" he asked flatly.

Dwyll chuckled, "It was an honest mistake. I hope you'll forgive us. In the meantime, I'm putting you up in one of our nicer rooms at our headquarters. You'll want for nothing and be our guest while we continue to look for your sister."

"I'll be able to leave with my sister once we're reunited. Right?"

"Of course," Dwyll said, bowing his head with a smile. He looked around the room. "Now, where the hell did our waiter run off to?"

Alex looked out the window, seeing the crowd had been dispersed, and a guard had placed a tarp over the body. Alex couldn't help but feel a chill watching people walk by the scene without even glancing over at what had occurred. Something was very off in this city.

Journey to the Airfield

Ethan hadn't been sleeping well the last few days with being in different environments. After hours of tossing and turning, he'd lost track of time and right when he had finally dozed off, someone dropped a metal tray in the cafeteria, startling him. He sat up, taking the noise as an alarm clock. He stretched, seeing Summer still asleep in a bunk across from him. The smell of freshly cooked eggs and sausage wafted into the room and he decide to put on his shoes and start the day.

The mess hall across the way was filled with a couple dozen people talking to each other. He didn't recognize any of them, opting to head over to the mission room to see if he could find Fletcher or Talia. He headed down the hall, finding people busy on the radio equipment.

"Morning!" Fletcher yelled, waving him into the mission room. "Glad to see you're finally up. Talia was just wondering when we'd see the two of you."

Ethan joined them at the mission table. "Sorry about that. I'm used to an alarm."

Fletcher shook his head. "No worries. We figured we'd let you sleep, given the hike we have ahead of us today."

Ethan didn't like the sound of that, but before he could ask more about it, Talia shoved two changes of clothing into his arms. "Here.

Go get changed into these, so you look like a local. Then go get your friend up and have her change as well. We need to make sure you two look like regular travelers going to the capital."

"Go get some coffee from the mess hall while you're at it," Fletcher said. "Looks like you could use some. We'll be going over the plan here in about thirty minutes."

Ethan nodded, heading to a bathroom to change. The grey colored slacks they handed him felt stiff compared to the relaxed jeans he had always been used too. The white, collared, button-down shirt was a good fit and relatively comfortable. He looked at himself in the mirror, not being a fan of the style, but if it kept him from being killed, he wouldn't complain.

He left the bathroom heading to the bunks and waved at a couple of people as he passed. They returned the greeting but didn't seem welcoming. He couldn't blame them. By now, word had gotten out that he and Summer weren't from Lunaria and it surprised him Fletcher trusted them enough to let them stay. By the time he got back to the bunks, Summer was sitting up. "Good morning. Sleep well?"

"Not really, but I don't think these cots were made for comfort." She smiled, taking in his new attire. "Looking sharp."

"Not something I'd generally wear, but thanks. They wanted us to blend in better." He handed her the change of clothing. "Talia had these for you. I'll be right outside so you can change." He grabbed his backpack off the ground, walking to the hallway and knelt, opening his pack. The Delphinium Key and journal were a welcome sight and boosted his trust in their new friends. He zipped his pack and waited for Summer to finish up.

A few minutes later, he heard her come into the hall and looked up. His jaw dropped. She looked stunning wearing the short sleeve, knee length dress giving her an hourglass figure. The top had a collar with decorative buttons going down to a thick belt, and her hair was up in a ponytail. She saw his reaction and blushed.

"How do I look?" she asked with a half twirl.

"You look amazing." He put his arm out for her to take. "Care to join me for some breakfast?"

"I am starving...so yes," she said matter-of-factly, taking his arm.

They headed into the mess hall, finding most had already finished their breakfast, leaving no line for them to get food and coffee. Once they had their meal, they scanned the room for a place to sit before Elise came running up to them. "Talia wanted me to find the two of you and have you eat in the mission room. I guess they're going to start going over the plan a bit early." She looked at the two of them with a smile. "Much better."

"Thank you," Summer said, smiling. "You look good too."

"I miss wearing dresses," Elise said, looking down at her outfit, heading for the hall with the two following. "I don't get too very often anymore. Not practical when you're always on the run."

"At least they're not having us wear heels," Summer said with a laugh.

"Yeah, I wouldn't be going on this mission if we didn't have flats."

When they arrived, Fletcher and Liam were already eating at the table, and Talia was looking over some papers, sipping coffee. The three of them took a seat as Fletcher grabbed a napkin, wiping his mouth, and got up from the table.

"Let's get this started," he said. "First off, sorry about the dress's ladies. They're temporary until we're in Heraldrin. Have to look the part when we're boarding an airship."

"Actually, I kind of like it," Summer said.

"Be that as it may, we'll need the two of you in appropriate attire when we infiltrate the Kriva Rasturna headquarters to get your brother out. Secondly…we had this travel vest made for you, Ethan," he said, grabbing it off the back of a chair and tossing it to him. "We had it altered with a hidden pocket on the interior of the back. It's big enough to hold both the key and your journal. Better yet, we've treated the fabric, so it's water resistant. That'll keep the sweat from ruining any notes you take as we hike through the woods."

"Thanks," he said, grabbing his backpack. He dug out the items and placed them in the hidden pocket, putting it on. He liked the muted blue-grey color and was surprised it fit perfectly, noting he didn't feel a lump where the journal and key were. "Fits nicely."

"That will get you past the security checkpoint at the airfield," Fletcher said, tossing him a pack that had a large strap and a fold over top. Ethan checked inside, finding various sets of rolled up clothing before Fletcher continued. "We treated a pocket in this pack similarly to be water resistant, but guards will be checking the bag thoroughly. For now, we can use it to hold the clothing changes we'll need later."

A guy in his early thirties wearing dark tactical gear quickly walked into the room, taking a seat next to Liam. "Sorry I'm late."

"You're right on time. Ethan. Summer. You met Caleb yesterday for a short bit when he helped get you off the streets."

Ethan nodded towards him. "Appreciate that."

"Don't think of it. Just doing my job."

Fletcher continued, "Caleb here is in charge of our backup team. They'll be escorting us to the airfield. If anything goes wrong, they'll jump in. You'll each be given a dagger for protection as we head over. Hopefully, you don't need to use them, but we expect there will be patrols on the way. Close to the airfield, there's a curve in the road not far before we get to the security checkpoint. It'll mask us enough to hand our weapons over to Caleb and his team, for obvious reasons. Any questions?" He paused to give them a moment. He looked around the table, making eye contact with each but no one spoke up. "Ok. The airships are a couple miles away and we're going on foot. Finish what you need to and meet outside this room in ten."

The meeting disbanded, allowing Ethan and Summer to finish their meals while the others prepared. A few minutes later, the team began to gather near the radio equipment. Fletcher emerged from the training gym with Talia, carrying a handful of daggers, and passed one out to each of the team. Summer and Elise tucked theirs into their belts, putting their cloaks on as much for warmth as to conceal the blade.

"This way, people," Fletcher said, motioning for the others to follow. They took a long corridor off to the left before coming to large, metal double doors bolted shut. Fletcher slid the massive bolt sideways and pulled on the handle. The door's weight made the hinges creak loudly in protest as it opened and cold air flooded the corridor. A large hand dug tunnel slanting upwards lay before them, revealing daylight.

Talia hugged Fletcher tightly. "Stay alert. Be safe."

Fletcher smiled. "We'll see you in a couple of days." She backed away, and he moved into the tunnel with the rest of the team following. The chill of the morning air enveloped them. "Be glad it didn't rain. This can get pretty slick when it does."

Ethan looked behind him, hearing the creaking of hinges as the door closed. The sound of grinding metal followed caused by the locking bolt sliding into place. He caught up to the others just as they were emerging to the surface. They had hidden the entrance well. Thick bushes surrounded it with the only opening having a large tree standing guard that hid the entry from sight. Fletcher checked the area, leading them to a gravel path just ahead.

Summer enjoyed hearing the birds and watching squirrels run around. The fresh air was welcome after being underground for so long. A zemper hopped away from under a nearby bush, startling her. "Those things are so cute. I'd love to have one as a pet."

Elise smiled. "Zempers are soft and cuddly looking, but they don't make good pets. Trust me. I've had friends that tried to domesticate them and unlike dogs or cats, zempers refuse to be potty trained. They just go wherever, and no amount of training seems to help. They also tend to rip into furniture with their claws when making dens and knock everything over with their jumping. One of my friends had their great-grandfather's urn knocked over. It was a mess."

Summer cringed at the thought. "I guess I'll pass on bringing one home then."

Ethan chuckled, then looked over at Liam, who seemed lost in his thoughts. "So, Liam. What made you decide to join up with these guys?" Liam looked a bit shocked to be asked. "Sorry," Ethan said, seeing his reaction. "If it's too personal a question, you don't have to answer."

"It's alright. It's good to talk about these things. Gets it off your shoulders, you know?" He took a deep breath, looking somber. "I joined up because I lost my mentor to the Kriva Rasturna. He was a great man who took me in when he didn't have to. Treated me like a son. I had been on my own since I was about twelve years old. Both my parents had died in an accident, and I was living on the streets for a few months. He saw me scrounging around for food one day and invited me over to share a meal with him. From there, he took me under his wing as an apprentice. Taught me about radio equipment, how it functioned and how to fix it. Turns out I had a knack for it."

"Sounds like someone that really cared," Ethan said.

"He was. Life was good for a while." Liam looked down at the ground. "Then the Kriva Rasturna came. The changes started small enough, like not being able to crack jokes like we had before, saying it was hate speech—whatever that means." He shook his head. "Then they moved on to peer pressure through bullying. My mentor and a few others saw what they were doing, knowing if you don't submit to their ideology, they'll try to ruin you."

"We've heard a little about how they go about it," Summer said.

"Yeah. They make it so you can't earn a living. Destroy your name or your business's name so no one will hire you. My mentor didn't care, though. He knew what was right and stood up against them during one of their rallies. He had me hang back away from the crowd and I watched, proud, to see someone standing against them and calling them out for what they were. Unfortunately for both of us, it didn't take long for things to turn ugly. A group of Greys started beating him. I thought they were going to kill him until a czar from the stage stopped it. I thought she was going to let him go, but instead, she had them hold him down while she injected him with scopshade. Then had him dragged off to the cathedral."

"Why did no one stop them?" Ethan asked, confused.

"Most were scared the same would happen to them. I must have waited outside the cathedral for hours before I finally saw him walk out the doors. He looked like hell, and I ran up to see what I could do to help." A weak chuckle escaped his throat as his eyes welled up. "He started spouting the same trash he had fought against at the rally. I couldn't believe it. I asked him what he was saying, and he backhanded me across the face. First time I'd seen him hit someone and there was no remorse in his eyes. It was like I'd lost my parents all over again." He wiped away a tear.

"I...I'm sorry," Ethan said. "Maybe I shouldn't have brought it up."

"No. It's good to remember what the Kriva Rasturna stand for and what they do to people. It wasn't long after that I left his home and found my way to the resistance. Whatever I can do to make them pay for what they did to him, I'll make them feel it." He looked up, noticing the others had been listening in. "I've been with these guys ever since."

The group walked in silence after the story, following the winding path to the airfield. After a while, Fletcher slowed, eventually coming to a stop. He cocked his head to the side, listening for a moment, and suddenly raised his fist up at ninety degrees. He turned to the group. "Hide!" he said in a stern whisper before dashing quickly into the woods. The team scattered with half following Fletcher to the left while others, including Ethan and Summer, banked to the right, ducking behind thick tree trunks or laying prone under bushes.

Ethan had just settled behind a large tree when he heard talking coming from just up the way. He peeked around the trunk slowly, seeing three guards and two TAKs walking towards them from around a bend up ahead. Remembering his last encounter with one of the creatures, he slowly slid his dagger out from its sheath. Looking over, he found Summer laying on the ground next to Elise behind some bushes and hoped the overgrowth of the forest would be enough to conceal them. He overheard the guards talking as they neared.

"I've been on patrol for the last twelve hours. My feet are killing me."

"Shut it! These Deplorables could be anywhere. Keep your eyes peeled."

"When we get into Kinsford, we should go to that deli near the market. You know, the one with the old man?"

"What of it?"

"Hear me out. I say we take one of the TAKs with us, demanding a free lunch as tribute to the Kriva Rasturna. They won't refuse with one of these guys with us, and if they do, we'll sic it on them and take what we want." The three guards laughed as they passed the tree Ethan hid behind.

Ethan's translator suddenly squelched loudly. He grimaced at the noise, but didn't make a sound for fear of being discovered. One of the TAKs stopped and jerked its head in his direction. The squelch from the translator stopped and the creature's ears moved, trying to pick up the sound again before a slow guttural growl came from its throat, grabbing the attention of a guard. The other TAK stopped and looked in the same direction.

"Hold up gents." The guard looked down at the TAK and over at the trees near Ethan. "What did ye find?"

"I swear to all that is holy, if this is another zemper, I am going to lose it at this TAK." The third guard laughed just as the translator squelched again. Ethan gritted his teeth.

The TAK pulled free of the leash, bolting towards the tree Ethan was behind. "What the!" a guard yelled in surprise. Before it could reach the underbrush, the other TAK let out a loud yelp as an arrow struck it in the eye. It shuddered and collapsed as the arrowhead pierced its brain. The TAK that had been charging skidded to a halt, looking back at its companion.

Fletcher yelled the order, "Attack!"

Ethan saw his moment of opportunity with the TAK looking confused as a half-dozen men emerged from the forest, attacking the guards. Ethan quickly stepped out from behind the tree, getting its attention, but before it could respond, he had already driven the dagger down into the creature's eye. It howled in pain, thrashing backwards, stumbling and falling over in convulsions.

One of the guards readied his rifle, firing into the group of resistance fighters charging them, hitting one square in the chest; the impact knocking the man backwards as though he'd just been hit by a car. An arrow flew past Ethan's head, striking one of the guards in the throat; the man producing a gurgling sound before he fell to his knees, dropping his weapon.

The two remaining guards panicked, firing into the woods blindly, forgetting about the resistance fighters fifteen feet in front of them. Ethan watched as one of the resistance fighters grabbed the downed guard's rifle, firing point blank into another guard's side, turning him into a rag doll, flung ten feet before smacking into a tree trunk. Fletcher finished the remaining guard, running his sword through the man's chest. The guard gasped, staring in disbelief before toppling over off the blade.

Fletcher surveyed the scene before yelling out to his men, "Clear! Report injuries!"

"Tomps is down!" one of the fighters yelled out.

Fletcher and a few others ran over, but it was too late. The damage to the man's chest was severe, causing death on impact. "Damn pulser rifles," Fletcher said. "Caleb. Help me get Tomps hidden off the road. You'll have to get him back to base on the way back." Caleb nodded, grabbing the man's legs.

Ethan walked up to the TAK he had killed, pulling on his dagger. The blade had embedded into the orbital bone of the creature's skull, making it difficult to pull free. He leveraged his foot on its head, yanking on the handle hard before the blade finally gave.

"No way!" Liam yelled excitedly, pulling a device out from one of the guard's pockets.

Elise quickly joined him. "What is it?"

"This guy had a portable D.R.S on him!" Liam proclaimed.

She looked confused. "A what?"

"A Dimensional Resonance Scanner," he said, starting to geek out. "It scans someone telling what dimension they're from. I never expected a guard to have one of these out here. They must really be locking down the airfield. I'm taking it."

"Good work taking that thing out," Fletcher said, addressing Ethan, "but what alerted it?"

Ethan pulled his translator from his ear. "This thing keeps squelching every few seconds. Hurts like hell."

Liam overheard Ethan and pocketed the D.R.S., "Squelching?" he asked. "Let me see it." Ethan held it out for him, and he started examining it just when another squelch started. The noise was loud enough to be audible to everyone within a few feet.

Summer joined them. "I can't believe you managed to kill that thing. Are you ok?"

He nodded, "I'm fine. I got it by surprise."

"You took that thing out with a—" she grimaced, not finishing her sentence, as her translator squelched as well. She grabbed at her ear, pulling the translator out.

Liam looked perplexed. "No way that this is a coincidence. Two malfunctioning at the same time? This has to be some kind of short-range interference."

The devices squelched in unison a couple more times before Summer noticed a blue glow from the back of Ethan's vest. "Would the Delphinium Key cause any kind of interference?" she asked, pointing to his back.

Liam turned Ethan around, seeing the blue light dim just as the squelch stopped. The light returned a few seconds later, followed by the squelch. He pulled a small screwdriver from his jacket and started slowly adjusting the frequency the translator would pick up. A moment later, another sound came from it, making Liam stop. He held the translator closer to hear better.

A few seconds passed before they heard a small voice. "Hello? Ethan... Are you there?"

Back at Home

Two Days Ago

Mason Burke helped his wife, Ellena, to the couch after she'd witnessed their son warp to another dimension. He called a family meeting shortly after to let his daughters know what had occurred and what they were dealing with. A couple hours later, they were in the living room, wondering what had happened, as these meetings were rare.

"What's the meeting about?" Aiza asked. "We haven't had one of these in a while."

Mason chastised himself for not having the conversation earlier. "I should have told you this right when you all inherited those journals. Told you all what they actually are and represent. Deep down, I had hoped to avoid the topic, but it seems your brother and his friend found a way to activate the key."

"What are you saying?" Lilly asked, raising an eyebrow. "How did he do that?"

He shook his head. "I don't know. I thought I'd prevented this from ever happening after burning the pages with the combinations."

"Wait," Aiza said. "Does this have anything to do with that compass looking thing Ethan had me scan?"

Mason nodded. "It has everything to do with it."

"Ethan told me he was thinking it could transport people across dimensions, but I didn't believe him," Aiza said. "Are you saying he's in another dimension?"

Ellena tried to put her thoughts into words, "He...uh."

Watching her struggle, Mason filled them in. "Your brother could be in serious danger. It really depends on which dimension he went to. He shouldn't have been able to go anywhere. I don't know how they discovered a correct combination so quickly."

"When did this happen?" Lilly asked in disbelief.

"This morning," Ellena said. "They were attacked last night by some creature. His friend, Summer, had stayed the night. Somehow, she activated the thing, causing a ball of light to surround her, and he was pulled in trying to get her out of it."

"Let me start at the beginning," Mason said. "We went over this with Lilly last night, but Aiza, do you remember the story of your uncle waking up in the middle of the forest when we were on that metal detecting trip?"

"I remember. I always thought he had a secret drinking problem."

"That's the night he found the key—that compass thing. The key is an object that allows the user to input a set of glyphs. Depending on what you input, it may open a door between dimensions called the Steradian Gate."

Aiza frowned. "I feel bad for thinking he had a drinking problem now."

"Luckily, your uncle had found the first code not far from where he found the key, which ended up being the code to our dimension. That let us know how many symbols were needed for a correct code and our way back if we went anywhere. Jerran and I must have put a hundred different codes into that thing before we finally hit on a combination that opened the gate," he said, shaking his head. "Turns out, I never could activate the thing. Apparently not everyone can so all my attempts at combinations were wasted."

"Ethan told me it had glowed for him," Aiza said, "but it never glowed for me when I touched it."

"Seems your brother and his new friend have the ability to activate it," Mason said, looking over at Ellena.

"That's what I saw," she said. "Summer was already in the middle of the thing when he had rushed out the back door."

"Well," Mason said, "The first place your uncle took me ended up being a dimension called Lunaria. It resembled the 1930s that we've all seen in history books. They had similar clothing styles and technology to that period. It almost felt like we had gone back in time, but with obvious differences, many of which your uncle sketched in those journals. It's also the first time I had seen a person with purple eyes."

Lilly looked skeptical. "The 1930s was the great depression. I remember learning there was a lack of food. You made it sound as though Ethan was in more danger than a rumbling stomach."

"The different dimensions have different histories. Unfortunately, this is where things take a turn. After a few more months of testing combinations, we found another for a dimension called Primula. They had slightly more advanced technology than we do now, but it was dark and dystopian." He looked grim, recalling the memory. "The people there were little more than slaves to a dictatorship called the Kriva Rasturna. The crap we saw authorities do to people was horrifying. It was like there were only two classes of people, masters, and slaves."

"You got lucky," Ellena said, shooting him a look.

"What does she mean, dad?" Aiza asked.

"I don't enjoy talking about it, but you should know what your brother may be up against. While we were in Primula, we watched as a couple of guards beat a child. I don't even know what would ever warrant such an action. We were about to intervene when someone stepped up to stop them before we could. A woman told them it wasn't right to harm a child. They pulled out some kind of gun I'd never seen before and shot her for her trouble."

"Oh my God," Lilly said. "How could they get away with that?"

"The other guard kicked the poor kid in the gut. I yelled at them from across the street. So stupid," he said, shaking his head angry at himself. "They started chasing us with these dog creatures. We ran for our lives and were lucky enough to lose them. We got the hell out of there as soon as we could. Then when we got back, I tore the combinations page from the journal and burned it. Your uncle didn't talk to me for a month, but eventually came around understanding my reasons. Your mom just found out last night. She's...not happy with me."

"Of course, I'm not happy with you!" she retorted. "You were traveling across dimensions and could have been killed! What would have happened to me and the kids if you hadn't had lost those guards?!"

He sighed. "I thought I had put an end to our adventures when I destroyed that page, but Jerran must have found the correct set of symbols to travel again. I should have grabbed the key out of Ethan's hands when I saw it and smashed it right then and there."

"He brought the key to me to have it scanned," Aiza said. "I haven't gone over all the data but did notice there seemed to be an interesting frequency coming from it. I have all the data saved at the lab, including a detailed scan showing all of those symbols. We could start creating combinations and see if you recognize any of them. Maybe we can figure out a way to go after him."

Lilly was tearing up. "He has the key with him, Aiza. We need that to open the gate." Ellena got up, joining her on the other couch and hugged her.

"What about getting that combination for our dimension again? You remember where that was in the forest, right?" Aiza asked.

"That part of the forest was developed a couple of years ago. The stone the combination was on is long gone."

"Dammit." Aiza got up and headed for the door. "I'm going back to the lab to take another look at those readings. There must be something in the data that can help us get him home."

One Day Ago

Aiza woke up in one of the most uncomfortable positions she remembered feeling. She pushed herself up, seeing a small puddle of drool on her desk. The last thing she remembered was having her computer compare the frequency coming from the key to other known frequencies. She decided she must have fallen asleep waiting for the computer to find a match.

She got up from her desk, walking to the kitchen, still groggy, and grabbed a mug from the cabinet. She placed it into the automated coffee machine and selecting the hazelnut blend she always enjoyed. Rubbing her eyes, she listened to the liquid pour into her mug. She picked up the mug when the coffee was done, cupping it in her hands, feeling the warmth, and brought it up to her nose, inhaling the aroma. She smiled, taking a sip, and walked back to her desk.

As she sat, she noticed her computer had finished its comparison, finding a close match to the frequency the key had given off. She put her coffee down, expanding the window with the results. The key's frequency was comparable to that of CB radio frequencies, but lower on the spectrum than what CB radios generally used, coming in at 24.85 Megahertz.

Curious, she slid her swivel chair to the next desk over, logging into her lab's operating system for the radio telescope. She typed in the frequency when prompted, having the computer search for it. After only a minute, the radio telescope successfully located the signal. She turned up the volume on the receiver, interested if she could hear anything from it, but there was nothing. Not even static.

"So, you're finding the signal, but nothing's coming through." She caught herself talking to the computer again. It was an odd quirk, but it helped her think. She pushed her chair back over to her desk to take another sip, hearing a blip of static come through on the receiver. It had only lasted a second, but the static had been there.

She thought to herself a moment. While their current setup wouldn't allow her to broadcast, maybe there was a way to modify it so that she could and get a message to Ethan. If the key was giving off the 24.85 Megahertz frequency, perhaps it was also listening to that frequency. The question now would be if she could open a line of communication.

She glanced at the clock on her computer, seeing it was just past eight o'clock in the morning. She was sure her dad would be up and want to help with this, but she needed to run her idea past her boss before ripping apart the equipment.

This Morning

Aiza had spent nearly all the previous day soldering, piecing, installing and tweaking equipment. Her boss was excited at the prospect of being able to send signals out through the radio telescope. She knew he had always been into the idea of extra-terrestrials and had leveraged that as a selling point for her idea. He was happy to let her try out the experiment, letting her know she had better be able to put it all back together the way it was afterword. The other selling point was that her dad was going to be the one buying the hardware necessary. Her boss had helped her with some of the modifications, but she stayed overnight, continuing to work until the modifications were complete.

She wanted to make sure the equipment worked before getting the hopes of her family up. Her mom had been depressed the last couple of days and she couldn't put her through any excitement should this fail. Having finished her fifth cup of coffee, she was finally ready for a test transmission. She booted up the computer to the radio telescope, checking to make sure the new hardware was recognized and did a mic test using the CB. The indicator light on the monitor fluctuated with her voice as she spoke. "It's working," she said excitedly, flipping on the receiver and finding the frequency again. She smiled, hearing the blip of static.

Typing in the frequency into the radio telescope, she ensured the wavelength matched exactly as the key had displayed during the scan. She turned the recording software on, grabbing the microphone and held down the button to speak, watching her monitor. "Ethan, are you there?" The indicator lights fluctuated with her voice, confirming she was broadcasting.

"Hello. Ethan? Ethan, are you there?" She paused, hoping to hear him respond, but nothing came back. She triple-checked all her settings before broadcasting again. "Ethan, are you there?" She waited a couple of minutes, but when there was still no response, she worried.

"Why isn't this working?" Her mind raced with questions. Maybe she had hooked up something wrong? Maybe the radio telescope wasn't powerful enough to get through? Was the transmission even getting to him? She recalled all the work she had done over the last day, going over every detail, confident it was setup correctly.

She needed to give it more time. Maybe he didn't know how to respond to her? She sighed, not wanting to give up but knowing it was a long shot. She held down the transmitter button on her mic again. "Hello? Ethan... Are you there?" She paused again. She held her breath, hoping to hear something—anything.

A crackling noise came from the receiver. "Aiza, is that you?!" Ethan replied.

***

Everyone in the group was looking at Ethan as Summer handed her earpiece to Liam. "Can you adjust mine as well?" she asked. Liam nodded, adjusting hers so she could listen in.

"Look at you, making the first interdimensional phone call," Ethan joked.

Aiza laughed, excited to hear his voice. "We've been so worried about you. Where are you!? Which dimension? Dad said that you're in danger, describing a place he's been to as essentially hell."

"We're in Lunaria. And yes, we're in danger. I don't have a lot of time. We've joined up with the resistance here to get Summer's brother back from some creepy cult called the Kriva Rasturna. In return, we're helping them find their Steradian Key so it doesn't fall into the wrong hands."

"Dad mentioned that group, but he said they were in a different dimension. I don't remember what he called it."

Liam finished adjusting Summer's earpiece, handing it back to her so she could be part of the conversation. Fletcher waved the group forward to keep moving. "Let's keep going guys. We don't need to miss our ride."

Ethan continued his conversation, following the group. "I don't know the entire history, but they started invading Lunaria a few years ago, which is why there's a resistance here to begin with. The crap they've pulled—"

"We're working to find the right combination to get back," Summer interrupted. "Wait. Maybe this call can help us? How did you do it?"

"I had to alter the radio telescope at my laboratory. Ethan was smart to have me scan the key when he did. My equipment found a frequency being emitted from it. I found a way to make it possible to transmit on that frequency. Was there something you had to do on your end? It seemed to take a while to get through to you guys."

"Your call came in at a bad time, coming in as a high pitch squelch," Ethan said. "We have a tech wizard here by the name of Liam that helped us out." He patted him on the shoulder. "He adjusted our translators to the frequency on our end, connecting the call."

"I can work on combinations on my side, but it's going to be difficult to test without a key or someone to activate it."

"Ethan," Fletcher said, "Wrap it up. We don't need to bring attention to ourselves if someone else comes along."

Ethan nodded. "I've gotta go. Love ya sis."

"Oh!" Summer said, "Please call my mom. I left her name and phone number on the coffee table."

"We found it and called her already. Ethan! Take care of each other and get home safe."

Ethan smirked. "You know me."

"Exactly," she said. "I'll reach out again tonight with everyone here. Love ya." The transmission disconnected.

Summer looked over at Ethan, seeing the enormous grin on his face. The conversation had given both of them a renewed hope they would be able to return home once they completed their tasks. "If I hadn't tried to activate the gate, we wouldn't be walking into a bad situation right now."

Ethan shook his head. "You were trying to find your brother. Don't worry about it. I'd have done the same if it were one of my sisters."

"I just—"

Ethan held up his hand, cutting her off. "Family comes first."

"Still. Thanks for helping. I'd have probably gotten caught back at the state archive. That woman gave me the creeps."

"She was something all right," Ethan agreed. "And that massive stick up her butt was insane." He held his hands out, giving a measurement, and Summer laughed.

Elise had been listening in on the conversation. "A stick up her butt?" she asked. "Like...an actual stick?" The look on Elise's face made Summer laugh twice as hard.

Proselytizers

Alex looked out over downtown Heraldrin from the window of his new apartment. The sun was rising, and he could see the bustle of the city below starting for the day. It was obvious Dwyll had provided him access to one of the nicer living quarters, given the large living room filled with expensive furnishings. This was luxury from what he was used to back home and from what he had seen of the city so far...this was better than how most here would ever live.

A knock came from the door, and he let out a sigh, uncomfortable with those that provided the room. Not just because of being jailed, but also due to some of the things they said and believed in. Before he could turn to head to the door, Dwyll walked in.

"Didn't mean to barge in on you, but I wanted to make sure you're happy with your current living arrangements?"

Alex looked around the apartment again. "It's really nice. Thank you."

"Good," he said, smiling. "We don't put just anyone in here, you know. We see your potential." Alex was curious about what potential he was talking about. "I'm sure you still have questions," Dwyll continued. "Come with me. We have a lot to show you today, starting with a short tour. After that, I'll introduce you to a couple others that are about your age. They're on the front lines of our information center."

Over the next half hour, Dwyll dragged Alex around the building. He could tell it was all a move to impress him, but couldn't have cared less about gyms, cafeterias, or meeting rooms. The building felt sterile, like he was walking around an empty hospital or museum. Still, he couldn't complain. It was better than being a prisoner.

The elevator dinged, and the doors opened to a hall leading to a massive, three-story room with large windows letting daylight beam in. "This way," Dwyll said. "Time to introduce you to your new team."

He followed Dwyll towards some couches at the center of the room and looked around, not seeing anyone. Nearing the couches, he turned around to find above the hall they had come through was a second story loft with a glass railing lining both the loft and a set of stairs on either side of the room. From what he could tell, the loft was filled with bookshelves and he could make out the top of someone's head sitting at a table, quietly reading.

"Proselytizers! Get down here," Dwyll demanded.

Alex watched a couple of heads jerk up and look out over the room. When they recognized who had called them over, four people quickly got up, scrambling down the stairs and lined up in front of the two of them. The eldest didn't look to be more than in their early twenties, with the youngest being a girl about his age.

"Good," Dwyll said, looking over at Alex gesturing towards the group, "These are the Kriva Rasturna's proselytizers. I think you'll be a good fit here." He glanced over at the four standing in front of him. "All, this is Alex, the Delphinium Catalyst, and I need one of you to explain what it is that you do here. Give him a better idea of everything from…our perspective. Maybe over some breakfast? He's going to be joining us as a new proselytizer until we can reunite him with his sister. Take him out and show him around the city as well."

He paused, looking the four of them over before pointing at the girl, "You. Girl with the glasses. How long have you been with us?"

"My name is Mei," she said with a tinge of angst. "I've been here for over a year now and you've known me for at least three months, Dwyll." Alex couldn't help but crack a smile.

"Alright, you get to show him around then. When you're out, be sure to swing by Remage's. He'll be expecting him." He looked over at Alex again. "I'm going to leave you in her hands. I've got a few things I need to take care of, and I'll be back later to see how things have progressed today."

The group remained quiet, watching as Dwyll strode towards the elevator. Once the elevator doors shut behind him, the group turned back towards Alex, staring at him. Mei took a step forward, holding her hand out. "I'm Mei Hirano. Try not to forget that."

Alex shook her hand. "Alex McKeown." He looked her over, thinking she was cute. She had shorter raven black hair with a thin blue stripe in her bangs that matched the color of her shirt. Then noticed her eyes were grey.

Mei continued introducing the group by pointing to each, starting with the eldest. "Over here in the red shirt is Casey. Purple shirt is Tyrone. Then last, we have Kalifa here in the green dress." Alex shook their hands. Tyrone headed back up the stairs, not interested in getting to know the new guy.

"How'd you land this gig?" Casey asked.

"I don't think I'm going to be staying long," Alex said.

Kalifa scoffed. "People would kill to get this career and you're going to just leave? I'm not sure you can do that, but whatever. We don't need another white guy, anyway. Dwyll should have gotten someone else."

Alex had to rerun what she had just said through his mind to confirm what he'd heard. "I'm just here till my sister catches up with me. Then I'm headed home. Happy to get out of your hair, though, All Mighty One."

"Oh, you did NOT just take attitude with me," Kalifa said, stepping forward.

Mei jumped between them, intervening. "So, did Dwyll show you where the cafeteria is?"

Alex nodded. "Yeah. I got an idea of where things are during a really boring tour."

"Tours suck," she said, grabbing his arm and leading him to the elevator. "But you'll have to be bored a bit longer." It didn't take long for the elevator to return once she pressed the call button. Kalifa glared as they got on and Mei selected the appropriate floor. "You didn't make a great first impression with Kalifa, but let's move on. How do you not know what we do? Do they not have proselytizers in Delphinium?"

"I've never heard the word before, but not a fan of here, given that I was kidnapped. Some crazy dog things cornered me, and some guards took me through a portal. Then they locked me up for a month and now have me joining your team while they look for my sister."

She turned to him with a curious expression, "You're really not from Lunaria?"

He shook his head as the doors opened. "No. Dwyll said my dimension is called Dolfen—"

"Delphinium," she corrected as they walked into the cafeteria. "Interesting. I thought Dwyll just made it up. Do you know why they took you?"

A short line had formed where breakfast was being served. "They think I can activate some key. I really don't know much about it." He picked up a tray, following her lead.

"You're a Catalyst then?" she asked, surprised.

Alex shrugged. "I don't know what that is. I just know my sister is running around trying to find me, and Dwyll said they would help find her so we can go back home." He held out his tray and the cook behind the counter put a couple of biscuits and what he hoped was gravy on top. They found a table and sat down to eat. "So what does a proselytizer do?"

"Oh, we're one of the more important arms of the Kriva Rasturna. The people must understand they need their government to be run by Kriva Rasturna policies. We own their elected officials already, but the people need to stand with us too. Not fight us. We also help fight social injustices and go talk to kids at schools."

"What do you talk about?"

Mei found she was excited to explain what she does. "For generations, some people here have benefited through inequity and others have suffered. We teach the kids that some of them are victims and others are oppressors because of this inequity. We hope they'll see the light and join us to prevent that in the future. Nobody wants to be an oppressor, right?" She smirked.

Alex was perplexed. "They're kids. How are they oppressing anyone?"

"Most don't realize they're oppressing, but they are just by existing," she said, still smiling. "It's up to us to teach them they have to repent for the sins of their existence."

"Doesn't teaching people that they're victims and others that they're jerks just cause fights? I mean, you're right that no one wants to be an oppressor, but saying they are one when they've done nothing wrong to begin with...that seems like you're wanting fights."

"Oh, we do. When they fight back, we know it's their racism and bigotry coming out and we use that against them. At that point, they can either join us or be removed from society. We make sure to point them out to Czars like Dwyll, who then put pressure on their birthing person to comply."

"Removed?"

"Remember our saying..." she said, smiling. "Peace through Compliance."

"Honestly, you're making the Kriva Rasturna sound like a fascist regime or a dictatorship. I had to do a report on this topic last year when I was studying World War II back in my dimension."

"No, no. You misunderstand. We aren't capable of being the fascists. The fascists are those that try to stop us from taking control. Don't worry though, you're new here. We'll get you sorted out. Why don't you hurry and eat and I'll take you on that tour of Heraldrin?"

***

Dwyll took the elevator to the upper floor. Large red banners with the Kriva Rasturna emblem hung from the rafters. A group of a half-dozen people sat around a desk to his right, going over the morning's intel. They pored over reports still coming in of factions hesitant about their teachings and what various resistance cells across Maraldi had been up to.

Dwyll neared a receptionist desk with a woman sitting behind it. She smiled at Dwyll as he passed her desk. "The meeting has already started, sir." He nodded, opening one of the large double doors in front of him.

Rusak sat at the head of a large table, taking up the center of the room. Prevara sat to his left with six representatives from the Maraldi government sitting around the table. All the representatives looked nervous, unsure of what to say or how to act.

"Ah, Dwyll," Rusak said in a low grumble. "Good of you to join us. You haven't missed much, yet." He nodded silently, walking to his seat on Rusak's right. "Newly elected President Robinson, and I were just going over the necessary donation from the Maraldi government to us, but he was voicing some concerns—says we've been impeding the rights of his people by ignoring their Constitution." He grinned. "Is that correct?"

President Robinson nodded, looking into Rusak's dark eyes. "That's correct. We can't have the Kriva Rasturna taking matters into their own hands anymore. We're a Constitutional Republic and the voices of the people have been heard via my election. I told them I would stand for them and that's why I've joined you here today. You've been a guest here in Maraldi…in Lunaria, and you've been overstepping your authority significantly over the past few years with gross misconduct. I'm sorry, but we will no longer pay the requested ten billion coin per year. It's time for you and the rest of the Kriva Rasturna to leave. And take your technology with you."

Rusak's grin faded. "I see." He leaned back in his chair, tapping the nails of his fingers on the desk. "What can we do to come to an agreement? Are you needing an extension to make the payment? Maybe we can get you a percentage off the top for your personal use? Perhaps women?"

"No, I'm happily married," President Robinson said, shaking his head, "and I'm not that kind of politician. Simply put, you're no longer welcome here. We formally request you leave Lunaria. All of you."

Rusak leaned forward in his chair, putting his weight on his elbows. "Do you agree with his sentiment, Vice President Malum? What are your thoughts?"

The slender middle-aged man stammered so much that his graying beard trembled when he spoke, "I...I sp—speak for the people. President Rob—Robinson is in violation of the peop—people's wishes."

President Robinson shot Malum a glare. "What are you up to, Malum?"

Rusak stood from his chair, unsheathing a large serrated sword. President Robinson turned, seeing the movement in time to watch the blade plunging into his chest. He yelled for only a second; the scream refusing to escape his lips. His arms slowly dropped to his sides as though his batteries were running out. Rusak smiled, watching the life drain from his victim's eyes before withdrawing the sword with a sickening sound. He placed the blood covered blade on the table, taking his seat. All the Lunarian officials, including Malum, looked like they were going to be sick. Rusak leaned forward on the table, looking Malum square in the eyes. "Congratulations, President Malum. I trust you'll take care of the donation quickly and that I can look forward to your support in the coming years."

Malum quickly nodded, never taking his eyes off the sword.

"Good," Rusak said, grinning. "You may leave. You may all leave."

Dwyll chuckled, watching the men practically run from the room. He hadn't seen a spectacle like that in quite some time.

Rusak leaned back. "Remember. Fear can be just as potent a motivator as scopshade. Sometimes more so." He sighed. "The masses always amuse me, thinking electing some new official with their ideals will save them." He shook his head. "Deplorable, naïve, and pathetic. That's the people we're up against here." He turned his attention over to Dwyll. "Speaking of, how goes the converting of our first Delphinium recruit?"

Dwyll smiled. "It's going well. I have him staying in one of our nicer apartments and I have Mei with our proselytizer team showing him around. I thought maybe she could woo the boy, if nothing else."

"I'm not sure he likes women," Prevara said with a smug look.

"Of course, he doesn't like hags that are twice his age. It's why he shot you down," Dwyll said with a chuckle. Prevara's smugness turned to anger. Dwyll looked back to Rusak, "I have the girl giving him a tour of the city and stopping by Remage's weapon shop later today. Weapon's training will begin shortly after."

Rusak let out a single laugh. "You've learned well, Dwyll. Give a boy a sense of belonging, a weapon and luxury—he'll be joining up with us by tomorrow at this rate."

"Once he joins us, we can start him on training with the Helenium Key."

Rusak nodded. "Be sure to question if he knows where the Delphinium Key is as well."

"I already have that covered." Dwyll grinned. "I believe his sister Summer and her companion, Ethan, have it. They came to Lunaria looking for the boy. Not only that, but our informant within the resistance has let us know they are making their way here as we speak. Seems they believe they can snatch him directly from our headquarters without a fight."

Rusak glanced at Dwyll. "You're sure they have the key?"

"One of them has it. There's no other way the two of them could have gotten here. I didn't see Jerran around helping them. If I had to guess, I'd bet they stole the Delphinium Key for their little rescue mission."

"You've increased patrols on the roads leading here?" Rusak asked.

"I've been told they're going to be coming by airship from Kinsford. I've doubled the guards on each flight heading this way. We can apprehend them in the air."

"Good," Rusak said, leaning forward, resting his arm on the table. "but I have another thought. When we have confirmation which airship they're on, I want it to be taken down. Send out one of the tempests to do the job. After the crash, take a team with a couple of TAKs in and search the debris. They'll be able to home in on where the key is."

"Sir," Prevara said hesitantly, "Couldn't the crash destroy the key?"

Rusak shook his head. "They've been through worse over the centuries."

"Then what about the guards on the flight who are loyal to the Kriva Rasturna?"

"If their loss means we gain the Delphinium Key, then their deaths will not have been in vain," he said, staring through her. "You are all secondary to the Kriva Rasturna getting those keys. Never forget that."

The Airship

The group had been walking for a couple miles, luckily without further incident. Ethan's feet were killing him and from what he could tell, most of the group was ready for this trek to be over with.

"We're nearly there," Fletcher said. "The airfield is just around the bend up ahead." He turned to the group. "Elise, Liam, Ethan and Summer...hand your weapons over to Caleb's team. Carrying them beyond this point will only cause us problems." Ethan took the dagger from his belt, handing it over and saw the others do the same.

Elise came up beside Summer. "I'm not looking forward to getting past the guards."

"Caleb," Fletcher said. "It's time for your team to get into position." Caleb nodded, pointing two of his men to head into the trees on the right while he and the remaining man would go to the left. As he walked by, Fletcher caught him by the arm. "Hey." Fletcher lowered his voice. "Don't forget about Tomps on the way back. He deserves a proper burial."

"He won't be left behind," Caleb said before heading into the woods.

Ethan watched as the four of them disappeared. He could hear the crunching of leaves under their feet for only a few seconds before it was silent again, proving they were practiced in stealth, making Ethan happy they were on his side.

"We're going to hold here for a few to make sure they're in position," Fletcher said. He pointed to Summer and Elise. "You two will head in first. Elise, you'll be buying the tickets. They will check your bags. Don't be alarmed or try to stop them." He looked over at Ethan and Liam. "You two are with me. I'll be buying the tickets for us. We're going to follow the girls in after a few minutes to give them time to make it through the checkpoint. That will help solidify the illusion of us not being with them. Ok, ladies. You're up. Good luck."

Summer placed her hand on Ethan's arm. "Be careful."

Ethan smiled, "You too. I'll see you when we land." He watched as the two of them headed down the path, around the bend, and out of sight.

"Remember," Fletcher said, "If things go south, we have Caleb and his team waiting to jump in if they're needed."

Though Ethan felt the wait to follow seemed to take forever, it was really only a few minutes. The cool morning air felt good regardless of his nerves. He kept thinking about what would happen if Summer were discovered. He hated to think of it, but had a good idea of what would happen to either or both of them should they be found out. Still, he didn't hear any signs of a struggle up ahead, giving him hope.

Fletcher looked at his watch. "It's been ten minutes. Let's move."

The three of them continued along the gravel path, walking around the bend. The thick trees thinned out, leading to a T junction with a large grass field just beyond, surrounded by a tall fence. An entrance to the airfield was directly ahead, where a small line of people had formed. Three guards were posted, selling tickets and checking bags for weapons.

Looking across the field, Ethan's jaw dropped as he saw three massive zeppelins anchored, sitting a few hundred feet from each other. In the distance, he saw Summer and Elise walking towards one of them, having gotten past security successfully. "Zeppelins...the airships are zeppelins! We haven't had these in well over a hundred years!"

Fletcher shot him a look, elbowing him in the arm. "Hey! Only reference these as airships. If someone hears you calling them something they don't recognize, it'll give you away. You'll be reported and apprehended. Airships only. Got it?"

"Yeah, of course. I just got excited. I've never seen one in person, let alone think I'd get to ride in one."

Fletcher's edge softened. "Then you're in for a treat. Just try to curb your enthusiasm before we get to the security checkpoint."

While they waited in line, Ethan looked around, seeing what looked to be an entry point through the fence every few hundred feet. Patrols of guards with TAKs walked the length of the fence, going back and forth between the security checkpoints. Fletcher stepped forward to the security table, with Ethan and Liam close behind.

The guard looked up. "Where to, and how many in your group?"

Fletcher smiled, pointing at Ethan and Liam with his thumb. "The three of us are headed to Heraldrin." Fletcher handed over the coin for the tickets.

Two of the guards came up to Ethan and Liam, doing pat downs for weapons. They each held out their arms, allowing it. The guard counted the money. "Well, you made it just in time. The airship for Heraldrin leaves in about ten minutes. Next one won't be for a couple hours." He finished counting, putting the money in a lockbox. He produced three tickets, handing them to Fletcher. "Your airship is the closer one just over there." He pointed.

Liam stopped holding his breath when the guard had completed his pat down, happy the guard had been sloppy at his job, missing his new device. The guard walked to Fletcher, starting his pat down. "What are you heading to the capital for?"

"We're having a guy's weekend," Fletcher said. "Planning to play some cards and have a few drinks."

The guard chuckled, completing the security check. "Just be sure not to lose all your money. Save some for the hotel or you'll be on the streets for the rest of your trip."

Fletcher shrugged. "I don't know about these two, but I plan on bringing home some winnings. Actually, let's see who can bring home the most."

The guard looked glum. "Wish we were going with ya. Be better than here." He waved them through the checkpoint before letting out a sigh, continuing with the next group.

As the three of them headed towards the airship, Ethan marveled at the details of the massive silver blimp. It blocked a majority of the sky, shocking him at how large it was up close, having only seen them in photographs before. He wondered if it hadn't been overcast, if the silvery exterior would have blinded him, reflecting the sunlight. The passenger decks appeared tiny compared to the blimp, but were still rather large the closer he got.

A young woman snapped him out of his thoughts as she greeted them. "Tickets, please." She held out her hand, standing at the bottom of the stairs to board the craft. Fletcher handed them to her, which she counted and punched, returning them. "Welcome aboard. It should only take about three hours to get to the capital. Please take a seat quickly, as we'll be taking off momentarily."

Upon entering the passenger area, it looked more like a fancy restaurant than what Ethan had expected. The interior stretched a few hundred feet with the width being about a third the length.

Along the sides were booths with a table sticking out from under each window and at the center was a raised floor with decorative railing along stairs leading up. Smaller tables with candles and flowers were lined at angles to each other while large potted plants were scattered about the room to add ambiance—even chandeliers were hanging from the ceiling every few dozen feet.

Ethan spotted the girls at one of the center tables with a waiter talking to them. Fletcher must have noticed them as well as he grabbed Ethan's arm, steering him away towards a booth off to his left. When they took a seat, Ethan found Liam smiling.

"When's the last time you've flown on one of these?" Ethan asked.

"I last flew with my mentor over to Heraldrin. He was teaching me the art of haggling," he said with some flare. "He loved to haggle. It was a game to him. I couldn't believe the deals he could get for parts from vendors." He sighed, "Geez, that must have been...six or seven years ago now."

"What about you, Fletcher?"

"It's been a couple years," he said, coming off almost angry. "Not good memories." He sat back in the booth, looking around to make sure no one was in earshot that shouldn't be. He leaned forward, talking in a hushed tone, "For me, it was getting away from Heraldrin shortly after the Kriva Rasturna came. I saw the writing on the wall rather quickly and had to get out of there."

Ethan shook his head. "How did it get to this—" Fletcher loudly cleared his throat, cutting Ethan off mid-sentence.

He gave a cheerful smile. "The first place I'm taking the two of you is the food market. It's the best place in Heraldrin for anything you could want to eat."

Confused by the change, Ethan heard someone come up behind him. A waiter bowed, introducing himself, "Good day. My name is

Ziff. I'll be your waiter for your travels. Excuse the intrusion, but I heard you talking about heading to the food market. Once there, you'll have to make it a point to try the Brioche Bakery about a block north of the statue of Sovereign Rusak. Just the memory of the smells coming from that shop makes me wish I could pick up a loaf or two." He paused a moment, appearing lost in thought before remembering what he was going to ask. "In the meantime, what can I get the three of you to drink?"

"Just water for me," Ethan said. "I'm trying to save my money for the cards we're going to be playing later."

"Good call," Fletcher said, nodding in agreement.

The waiter looked at Liam. "Water for you as well, sir?"

"Please," he responded. "I don't want these two having an advantage."

The waiter grinned. "Very good." He clicked his heels together as a formal salute and headed towards the kitchen.

Ethan watched as the conductor that punched their tickets earlier entered the craft. She closed the door, locking it into place and quickly pulled a string above her twice, setting off a bell that notified the pilots they were ready for takeoff. He looked out the window, watching various crewmen untying ropes that anchored the airship.

Large safety clamps holding the airship in place released jolting them skyward. Ethan's stomach lurched, causing a moment of nausea as the landscape shrank under them. A second later, the hum of motors increased, speeding up giant propellers and pushing the airship forward. They were officially on their way.

***

Dwyll entered the communications room at the Kriva Rasturna headquarters, quickly making his way past the guards and ignoring their greetings. He needed confirmation from his contact in the resistance. "He had better have come through," he muttered under his breath.

He approached the desk of one of the clerks deciphering Morse code over radio signals. The clerk continued scribbling letters as quickly as he could, double checking his work before he noticed Dwyll looming over him. He jerked back, startled, "How...how can I help you, sir?"

"Has there been any updates from our contact within the resistance? I need to know which plan I'm to move forward with, and he was to have updated us by now."

"Uh," the man said, flipping through his paperwork.

A second clerk stood up, peering over the divider that separated their desks. "I've got your message, sir. Came in just ten minutes ago."

"Well? Spit it out."

"Word is, they just took off from Kinsford an hour ago. It'll be another couple before they've arrived. I did try to get the message to Sovereign Rusak when it first came in, but he had already returned to Primula."

Dwyll rolled his eyes, hearing a familiar voice from behind.

"Hey boys," Prevara said as she strode in. She noticed Dwyll already talking to the clerk about the message. "I see you've finally showed up."

Dwyll couldn't stand the sound of her pointed heels clacking on the tile wherever she walked. He turned, looking at her with disdain. "What do you want?"

She smiled, enjoying that her mere presence was enough to annoy him. "Whatever you're going to do, you'd better do it quickly. Rusak won't abide failure."

"Actually," he said with a sarcastic grin, "Once you're done babbling, I'm going to be getting ahold of the Harriers. Taking down an airship should only take one, maybe two tempests?" He stroked his goatee, remembering the firepower statistics of the smaller airships.

Prevara raised her brow. "Don't you need that girl to keep Alex in check? Killing his sister might piss him off."

Dwyll snickered at the thought. "Reuniting them was never my intention. She's obviously joined the dissidents. That makes her and her friend our enemy. Besides." He waved his hand dismissively. "The Delphinium Key will survive a fiery crash. Better to sift through the rubble as Rusak said, than let them run and hide it from us."

"Too bad they don't have the tech here to video record the crash," Prevara said flatly. "I've always wanted to see one of those airships go up in flames."

***

Summer and Elise had been busy talking for the last hour about Summer's past, her brother Alex, and what they had been through over the last few days. It wasn't until Summer started looking for their waitress to get a refill that she noticed most of the surrounding tables were empty. "I expected more people to be riding."

"That's because few people want to visit Heraldrin anymore. It's become a dangerous place for those that don't hold the same viewpoints as the Kriva Rasturna." She saw how uneasy the information made Summer. "Don't worry. Between Fletcher, Liam and I, we'll keep you safe. I'd wager Ethan will too," she said, smirking.

Summer glanced in Ethan's direction, but could only see the back of his head. It looked like the guys were laughing about something from across the room.

"Given that we have all this space around us," Elise said in a hushed voice, "I'm wondering what it felt like to travel between dimensions. Were you ever dizzy or did you pass out when you first came into contact with the key? I've read that it can be a side effect for Catalysts that have never held one before."

"I never passed out, but I did feel a bit sick after we crossed. I think that was because I was lifted off the ground when crossing, almost like there was no gravity. Felt weird."

"No gravity?"

"I don't know. I just...started floating shortly after the light bubble surrounded me."

"There's been no mention of that in any of the documentation I've pored over. Of course, there's been no mention of what it was like to travel between dimensions at all."

"So how long have you been, you know...with..." Summer stopped herself, realizing if she had finished the question, it could put them in danger.

"About a year, I guess," Elise said, understanding. "I joined up shortly after my mom was injected with scopshade." She sighed. "We lived in Roris, a small town northwest of Lake Aestatis. She used to take me to the library on Saturdays. We'd pick up a couple of books and go to the lake to read. There was usually a nice breeze and a large tree nearby providing shade. It was relaxing and we would tell each other about the stories we read and what interested us about them."

"That sounds nice."

"It was those Saturday reading sessions that started me in learning all I could about the Steradian Gate and the keys. She saw I had an interest in reading and researching and showed me some of the work that she, my dad, and my grandfather had already done on the keys. Initially, I thought it was fiction or a joke. Then she pulled out a dusty box of research papers. She explained that the three of them had been looking for the key, trying to learn as much as they could for years. My grandfather had been researching since my mother was a child. Sadly, he had passed away from old age shortly after she brought me into the fold and then, a year later, my dad died from an illness. She stopped her research and focused on work to make sure I was taken care of. She missed him so much."

"Did she get back into researching it with you later?"

"She did," Elise said. "Always pushed me to learn as much as I could about it—saying one day I'd become a renowned archeologist, making a name for myself." She looked up, noticing Summer intently listening, "I'm sorry, I'm probably boring you with all of this."

"Not at all," she said.

Elise sighed, "It wasn't long after that, maybe a couple months, when we heard about the Kriva Rasturna invading Maraldi, starting with Heraldrin. Another few months after that and they had spread to Devon Falls and then Kinsford. Much like what Liam described, happened to my mom. They even called her a terrorist because she didn't share their beliefs. She was arrested at the library right in front of me, released a few days later as a Grey. It's so hard watching someone you love no longer be themselves. No longer interested in anything they used to be or even having hope."

"I'm sorry."

Elise shook her head. "I haven't given up. There must be an antidote somewhere or one I can make. We just haven't found it yet.

I'll get her back." She let out a single nervous laugh, not wanting to cry. "Let's talk about something a little more upbeat."

"Of course," Summer said.

Elise managed a mischievous grin. "Seems pretty clear Ethan has a thing for you. How long have you had a thing for him?"

Summer felt her cheeks go flush. She glanced towards him again, seeing he had looked her way as well, with a goofy grin on his face. She smiled. "I thought he was just some nice guy helping me research how to get Alex back, but it's been a bit of a whirlwind this last week."

"But you do like him?"

Summer couldn't stop smiling and nodded. "It's more than just being stuck here together. I don't know what it is, but we…we click."

"Have you told him?"

"What? That we click?"

"No. That you like-like him."

"Being on the run constantly isn't the best time for romance."

"Well, if you ask me—" Elise started.

"Hold on," Summer said, peering past her out the window. Something had flown by that she didn't recognize, and it was certainly not an animal. An object came into view a hundred feet off in the distance, hovering. Concerned, Summer pointed at it. "Have you ever seen something like that before?"

"What is it?" Elise asked, turning in her seat to get a better look.

"Are there other flying vehicles in Lunaria?"

"Yeah. It almost looks like…a tempest." She stood up, fixated on the object, before realizing what was about to happen. "Oh…no…" she said under her breath, just as the window exploded from a hail of bullets.

Summer looked in horror, seeing a waitress scream just before getting struck by a bullet, knocking her to the ground. Everything was happening in slow motion. Passengers screamed, running for cover. She felt a tug at her arm as Elise pulled at her. The stream of bullets rose out of the cabin, giving a temporary moment of relief while alarms blared. Ethan came running with Fletcher and Liam.

"We've been discovered!" Fletcher yelled over the chaos.

Bullets came pouring back into the cabin, causing a second explosion of splintered wood, shattered glass, and shards of broken pottery to fly across the room. Ethan grabbed Summer's arm, bringing her behind a dividing wall, and covered her face.

"We need to find better cover!" Ethan yelled over the deafening sound.

The four guards posted on the airship had taken positions at the windows, firing back at the tempest with pulser rifles. "Why the hell are they shooting at us!?" yelled one of them.

"Doesn't matter," another said. "It's us or them."

Ethan pointed towards the kitchen at the back. It was fully walled off from the attack. "There!" The bullets dipped below the cabin area, giving them an opportunity. "Now! Move!" Ethan yelled. The group ran as quick as they could past scared passengers and dodging around lifeless bodies. The bullets entered the cabin again, striking another passenger just behind them. More screams followed.

They reached the kitchen, diving behind equipment right when the hail of bullets ripped past the doorway they'd entered; bullets ricocheting off the metallic cooking equipment nearby.

"Is there a way off of this thing?" Ethan asked. "A secondary escape craft...or...or...parachutes?"

"These are supposed to be luxury vehicles," Elise said. "They're well maintained for safe travel. They aren't built for combat."

"Nothing for emergencies?" Summer asked.

Fletcher shook his head. "Nothing that I kno—"

A jolt came when a clamp holding the cabin to the rest of the airship's structure gave way. Liam looked through the kitchen door at the guards, watching one of them lose his balance. The guard tried to grab on to the windowsill to regain his footing, but it was too badly damaged, and he fell out the window screaming just as a massive explosion rattled the cabin. Cracks started forming at the back wall of the kitchen and fire engulfed the main seating area they had just escaped.

The rush of gravity pulling at them shoved their stomachs into their throats. They were dropping quickly, causing the back wall of the kitchen to give way with a metallic, screeching tear. Ethan watched the wall give way, disappearing and opening the kitchen to oblivion. A cook who had been hiding at the back tried to grab hold of a bolted down table, only to be sucked out of the new hole and into the open sky.

The doorway to the kitchen now acted as a wind tunnel, pushing them towards the gaping hole in the craft's side; the wind ripping past each of them in a deafening roar. Kitchen utensils and food flew around the room, getting sucked out. Each of them grabbed hold of bolted down equipment as the airship began to corkscrew. Ethan looked at the void, seeing the tops of trees near what looked like the start of a lake.

"Look!" Ethan yelled. "That lake is our best bet!"

Summer screamed, losing her grip on the cooking range. She flew backwards towards the opening, but managed to grab hold of cabling hanging through the half-destroyed ceiling. Ethan saw her wrap the cabling around her arm to better secure it before seeing what lay beyond her. Open sky had replaced the trees and the lake through the opening. He focused back on her, seeing her hands slipping against the pull of the wind while her feet dangled behind her.

Another cable flapped around in the wind near Ethan. Grabbing hold of it, he made his way towards her. Seeing her panicked, he quickened his pace, eventually reaching out and grabbing her forearm, pulling her close.

"Grab onto me!" he yelled. She wrapped her arms and legs around him, holding tightly. He motioned for the others to grab a cable and make their way towards them before he saw the view of trees about a hundred feet down move to the sky again, with the airship continuing to corkscrew. Flames licked up the walls surrounding them. He knew they were running out of time and needed to act. The others had finally reached them.

"We need to time this right," he said, making sure they could hear him over the screeching metal and wind. "When you see the lake below, you'll need to let go! Let yourself get carried out and aim for the water while you fall! Get ready!" Liam vomited his breakfast, still holding onto his cabling tightly.

The tops of trees began to show, looking to be only about forty feet away. Then the large body of water came into view below. "Now!" Ethan yelled, releasing the cabling. He and Summer were flung out into the open air. She tried her best to hold on to him, but the force of falling proved too much, ripping her away from him.

Ethan had only a second to look around to get an idea if the others had made it, seeing them free-falling with him and the airship flying forward. He looked down and the water below rushed towards him, giving him barely enough time to take a deep breath.

Remage

The cold water enveloped Ethan as he went in feet first. There was no telling how far down he'd gone, but his ears ached from the pressure. He felt his body slow and swore he could make out a muffled rumble followed by an impact wave pushing against him like a strong current. Opening his eyes to make sure it wasn't some creature, he found only a dark blue blur surround him. He remained motionless, letting his body naturally float upwards to regain his bearings before swimming upwards. His lungs started to ache, making the light shimmering through the surface a welcome sight. He broke the surface, gasping for air.

He twisted in the water, looking for the closest shore, and then he saw it. A hundred feet ahead of him were the remains of the airship; the tail end of the craft lay in the water, with the majority of it a mangled burning heap strewn across the beach, stretching well into a grouping of trees beyond. The flames reached upwards of forty feet and were so intense he could feel the heat even from where he was. His focused shifted, finding Fletcher treading water, looking at the wreckage as well. He didn't see anyone else. "Are you alright!?" he yelled over the crackling inferno and screeching metal.

Fletcher turned. "I'm fine. Have you seen the others?"

Ethan shook his head, frantically searching the top of the water just in time to see Elise surface, sputtering for air. Fletcher swam to her to help get her out of the water while Ethan continued searching. After a few seconds, something floated to the surface. It only took him a moment to realize it was Summer's back. When he reached her, her face was still under the water. He flipped her over and checked her breathing, but the unsteady water made it difficult to confirm. Knowing he had little time to help her, he swam to shore, pulling her along, and saw Liam lifting himself up on the beach with Fletcher kneeling next to Elise. "Fletcher! Need some help!"

Fletcher looked over and jumped back in the water, swimming towards them. They pulled her the rest of the way out, laying her on the wet sand. Ethan got to her side to check her pulse, finding it was faint but still there. He immediately began chest compressions.

"Oh my God," Elise said, rushing to join them.

Fletcher was hunched over, catching his breath. He knew all too well situations like these rarely had good outcomes. "Let's just give him some space. That's all we can do for now." He slumped into the sand and Liam joined them, wincing at his arm.

Ethan tilted her head back, giving a couple of breaths, repeating the process once more before Summer finally coughed up water. He turned her to her side, and she coughed up more before gasping to fill her lungs with air. Her eyes shot open.

"Summer, can you hear me!?" Ethan asked as she sat up.

"Yeah," she wheezed, "Drowning doesn't make you deaf."

Elise knelt next to her, smiling. "You had us all scared."

"Let's still give her some room. Glad to see you made it," Fletcher said with a nod.

"I can't believe we all made it off that thing alive," Liam said, clutching his arm.

"We got lucky," Fletcher said, looking over at him. "Is your arm, ok?"

Liam shook his head. "I think it's broken."

"We'll figure out something before we continue. The fire is dying down. Let's just take a moment."

Elise bent over, hugging Summer. "I thought we might've lost you."

"I just need a moment, I think."

A thunderous screech of metal followed by an eruption of flame came from the wreckage as a sizeable chunk of the frame collapsed inward. Ethan brought his arm up to block the heat and got up, looking at the burning wreckage. "Did anyone else survive?"

Fletcher lowered his arms as the flames died down. "No one would have survived that impact." He looked along the beach at a few lifeless bodies. "Elise, come help me check these two out over here. Maybe they'll have something we can use." She hesitated at the grim prospect but did so anyway.

Summer pushed herself up, her soaked dress making the task harder than it should have been. She wrapped her arms around Ethan. "Thank you," she said, squeezing him tighter. "I keep having to say that, don't I? This trip has sucked."

He smiled, hugging her back. "I'm just glad you're ok."

The two were suddenly aware of the others watching them with a sly smile on Elise's face. Feeling awkward, they stopped hugging and took a step back from each other.

Fletcher broke the silence. "It's pretty obvious no one else made it."

"Aside from Liam's arm, is everyone good?" Ethan asked. Everyone confirmed they were ok, having only endured a few minor scrapes and bruises.

Fletcher walked over, patting Ethan's shoulder. "We'd probably have died like the rest here if it weren't for your quick thinking. We all owe you our lives. Where'd you learn how to bring back a person from drowning? I don't think I've ever seen that before, at least not successfully done."

"It helps that my mom's been in the medical field since before I was born. She and my dad passed down different survival skills like that."

"I guess we have that in common," Summer said. "My mom was in medical too."

"Where'd it go?" Liam butted in.

"Where did what go?" Elise asked.

"The tempest that shot us down. It's gone."

"Well, it did what it came to do," Fletcher said angrily.

"Why shoot us down in the first place?" Summer said, irritated. "If they wanted us so bad, why not just wait till we arrived in Heraldrin to arrest us?"

Fletcher shook his head. "I don't have an answer. My question is, how did they know we were on it? The guards at the checkpoint wouldn't have let us pass if they suspected us."

Luggage had been scattered across the beach, with some still floating in the water, being pushed up by the waves. Summer opened a nearby suitcase, shuffled through it and grabbed a shirt, taking it to Liam. "This might hurt a moment, but it'll help." She ripped the shirt, creating a makeshift sling for his arm.

"Appreciate that," he said.

Elise held up her pack with their change of clothes. "Hey Summer, I don't know about you, but I don't think this dress is going to do me much good from here. Want to change?"

"Are the clothes dry?"

Elise opened the pack, remembering it had a semi-water-resistant lining. "They're dryish," she shrugged. "Dryer than what we have on now. We can change over here for some privacy." She pointed to some thick bushes jutting out onto the beach.

"No peaking," Summer teased as she passed Ethan heading towards the bushes.

"Oh, I wouldn't dream of it," he said with a smirk, pulling off his vest to ensure the Delphinium Key and his journal were still with him. An involuntary sigh of relief escaped him seeing the objects still tucked away in the hidden back pocket. He checked the journal, amazed it was still dry. "Any idea where we're at?" he asked, putting it back on.

Fletcher nodded. "I think this is Lake Thera. It's about a three-hour hike from Devon Falls. We have a resistance cell we can meet up with there," he said, pointing to a ten-foot path cutting its way through the forest. "Over there should be the main road."

"Word of a crash like this will spread quickly," Liam said. "That smoke can probably be seen for miles."

After a few minutes, both Summer and Elise rejoined the group. "Sorry for the wait," Elise said, "but it takes longer to change when the clothes are wet."

"And these are still damp," Summer said, still adjusting her shirt.

"They'll dry on the way. We should get moving before guards show up," Fletcher said, starting towards the opening in the trees. "Let's get moving. I don't enjoy lingering around the dead."

***

Mei led Alex down a busy street on her tour of Heraldrin, passing shops of all kinds. Occasionally, a teenager would come running up to her to shake her hand or give her a hug. He watched as she finished hugging some random pre-teen girl who squealed upon seeing her.

Alex couldn't help but chuckle to himself as the girl was so excited, she could barely form sentences before squealing again.

"There's no way my friends will believe that I got to meet…The…Mei Hirano," she said, gushing. "I'm SUCH a big fan!" She squealed again, loud enough to hurt Alex's ears, making him cringe.

"It was great to meet you," Mei said with a smile. "Keep reading and listening." The girl waved excitedly before running off to tell someone about the encounter.

"Does that usually happen this often?" Alex poked fun.

She waved her hand dismissively. "You have to understand that those of us in the role of proselytizer are a bit like…well…celebrities. While we work to inform people of the good the Kriva Rasturna strive for, we also get to say what's going to be popular. It's only natural these kids look up to us."

"And how old are you?" Alex asked with a smirk.

"I'm fifteen, but that doesn't mean I can't be a role model," she said defensively. "Besides, people meeting us out on the street like this is beneficial for them. It boosts them in their social circles and it's also good for us because it puts the Kriva Rasturna in a good light, generating positive word of mouth. That way, people are more willing to accept the Czars, and of course, Sovereign Rusak as we spread the word."

"You know I was just kidding, right?"

Mei pointed to the building on their right. "Here it is." A three-story building with bladed weapons on display in the windows took up half the city block. Above and to either side of the arched entrance hung enormous banners displaying the emblem of the Kriva Rasturna and a wolf with spikes protruding from its head, which Alex had learned was the emblem of Lunaria.

"What's this place?" Alex asked.

She smiled. "Dwyll wanted me to get you weapons ready and start your training. Everyone knows the best person in Heraldrin to do that is Remage. He's been training people in swordsmanship longer than I've been alive and is one of Maraldi's, if not all of Lunaria's finest mentors. This is both his shop and training facility. Dwyll already let him know to expect us."

"Weapons training?" Alex asked, slack jawed. "Like, I get a sword?"

"I'm sure it won't be just any sword," Mei said. "Remage helps the wielder find the right sword for them. Also, it's an honor to be trained by him as he usually only picks the best with proven raw talent to move forward with."

"I've never used a sword before," he admitted.

"Then you should thank Dwyll next time you see him for setting you up as Remage's apprentice. He wouldn't be teaching you otherwise. Come on." She opened the door for him.

Alex was amazed upon entering the shop, having never seen the number of swords, axes, and other bladed weapons displayed. Large, curved stairwells led up to the second and third stories from either side of the large room and hanging above were more banners displaying Lunaria, Kriva Rasturna and a third emblem he didn't recognize. "What's that banner represent?" he asked, pointing.

"That would be the symbol for the fine country of Maraldi in which you find yourself," came a booming voice from behind, startling him. He turned, seeing a tall, muscular man bowing slightly to Mei. "Good to see you again, Miss Mei. Is this the one?"

She nodded, giving Remage a quick hug. "Good to see you too, Remage. This is Alex."

"Alex!" he said in his booming voice, smacking Alex's shoulder. "It's good to meet you. I'm sure you heard, but I am Remage. Dwyll informed me you're going to be starting your weapons training and

I'll be the one training you." He sized Alex up, frowning, "Hmm. It would seem we're going to have to work on your upper body strength first."

Alex held out his arms looking at himself, "Gee...thanks."

"Better late than never," Remage said with a laugh. "In all seriousness, though, you'll need to select which weapon to train on. We have anything you'd ever want here; longswords, claymores, cutlass, rapiers, sabers...name it and I can train you in it." He gestured towards the various shelves filled with weapons.

"I honestly haven't ever used a weapon," Alex said, feeling embarrassed.

"You don't say," Remage said, looking at Alex's thin arms again.

Mei chuckled, making Alex feel worse.

"Don't be too annoyed with us," Remage said, putting an arm around him. "Understand that here in Maraldi, most boys start their sword training no later than age ten—usually far earlier than that if their fathers have anything to say about it. Don't worry though," he said, slapping his shoulder again, "I'll soon have you trained up like you haven't lost any time at all."

Mei saw the lack of amusement on Alex's face, wanting to restore some of his confidence. "Dwyll told you Alex is from Delphinium, but did he also mention we believe he's a Catalyst?" she boasted.

Remage looked down at him, impressed, "A Catalyst, huh? No wonder he's wanting you trained up. Very well, follow me and we'll get you started," he said, walking towards the stairs. "Your training starts with the selection of a suitable weapon. For a Catalyst, you'll need a weapon that also looks the part. Something that will be recognizable to others of the importance you hold. None of the weapons down here are for someone of your stature."

"Lead the way," Alex grumbled, still stinging from the insults. He followed Remage up to the second floor, where it was immediately clear this was a higher class of weaponry. To Alex's surprise, the weapons seemed to be color coded as well.

"You've noticed the color coordination up here?" he asked.

Alex nodded. "I was just about to ask, actually."

"Good," he said. "These weapons are sorted like this to reflect the different dimensions matching their respective Steradian Keys. As you're from Delphinium, may I suggest those with blue decoration? Many have sapphires and even rare blue spinels embedded in the handles. Of course, if you're not a fan of blue, you're not forced to choose that color."

Mei looked over the wall of weapons in amazement. She'd never been able to see the craftsmanship of these before. "They're beautiful, but why wasn't I allowed to choose from these when I was recruited?"

"Don't take offense," Remage said. "These weapons are reserved specifically for Catalysts and those higher up in our military ranks, which are now controlled by the Kriva Rasturna. Even Dwyll got his long sword here. It has orange sapphires and spessartites embedded, representing Helenium. I had initially made the Lunarian set and was incredibly saddened when the Lunarian Catalyst was executed. Horrible loss of life and we had used the most extraordinary amethyst gems ever seen in these weapons." His eyes lowered. "I fear they'll never be properly wielded now."

Alex walked down the aisle looking at the various weapons in wonder. "So, I can have any of these and you'll teach me how to use them?"

"Yes, of course," Remage said, bringing himself back from his thoughts. "We have an actual Catalyst in front of us now. Let's make sure you get the weapon you need. Now," he said, clearing his throat, "We have long swords and broadswords, but I think those may be a bit too heavy for you until you build up that upper body strength."

He saw Alex getting defensive again and quickly added, "That's not a slight young man. You're still quite young and the kind of upper body strength to wield such weapons isn't usually acquired until someone's early twenties or so."

Alex accepted the reality of the situation. "Alright, so what do I do?"

Remage pointed to another weapon on the wall. "I recommend choosing from one of the many other types of weapons we have. Here, we have the naginata. It's essentially a bo staff with a curved blade at the end. It gives you the range, but will also require more balance by the wielder." He pointed to the next, showing a pair of short, three-pronged weapons with beautifully decorated handles. "These sai are meant for short range attacks but can also be well suited to block incoming sword attacks and even disarm your enemies."

Mei pointed to an oddly shaped weapon on the wall that looked like two sticks chained together with a scythe attached to the top. "What are these?"

"Ah," Remage nodded, "That is a double chained kama. I don't recommend it for beginners." He pointed to another sword on the wall. "This, on the other hand, would befit a Catalyst and be a sword that, with practice, could be something for enemies to fear. This is a katana; an ancient type of sword reserved for those with honor." He lifted it from the wall, unsheathing it. "You'll notice the blade is slightly curved. It's thin in comparison to many of the other swords here, but make no mistake, this is a worthy weapon that is sturdy and will handle well during battle." He sheathed the sword, replacing it on the display with reverence. "So, what weapon has your attention? Which would you enjoy learning?"

Alex took a step back, admiring the selection. There were so many that it made the choice difficult. He walked down the aisle looking at the different options before finally moving forward towards the green Alchemilla section. He picked up the pair of sai, turning them in his hands, amazed at the craftsmanship.

"These green gems really pulled me in," Alex said, smiling. "What are they?"

"Interesting," Remage said, raising an eyebrow. "Those gems are chrome diopside and chrome tourmaline. They're incredibly brilliant, are they not?"

Alex smiled ear to ear, not taking his eyes off the weapons. "They're amazing."

"Is that your choice, then?" Remage asked.

Alex nodded, "Yes. How much do I owe you for them?"

Remage smiled, "Excellent choice. Your first weapons from here are a gift to you from the Kriva Rasturna. Enjoy them, but be warned, they are not toys. They can and will kill you or those around you if used improperly. Pay attention to your surroundings. Pay attention to your instruction, and of course, respect the weapon."

Alex looked down at the pair of sai and back to Remage beaming, "Thank you."

"You begin your training later tonight after my shop closes," Remage said. "I expect you here no later than five o'clock. The first few days of training will be hard, so prepare yourself and be sure to eat well before arriving. You'll need your strength."

Revelations

Ethan looked back, seeing the smoke of the wreckage still clearly visible after walking down the path for the last hour. The path hadn't been traveled in some time, with saplings having sprung up and thick grass covering what used to be tracks. Trees hadn't been trimmed back either, growing overhead, providing spots of shade as they continued. A branch came swinging back, hitting him in the face. He grunted, not expecting the sting.

Summer looked back apologetically. "Sorry, I didn't think it'd swing back that fast."

"When's the last time you think someone's been through here?" Ethan asked, rubbing his cheek.

"We're nearly in what would be the off season," Fletcher said, "but people haven't been able to go to the lake the last few years. Normally, they would only shut it down during winter, but the Kriva Rasturna closed off public access to lakes across the country indefinitely. They didn't bother telling us why."

"At least it's not spider season," Elise said. "I hate it when there's a lot of huge spiderwebs in the trees and bushes. Gives me the creeps."

Liam involuntarily itched the back of his neck. "I'm not a fan of spiders, either."

"How's your arm feeling?" Summer asked.

"It hurts like hell, but I'll get through it."

Ethan heard some faint static from his translator. "Are you guys hearing that?"

Summer nodded, "I am."

"Are the translators water resistant?" Ethan worried.

"Yeah," Liam said with a nod. "We've tested them up to fifty feet down and they worked just fine after."

Aiza's voice broke through the static. "Hello? Ethan?"

"Thank God this thing still works. Aiza, good to hear from you."

"Did you ever doubt me?" she said sarcastically. "Once I have something working, it usually stays functional."

"Kiddo?" came Mason's voice.

"Dad!?" Ethan said excitedly.

"We're all here," Mason said.

"You're not hurt, are you?" asked his mother, Ellena.

"No, I'm ok."

Lilly broke in. "Have you seen any of those tiny kangaroos?"

"More important things first," Mason said, interrupting. "Aiza had let us know you've had a run in with the Kriva Rasturna. You need to stay far away from them. I've been to their dimension, and I've seen what they do once they have power."

"I know, dad, but I don't have a choice in this. They're the ones that took Summer's brother, and we're getting him back. We're not alone though. We made some friends here who are helping us out. Plus, we have the element of surprise, now that they think we're dead after they shot down our airship."

"Shot down your airship!?" Ellena asked, startled. "You said you were ok! That's not ok!"

"We're fine. Hit a couple rough patches, but we're fine."

"Hi everyone," Summer chimed in. "This is Summer. I just wanted to say I didn't mean to get Ethan into this mess. He's been incredible with all of this, helping to find my brother."

"Family is everything, I get it," Ellena said, "but what you did was reckless. Activating a portal to God knows where without a way to get back? What were you thinking?"

"I'm sorry," she said defensively. "I needed to see if it would work and by the time I knew it would, it was too late and I couldn't stop it."

"Ok. Let's take a step back," Mason said, trying to calm things. "The two of you are ok. Ethan says you have help. Who's helping?"

"That'd be the resistance here," Ethan said. "They've taken a stand against the Kriva Rasturna and from the sounds of it, Uncle Jerran had a hand in founding them."

"He made himself a legacy after all," Mason said. "So, what's your plan? It won't be easy going up against that cult, from what I've seen."

"We're still working on the details, but after we break out Summer's brother, we promised we'd help at least look for the Lunarian Key. From what Fletcher told me, it's in everyone's interest to keep the Steradian Keys away from the Kriva Rasturna, and I agreed. Seems they go from dimension to dimension trying to enslave the population."

"What's the Lunarian Key?" Lilly asked.

"You know that compass thing I got from Uncle Jerran? It's the Lunarian version of that. Our dimension is called Delphinium, and I inherited the Delphinium Key. We're currently in Lunaria, so—you get the picture. Each of the five dimensions has their own and the Kriva Rasturna already have two of them."

"We believe that's the reason they took my brother," Summer said. "They think he's one of the few that can activate the keys, calling them Catalysts, but it seems they were really after me instead. They made it clear they'll either recruit or kill every Catalyst, making sure they're in control of all interdimensional travel."

"That's a lot to take in," Lilly said.

"I'm still working on finding a way to test combinations to open the portal," Aiza said. "It's been slow going, as I don't know how the keys work. I have the detailed scans, but that's not really telling me much about its power source or how it activates. The characters themselves, the ones on the outer ring, look close to Paleo-Hebrew or Phoenician script. Not identical by any means, but they're really close."

"The combination is probably something we're going to have to work on from our end, Aiza. I don't know how you're supposed to figure out combinations for traveling between dimensions without one of the keys."

"Oh!" Elise said excitedly. "It's quite likely that the combinations for each dimension would be listed somewhere in the lost city of Mystell. It was a hub for traveling between the dimensions back when Mystell was at its peak. We can keep a lookout for them when we get there."

"We've got a lead then," Ethan said.

"You should also know Ethan's saved my life after the airship went down. He saved all our lives. You should be proud of him," Summer said, looking over at him.

"We've always been proud of him," Mason said.

Fletcher held up his hand, stopping in his tracks. "Quiet." He tilted his head, listening for a moment. "It's a tempest!" he said in a hushed tone. "Everyone under cover. Now!" he ordered, pointing to the thick woods surrounding the path.

Ethan darted under the canopy of the trees, with Summer pressing his back to a tree trunk. "I need you guys to stay quiet for a bit. I'll let you know when I can talk."

The humming of the tempest's engines grew louder, coming from the direction they were headed. Ethan and Summer looked up as a smaller sleeker airship flew overhead with dual propellers, followed by another, then another. A total of seven tempests were headed to the wreckage.

Fletcher came out from behind a tree after they'd passed. "We should be good. I'm betting that was a search party. Our flight should have arrived by now and the smoke is probably visible all the way to Devon Falls. Let's head out." He waved his hand forward.

Ethan put his hand up to his ear. "Are you guys still able to hear me?"

"What happened?" Ellena asked.

"Just avoiding some trouble. Not sure if you heard, but Elise believes the combinations could be where we're heading. Might be a two for one."

Aiza agreed. "Yeah, but keep in mind, it's also possible they kept the combinations for travel separate from the keys to prevent people from abusing it. I'll keep working on my end until you're able to confirm you have the com—"

Static filled his ear, garbling the rest of Aiza's sentence. "Aiza?" The static continued, eventually cutting her off entirely. "So much for long-distance calls."

"Your family hates me," Summer said with a sigh.

Ethan shook his head. "They don't hate you. Angry with you? Sure, but that's from the decision you made ending with the two of us here. Not liking your decision and not liking you are two different things. They'll get over it in time. Unless we die, of course."

"That's reassuring, but I get it. Killing us doesn't make a great first impression."

"Yeah. Let's try to avoid that."

"I really want to know how your sister made it possible to talk with you from Delphinium," Liam said. "You think she'd teach me how?"

"I don't see why not. She's always been smart like that."

Liam pulled the D.R.S. from his pocket, admiring it. "We're so behind in technology. Hey...do you mind if I scan you to make sure this thing still works after the dunk in the lake?"

"We don't have a lot of time for this," Fletcher said, halting the group.

Liam looked saddened. "Ah, come on. This will come in handy, and I've been wanting to try out one of these for months."

"Fine," Fletcher said, "but make it quick."

"What do you mean, scan me?" Ethan asked.

Liam held up the device. "This thing is supposed to be able to scan a person telling you which dimension they're from. I know you're from Delphinium, so when I scan you, it should light up the corresponding emblem. For you, that'd be the compass. Here, I'll scan myself to show you."

He held it out, pointing the clear rounded end, which Ethan guessed was the front, at himself. Ethan could make out the five different emblems he recognized from his key surrounding one in the center he knew stood for the Kriva Rasturna. Liam pressed a button on the side and a thin orange beam came from it, moving from his mid-section to his head and back down to his feet in a half second. The device hummed for a moment, letting out a beep as one of the five symbols illuminated a lavender color.

"Sure enough. The Guardian lit up. You ready?" he asked, holding the device towards Ethan.

"I heard Elise mention the Guardian when she first saw my key. Is that the wolf?"

"The Guardians are a legend we have in Lunaria," Elise said. "They're kind of like a wolf, but much bigger, with spikes along their spine. Legend had it you could summon them, asking for their help in protecting someone or something, and if they deemed it a worthy enough cause, they would assist. It's all legend though. There haven't been any recorded sightings that I'm aware of and no remains have ever been found, but they were revered enough that our ancestors chose them to represent our dimension." She looked over at Fletcher, knowing he wasn't pleased with the delay. "We can dig into the history of them more later."

"Alright Liam, scan away," Ethan said, holding his arms out and shutting his eyes, not wanting the beam to mess with his vision. A moment later, he heard a beep and looked down, seeing one of the emblems illuminated in a blue color.

"Seems to work," Liam said, excitedly turning to Elise and scanning. It beeped again, illuminating the Guardian. He nodded and turned, scanning Summer.

"Hey!" she snapped, taking a step back. "Maybe ask first."

"Oh," he said, looking up from the device as it beeped, "Sorry, I was just so excited to finally have a piece of tech that..." he trailed off, looking at the result.

Ethan looked at the device, seeing one had illuminated greenish-teal. "What dimension is that emblem for?"

"Alchemilla," Liam said slowly. "That can't be right."

Summer backed away, nervous with everyone looking at her. She saw Ethan's puzzled look, wishing she'd told him earlier, "I...I didn't want to tell you when we first met, Ethan, because I didn't trust you yet. I don't want you to think I've been hiding anything from you."

"Hiding what?" Fletcher questioned. "We can't afford to have some Kriva Rasturna spy following us around."

"No, I'm not with them," she said, holding her hands out to try to calm the situation. "I honestly didn't even know they existed until we got here. I'm no spy...I'm...I'm just not from—"

"When were you going to tell me? We've been together for how many days? Seems like your knowledge of different dimensions might have been important to know after we got here."

She shook her head, "You knowing I'm from Alchemilla wouldn't have changed anything. I don't know much about the dimensions other than they exist."

"I just wish you would have felt comfortable enough to tell me. That's all."

She sighed. "So Alex and I are originally from Alchemilla. It's not a big deal. Once I knew you better, I didn't know how to tell you and then we were so busy trying to find my brother and simply survive that it just never came up."

"Wasn't Alchemilla taken over by some kind of plague?" Elise asked. "Pretty sure that's what was broadcast for them having no intentions of going there. I think that was the one thing I could respect them for—not wanting to spread a plague to the other dimensions—wait..." She paused in realization, taking a precautionary step back. "We're you infected?"

Summer wrapped her arms around herself and looked down at the ground. "About ten years ago, my parents sent me and Alex to Delphinium to escape the plague just before it started to spread. He doesn't really remember anything about Alchemilla, only that we lost our parents when we 'moved'," she said, looking heartbroken. "We were moved before anyone in our family got infected. I remember my parents watching the news all the time. It just kept getting worse and worse until there was an announcement that the virus was going to spread globally."

"How would they have had access to the Alchemillan Key?" Fletcher asked.

She shook her head. "I don't know how they got it, but they did. It's foggy, but I remember the day we left. Me, Alex and my parents were at our house in the light sphere getting ready to cross the gate, when I saw people grab both my parents pulling them out. My dad struggled against someone pulling on him, but he couldn't break free. I reached for them and then Alex and I were in the middle of a field in Delphinium—alone in a world we didn't know."

Everyone fell silent, taking in the information before Ethan spoke up. "Have you been able to contact your parents since?"

"No," she said, looking back at the ground, "I...I don't even know if they're alive...or if anyone from Alchemilla is alive."

Elise moved forward, giving Summer a hug. "That's horrible." She released her. "I'm so sorry you had to go through that."

"Any idea who pulled your parents out at the last minute?" Ethan asked.

She shook her head. "I don't know who they were other than they were dressed as military officers. I'm not sure why they were there or even how they pulled them out."

A low rumble sounded in the distance, taking Ethan's attention. He looked up the path, seeing three vehicles just as a nearby tree trunk exploded from a pulser shot. He raised his arm above his eyes, blocking the splintered wood.

"Ground patrol on revbolts! Into the woods! Now!" Fletcher yelled.

They entered the wooded area, looking for cover with more shots flying past them. Another trunk splintered, followed by another. The pulser shots kept getting closer before another tree fully collapsed nearby. Ethan had lost track of Fletcher and Liam, focusing on following Summer with Elise just ahead of her. He continued swatting away tree branches from his face as they ran, leaves crunching under their feet. He hopped over an old rotted tree trunk when the sound of tires skidding across gravel could be heard back on the path, followed by someone barking orders.

He spotted a massive seven foot tall moss-covered boulder amid many large trees and grabbed Summer's arm, getting her attention. "Hey!" he said in a stern, hushed voice. She turned, seeing him point to the boulder, "Hide behind there."

"What are you going to do?"

"I don't know. I'll come up with something. Go."

She scrambled towards the boulder. "Elise! Over here."

Ethan took cover behind a thick tree trunk. She was right. He needed a plan, and his options weren't good without weapons. He looked at the ground, finding a rock partially covered with leaves. Brushing them aside, he picked up the softball sized stone, feeling its weight in his palm. He took slow, deep breaths, trying to calm himself, knowing what was coming as he waited for their pursuers. It wasn't long before a pair of footsteps crunching leaves approached.

"They've got to be here somewhere!" said a deep voice.

"We'll find 'em," the other said. "Maybe have bit a fun before we kill 'em."

"Just remember, they want the girl alive," said the deep voice. "You can kill the boy."

"Grab that stick," Summer whispered to Elise before slowly getting up. She quietly climbed to the top of the boulder, finding foot and handholds as she went. When she got to the top, she kept as low as possible to see how many pursuers there were. Elise stayed below, readying to hit anyone coming towards her. Summer saw the two guards with Kriva Rasturna markings on their gear. One was moving to her left, nearing a large tree, where she saw Ethan waiting on the other side.

Ethan took another deep breath, hearing the footsteps get closer until the muzzle of a pulser rifle become visible. He quickly grabbed the muzzle, startling the guard. "The fu—" the guard said, firing the rifle before feeling the rock smash into his skull like a hammer. The shot hit a tree in the distance as the man collapsed, holding his fresh wound. He looked up at Ethan, horrified as he was struck again.

Ethan reached for the pulser rifle, content the man wouldn't be getting up anytime soon, but before he could grab it, he heard a grizzly voice.

"Hold it right there. Pick it up and I'll fire."

Ethan paused, looking at the man, "Why were you firing at us?"

"The only reason you're still breathing is because my pal knocked out on the ground over there was a huge pain in my ass and deserved a wallop. That said, we have our orders to bring a couple of travelers back to Heraldrin. You can cooperate and live, or you can die. We only need the girl."

"What girl are you looking for?"

"We're looking for the bitch from Delphinium with red hair. Looks similar to someone you were walking with."

"Lost track of the people I was with when we ran from the trail."

"You come from that wreck just down the way? She would have been on there."

"I was at the beach with some friends. Nearly came down right on top of us. No way anyone survived that."

"Shit," the guard said, lowering his rifle. "Looks like you just volunteered to help search the wreckage fo—" Ethan watched in amazement as Summer leapt from the top of the boulder, her body slamming into the guard, knocking him backwards. He dropped his rifle, swearing, and pushed Summer off hard. "Well, you got some balls." He started to get up.

Ethan rushed forward, shoving the guard to the ground, but it only seemed to enrage the man who quickly got up, ready to fight. Ethan swung hard, but the man deflected, punching him in the gut. He staggered backwards, catching his breath and wished he had kept hold of the rock. The man grinned menacingly at him. "Pathetic. No wonder you were hiding behind a tree like a child. You can't fight for shi—" Summer swung a baseball bat sized stick hard into the man's head, knocking his helmet off.

"You talk too much," she said, bringing the stick down again. He caught it in his palm, wrenching it away from her.

"You won't catch me unawares again, luv," he said, backhanding her. She toppled backward, landing on her back. "Just sit this one out, girl." He turned his attention back to Ethan just in time to feel a fist smash into his throat. Ethan grabbed the stick from him while he choked, hitting him in the face hard with it. He staggered into the large boulder, catching himself before getting hit in the face again, knocking his skull into the hard stone with a sickening crack. The man fell over, leaving a streak of blood on the stone where his head split open.

Ethan stepped back, catching his breath, waiting for the man to get up again. When he looked closer, the man wasn't breathing. Ethan dropped the stick, turning to Summer. She looked at him, shocked at what had just happened. "Are you ok?" he asked, helping her up.

"I was just about to ask you the same." She wiped the debris from her clothes. "Where did that come from? I've never seen you look like that."

"Sorry, I just kind of lost it when I saw him hit you." He turned, looking at the man and then at the other he had hit with the rock earlier. "I think I'm going to be sick."

Elise came from around the rock, hearing her friends. "Are you guys alright?" she asked, coming around the boulder. She slowed, seeing the guards on the ground. "Oh..." She looked over at Ethan, seeing the look on his face while he contemplated what he'd just done. "You know you probably saved us, right? They were trying to kill us. You shouldn't feel bad for defending yourself or your friends." He nodded, still in shock.

Summer hugged him. "You'll be ok."

"Did either of you see where the others ran off to?" Elise asked just as yelling coming from the road. She picked up one of the pulser rifles. "Let's go save the boys."

The three of them started back to the path, slowing as they neared. Elise raised her rifle, seeing movement near one of the revbolts thirty feet away. They ducked under branches, taking cover when Fletcher moved around the back of the vehicle, engaged in a fistfight with one of the guards. Fletcher was hit hard in the stomach but recovered quickly, punching the guard in the face. The man stumbled, but Fletcher didn't let up. He pummeled the guard repeatedly in the gut before grabbing him by the back of the head, smashing his face into the side of the parked revbolt, tossing the unconscious man to the side.

Distracted by the fight, they didn't hear a revbolt coming down the way. A pulser shot flew by where they hid, striking the back of one of the parked vehicles, the impact causing it to cartwheel with bits of plastic and metal flying off. Fletcher dove out of the way as it came crashing down on its side where he had been standing.

The incoming revbolt drew near to Ethan, and the driver fired again with the shot going wide. Still feeling the adrenaline, Ethan rushed forward, tackling the driver. The two tumbled to the ground and the guard's helmet flew off. By the time the two came to a stop, Ethan had the wind knocked out of him while the armor wearing guard was more angry than hurt. He elbowed Ethan in the face, quickly getting to his feet, pulling a hand pulser from his belt. "Where the bloody hel—" he said, before being flung backwards hard into a tree. Ethan sat up, seeing Elise standing at the tree line still pointing the pulser rifle at the guard's body.

Summer ran forward to him. "What were you thinking? It's like you enjoy getting hurt."

Ethan smirked and got to his feet with a bloodied nose. "Not sure I'd say I enjoyed it." He looked over at the incoming revbolt, which had stopped, having gone into the ditch. "Let's go see how the others are doing."

Fletcher had gotten to his feet and was dusting himself off, surveying the area for any further threats.

"Where's Liam?" Elise asked, worried.

Fletcher gave a sigh of relief, seeing them. "Glad you guys are ok." He looked at the tree line and back to her. "He's around here somewh—Liam! Come on out. We're good for now." The rustling of branches came a moment later, just a few feet beyond the path.

Liam walked out from behind a tree, tripping lightly over a stone when crossing the shallow ditch. "You guys made it," he said, catching himself. The stumble being enough to make him wince at his arm.

Fletcher gestured towards the revbolts in front of them, the one on its side damaged to the point of no longer being functional. "We have our ride to Devon Falls. Should easily make it to town before nightfall now."

"You want this?" Elise asked, holding up the rifle.

"I'll take it," Fletcher said. "Thanks. We'll keep it on hand till we get closer to town and ditch it before we arrive. Don't want to raise suspicion." He hopped onto the closest of the revbolts, holstering the rifle in a pouch on the side of the seat. "Ethan, how about you drive one of these? Elise, you drive the other. Liam and Summer, go ahead, and hop on with whoever you want to ride with. Let's get out of here before these guys come around." He turned the ignition key, and the engine roared to life.

Ethan pulled the revbolt out of the ditch and hopped on, finding the engine still running. His spirits rose. "Oh man, I finally get to drive one of these."

Summer jumped onto the back, putting her arms around him. "You're going to drive safely on this thing...right?"

"Of course." He grinned, looking back at her with confidence.

Fletcher and Liam drove off, with Elise not far behind. Ethan revved his engine and followed. He smiled at the acceleration and wind against his face as he sped off to catch up with the others.

Devon Falls

Mei walked with Alex on the way back to headquarters. He kept staring at his new sai, admiring it and she found herself jealous, wishing she was given the opportunity to pick a similar weapon. "I think you're going to do well as a proselytizer after we get you trained up," Mei said, "but you're going to have a couple hurdles to worry about."

"Hurdles?" Alex asked anxiously. "I mean...I know I'm new, but I'm a quick learner."

"No." She shook her head. "You're a guy, right?" She gave him a moment to catch on, but realized he didn't get it. "We really have to get you caught up on how things work around here. To start, you being a guy means a lot of our listeners are going to have a difficult time taking you seriously. You're part of the patriarchy and because of that, you take responsibility for everything men have done. That means you must publicly admit guilt and ask for forgiveness."

He tucked the sai in his belt opposite the other, not liking what he was hearing. "Why am I responsible for what others did?"

She ignored him, continuing with her explanation. "Add on top of that, you're an uncleansed white. You have an uphill battle, but nobody's perfect." She smiled innocently.

He glared at her. "That's really racist. Also, sexist," he said sternly. "You're supposed to judge people for who they are. What they say and do. Not by what they look like or if they're a guy or girl. I can't believe you actually just said that crap." He shoved his hands in his pockets and continued to walk, irritated.

She quick stepped in front of him, putting her hands up. "Whoa, hold on."

"What?!" he snapped.

"You're not from here, so you need to understand and accept our truths if you're going to join our ranks. First off, you can't be sexist against men. Second, you can't be racist against whites or the uncleansed and you're both. That's our truth and the truth you need to be pushing to others. You either accept that, or you'll never be one of us," she said darkly.

"You just pointed out that I'm not even from here, but I'm somehow to blame for your social crap because I'm a white male?" Alex was angry and disgusted. "My mom taught me what real racism was when I was a kid, and what you said just then...was racist...no matter how much you say it's not. Your belief system, or whatever you want to call it, has lied to you. It's complete BS if it teaches what you just vomited out."

"You don't know what you're talking about!" she yelled, sounding just as confused as she did angry. "Find your own way back to headquarters!" She turned, storming off.

It was difficult to get him this angry, but he wondered if he'd pushed back too hard. He didn't want to piss off the only person he'd considered a friend here, but he also didn't want to be friends with someone that saw him as some kind of lower lifeform, either. He looked around, suddenly glad he'd been paying attention to the layout of the city as they'd left that morning. It wouldn't be difficult to get back. He noticed a few people who had been within earshot glaring at him and decided it was best not to stick around. His stomach grumbled as he continued down the road, and he hoped something good had been served for lunch back at headquarters. He was happy to see the tall building just up the hill about a block away.

When he got to the top of the hill, someone was standing outside the main entrance waiting for him. He tried to make out who it was, only able to recognize Dwyll once he got closer. He watched Dwyll push himself off of the side of the building to meet him.

"I can't believe she already had time to tell on me," Alex muttered to himself.

Dwyll gave a doleful wave as he got closer. "Alex, I'm afraid I've a bit of bad news." Alex looked confused for a moment, not saying anything. "Why don't you come have a seat with me in the lobby?" He put an arm around Alex, leading him to the main entrance.

When they stepped inside, Alex felt his stomach sink, seeing that aside from them, the only others in the lobby were a couple of guards at the front desk. He couldn't believe they were going to lock him up again for standing up to Mei.

"Have you seen the news today?" Dwyll asked, gesturing towards the couch.

Alex shook his head. "No. Mei and I were just at Remage's, where he had me pick out my weapons to train with." He pointed to the pair of sai tucked in his belt. "He said they were a gift from you guys, so thank you."

Dwyll glanced at the sai, smiling. "Good choice. I had a friend once who was trained well with the sai and you're most welcome." He bowed his head slightly. "Unfortunately, there's been a situation that you should be made aware of." He cleared his throat, seeing Alex wasn't going to bother sitting. "Earlier this morning, there was an attack on an airship heading this way from Kinsford. Rescue teams responded as soon as we were made aware. They did a sweep, looking for any survivors, but the wreckage was extensive. They spent hours searching before sending in the report, and sadly, no one was found alive. Your sister...was on the airship at the time of the incident."

Alex's face glazed over; the words feeling like a physical punch as he took a step back. "No..." He shook his head and grabbed the back of the couch for support. "There must be some kind of mistake. You didn't even know where she was. Guards were still looking for her."

Dwyll sighed. "I had meant for tonight to be a happy reunion for the two of you. I had sent out a description of your sister based on what you'd given us and was informed yesterday she had been seen in Kinsford. Once we confirmed it to be her, I told the guards to escort her and her friend to the airfield for transport to us. The earliest they could come was this morning's flight."

Alex blinked, not able to talk or even think.

"It's little in this trying time, but we know who's responsible. Our team intercepted communication from the dissident factions just before the crash. It seems they had put out orders to bring down any airships headed here in order to send us a message. They call themselves a resistance, but in truth, they're terrorists. They don't tolerate the freedoms the Kriva Rasturna provide and don't care who they kill so long as we're hurt in some fashion."

Alex's eyes burned with hatred when he had finally found the strength to look up at Dwyll. "We're going after these terrorists, right?"

"We already have teams sweeping both Kinsford and Devon Falls, as those would likely be the places the attack would have originated."

Alex started pacing. "I want to join the search."

"How about you take the evening to digest the information?" He motioned to the elevator. "Go get some food or a stiff drink from the cafeteria. I'll let Remage know to expect you for training in the morning instead—"

"No. I want to train tonight. I need to bring these bastards down." He stopped and took a deep breath. "I need to blow off some steam." He headed out the main doors to get some fresh air.

Watching Alex storm away from the building, Dwyll's mouth contorted into a malevolent smile.

***

Ethan slowed the revbolt upon nearing Devon Falls, eventually coming to a stop next to Fletcher and Elise. Off in the distance, a waterfall cascaded into a clear teal lake with a river snaking out from it, going around a tree covered cliff. Ethan could make out the occasional building poking out from behind leafy branches when the wind blew.

"It's so nice to be back," Elise said. "I loved visiting the falls as a kid."

"I think I want to live here," Summer said, looking in awe at the beautiful green landscape.

Ethan pointed to a bridge spanning the crest of the waterfall. "How high do you think that is?" He brought his other hand up to block the glare of the sun.

"That's the central waterfall," Liam said. "It's more than forty feet up, but there are more waterfalls than that. It's just the one that greets travelers. They built the city to integrate as many of the waterfalls as they could."

"No time for sightseeing, guys," Fletcher said. "We have to get your arm checked out, Liam. Once we're settled in with the resistance cell here, we can give a tour." He revved his engine, taking off down the road.

The scenery heading into the city was breathtaking, with a misty fog created by the waterfall enveloping the lush mountainside. It gave a sense of mystery that Ethan found intriguing. Opposite the falls was an open field. Animals of all types leapt away into the hidden depths of a large thicket of bushes at the sound of the revbolts speeding by. The road continued around the mountain, leading to a decorative wooden bridge, providing a way across the river.

They slowed, nearing the open and inviting main gate, passing two guards busy talking with each other. Fletcher slowed further as the road changed from dirt to paved, crossing the threshold into the city. Busy shops lined the main street with children running along the sidewalks after each other playing.

Ethan smirked seeing, who he assumed was a child's mother, grab a boy by the back of the coat, making it so he couldn't join in. The young boy looked sullen, following his mother into a nearby shop. He turned his attention back to the road, following Fletcher a couple more blocks until they parked in front of a building with a medical symbol above its door.

Fletcher got off his revbolt, dusting himself off. "Once we get your arm looked at, Liam, we'll find our friends. The rest of you feel free to look around but stay close and don't draw attention to yourselves." Fletcher waved Liam over, who looked as though his arm hurt more after the ride.

Summer looked up and down the street, not sure how long the doctor's visit would take. "What do we do while we wait?"

Elise pointed to a deli across the street. "I could go for some food." She got off the revbolt and started walking across the street before they could reply. She headed into the deli and the two followed her inside. Ethan was happy to see the place was mostly empty.

The smell of freshly baked bread wafted through the air and the lobby looked inviting, with potted green plants hanging from the ceiling and neatly made tables ready for patrons. The glass counter had various meats, cheeses and vegetables displayed, showing the freshness of their produce.

"Welcome to Devon Deli," said a young woman from behind the counter. "What can I get for you?"

Elise looked back at Summer and Ethan. "Do you mind if I order for us? It'll be quicker." They both shook their heads, not really knowing the names of the foods posted on the menu.

"I'll trust your judgement," Summer said.

Elise turned back to the woman at the counter. "I'll take five spuckies please. Hold the carrot salad."

The woman nodded, getting to work. "Did you hear about the airship crash that happened not too far from here?"

Elise shook her head, not knowing what would happen if she answered yes. "No. We've been out driving around today. Sounds horrible. Were there any survivors?"

"Given what the news said, it doesn't sound like it."

Another worker came out from the back restocking some freshly cut vegetables. "Horrible tragedy. The news says it's believed the dissidents shot them down."

"I don't think that sounds like the resistance," the woman said. "They've never gone after civvies before. Why would they start now?"

The worker glared at her. "You're questioning the Kriva Rasturna? The reporters got their information directly from them."

She suddenly looked fearful. "Of...of course not. I was questioning the news, not the Kriva Rasturna."

"You know it's one and the same. If I hear you question them again, I'll report you to the guards." He turned his attention to the three of them. "I'm sorry for my worker. She's new and still learning. Please know we're an ally. The sandwiches are on us for the offense." He finished stocking the various vegetables, looking back at the girl. "Finish those sandwiches, quickly...and keep your mouth shut." He walked to the back room, leaving the girl to her work.

When Ethan was sure the guy was out of earshot, he whispered to the others. "What just happened?"

The girl looked up directly into his eyes nervously. "He's scared," she whispered back. "Many of the shops are working in fear they'll be boycotted if they speak against the Kriva Rasturna. They control a lot of minds here. Every day, people have been vandalizing shops whose owners have spoken up. Some of the owners lose everything, but it's worse. They often get death threats from followers. Threats against their families too. It's meant to shut everyone up and I'm sad to say it's working."

"Followers?" Ethan asked.

"It's not even just those calling themselves the Cleansed. Some are just bad people, joining them to cause chaos because they know they won't be held accountable for their crimes."

"You mentioned families? You're saying they'd come after children?" Summer asked.

The girl nodded. "They do. Many followers don't think clearly anymore. They don't value family or children unless they can use them to gain power. That's all they care about...power and control. They've even gone so far as to call parents 'terrorists of the state'. Many parents here have been arrested and their children removed—taken by the followers." A woman entered the shop with her young daughter and the conversation abruptly ended. She finished wrapping the last of the sandwiches and handed them to Elise.

"Thank you," Elise said. "I hope you don't get in much trouble with your boss."

The girl shook her head, smiling, "He's one of the good ones. Really. He just fears for our safety, not wanting any violence or vandalism."

"Luck to us all," Elise said, waving before heading to the door.

The woman nodded, turning her attention to the mother and child. "Welcome to Devon Deli. What can I get for you?"

"Your prices have gone up so much," the woman said.

"Apologies. We're trying to do the best we can with the way inflation has gotten out of control."

"Can I have a spuckie, mom?" the little girl asked. Summer slowed, overhearing.

"No Dear. We can't afford it."

"Sorry," Summer said, "I don't mean to pry. Do you have food at home?"

"We make do," the mother said. "We'll have to go to the market from here."

"I'm not horribly hungry. Here," Summer said, holding her sandwich out. "You can have mine. I wouldn't have been able to eat all of this, anyway. I wouldn't want it wasted."

"That's very kind of you," the mother said, accepting it.

The little girl hugged Summer's legs. "Thank you!"

"You're very welcome." She smiled and kneeled, giving a quick hug in return. She left the deli, joining the rest outside near the revbolts.

"Where's your sandwich?" Ethan asked.

"Someone else needed it more. I didn't imagine things being this bad."

Ethan shook his head. "It seems to just get worse the closer you get to the capital." He handed half his sandwich to Summer.

"It makes sense. They're headquartered in Heraldrin and their influence radiates out from there," Elise said, taking a bite.

"How do you fight back against an evil that has that much power?" Ethan asked.

She covered her mouth, still chewing. "All we can do is try."

The door to the doctor's office opened behind Ethan with Liam mid-sentence, "...doctor said I was lucky to not have broken my neck falling off the revbolt."

"We all got lucky," Fletcher said with a pat on his good shoulder. "Ah, looks like you guys got some food. You didn't forget about us, did you?"

Elise tossed him a sandwich. "Of course not." She handed the last to Liam as he sat next to her. "They're all the same."

"Let's walk and eat," Fletcher said. "We need to get off the streets before curfew, which is only a couple hours off. It's been a few of years since I was here last, but I think I remember where I'm going."

"What about the revbolts?" Ethan asked.

"Leave 'em. They're only going to draw attention."

The group followed the road as Fletcher gave a mini tour of the town. They passed over a moderate sized river that was made a central part of the city with many bridges crossing it. Flowers of all colors bloomed on its banks with ferns and other vegetation. They stopped a moment, enjoying the view, and finished their meal.

After a few minutes, they continued towards the town square. Fletcher pointed out city hall, a guard station and the cathedral. He also pointed out a bakery. "That there is one of the best bakeries in town. We should definitely make a visit in the morning. The buttery croissants they make are some of the best I've had."

"Sounds good to me," Ethan said, seeing two pairs of guards patrolling the square. They looked to be keeping a watchful eye on everyone, with Ethan noting he hadn't seen any TAKs since entering town. There weren't many people out either, but Ethan guessed that was due to the town nearing curfew. Those that were still out seemed to all be headed to the cathedral, which he found strange.

Fletcher slowed the group, seeing a middle-aged woman swaying back and forth, mouthing something to herself. He spoke in a hushed tone, "Looks like there's one of the more unstable Greys across the way. Let's try to give her some space." The woman looked up, taking notice of their change in direction as Fletcher lead the group away towards the bakery.

Out of the corner of his eye, Ethan saw her start towards them, picking up speed and almost jogging just to catch up. Ethan could see the hint of a smile on her face as she body checked Summer in the shoulder.

"Hey!" the woman said, acting startled. "What are you doing knocking into me!?"

"I'm...I'm sorry, I didn't see you," Summer said, visibly confused.

Ethan watched as Fletcher turned, seeing the interaction. The look on his face saying something was off before he went to grab a sword on his belt that wasn't there. Fletcher cursed under his breath while Elise and Liam both started backing away from the woman slowly.

"You think you're better than me!?" the woman snarled.

Ethan stepped between them. "I saw you practically running towards us before you collided with her. If this is anyone's fault, it's yours. She said her apology. Now go."

The woman almost had a look of glee in her eye and Ethan thought he saw a flash of a smile before he heard her slowly whisper, "Bigot..." She suddenly wobbled back as though she had been shot, clutching at her shoulder, "Bigots!" she yelled. "Bigots! The lot of you!" She let out a startling, shrill scream as though she were a wild animal that had just been wounded. The attention of everyone in the square was on them.

Ethan shot a look of confusion at Fletcher, shaking his head, not knowing what was happening. He kept Summer behind him and backed away. The woman lunged at him, hitting at him over and over. He blocked her blows while she screamed, "Bigots!" with each hit. To Ethan's horror, he started hearing the chant spread to others, like a viral insanity.

"We gotta move!" Fletcher yelled.

Ethan looked back in time to see a dozen people converge on them and start attacking Fletcher, Elise and Liam; hitting at them with whatever they had in their hands. A man in a brown cloak grabbed Summer, pushing her away from Ethan. She stumbled, tripping over something in the road and fell, hitting the ground hard.

Liam howled in pain when someone hit his bad arm with a stick, but no one could help, too busy fending off the masses. Ethan saw the man that had tossed Summer start towards her. Knowing he didn't have time to deal with the woman hitting him, he shoved her hard, knocking her over before turning and sprinting full force into the guy. He tackled him and the two hit the ground, rolling.

The attackers stopped, momentarily shocked that anyone would dare to fight against them. Their lapse gave Fletcher and Elise enough time to subdue a couple of them before guards joined the fray. One of which struck Liam in the back of the head with a baton, knocking him unconscious, while a couple of others focused on Elise and Summer.

Fletcher rushed the guard that had hit Liam, punching him hard in the face, causing him to stumble backward, holding his nose as blood started pouring out. Fletcher snatched the baton from his hand, pushing him to the ground.

Summer rolled to her side to get back up, only to feel the wind get knocked out of her as a guard kicked her in the stomach. The pain was excruciating, making it so she couldn't move, let alone breathe. The guard chuckled, scooping her up, and slung her over his shoulder. He headed towards the cathedral, shifting her weight.

Ethan looked up from his fight, seeing Summer being taken away. He grabbed the back of the man's head and smashed his face into the ground before refocusing on Summer. He pushed himself to his feet just as a searing pain emanated from the back of his head. His vision blurred, making him stumble and then fall to the ground. Unable to move, he watched as Summer was dragged into the cathedral before darkness engulfed him.

FUGITIVES

Alex slumped into a chair, winded, feeling exhausted. He hadn't expected the training to be so intense regardless of Remage's warnings. He had been so focused on training to get revenge that he'd overdone it and could barely move his arms—the nearby pitcher of water looking inviting.

Remage watched him shakily pour himself a glass of water and sat next to him. "I think that's enough for tonight. You need time to heal. Both your body and your mind."

"What I need," he said with an edge, "is to get better. I need to take out the bastards responsible for killing my sister."

Remage let out a slow sigh. "I know you're hurting, but it would be best to take a step back. Rest for a moment to regain clarity. If you go into a fight fueled by rage, you might win...or...you could just as easily lose. Without clarity in a fight, you make mistakes. If you make mistakes, you will lose and the fights I'm training you for..." he took a deep breath, sitting back. "If you lose, you die."

Alex finished chugging the water. "I won't lose with your training."

"Part of the training is learning how to fight with clarity. How would your death gain justice for your sister? Are you sure you even know who is responsible?"

His eyes narrowed. "Dwyll told me the dissidents shot down her airship. That's my best lead and I'll hunt them down, at the very least, for answers."

Remage gave a nod. "In my many years, I've found not everything is as it seems. Let me ask you...what if Dwyll is incorrect in who is responsible? Could you live with yourself if you killed an innocent person?"

Alex looked down at the ground for a moment, thinking. "I...I don't know."

"If you're unsure, then it brings me a bit of hope that you'd do the right thing. Killing someone—it changes you. Being responsible for the life and knowing you've robbed that person of any future happiness they may have otherwise had. If you intend to kill someone, it should only be to protect yourself, your family, or your friends and only in the worst of circumstances where there's no other means of escape. Killing is a burden on the soul. Don't let your rage and a need for vengeance forever change you."

"Someone has to pay," Alex retorted.

"If that's the case, make sure the right person is paying for the deed. Now." He clapped his hands. "Let's call it a night. You need your rest, and so do I. We'll continue your training tomorrow evening."

Alex got up, still a little shaky after the last few hours. "Thank you for everything."

"Of course," Remage said, bowing his head slightly. "Reflect on our conversation tonight."

Alex made his way out of the training facility and onto the streets of Heraldrin, glad it was a short walk back to headquarters. The stroll in the cool air gave him time to think of everything that had happened over the last few days. Up ahead, a guard walked towards him with a leashed TAK. They still made him shudder, regardless that he knew they wouldn't attack him now.

"Hey," the guard said with a nod, "You best be getting back home. Nearly curfew."

Alex nodded back. "I'm heading back to headquarters now."

The guard had a brief look of surprise. "Headquarters? Ah, you must be the new proselytizer. What's the name?"

"I'm Alex. Just got done getting some training in from Remage."

"Ah, he's one of the best. You'll be killing our opposition and well on your way up the ranks with training like that. Might even make Czar with as young as you look." The guard grinned. "Well, hurry along. Good to meet you."

Alex waved, continuing up the road towards headquarters, lost in his thoughts. There was something off about the way those in the Kriva Rasturna acted. He just couldn't put his finger on it. Was it right to align himself with people that had kidnapped him only a month before? Then what about Mei's weird outburst earlier today? It made no sense. He looked up, seeing the building ahead; the lights dimmed in the lobby.

He looked around, suddenly aware of how eerie it was being out in the evening twilight with so few others around. Storm clouds loomed, and the wind had picked up. Dogs barked in the distance, breaking the silence occasionally. He neared headquarters when a scuffle between two homeless men started in an alley behind him. The guard he had just spoken with moved to intervene. "Hey!" he heard the guard yell as he opened the door, taking one last breath of fresh evening air before heading in. Aside from a guard at the desk, the lobby looked deserted. Then he heard a voice to his left.

"Hey Alex," Mei said quietly, getting up from her chair.

He really didn't feel like having this conversation. "Hey, I'm pretty tired after training and not up for any debates right now. I'm going to head up to bed and get some sleep." He gave her a wave and headed for the elevator.

"Wait," she said, hurrying to catch up. "That's not the reason I'm here. I...I wanted to say I'm sorry about your sister. If you need anyone to talk to, you know you can talk to me, right?"

He forced a lazy smile, not wanting to give her an answer. He pressed the button and the elevator doors opened. "Right now, I need some sleep. I'd rather this day just be over with," he said, getting on the elevator.

"Oh...ok. We start your proselytizer training in the morning. Will I see you for breakfast before?"

"I dunno," he said as the doors shut.

***

Ethan's head ached so much that he didn't want to open his eyes. He could feel the cold, hard floor under him and heard shuffling nearby. Someone was speaking, but he couldn't make out what was being said. He slowly opened his eyes, the world remaining a blurry mess. There was very little light, which he was thankful for as he looked towards the sound. Two blurs were looking out of a window, whispering to each other. He sat up, wincing as his whole body ached, but the worst of it was at the back of his head. One of the figures approached him and crouched.

"Try not to move too much," he heard Elise whisper as his eyes finally focused. "You took a nasty blow to the head yesterday. You've been out of it for hours," she said with a sympathetic smile. "Stay quiet. Guards have been searching for us ever since."

Ethan looked around, only seeing Fletcher aside from the two of them. "Where's Summer and Liam?"

Elise looked away, shaking her head. "They...they were captured yesterday during the fight. If it wasn't for Fletcher here, we'd all be captured. He even scooped you up and carried you with us."

Fletcher came away from the window, taking a seat next to them. "We barely managed to lose them. If they had had TAKs with them, we wouldn't have stood a chance." He pointed to Ethan's vest, that was strewn over the back of a chair. "The key and your journal are still there. Elise was nice enough to take it off you, so you weren't sleeping on them all night."

"Appreciate that." The pain at the base of his skull throbbed, making him instinctively reach back, feeling a dried crustiness in his hair. Pulling his hand back, he found flecks of dry blood on his fingers. "Geez."

"I got the bleeding stopped as best I could when I got here," she said. "You really had us worried. We didn't know if you'd wake up."

"We need to go after them," Ethan said, wincing again as he pushed himself up to stand. He felt dizzy bracing himself against the wall. "We can't just leave them behind. Do we know where they are?"

Fletcher stood, helping to steady him. "First things first. You can barely stand, let alone walk. We need to get you checked out. We're still a couple blocks from the resistance cell here. Getting to them first is our priority. We can get you fixed up and get reinforcements."

Ethan felt weakened but was willing to take the risk. "No, we need to get Summer and Liam back now. They're our priority."

"How are we supposed to do that?" Fletcher shot back. "If we don't think this through, we're going to get caught or killed. We need weapons. We need backup. Most importantly, we need a plan. All of that, we can get from the local cell here."

Elise put her hand on Ethan's arm. "We want them back too, but Fletcher's right. We need help if we're going to have a chance."

Ethan let out a sigh, conceding. "I have your word they'll be the priority after?" The dizziness began to subside, and he felt sturdier.

Fletcher nodded. "Liam and I go way back, so you bet your ass we're going after them."

"Ok." He pushed himself off the wall. "Then how do we get to the local cell from here?"

"That's the tricky part," Fletcher said. "After our fight last night, the guards are still on high alert, searching for us. What's worse...they brought in a few TAKs."

Ethan walked to the window, staying low. Outside, patrols of guards walked up and down the streets. At least two TAKs were busy sniffing everything in sight, trying to locate a trail for their masters. "I hate those things."

"We all do," Elise said, joining him at the window. "They aren't natural. At least, not from Lunaria. Rumor is they're made in a lab from one of the other dimensions."

"All that matters is we know they'll kill us," Fletcher pipped in. "We need to avoid them at all costs. That means we stay low, and we stay quiet." He looked over at Ethan, who seemed to improve more with time. "Are you able to keep up?"

Ethan nodded, flinching at the slight motion. "Yeah, it just hurts like hell."

"It'll hurt worse if one of those TAKs tears you apart. Are you sure?" Fletcher asked. Ethan grabbed his vest, putting it on, and felt the weight of the key pat him on the back. "Alright, good." Fletcher pointed to an alley across the street. "We need to get to that alley first. Staying off the streets will be our best bet. The alley up ahead turns north. We can follow it for at least a block, getting us halfway there. We just need to time it right."

"Shhh!" Elise whispered. "A guard's coming." She ducked below the window while Ethan and Fletcher hid behind a desk. A shadow appeared through the glass and Elise held her breath, making sure she didn't make a sound to attract the guard's attention. The shadow lingered for what felt like an eternity before finally moving on. She exhaled, relieved to take a lung full of fresh air.

Bracing herself to look out the window, she froze at the sound of sniffing that came from under the wooden door. She imagined the creature's sharp jaws being just on the other side, forcing a chill up her spine. She heard it snort and its claws scratch against the wooden frame. Elise was sure it knew they were there, feeling a bead of sweat run down her forehead. Her stomach twisted into a knot, and she held her breath again.

"Ay! Come away from there, ya mutt!" the guard yelled at the TAK. "You're not getting any food from there." The sounds of the creature at the door were replaced by fading footsteps as they continued down the road.

Fletcher appeared from behind the desk, moving to where Elise was crouched under the window. "Good eye." He peered out, seeing no guards nearby. "Now's our chance, you two." He quietly shuffled to the door, cracking it to look out. The guard with the TAK was nearing the end of the block and still walking. He peered his head out to the left, not seeing any guards that way, either. He dashed across the street into the alley, with Ethan and Elise close behind.

Ethan stopped and peered around the corner, making sure they didn't catch any attention. He was relieved to see the guard continuing down the road and looked back, seeing Fletcher waving him over at the other end of the alley. He sprinted to them, catching up.

Fletcher looked down the alley in both directions, seeing they were clear, before motioning them forward. They moved quickly, heading to the left before stopping behind a large stack of crates a nearby shop had stored there. Just beyond, lay a large garden area that had been cleared of people with the nearby shops temporarily closed. Decorative trellis' with all kinds of flowers growing through them outlined the beautiful garden. Raised flower beds and elaborate fountains with statues scattered the area, with an occasional bench placed for enjoying the scenery.

Fletcher signaled them to stay still, seeing two guards patrolling the gardens. He pointed to his right, past a trellis to a tailor's shop. "There. That's where we need to go." Footsteps approached, forcing them to take cover behind the crates. A guard had stopped on the other side.

"I'm sick of this," the guard said. "This is a waste of time. They must've skipped town last night. I'm heading to the market to get some food."

"There'll be hell to pay if you're caught not patrolling," said another guard.

"I'm on break. They can deal," the first sneered before the two walked off.

"Thought he was going to find us," Ethan whispered. "That trellis should be able to give us some cover with only the one guard."

Elise shook her head and pointed to the gravel covered road. "We won't be quiet enough. He'll hear us even with us just walking. We can't chance leading him to the entrance."

"I've got an idea." Fletcher smirked. He picked up a metal pipe laying near the crates, feeling the weight of it in his hand. "This should do."

"You still have to get close enough to hit him with it," she said, keeping her voice low. "You have a pipe. He has a pulser rifle. Who do you think will win that fight?"

"Ah, that's where you two come in. You two play the role of the couple on an afternoon walk to the gardens, unaware of the lockdown. Worst that happens is he goes to arrest you. I'll be hiding in wait behind that trellis on the left," he said, pointing to it with his thumb. "Give me a moment to get in place." He peered around the crates, seeing the guard move away, and started to make his way to the trellis as quietly as possible. A few moments later, he was in position, giving a thumbs up.

Ethan stood, holding his hand out to Elise. "I suppose we should sell it, huh?" As they stood, he pushed out his elbow, signaling for Elise to take his arm.

She took it, looking at the guard, who still had his back to them. "I don't like this. What if he just shoots us instead?"

"Fletcher has us covered," Ethan said with a smile. "Remember, we're out for a romantic walk. Look like you're enjoying yourself or he may not believe it." She nodded, putting on an exaggerated smile, tilting her head sarcastically. Ethan rolled his eyes. "Absolutely stunning," he whispered, leading her towards the garden.

Elise chuckled. "I can see why she likes you."

"Who?"

"Who do you think?"

"Hey! Stop right there!" the guard yelled, jogging over to them. "This area is off limits while we search the area for last night's troublemakers. What are you doing out?" Elise put her hand up to her chest in shock, gasping.

"I'm so sorry, sir," Ethan said in a cheeky tone. "I was just taking my lady out for a walk in the gardens and didn't know it had been closed off."

"Hold on," the guard said, raising his rifle at them. "You're about the age of the people we're looking for. Where's your friend?" The guard looked behind them suspiciously.

Ethan stared at him blankly. "I only brought my girl here. I don't know who you're referencing."

The guard lowered his rifle, double guessing his intuition. Ethan saw a blur followed by a cracking sound, and the guard crumpled in a heap on the ground. He quickly picked up the pulser rifle.

Fletcher wore a smug grin, being overly proud of himself. "Come on. We don't want to get caught." He jogged up to the tailor shop and rapped his knuckles on the door. When there was no answer, he knocked again, making sure anyone inside would hear. Another minute passed before he finally saw movement through the glass.

The door opened, and an older man looked out at the three of them. "I'm sorry, but we're closed while the guard conduct a search. Please come again tomorrow." He started to shut the door, but Fletcher put his hand up, stopping it. "I've already told you—"

"I'm looking for a chartreuse colored hat for my friends and I," Fletcher said seriously.

The tailor tilted his head with a look of understanding. "I see... What kind of hat are you looking for exactly? I can check to see if we have it in stock."

"Needing a derby hat," Fletcher replied.

The tailor nodded, opening the door the rest of the way. "Please, come in." The three of them quickly entered, and the tailor shut the door behind them, locking it. "You can't be too careful these days," he said with a smile. "You made quite the mess last night, from what I hear. Follow me to the back and we'll get you sorted."

The three of them followed past racks of clothing to a back room full of boxes ready to inventory. To the far side of the room were a half dozen seven-foot-tall, metal filing cabinets with rolled up paperwork laying on top. The tailor walked to a desk against the wall, opening the top drawer and pressed a button hidden a couple inches in at the top.

Ethan heard a barely audible click come from the cabinets, watching three that were connected swing open, revealing a hidden room. "Ok, that's cool," Ethan said, smiling for a second before realizing the room appeared empty. A knock came from the door at the front of a shop, followed by some muffled yelling.

"Quickly," the tailor said. "Once I close this back up, press the button on your right." The three of them shuffled in and they heard a second knock at the door. The tailor shut the cabinets, and with a clicking sound, they were surrounded by darkness.

"I'm coming!" they heard the tailor yell; his footsteps fading while their eyes adjusted. Ethan's eyes wandered around the darkness for any kind of detail before spotting a small green light blinking on the wall. He watched as a hand pressed the light in like a button, and the floor lurched, slowly descending.

"Is this a standard feature with all your bases?" Ethan joked, seeing a dim light surrounding the edges of the platform.

Fletcher smiled. "You heard what he said up there. You can't be too careful these days."

Happy to have some sight restored, Ethan watched the cement wall ahead of them open to a narrow passage and the lift came to a stop. The passage was barely shoulder length in width with emergency lights setup every few feet. At the corridor's far end, a sealed metallic door with a circular locking mechanism awaited.

Fletcher moved forward, with the others close behind. The cold air almost felt like a mist that floated around them, making Elise shiver. When they neared the door, Fletcher pressed a button on the wall. They sat waiting in silence for a couple of minutes before the locking mechanism began to turn. The door swung open, revealing two resistance members at the ready with unsheathed swords.

"Fletcher!?" one said, surprised. "Thank God, we thought they got you. Come in!"

"They almost did," he said, walking in.

"Who's this?" one said, pointing a thumb at Ethan.

"He's with us," Fletcher said.

"We'll have to search him before he can enter further."

Ethan agreed, moving forward and putting his arms out, allowing a pat down.

"Fletcher!" said a familiar voice. Talia rushed towards him, throwing her arms around his neck, hugging him tightly. He hugged her back, picking her up and spinning her around.

"I thought you had been killed in the airship crash!" she said.

Fletcher cracked a smile, putting her down. "Our newest recruit has a few tricks up his sleeve," he said, gesturing to Ethan, who just got done getting checked. "He got us off the airship alive. Seems to know what he's doing in a tight spot."

Talia hurried over to Elise, giving her a hug as well. "I'm so glad you guys—" She stepped back, looking around Elise for the others. "Where are Liam and Summer?"

"Those bastards back at the cathedral took them," Ethan said angrily.

"The doctor needs to check Ethan's head too," Elise said. "They hit him hard enough that he was out for a long while."

"I'm fine," he said. "We need to start on a plan to get them back."

"We'll set up a meeting with Cormack," Talia said, looking to Fletcher. "We also need to catch you up. One of the reasons I'm here is we've found we have a mole in the Kinsford cell. I don't know who it is yet, but I'm hoping Cormack can help us out."

"A mole?" Fletcher said, surprised. "Who the hell would turn their backs on us?"

She shook her head. "I don't know, but somehow, they knew exactly which airship you guys were on and there were only a handful of us that knew."

Best Laid Plans

The door swung open, and a guard held out a cooking pot, striking it three times with his baton. "Wake up, trash!"

Summer jolted at the noise, grimacing, and rolled to her side, pushing herself off the hard floor. Her hands had been chained, making the process more cumbersome. The dimly lit room looked to have been used for storage, with boxes stacked against the far wall. She looked along the ground where she had been laying, seeing what looked like dried blood. Two more guards walked in, grabbing her roughly by the shoulders, forcing her to stand.

"Hey!" she protested.

"Shut it!" a guard said, punching her in the gut. He held her upright while the other unlatched her chains from the wall, using his key; the metal chains falling to the ground clanking.

The guards dragged her out the door by the arms as she still gasped for air, shoving her hard against a wall. Her translator fell off her ear, attracting a guard's attention. "Sneaky. Won't be needing that anymore," he said, smashing it with his foot. A yell echoed in the wide hall and she looked to her right, finding Liam doubled over, having just been hit in the arm by a guard. Still catching her breath, she surveyed her surroundings. There were multiple guards; two of them holding TAKs at bay, which snarled, pacing back and forth, ready to strike, taking her idea of making a run for it off the table.

One of the guards yelled at Liam, "Get up!" He hoisted Liam, shoving him hard against the same wall next to her. "The Czar wants to speak with both of you."

"Leave him alone!" Summer yelled.

"Tsk, tsk," said a man approaching her.

She turned to see a hooded man in a black leather trench coat stop directly in front of her with a smug smile. His goatee gave his already pointed chin the appearance of a dagger, while he focused his orange-hued eyes on her.

"Did you really think you could hide?" he said snickering.

"You!?" She felt resentment boil up in her, recalling their previous encounter. "How's the shoulder?"

"Cute," he said, unamused, pacing in front of them. "The Kriva Rasturna owns everything and everyone across three dimensions. Some just can't accept it." Without warning, Dwyll hit Liam's injured arm, making him howl in pain.

Summer charged at the czar, but a guard stopped her with the butt of his pulser rifle across the cheek. Not expecting the hit, she shrieked, falling to the ground and landed on her shoulder. Her world spun and her jaw throbbed.

Dwyll laughed. "What did you think you were going to do with your hands chained up, sweetheart?" He nodded at the guard, who got her back to her feet, shoving her roughly against the wall again. Her eyes watered uncontrollably at the metal cuffs rubbing against her wrists. "I'll give you this. You have spirit. Much like your brother."

"What have you done with him?" she demanded.

"He's joined our ranks," he boasted with a crooked smile, spreading his arms out. "He's being trained as our new proselytizer. As soon as he heard the dissidents had shot down your airship, he jumped at the chance to find your killers. And...I...was more than happy to help him do it." He walked over to her, staring into her eyes. "The people of this country have fallen, as will the rest of this dimension, and he'll help us finish the job of destroying any hope they have left before we move on to Delphinium."

"He won't help you once he knows you're the ones that shot us down!" she said defiantly.

"You might get the chance to tell him yourself if you give me what I want." He smirked. "Where's the Delphinium Key that you and your boy toy...Ethan...used to get here?"

She glared at him. "I don't know what you're talking about."

He rubbed his temples with his fingers; his smile fading. "Playing stupid?" He shook his head and sighed. "Very well. We can do this the hard way. Captain!"

One of the guards stepped forward at attention. "Yes, sir!"

Dwyll never took his gaze away from her, "If she doesn't give me an answer by the time I count down to zero, I want you to go to the comm room at the cathedral, radio Heraldrin headquarters, and pass along my order for our new proselytizer to be killed. Ten!"

"Understood, sir!" the captain acknowledged, standing by.

"Nine!" he continued. "Eight! Come on girl, you want him dead? Seven!"

"Stop it! You said you wanted him to do your dirty work."

"He's expendable," Dwyll shrugged. "A means to an end. Six! That end is getting the Delphinium Key and his death is your choice. By my count, you have five seconds to decide."

"Don't tell him anything," Liam said weakly. "He'll kill us all, regardless." A guard nearby punched him in the arm again, forcing another howl.

"Seriously..." Dwyll said, looking annoyed. "Shut him up." The guard nodded, raising his pulser rifle, clocking Liam on the back of the head. He let out a grunt, crumpling to the floor, unconscious.

"Stop it!" Summer pleaded. "Just stop it!"

"Well, looks like your time is up," Dwyll gestured. "Capt—"

"Wait!" she yelled. "I'll...I'll tell you. Just don't kill Alex and stop hurting Liam."

Dwyll held up his hand to stop the captain. "Continue." He relished the forced win. Summer looked at the ground, not sure what to say. Dwyll's look of amusement faded as the seconds ticked by. "I'm not a patient man. Tell me now or I kill this one," he said, pointing to Liam. "Then I'll kill your brother too," he sneered. "Don't play games."

She looked up at him with resentment. "I don't have it. We left it in Kinsford with the resistance. Our plan was to get Alex, return to Kinsford, and go home."

"Interesting," Dwyll said, raising an eyebrow. "Captain. Get in touch with our guards over in Kinsford and turn that place upside-down. Question everyone and, if any refuse questioning, make an example of them. In the meantime, I'll be in contact with our...resource."

"Those are innocent people!" she said, appalled. "They won't know anything!"

Dwyll backhanded her across the face. "They aren't innocent if they know those connected with the dissident movement and haven't reported them. That's harboring a terrorist, girl," he snarled. "And if I find out you've lied, I'll bring Alex here and kill him in front of you." He turned to the captain. "Get these two back in their room." He kicked Liam's shoe. "When this one wakes, question him on where the dissidents would keep the key."

***

Alex woke up sore. He had strained to get moving this morning but managed to get showered and dressed for the day. He felt sick at the thought of Summer's death, wondering how he was supposed to explain everything to his mom when he got back home. Would she even believe him? Alternate dimensions. Weird creatures. Without seeing it herself, he didn't think she would.

He sat slumped in a chair looking out the window, pondering, when a knock came from the door. He wasn't in the mood to be around anyone and ignored it when a second knock came. A couple minutes later he heard the door open, and someone enter, walking towards him. He didn't bother looking at who it was.

"Hey," Mei said. "I wanted to check up on you after everything that happened yesterday. I...I brought a peace offering." She placed a breakfast tray on the coffee table next to him, taking a seat. "I don't want the argument from yesterday to ruin a friendship. I'm sorry."

Alex sat up in his seat, looking at the food. "Well, you did bring bacon."

"Only the best, right?" She watched him stare at the food before he picked up some bacon and took a bite. "So, we're still friends...right?" she asked nervously.

"Yeah, still friends."

"Good, because today we're going to be training your mind. We need to get you caught up on the different problems we're facing and how you can help. Our biggest problem right now, of course, are the dissidents." She saw a flash of anger cross his face at their mention. "Hey..." she said softly, "Try not to focus on your sister. We'll get them for what they did, but right now, we need your focus to be on learning how to be a proselytizer. That's what's going to hurt them the most."

He took a deep breath. "You're right." He sat up and grabbed another piece of bacon. "Where do we start?"

"We start in the knowledge center."

After a few bites of breakfast, she led him to the elevator, taking it down to where she did most of her research. When they entered, he could smell freshly brewed coffee. The tall windows had the drapes open, allowing the daylight to enter the room. Alex looked over at the massive bookshelves lining the wall, still amazed at the sheer number of books the knowledge center had. Walking over to one of the more comfortable looking chairs, he looked over at one of the proselytizers sitting at a desk, reading with a stack of a couple dozen books in front of him.

"What's he researching?" Alex asked.

Mei glanced over. "Casey? He's going over Lunarian history making corrections. We have to help them see their history through the lens of our truth. That way, future generations can know they come from a hateful people and need to repent. That's just one of our many projects, though."

"Seems kind of extreme to say everyone in this dimension comes from hate."

Mei nodded. "It was hard for me to understand at first as well. We all want to believe there are good people, but you have to remember, if they aren't with us, then they aren't good people. We have to assume they're with the dissidents, or at least not with us, until they prove they are. It's the only way we can make sure our worldview becomes dominant. I hate to say it, but the dissidents can recruit random people off the street just as easily as us. Those recruits could be responsible for your sister's death. It's a battle for the minds of the people."

Alex shook his head. "Specific people killed my sister—those within the dissident groups." He walked over to a window looking out over the city. "The others, the workers, the kids running around out there, they didn't kill her. The dissidents did. You think I'm a good person, but I was a prisoner less than a week ago. You'd have hated me as much as them by your own logic."

"That's different," she said, smiling. "You're from another dimension entirely, and you were taken in order to help us. You're special. That said, we have a lot to cover to get you caught up."

"Are you from here, or from one of the other dimensions?" he asked.

She walked over to one of the sofas, motioning for him to come sit with her. "I'm from here. I remember when the Kriva Rasturna first came to Lunaria. They had a different way of thinking, and it scared most people, my parents—sorry...my birthing people included—still getting used to that. They went to rallies protesting the changes the Kriva Rasturna were making and eventually got arrested. They were held for a couple of days before being released, and when they got home, they were different. Better. They told me they had been wrong, and that the Kriva Rasturna were here to help us. Rusak's men even supplied them with free medicine to help inoculate their loved ones. Everyone was offered the medicine for free. My birthing person injected me with a dose that night and you know what? I don't recall being sick ever since."

"Birthing person? You mean your mom?"

"We used to refer to them as mothers, fathers, and parents, but those words are now considered offensive and assume too much, including the assumption that they would have rights over their offspring. The words obviously had to be changed."

"That seems—" He stopped himself, not wanting another fight. "What made you decide to join them?"

She smiled. "I was in grade school the first year they had arrived. Kids in class would question something the Kriva Rasturna did, and

I was quick to correct them. I'd let them know how they've helped us stay healthy, get past our evils and learn to grow together in thought. When a kid would argue with me, I'd simply report them. It wasn't long before someone from the reeducation department would reach out to their families. Usually a day or so after, I'd check up on them and they'd be like a new person—ready and willing to help our cause. Even their birthing people would become active and vocal, joining in protests against the hate they used to spread themselves," she said, almost giddy. She leaned back on the sofa, remembering. "It was the Kriva Rasturna that reached out to me once they saw how many I had helped bring into the fold. I became the youngest proselytizer they'd ever recruited."

"Did you ever question why those families turned on their beliefs so quickly?"

She shook her head. "I never really gave it much thought, but we don't use the word 'family' anymore either, unless referring to the Kriva Rasturna...our true family."

Alex tried to grasp how she was ok with the odd language changes and ideas being presented. "What happened to the people that never accepted the Kriva Rasturna? Did everyone at your school just end up changing their beliefs?"

"Oh no. No. No," Mei said with a laugh. "There were a lot of birthing people that were angry that Kriva Rasturna beliefs were being taught to their offspring. They would come to meetings trying to slander the school or the teachers."

"What happened to them?"

"Our government did the right thing. The birthing people that wouldn't allow their offspring to be taught the path of the Kriva Rasturna had their offspring removed from them. The offspring were put into reeducation camps for a few months, teaching them much of what they should have been learning in school already."

"What about the parents? Did they ever get their kids back?"

"Birthing people..." she corrected him. "And sometimes. Sure. Those who wanted their offspring back had to admit publicly their wrongdoing at their local cathedral and repent, asking forgiveness from Sovereign Rusak and the Kriva Rasturna as a whole. If they embraced their shame in front of everyone and did reeducation sessions themselves, then they had a good chance of getting the offspring back. Sometimes birthing people decided not to repent, but I don't know what happened to them. We just never really saw them again."

Alex swallowed his disgust at the revelation, doing his best to hide his reaction. "That, um...that doesn't seem right on any level." It was clear to him he needed to leave directly after avenging his sister or risk becoming a prisoner again.

"It's a lot to take in when you're new," she said, understanding.

"Let's switch topics, then." He couldn't believe how oblivious she seemed of the horrible wrongs she spoke about so proudly. "What does a proselytizer do exactly?"

"We preach our truth—the Kriva Rasturna's truth. It can happen through public speaking at events or even just on the street to let people know that we're here helping them. Most often, though, we broadcast over the radio for large audiences to listen in. Sometimes we talk about a change that's needed and what our steps will be to get to that goal. We let the people know we need them to join us."

"What happens if they don't join us?"

"I don't know. We simply report them."

***

After getting Ethan's head checked, Talia led the three of them through the facility. The Devon Falls headquarters was much bigger than Ethan expected, and he marveled at how organized everything was. The radio room was busy with people sitting around two large tables at the center scribbling down incoming messages, with a couple pointing at maps up on the wall. They passed three massive bunk rooms with personal lockers lined up, and the training room had more weapons than Ethan could count.

They moved on, walking past a hanger with two small airships that caught Ethan's attention. "What are those?" The airships were twenty feet long, with a centered pilot's seat having two short rows of seats behind it. The left side of the craft was open for quick deployment of troops and the wings stuck out with thick helicopter propellers jutting upwards from them, allowing for vertical takeoff. Large machine guns were braced under the cockpit, pointing forward.

Talia stopped and looked with a smile. "Those are our tempests. We believe a Kriva Rasturna squadron called the Harriers used a tempest to bring down your airship. You'll get to meet Samuel here in just a few minutes. He was responsible for planning the mission that got us these. With the help of Armond, of course. He's one of our best pilots. I'm sure he'd be happy to tell you all about how he stole them from under the Harriers' noses later." She looked over at Ethan, who was still studying the tempests. "Meeting is going to start soon. Let's not be late," she said, continuing down the corridor.

He turned to follow, nearly running into someone hurrying in the opposite direction, barely having enough time to sidestep out of the way. "Excuse m—" he said, but the person was already halfway down the hall, having ignored him. He stayed to the right of the corridor, following Talia while people hurried past them, making him wonder what was going on that had everyone in a frenzy. "Are people running through the halls pretty usual in the resistance?"

Talia shook her head. "Something's going on, for sure. I just don't know what. Cormack will fill us in if it's something we need to know."

They eventually came to a large meeting room with a long, centered table. At the head of it sat a burly man with greying hair and mustache, intently going over some fresh intel with a communications officer. He shook his head angrily, "Dammit." He tossed the report on the desk and stood up. "Radio to the Kinsford cell that they need to evacuate to their secondary location. Let them know we're getting a team together and will send help soon. The communications officer nodded, running out of the room, past Ethan and the group.

"What's happening in Kinsford?" Talia asked, worried.

The man looked up, seeing the group at the door. "Please, come have a seat. We'll go over it shortly."

As the group filed in, Talia made introductions. "Ethan, I'd like you to meet Cormack. He's the leader of the Devon Falls resistance cell."

Ethan leaned over, shaking his hand. "Good to meet you."

"You must be the guy from the dimension next door, huh?" Cormack said with a smile. "Glad to have you with us." He turned his attention to Fletcher and Elise. "It's good to see the both of you again as well. I feared the worst when Talia radioed over, telling us your airship was the one that had been shot down."

"We barely made it out of there," Fletcher said.

"Talia insisted on coming over to help search for you. Glad we had the tempests at our disposal to get her here quickly. Come. Sit. We have some disturbing developments coming in from Kinsford that I'm sure you'll want to be informed of." They all took a seat at the table before he continued. "The Kriva Rasturna have moved more than three hundred guards into Kinsford a couple of hours ago. You may have noticed our personnel working to get a team and supplies put together in case our assistance was needed."

Fletcher cursed under his breath. "Any idea why the hell they're making a move like that?"

"Their end goal appears to be finding your friend's Delphinium Key," he said, gesturing towards Ethan. "They believe it's located in Kinsford and that we have it for some reason. The report we just received says they've started arresting dozens of people for questioning. Anyone they believe might have a connection to us, they're herding like cattle. Due to the nature of this, we're sending in a team to help move your troops."

"Where'd they get their intel?" Talia asked.

Cormack shook his head. "We've come up with three scenarios. The first is they're guessing and trying to make a show of force in a smaller town to incite fear. I wouldn't put it past them. Second, we have word that two of your people were arrested recently. I don't know how well either would stand up to torture, but they could have talked."

"Summer wouldn't knowingly put anyone in danger," Ethan said.

"Then that leaves our third idea," Cormack said grimly, "Your mole has become a bigger problem than we thought. He may have tipped them off as an exit plan to leave the resistance. We may never know what was said or by who. God willing, we'll arrive in time to help the rest of the Kinsford cell get out of there and transferred to the secondary base out of town."

"We appreciate the help," Fletcher said.

Cormack nodded. "We have to watch out for each other. It's the only way we'll survive." He sat back with his steepled hands in front of him. "Now, we have an opportunity to work together against the Kriva Rasturna and hit them hard. A few days ago, we had a team infiltrate their base at the cathedral across town. We had good information they've been working on a new weapon; God knows what it's capable of. The team were to infiltrate the base, destroy the plans as well as any prototypes found and get out before being discovered. Unfortunately, they were captured before fulfilling their mission. We know this because one of them, Phillip, was publicly executed two days ago. We can only hope the other two are still alive."

"I'm so sorry," Talia said sympathetically.

"It's tough to lose friends, but we have to keep moving forward and speaking of, we got word that Liam and your friend were seen being taken into the same facility. That means this has now become a two-part mission. We get our people out, all of them, and we destroy their plans."

"...you know that!" someone said from the hallway. "I could out fly anyone."

"You could not," said a woman. They immediately stopped talking upon entering, seeing the meeting had already started.

"Ah!" Cormack said, standing. "Let me introduce you to a couple of our best," he said, gesturing to them. "Armond, here is our lead pilot for the tempests. He and his team will be getting you in and out for the mission."

Armond had a sly grin. "Yes, I'm truly one of the best, as I was just—"

Cormack cut him off. "We know Armond. Trust me." Ethan chuckled at the hurt look on Armond's face. Cormack continued, "And this is Marion, one of our best infiltration agents." They both took a seat, with Marion shaking Ethan's hand as she sat next to him.

"I didn't think someone influenced by scopshade would be able to join the resistance," Ethan said suspiciously, seeing her eyes were grey.

Marion smirked. "I forgot I had these in." She poked at her eye, making Elise gag at the display.

"What are you...doing!?" Elise asked, forcing herself to hold down lunch.

"I made these eye covers that make it look like I've been turned." She removed a small flexible plastic circle from her eye.

Ethan looked again, seeing her eyes were actually purple. "You have contact lenses?"

"I haven't named them yet, but they do a great job of fooling the guards."

Elise was impressed. "Can you make me a pair of those?"

"I'd be happy too, but I'm not sure your stomach could handle it. If you're around a while though—"

"I doubt we will be," Talia interrupted. "With everything going on in Kinsford and talk of a new weapon being made, we're running out of time. We need to refocus on finding the Lunarian Key. If Rusak and the Kriva Rasturna are coming down this hard on hearsay," she shook her head, frustrated. "We can't afford for them to get another jump on us by getting to the key first."

"Hold on," Ethan said, "You told us you'd help get Summer's brother away from the Kriva Rasturna. Now you're going back on that?"

"Of course not," she said. "We're not leaving him in their hands. We're just far closer to where Elise believes our key is located. It makes more sense to get the key first."

Elise nodded in agreement. "We're maybe a two days' hike to get to where I think the lost city is if we follow the Bonitatis River. If we go to Heraldrin first, we're adding a third day from the terrain."

"Maybe we can help with that," Cormack interjected. "Why not have Armond here fly you to the coordinates near the lost city, then get you over to the capital? That'd save you the hiking time."

"That would be incredible," Fletcher said. "What do you think, Ethan? That's a pretty good deal. We basically wouldn't lose any time getting to her brother had we gone on foot."

Ethan looked at the faces of everyone around the table. "I guess I don't have much of an argument left."

"Then it's settled," Fletcher said. "Now we need to focus on getting our people back. They've been in custody since last night. We need to get them out now." Fletcher stood up.

"Wait just a minute," Cormack said. "I appreciate your enthusiasm, but they're going to have to stay put for another few hours, at least until well past nightfall. We have a team leaving shortly to Kinsford, remember, and the Tempests won't be back until then, anyway. A night mission gives us the element of surprise, but I also want as few guards alert as possible. You should know that to make things easier tonight, we have an ace up the sleeve, so to speak. Marion used to attend service and was an active member, volunteering at this cathedral before it was taken over. She'll know the layout."

Fletcher sat back down. Marion grabbed a dark marker and a large piece of paper, folding it out over the conference table. "I can't stand that they've desecrated our cathedral." The marker squeaked as she angrily drew an outline of the different floors.

Someone jogged into the room, breathing hard, taking their attention away from the noise. "Everyone, this is Samuel," Cormack said. "He's one of our best tacticians."

"Sorry I'm late. I was getting an update on the Kinsford situation." He took a seat next to Fletcher, patting him on the shoulder. "Good to see you again, man." Fletcher nodded before Samuel continued. "They haven't discovered the main Kinsford base yet, but they could at any time. Everyone has been busy tearing down radio equipment and boxing up supplies for transport. They'll be using the back tunnel that leads out to the forest."

"At least they're getting out quickly," Talia said.

Marion completed the outline, showing two distinct floors, and pointed to her sketch. "I believe the most likely place they'll be holding our people is in the upper rooms. It would make a front door rescue attempt nearly impossible. These used to all be classrooms for children's church. This room here and over here," she said, marking them with an X, "both have skylights. That gives us access to the upper floors. The only thing to stop us from getting in are simple padlocks that can be cut. Now, what they have in each of these rooms, I have no idea. We may go feet first into a bunk room full of sleeping bad guys."

"How big are those skylights, Marion?" Samuel asked.

She shrugged. "I don't know actual dimensions, but if I had to guess, I'd say two people could fit through it pretty easily."

"Ok. Whichever point we enter at will be our escape route as well. We'll bring a rope ladder and secure it before dropping in. Hopefully, we can avoid a fight."

"Good," Cormack said, "Armond, you'll be getting our team to the cathedral rooftop with another pilot of your choosing. Each of these craft can only hold the pilot and four passengers, so we'll need both tempests on this."

Ethan didn't look convinced, "We heard tempests from miles away flying towards us on the way here. Won't the sound of the engines give us away?"

"Not our tempests," Armond smirked. "I've been working with my team on making modifications to them to make them near silent. Even reached out to Liam, who pointed us in the right direction a couple times, saving us months of guesswork. The only thing we'll really have to worry about is the wind gusts given off the rotor blades. The best we can do to avoid that is to be about thirty feet up from the roof. That means you'll have to fast rope down from the tempest to the roof and you just so happen to be the only one here that I'm not sure can do it."

"What's fast roping?"

Armond gave a deadpan stare. "We have work to do."

Fletcher chuckled. "It's like rappelling, but much quicker. You're not connected to a descender like you would be if you were rappelling down a cliff. Instead, you'll have thick gloves to use as your breaks." Ethan didn't like the sound of that, and it showed.

Armond smirked. "Don't worry. We'll get you trained up before dinner."

"You'll do fine," Elise reassured. "Compared to jumping from a crashing airship, this will be a walk in the park."

"It sounds like our plan is coming together," Cormack said. "I still want to go over some of the details again to make sure we have it down, but this is a good start. I know most of you have gone over fast rope training before, but I want everyone to work with Armond after this as a refresher. We don't need accidents tonight."

"It's been a while," Elise said.

"We don't have the benefit of training with tempests in Kinsford either," Talia said. "We'll go over hand to hand and sword combat refreshers as well. There's a lot to do."

"Agreed," Fletcher said. "Let's make sure the tempests are fully stocked with medical supplies. At the very least, we'll have Liam's arm to worry about. I expect worse though. We've seen what they do to their prisoners."

"That's not very reassuring," Ethan said. "Is Summer going to be, ok?"

"Don't worry, Ethan," Cormack said. "We've done a few rescue ops before. We know what we're doing, and we have the right people for this to go well." He stood up. "Alright, we know what needs to be done. Let's get to work."

Operation Cathedral

S ummer's wrists burned from the metal cuffs constantly scraping against her skin. The guards had chained her to the wall again shortly after her conversation with Dwyll hours prior. She looked around the small room, finding two stacked desks and a couple of chairs off to one side. A window had been bordered up, making the only light source coming from under the door. Regardless of the poor lighting, she could tell this used to be a child's classroom. She could make out numbers and letters lining the top of the walls with some art hung up near a chalkboard.

Her stomach growled. A guard would bring her some water every couple of hours, but never any food. She looked over at Liam, who hadn't moved since they tossed them in here. She could still see his chest rise with each breath, giving her hope he'd recover.

A guard would walk by the door with a TAK every half hour. It snarled every time it passed, but it was the clicking of its claws on the wooden floor that made her skin crawl. It was about that time and she could hear the claws click with two sets of footsteps approaching from outside just before the door flung open. Dwyll walked in, followed by a guard while the TAK stayed out in the hallway staring her down.

"My guards have been turning Kinsford upside down looking for your little dissident friends," Dwyll said smugly. "More than two hundred have been arrested because you refused to tell me where their base is. Tell me...where it is." She refused to speak, deciding simply to glare at him. "Very well. Pick this creature up."

The guard walked behind her, roughly grabbing her by the arms, and lifted her. She stomped on his foot, making him curse, and ran forward, forgetting she was chained to the wall. She yelled as the cuffs cut into her wrists further.

"You have to watch out for this one," Dwyll smiled. "She's got a bit of fight in her that still needs to be broken." The guard regained control of her, and Dwyll slugged her in the stomach. She doubled over onto her hands and knees, gasping. Dwyll grinned, watching a tear run down her cheek. "Pathetic."

She regained her breath, pushing herself into a sitting position, and Dwyll crouched next to her, moving his hand to wipe away her tear. She immediately recoiled. "Don't...touch...me."

He let out a laugh. "That's amusing, really." He violently reached over, gripping her throat, and squeezed. She grabbed his wrists, trying to wrench free, but it was no use. "You are our prisoner. We own you," he said, spitting the last words out. He shoved her back, releasing her neck. Her eyes watered and she coughed, taking in as much air as she could. He smiled at her discomfort. "I still need information, but I'll make this easy for you, hmm? You can tell me where the dissidents are located, or I can let this TAK feed on your unconscious friend in front of you. I'm sure it's just as hungry as you are." He continued to grin, enjoying the psychological games.

Summer glared at him; another tear rolling down her cheek. "I already told you, I don't know where they are. We were running from your stupid guards. I remember passing a large fountain and running down an alley past a maroon building before we got grabbed by them and pulled into what looked like a warehouse. I don't remember where it was."

Dwyll stood up, thinking for a moment, and looked down at her. "That's good enough for now, but remember what happens if I find you've lied." He turned, heading out the door and gestured for the guard to follow. As they left, the guard slammed the door. She could still hear Dwyll bark orders from the hall, "Get me a tempest ready within the hour. I believe I know where the base is. Radio ahead to the platoon in Kinsford and let them know to expect me."

She sat back against the wall, trying to think up a way to get both her and Liam out. She knew these psychos were going to kill them both. It was just a matter of time. She looked around, not even able to find a way to get herself out of the cuffs. Feeling helpless, her eyes welled up, wishing her brother had never gotten kidnapped, or that she was here in this cell. A tear rolled down her cheek, and she wished Ethan was with her. He'd at least be trying to cheer her up. She wiped another tear away with the back of her sleeve, noticing her wrists had been bleeding again.

Movement came from across the room. When it happened again, she was happy to see it was Liam's arm. "Liam," she whispered. There was no response. "Liam, can you sit up?" He finally moved, propping himself up on his good arm, and leaned against the wall. His breathing was shallow and raspy, and she could see dried blood smeared across his face where they had broken his nose. "Oh, my God."

"They really did a number on me, huh?" he asked weakly.

"Don't try to speak. We need to get out of here." She looked around the room again, seeing the window was the best bet aside from the door. "Can we get this wood away from the window enough to get through?"

He shook his head, lifting his good arm. "Chains."

"There has to be something we can use to get out of them."

A guard opened the door. "Shut up in here! Better get some sleep while you can. I doubt you'll have a good day tomorrow." He laughed, slamming the door. They heard a lock turn into place and fading footsteps.

Rain started hitting the window, and she began to cry again, burying her face in her arms. Liam looked up at her, knowing their situation was grim. "Hey," he whispered, "Don't give up yet. I'm betting Fletcher and the rest are working on a plan to get us out of here. Their first move would be to reach the resistance cell here—get some help."

Summer felt defeated. "We don't even know if they're alive."

"During our scuffle, I overheard some Greys yelling they were getting away. If they got to safety, they'll come for us, and from what I've seen, Ethan will do whatever it takes to get you back." He chuckled a bit before realizing it hurt to laugh.

"What makes you say that?"

"I've seen the way he looks at you." He tried to smile, but even that hurt. "It's pretty obvious how he feels." He coughed, grimacing. "Yeah, he'll come."

Summer smiled, wiping away the tears with her sleeve, and felt a glimmer of hope.

***

Alex rubbed his eyes, laying back in his chair. He felt like he'd just studied the entire internet for a quiz at school the next day. He didn't agree with a lot of what he was reading, but he was in a different dimension. Perhaps he just needed to get used to the idea of how they do things in Lunaria. Still, a lot of it was steeped in hypocrisy. He was looking forward to getting back home and leaving this all behind. Lost in his thoughts, he didn't hear Mei approach.

"You look like crap," she said, startling him.

"Yep. That's what I was going for," he said sarcastically.

"I know it's been a long day. I brought us some food." She handed him a tray.

He sat forward, seeing what he presumed was chicken and some kind of vegetable. He had lost track of time, unaware of how hungry he'd gotten over the last few hours. "I guess I studied right through dinner, huh?"

"Yeah, but the information is necessary." She sat next to him, placing her tray in her lap. "I have some good news," she said with an enormous grin.

"Oh?"

"I got the go ahead from Prevara to have you broadcast your first segment...tonight!"

Alex sat up, choking on the bite he'd just taken, grabbing his glass of water to help it down. He shook his head, finally able to speak. "I'm not ready for that! I barely know any of this. Definitely not enough to do a segment!"

Mei rolled her eyes. "Overreact much? You'll be fine! We're having you do your first, later tonight when fewer people are up and listening. It's a way to ease you in. We'll even have bullet points for you, so you don't get lost...and if you end up going off script or forget something, no biggie."

He didn't want to preach stuff he didn't agree with. He just wanted to avenge his sister and leave. "I don't know," he said, slumping back into the couch again.

"Most people our age dream of getting an opportunity this big, and...well...think of it like this. We're recording your segment. If you do well, we'll replay it in the morning to a larger audience. That'll get your name out there and the public will know that you're with us. That you're with them. It'll build trust." She giggled when a thought crossed her mind. "Then you'll be the one with girls running up to give you hugs." She playfully punched him in the shoulder.

"Alright. Aright. I'll give it a shot. No promises on being any good, though."

Mei excitedly clapped her hands. "Great! We've already booked you one of our studios on the communications floor. We'll get you set up when you're done eating."

"What's the topic?"

"This will be an easy one for your starter. It's going to be on how the dissidents lie when they say they're helping the people of Lunaria. The hard part is going to be tying that together with the airship crash and reminding the people that the dissidents are responsible for shooting it down and killing your sister. It'll be emotional, but we can use that to our advantage. Make people empathize."

Alex sighed, knowing she meant the advantage was manipulating people. He hated it, but had little choice. "If it helps bring those bastards down, then I'll deal with the emotions."

Mei nodded. "Good. We need you to connect with people by telling the story of your loss. Express the emotions you're feeling. Then we need you to ask that any with information on the dissident's whereabouts or those connected with them come forward to help get justice for your sister and the rest who died in the crash."

"If my segment ends up getting us good information and we find the people responsible for killing her, I want to be there when they're captured."

"We know how much this means to you. Don't worry, you will be there."

***

Ethan's legs felt like rubber. Armond and Fletcher had him jumping from a three-story ledge in the tempest bay for the last hour, training him on fast roping. He was thankful they setup mats to land on or he'd probably have already broken his legs. The first couple jumps nearly killed him, making him learn quickly to grip the rope tighter. He followed Fletcher to the mess hall for dinner, surprised by the number of people there when they entered. The chatter was loud enough he couldn't make out what Fletcher was saying to him.

"What!?" he asked.

Fletcher leaned in, pointing to a table where Armond, Elise, and Talia were sitting. "We've got your food ready for you!"

About halfway to their table, Ethan was suddenly aware it had become eerily quiet. Ethan looked around, unnerved that everyone was staring at him. "Why are they all staring at me like that?"

Fletcher leaned a bit, whispering. "You're the first person they've seen from another dimension since your uncle that's here to help us—not enslave us. Just keep walking." Once they took a seat, the ambient noise raised a bit.

Armond spoke while chewing, "You did pretty good for a first timer."

"Hopefully, my legs don't give out on me during the actual rescue. My knees are killing me."

"It'll be a couple days before you start to feel normal after that many jumps," Fletcher said. "Only one more to go, and you shouldn't have to do it again. At least, not for a while."

The group ate quickly, knowing they would head out soon. It wasn't long before Cormack joined them, coming up behind Ethan and Armond. "Fletcher. Talia. You'll be happy to hear we got word the rest of the Kinsford cell has evacuated successfully with their equipment. If the Kriva Rasturna find the base, they'll find it empty and if the secondary is discovered, they're prepared to scatter."

"Thank God," Talia said, "We can't afford to lose any more people."

"I couldn't agree more," Cormack said, looking around the table. "Is the team ready to go get our people back?"

Ethan smirked, "Oh, you mean jump into the face of danger, freeing our friends from the gnashing jaws of mutated creatures that look straight out of a horror movie before we blow the place up? Yeah, I'm ready."

Cormack let out a laugh, slapping Ethan on the back. "Glad to hear it! Armond. Once you're done here, have your flight team double check the tempests are ready to go." Armond nodded. "The rest of you, gear up and meet in the tempest bay in thirty minutes." Everyone gave a nod and Cormack left them to finish. Ethan's back still stung from the slap.

Samuel cracked a smile. "Seems the boss likes you. Maybe you and your friend should stick around and help us regain our freedom from Rusak and his brainwashed army."

"Not sure how long we'll be staying, but we agreed to help find the Lunarian Key. After that, who knows?"

"And reclaiming the Lunarian Key," Fletcher said, "will land a serious blow to Rusak."

Ethan had been unaware of how many in the mess hall had been listening in on their conversation until half the room erupted in cheers. He could feel the noise reverberate through him and couldn't help but smile at the infectious enthusiasm.

Fletcher stood. "Alright, let's go get our people. Grab your gear and head to the pad."

Ethan followed Fletcher to the bunk room assigned to the Kinsford cell, sitting on his bunk and relaxing while he had the chance. Elise walked in with Talia shortly after, each holding a new pair of boots. They sat on a nearby bunk, lacing them up.

"Glad we're all here," Fletcher said. "Elise, I'm having you sit this one out. Your knowledge of where the lost city might be is too valuable and if we're not successful, the Devon Falls resistance will need your help to recover the key."

She looked disappointed. "I understand. Just," she looked up at him, "don't leave Liam behind. Even if he's...you know...bring him back."

Talia wrapped an arm around her. "We'll get him back and he'll be alive. You just wait for us back at the landing pad to greet him."

Ethan still felt the weight of the Delphinium Key pressed against his back. "Hey," he said, walking over to them. He took off his vest, removing the key and his journal. "How about you hold on to these for me, Elise? It'll give you something to keep busy." He handed them to her, and her mood shifted to excitement. "Can't chance these ending up in the wrong hands, right?"

"Oh, my gosh! Thank you! I've been wanting to take another look at it."

"Just remember, I expect those back when I return." He smirked, seeing she was already too busy examining the key to have heard him.

"Good thinking," Fletcher said. "Elise, keep that close. If we had a mole in Kinsford, they could have one here too."

Hearing her name broke her concentration. "Of course."

"I spoke with Samuel and Marion earlier," he continued. "They said they'd have all sorts of weapons to choose from ready for us at the bay. Let's go see what they have."

The three of them got up and headed down the hall, leaving Elise with the Delphinium Key. While making their way towards the tempests, Ethan noticed the radio room was just as busy as earlier, with four people monitoring communications. They passed a second meeting room where their backup team was getting briefed before reaching the tempest bay where a group of a half-dozen people were doing systems checks on both airships.

Samuel and Marion were laying out different weapons on tables, making sure they were in good working order. Meanwhile, Armond finished latching the end of the training rope to an anchor on the closer tempest, tossing the rest of the coiled rope inside the cockpit under a seat.

Armond saw the three of them enter. "Both tempests are fueled up and ready to go. Kaylah will be the second pilot for the mission. She's good—not as good as me," he smirked, "but she'll get you to where you need to go."

"Oh, ha ha," Kaylah said. "Last week's race says different."

Ethan walked over to the weapons table where Samuel had just sheathed a short sword. He looked over the options, picking up a pulser rifle. It looked similar to the semi-automatic rifle his uncle had taken him to shoot a few years prior, but instead of black, it was a light grey color and oddly, no magazine or ejection port for the rounds. He turned it in his hand, finding a dial on the side along with a vent.

Samuel looked up, seeing his confusion. "Here," he said, taking the rifle. He pointed to the vent on the side. "The rifle has an air intake here. It concentrates the air into a controlled burst that acts like how our bullets did before all guns in Maraldi were confiscated." He pointed to the dial. "The biggest difference between the two is here. Turn the dial to alter the amount of damage the pulse will do to the target. You can have it turned down to 'focused', which acts like a bullet, or 'spread', causing mass damage." He rotated the dial, moving the pointer along the scale, demonstrating the increase in damage. "Just be sure you know what setting you're on." He handed Ethan the rifle back.

Ethan placed it back on the table, grabbing a tactical recurve bow instead. It was equipped with three arrows attached on either side of the riser. He pulled back the bowstring, testing the draw weight.

"Deciding to go stealth, huh?" Samuel said with a grin. "Good, that'll come in handy. I recommend a short sword for close combat as well. I've checked all of these if you want to swing a couple to test which feels best." He tossed Ethan a shoulder harness. "Wear one of these for your sword. With everything we're doing on this mission, having your sword on the back might prove a benefit. Just have it at the ready as soon as we get inside, or you'll leave yourself open to an attack, fumbling to get your weapon out."

"Appreciate it," Ethan said, placing the bow down and putting on the harness. He picked up one of the short swords, stepping away from everyone else and unsheathed it, taking a couple of swings; the weight feeling good in his hand. He placed the sword in the scabbard at his back and picked up the bow again.

"You definitely need more practice," Marion said, half joking.

"Yeah, I'm still pretty new to swords. Talia showed me a few things back in Kinsford, but I'm still a long way off from being decent."

Talia joined him at the table. "You'll get there. Don't give up on it."

"Gather around everyone!" Fletcher announced. The team assembled in front of him, waiting to hear the speech he'd prepared. "Let's go over this one more time. Samuel. No offense, but with you carrying the explosives for this mission, I'm going to have you in the tempest I'm not in."

Samuel laughed. "I don't blame ya. I'd have me go in the other one too."

"I'll go with you, Samuel," Talia said. "Just...be careful."

Fletcher continued. "Ethan and Marion. That means you're with me flying with Armond."

"Sure," Kaylah said. "I get to be the one flying the bomb." The group laughed.

"Just take it nice and slow," Samuel said with a smile.

Fletcher handed Ethan a large pair of bolt cutters. "Ethan. You'll be responsible for clearing locks and gaining entry. Once we're in, Talia and Ethan will work to find where the others are held and free them. Remember, we're looking for four survivors. When you free them, get them back to the tempests for evac. The rest of us are going to be looking for weapon plans and prototypes to destroy. After the charges are placed, we head out and once we're airborne, Samuel will use the remote detonator. We should be safe at that point. Any questions...? No...? Ok. Let's do it, people."

Armond and Kaylah headed to their tempests going through their preflight checklists while the rest of the team grabbed weapons and boarded. Ethan had never flown in anything other than a passenger airliner and was taken aback by the number of buttons and switches he saw in the cockpit. The rotating blades started up, and he buckled into his seat, putting his hand up to shield his eyes as the wind grew more intense from the whirling blades. To his surprise, he found the modifications Armond spoke of managed to make the tempest far quieter than the ones he'd heard before; barely producing any sound.

A loud metallic click followed by a grinding noise came from above. He watched the ceiling of the bay split down the middle with each half retracting slowly, revealing the night sky. A drizzle of rain wet the floor, and he felt the jolt of the tempest taking off vertically;

the floor beneath him falling away. He looked up as they cleared the roof of the base, excited to see the dim glow of Devon Falls beyond the treetops. He shivered, unsure if it was from the chilly night air or the sheer exhilaration of knowing he'd be speeding through the sky at any moment.

He estimated they were a couple hundred feet above the ground when Armond called back to the group, "Hold on!" The tempest jerked forward, knocking them all back into their seats. The sensation of gravity pushing against his body made him queasy for a moment before he finally got used to it. He watched as the tops of trees flew past just underneath them; some being only a few feet from the landing struts. The trees broke away, revealing one of the larger waterfalls shimmering in the moonlight, but the incredible view was short-lived as they entered the downtown area. The streets were completely empty except for a few guard patrols here and there.

Ethan leaned over to Marion. "You have curfews here as well?"

She let out a sarcastic laugh. "Yeah. When the Kriva Rasturna first arrived, they wasted no time using scopshade on dozens of people. Then they instructed them to riot, using that as the excuse for the curfews. Imagine a group of about a couple hundred Greys going around smashing and burning whatever they could in the name of social justice," she said, using finger quotes. "Then they implemented the curfew, saying it was for the safety of the citizens. Nothing quite like a corrupt government creating problems and then saying they're here to help."

"There it is!" Armond said, pointing to the cathedral. He slowed the tempest as they neared until they were hovering directly over the rooftop. The other tempest pulled up alongside them shortly after.

Ethan looked down at the roof, not seeing any security posted. "Where's the guards?"

Armond chuckled. "They never expect to be hit from the air. They think they're the only ones with the ability to fly."

Fletcher grabbed the rope, pulling it hard to ensure it would hold before tossing the coil over the side. "At least it stopped raining. That'll make going down easier." He finished putting on gloves and grabbed the rope. "See you at the bottom." He smiled and jumped out of the tempest. Ethan watched him glide down, hearing the unmistakable sound of the gloves grinding against rope. Ethan put his gloves on, motioning for Marion to go next.

"Oh no," she said. "You're next. I hate doing this."

Ethan looked down, seeing Samuel touch the roof from the other tempest. He nervously grabbed the rope, not liking the idea of jumping from an object that could move at any second. Fletcher looked up at him, giving him a thumbs up. He gripped the rope hard and jumped out into the night.

"Any time now," Marion said in a mischievous tone. He looked over, staring directly at her, and realized he was gripping the rope so tightly that he wasn't sliding at all. He loosened his grip slowly and began to descend. His muscles ached, having not fully recovered from the training, but still controlled his descent well enough, relieved when his feet finally touched down.

"You're practically a pro now. Good work on not falling to your death," Samuel said.

Ethan looked up at the tempest, signaling to Marion he was clear when Talia had just touched down next to them. He walked over to the side of the building and looked out over the street. A couple of guards with TAKs were stationed at the front of the cathedral. He was happy to see neither the guards nor the TAKs appeared to be aware of them and, even better, one of the guards was nodding off. He turned around, hearing Marion land on the roof. She gave a thumbs up to Armond and the two tempests rose into the air a few dozen more feet to stay out of sight.

Samuel scouted ahead, finding the skylight and waved them over. By the time they caught up to him, he was already tying off the rope ladder to an anchored metal bar outlining the skylight. "We're set to go," he said.

"There's another reason they don't have guards on the roof," Fletcher said, pointing at the two padlocks holding the skylight in place. "You have it right?"

"On it," Ethan said, pulling the bolt cutters from behind him and cutting the locks off.

Fletcher helped Samuel lift the skylight as quickly and quietly as possible, peering inside at two soldiers listening to radio equipment and a TAK curled up sleeping. This was not the luck they needed tonight. "We pulled the short straw," he whispered. "Two guards and a TAK. We're going to have a hell of a time keeping this quiet if we wake that thing." The TAK's ear twitched.

"I think I got this," Ethan said, readying his bow.

"You...think?" Fletcher asked.

Ethan shrugged. "I guess we'll see."

Samuel came up beside him, taking aim at the TAK with his pulser rifle. "It's good to have a Plan B for these situations."

Ethan took aim, pulling the bowstring back till it touched his cheek. He let out his breath and loosed the arrow. The TAK quietly yipped and lay still; the arrow having pierced its eye. He studied the TAK, making sure its chest stopped rising.

Samuel patted him on the shoulder. "Color me impressed. I honestly didn't think you'd be able to pull that off."

Fletcher had already begun lowering the rope ladder. "Quickly, before those comms officers decide to look behind them." Samuel headed down first, followed by Fletcher and Ethan. Ethan steadied the roped ladder for Talia and Marion while Fletcher and Samuel quickly made their way towards the communications officers.

In a flash, Samuel grabbed the guard on the left, putting him into a choke hold from behind. The officer started thrashing, trying to hit his attacker when the other quickly stood fumbling for his sword before getting cracked in the back of the head by the stock of Fletcher's rifle. By this time, Samuel had already dragged the man from his chair to the ground and was squeezing tighter until the guard passed out.

"So far, so good," Fletcher said, just as a snarl sounded from the open doorway. "Shi..." Fletcher said, slowly backing away. A large TAK took up half the door's frame. The guard patrolling with it looked into the comm room, hearing its reaction.

"What are you on abo—What the hell!?" the guard said, releasing the leash. Ethan took aim with another arrow as the TAK readied to strike. It lunged just as Ethan loosed his arrow, but instead of hitting the eye as Ethan had hoped, the arrow burrowed into its neck. The beast yelped, smashing into Fletcher, knocking him backwards.

Samuel pulled his sword free to help, and the guard raised his pulser rifle, taking aim at him. Seeing what was happening, Ethan rushed the guard, slamming into him, knocking the weapon away, but the guard was much bigger than he expected and quick to react. He lifted Ethan by his shirt, punching him hard in the face. Ethan's world blurred before he was shoved backwards. He stumbled, not able to catch his footing, and fell to his back.

The guard pulled a dagger from his belt, bringing it down quickly over Ethan's chest, but was stopped as Ethan grabbed his arm with both hands. The guard had the advantage, using his bodyweight as leverage while Ethan tried to wriggle free from under the bulky man pinning him down. To better the advantage, the guard punched him hard in the side again and again. Ethan could feel his arms growing weaker and the cold tip of the blade press against his chest. Ethan readied himself for the end, seeing a blur of motion. The guard flew off him and the dagger hit the wall with a clang. Fletcher had tackled the man, followed by a blast that stopped the scuffle. Fletcher pushed the guard's body away from him in disgust, seeing a pool of blood forming.

Talia stood at the bottom of the rope ladder, holding a pulser rifle. "What happened to being as quiet as possible during this op?"

Samuel helped Ethan up. "Good shot on that second TAK. You hit an artery. That slowed it down enough that I could finish it off." Samuel looked down at the blood on Ethan's shirt. "Are you ok?"

Ethan looked down. "He must have got me with his knife." Not sure if he wanted to see the damage, he lifted his shirt, exposing a minor wound where the dagger had cut.

Fletcher walked over, inspecting him. "You'll need a couple stitches when we get back to base. I'm afraid you'll have to deal until then. Appreciate you saving my ass, though."

Ethan smirked. "I was aiming for its eye, but then the thing jumped."

"Then I'm luckier than I thought," Fletcher said. Marion was motioning towards the doorway. "Let's hope we didn't attract more attention." He joined her to make sure they were clear.

She poked her head out, looking down the hallway, happy to see it deserted. "We're good for now. There are more classrooms and offices up ahead to the left. To the right are some stairs leading down to the lower floors. Before you hit the stairs, there's an opening that overlooks the main lobby below." Talia and Samuel had finished tying up the two communications officers before joining the others.

"Talia and Ethan, I want you two checking out the rooms up here for the prisoners," Fletcher said. "The rest of us will look for the weapon prototype and plans."

Talia looked at the blood on Ethan's shirt. "Are you still up for this?"

He nodded, "I'm good." They headed down the hall, stopping short of where the hallway jutted off to the right. Ethan peered around the corner at a guard laying back in a chair snoring, posted just outside of two doors. The guard's pulser rifle laid across his lap unsteadily, looking like it could fall to the ground at any moment.

"How much you want to bet?" Talia whispered to him as she tiptoed closer. Ethan followed, holding his breath when the floor creaked. He expected the guard to wake, but the heavy sleeper never got the chance. Talia smashed the guard in the face with the stock of her rifle, toppling him over with Ethan grabbing the rifle before it fell. To Ethan, it looked like the guard was still asleep, having never woken up, and he checked the guard's pockets, finding a key.

"Let's check out one of these rooms and get this guy moved to it," he said, unlocking the nearest door. He opened it slowly, finding two people chained to the wall that he didn't recognize. "Talia," he whispered. She crept over to him, looking inside before rushing to a person laying on the ground. Ethan grabbed the guard's foot, dragging him into the room.

Talia crouched next to the man, recoiling at the smell of urine. She nudged him awake. "Hey. Stay quiet. We're here to get you out of here." The thirty-year-old was too weak to even speak, but she could see the relief in his eyes. He tried mouthing something, but she couldn't make it out. "Let me check the on other. I'll be right back," she said, getting up while Ethan finished tying up the unconscious guard. "Ethan," she whispered. "Get his chains off. We'll have to carry him back to the tempest."

He pulled out the bolt cutters, snipping the chains off the man, and helped him into a sitting position before joining Talia. She checked the pulse of the other, shaking her head angrily. "Dead. Starved, dehydrated and brutally beaten. Bastards."

Ethan put a hand on her shoulder. "Let's go check the other room before we move him. Summer and Liam can't be far off."

She stood whispering to the man. "We'll be right back."

They checked the hallway and headed to a door on the other side of where the guard had been napping. Ethan unlocked it and slowly opened it to find Summer lying on the floor, chained to the wall. Scanning the room for guards, he found Liam, but couldn't tell if he was moving. Pushing the door open further, he quietly moved to Summer, crouching next to her and put his hand on her back. He was relieved to feel her breathing and nudged her lightly. "Hey."

She instinctively recoiled, backing to the wall before sitting up, looking ready to strike. "Stay away from me."

"Hey, it's me. It's Ethan. We're here to get you out." He moved closer to get a better look at her injuries.

"Ethan?" she asked, rubbing her eyes. Recognizing his face, she leaned forward, wrapping her arms around him, squeezing him tightly. "You came for me?"

He hugged her back. "Of course I did."

"I told you," Liam said from the other side of the room. Talia had helped him up, making sure not to hurt his arm further.

"Are you hurt?" Ethan asked her, letting go. She held up her chained wrists, making a face as the wounds bled again from the movement of the metal against her raw skin. He stood, grabbing the bolt cutters and removed her chains. "Can you walk?" he asked, holding out his hand for her.

"Yeah." She took his hand, getting to her feet.

"How about you Liam?" he asked, walking over and cutting off his chains. Both Ethan and Talia helped steady him.

"I...I think so. Mostly my arm, my face, oh, and my ribs hurt. For some reason, they didn't hurt my legs," he said, trying to smile, but grimaced instead.

"Let's get you guys to our evac room," Talia said.

Ethan hugged Summer again. "You guys go ahead. I'll get the other guy." He rushed over to the other room and looked down at the man, who seemed to have regained some energy at the thought of escape. He knelt next to him, hearing the others in the hallway. "I'm going to pick you up. Sorry for any pain, but we need to get you out of here." The man weakly nodded, still unable to speak. Ethan picked him up in a fireman's carry, hearing him groan, and headed out the door. By the time he reached the communications room, Talia had one of the radio headsets on, listening in.

"You're going to want to hear this, Summer," Talia said, looking discouraged. She lowered the volume and unplugged the headset so everyone could hear. "The person speaking introduced himself as Alex. That's your brother's name, isn't it?"

Summer stepped forward, listening for a moment. "Yes! That's him. He's alive!"

"Don't be too happy," Talia said. "From the sounds of it, he's one of them now. He's acting like one of their proselytizers—spreading their lies to convert others."

Summer shook her head in disbelief. "No way he would side with these psychos. There must be an explanation." She paused, holding up her hand for quiet so she could hear what he was saying.

Ethan gently lowered the man to the floor, propping him up against the wall. "Is it possible to turn that up so we can hear what he's saying better?" Talia turned a knob, raising the volume slightly.

"—the wake of the recent airship crash that killed my sister. I have joined with the Kriva Rasturna to spread the word that we need your help. We've received report from the crash investigation that the dissidents are responsible for the horrible loss of life. We need you to help find where they're located so they can't kill other innocent people again."

Summer was stunned. "He doesn't even know I'm alive, let alone that they're the ones that shot us down! They've been lying to him!" she said angrily. "Liam. Is there a way for me to talk to him on this thing?"

Liam walked over to the radio and picked up the microphone. "All you have to do is hold down the button on here while you talk. He should hear you just fine. The only problem is that they'll know where the transmission is coming from. We won't have a lot of time once they figure out where we're at."

"I have an idea of how to kill two birds with one stone," Talia said. "Summer, I want you to tell your brother that we're heading to the Fresnel Woods, just north of Devon Falls. We can meet him where the river forks to start looking for the Lunarian Key. Tell him to meet us there tomorrow afternoon. The Kriva Rasturna will jump at the chance—probably use him as a bargaining chip."

"Isn't that a bit of a risk? What if they kill him?" she asked.

"They won't," Talia said. "They'll need your brother alive to have a chance at the key."

"And if they get to the key first?"

"We'll have to cross that bridge when we get there. Liam, can you get up the ladder with one arm?"

"Yeah," he said, nodding. "Just don't stand under me in case."

"Then get your butt up the ladder," she ordered. An alarm sounded, startling everyone. "It's now or never," she said to Summer. Ethan held the rope ladder steady for Liam.

Alex's voice continued to drone on, "—Rasturna is currently looking in Kinsford. Please come forward with infor—"

Summer took a deep breath and held down the broadcast button. "Alex. Alex, it's me. Summer. I'm not dead." She released the button, hearing static for a few seconds.

"Summer?!" Alex asked. "I thought you died in the crash!"

"No, I'm alive. The Kriva Rasturna are the ones that shot us down. They captured me after trying to kill me."

Alex sounded confused. "What?! No, they wouldn't try to kill you. They said they were looking for you to bring you to me. They were helping us get home."

"They've tried to kill me more than once," she said. "Even after they knew I was your sister. They had no intention of bringing me to you. I...I don't know what all they've told you, but it's been lies." She looked over at Talia, seeing her motion to wrap it up. "I don't have much time. I need you to meet us in the Fresnel Woods, north of Devon Falls. We're heading there tomorrow to look for the Lunarian Key. Meet us where the river forks in the afternoon." The alarm continued to blare, and she heard footfalls coming from the hallway. "Alex. Remember, I love you. I'll meet you there!"

"I'll talk with—" The broadcast was shut down, cutting him off.

Fletcher and Samuel came running into the room, slamming the door behind them, locking it. "We need to go. Now!" Fletcher said.

"Where's Marion!?" Talia asked.

Samuel slammed his fist into the door. "She was shot!" Tears rolled down his cheek. "She's bleeding out, holding the remote detonator as long as she can, but it won't be long." He yelled, punching the door again.

Fletcher pushed him towards the ladder. "I'm sorry, but we don't have time to grieve. Go!" Fletcher grabbed the man on the ground, tossing him over his shoulder. "Keep the ladder steady for me." He followed Samuel up, ascending as best he could with holding the extra weight. Ethan held the ladder steady.

Summer began climbing as the sound of snarling came from the other side of the door, something slamming against it, cracking the frame. Samuel helped pull her to the roof and pointed at the two tempests hovering in place just at the edge. Fletcher was already putting the other man onboard one of them. "Go get on one. I'll be right behind." He turned, helping Talia up.

Two guards broke down the door, the frame breaking free of the wall. Seeing Ethan at the bottom of the ladder, they drew their swords and charged towards him. The building suddenly shuddered, and the wall exploded inward; splinters of wood flew into the room. Ethan clenched his eyes shut, gripping the rungs of the ladder as the concussive force pushed him against the ceiling. The explosive heat was almost unbearable, but he held tight as the ladder swayed. Daring to look, he saw the floor had crumbled away, replaced by heaps of burning wood and other debris two stories below. The guards that had entered the room moments before were lost in the chaos.

Talia and Samuel pulled the ladder up as the rooftop continued to disintegrate. Flames roared three stories above them from a gaping hole in the cathedral's side. They pulled Ethan up, pointing to the tempest. He could tell they were yelling, but could only hear ringing. Samuel grabbed his arm, pushing him towards the tempest. More of the rooftop cracked and splintered before breaking away, falling into the burning abyss.

The three of them ran, trying to reach their escape, when Samuel dropped to his knee. He felt a searing pain in his arm, making him instinctively grab at it. He felt warm liquid and knew guards firing from below had gotten a lucky shot. Ethan motioned for Talia to keep going, checking on Samuel. Seeing his injury, Ethan pulled him to his feet and ran the rest of the way with him before helping him into the tempest. He jumped in after him, grabbing some spare rope from the floor to create a tourniquet.

"Go!" Talia yelled. The tempest rose into the air, turning towards the woods.

Ethan looked down at the building below, watching as more of the roof gave way crumbling into itself; smoke pouring out endlessly. Guards down below continued firing, hitting the side of the tempest while the airship turned.

Samuel yelled and reached for his side. Blood poured from a fresh wound. The tempest lurched forward, and he rolled out of his seat towards the open air. Ethan grabbed his wrist, catching him with one hand while holding onto a handle from the interior of the craft. "Help me pull him in!" he yelled.

Talia reached down to Samuel. "Give me your other hand!" There was no response. "Samuel!" she yelled, but still he didn't respond. His body swayed in the wind as the tempest flew, making Ethan's grip more difficult to maintain. She reached down, grabbing the arm Ethan had a hold of and helped pull him in. They checked his breathing.

"What the hell's going on back there!?" Armond yelled.

Talia shook her head, seeing a one-inch hole through his side. "We have wounded!" She began applying pressure on his side. Armond looked ahead, determined to get back to base quickly.

Having gotten into the tempest opposite of Summer, Ethan looked out over the forest, hoping she was doing ok. After a few minutes, the top of the base came into view. The craft slowed until hovering directly over the opening to the base and descended quicker than he liked. He could see a group of people waiting to celebrate their success after he was sure they heard the explosion.

Once the tempests touched down and the wind subsided, Cormack came forward to congratulate them. Ethan took over applying pressure on Samuel, while Talia and Fletcher hopped out to debrief Cormack. Ethan watched as his expression went from excitement to pained at the news that two of his people had not made it out.

A team of medics rushed both tempests, getting both Samuel and the survivor they'd recovered onto gurneys. After providing the medics an update on Samuel, Ethan got out of the tempest joining the others. "I'm sorry. I never knew the one we found dead, but Marion was becoming a friend. She was a good person."

Summer walked up to Ethan, taking his arm. "I can't thank you enough for coming to get us. If you hadn't, I'm sure they would have killed us all."

Liam joined her, looking somber. "I feel like this is my fault."

Cormack stepped forward, putting a hand on his shoulder. "No. This isn't anyone's fault but that of Rusak and the Kriva Rasturna. They are responsible for the pain we've felt and the destruction they've caused." Putting his arm down, he turned to address the crowd that had assembled. He raised his voice so all could hear. "We all know the risks when we go on missions. We all accept those risks to make a better future. Sometimes the worst outcome happens and when it does, we honor those that have fallen defending our freedoms and our God-given rights. Tomorrow we will mourn those that were lost, and we will celebrate those that have returned."

THE FRESNEL WOODS

Dwyll sat at his desk at the Heraldrin headquarters, annoyed. He had, indeed, found the dissident base in Kinsford shortly after arriving, but it was completely empty. The guards had found various odds and ends left by those in their hurry to evacuate, indicating the base had been in use for some time. They'd been smart, though. No papers of importance, no equipment left and no one to arrest.

He slammed his fist on his desk, swearing under his breath. Rusak didn't tolerate failure, but perhaps he could come up with something—spin this to look like an accomplishment. After all, he still had the girl and her dissident friend chained up in Devon Falls. It shouldn't be hard to come up with a story he could tell the proselytizers to spread. Maybe he could plant the bodies of his captures at the Kinsford base, saying they were planning a terror attack on a shopping district. "Yes," he said, smiling. That would be exactly what he would do. A knock came from his office door, jarring him from his thoughts; the sound echoing through the large room. "What is it?!"

Mei entered, hurrying to his desk. "We have a problem. Alex was giving his first broadcast late last night, but in the middle of it, his sister spoke to him. I don't know how—not important. Anyway, the good news is that she's alive. The bad news is that she told Alex we're the ones who shot her airship down and that we've tried to kill her. He was pretty pissed."

He stared at her blankly. "What did you tell him?"

"Well, I told him she was either lied to or is lying."

Dwyll continued to stare. "Did he believe you?"

She shrugged. "I...I don't know."

Dwyll rubbed his chin, not in the mood to fix another problem. "You're supposed to be selling that we're on his side."

"I thought we were...on his side. We were trying to find his sister until the dissidents shot her down. Right?"

Dwyll's stare turned cold. "You are to do what I've told you to do—not question me."

"But, I thought—" she said, confused.

Dwyll slammed his hands onto the desk. "I don't care what you thought. If you can't persuade him, then I'll toss you back in the gutter I found you in. Maybe hire some young upstart girl willing to do whatever it takes to be in your position, maybe even entice the boy to keep him in line. You're replaceable. Never forget that!" Mei looked away, tearing up. "If enticing the boy is what you must do to get his trust back, then DO...IT..." He sat back in his chair and started rubbing his temples, trying to ease a headache. "We need to keep him distracted. Keep his mind off of what she said."

Mei wiped away a tear. "There's more."

Dwyll didn't want to deal with this crap, but he needed the full scope regarding his pawn. "Go on."

"His sister said she's going to the Fresnel Woods with a team to look for the Lunarian Key. She wanted him to meet her where the river forks later today."

Dwyll placed both hands on his desk and stood up slowly—a dark smile forming. "Well then. Let's reunite Alex with his sister. I want you to get him ready to hike out. The both of you are going on this little expedition."

Mei bowed slightly, happy to be back on Dwyll's good side. "We'll be ready shortly."

"Good. Now leave. I have some planning to do."

He watched her scurry away and was excited to finally have a lead on the Lunarian Key. He had been worried it had fallen through his fingers after the failed scopshade attempt on the Lunarian Catalyst. Now, though, he had an opportunity to impress Rusak. He walked around his desk to a painted portrait of the sovereign hanging on the wall.

Entering a code on an embedded keypad, the portrait slid to the side, revealing a hidden safe. He placed his hand on the biometric pad, releasing the lock with a familiar click and a panel on the front of the safe lowered, revealing the Helenium Key. He grabbed it, heading out of his office to the Gate Room down the hall.

A communications officer nearly ran right into him as he was leaving his office. "Czar Dwyll! I was just coming to see you."

Dwyll stopped short, raising an eyebrow, "What is it?"

The officer looked nervous, trying to find the right words, "Umm...the...the—"

"Spit it out," Dwyll sneered.

"The cathedral in Devon Falls...it was destroyed. We expect the dissidents are behind it, freeing the prisoners. Guards are still combing the rubble for any survivors."

"What of the weapon plans we have there!?"

"Czar Prevara has a copy of them, but the prototype was destroyed with the building."

"Hmm...I'll report this to Rusak directly," Dwyll said. "He'll want to know of Prevara's failings. Keep me apprised of any updates." The officer gave a salute and headed back to the elevator. He smiled to himself at the new bit of information. He didn't particularly care about the escape of Alex's sister or that other stooge, but could pawn the destruction of the cathedral on Prevara and watch her career topple. It was the type of news that made his day.

He continued down the hall appreciating that all Kriva Rasturna headquarters were built identically for each dimension and in the same spot geographically. It saved him time, making it far easier to move from one dimension to another. He recalled how they had to spend the first year in Lunaria building their headquarters to the same height as the others to ensure the Gate Room of other locations wouldn't leave any visitors falling to their death. He chuckled to himself at the thought of Prevara flailing in the wind for the last few seconds of her life.

He entered the Gate Room, moving to the center where a circular outline was etched into the floor. Tapestries lined the walls, each displaying an emblem representing one of the five dimensions, with the Kriva Rasturna's emblem centered. On the wall just ahead of him, he could see the displayed glyph combinations for each dimension.

He held up the Helenium Key and began rotating its outer ring, entering the combination for Primula. The Primulan emblem illuminated on the key in grey and he pressed his thumb to the orange stone at its center. The etched circle he stood in the middle of lit up and a dome of light appeared over him. Wind swirled, creating a funnel that extended towards him. The wind became more intense, and he felt the familiar sensation of being lifted off the ground. He squinted just as a flash of light burst through the room before gravity once again took over and he landed abruptly, steadying himself. The dome of light was gone, and the tapestries had been replaced with a statue of Rusak.

He left the room and headed down the hall, looking at the various art pieces; each displaying paintings from the three dimensions they'd conquered or encroached on. As he neared Rusak's office, the door opened. A guard was escorting a girl out; her bare feet slapping against the marble tile. She looked to be a fair-skinned young woman in her early twenties wearing a long dirty and tattered pillowcase as a dress. She looked ill with her cheeks sunken in and her brown hair matted into a rat's nest. Dwyll nodded to the guard, catching the already open door, and knocked on it.

Rusak looked up from some paperwork on his desk, "Dwyll...what brings you to Primula? Have you killed off the dissidents in Maraldi yet? We need to start expansion to other countries in Lunaria."

"Not yet, I'm afraid, but I have plans in motion that have already destroyed one of their bases. I've also begun looking at expanding our efforts outside of Maraldi." He looked back at the door and then at Rusak. "If you don't mind my asking, sir, who was the girl just now?"

"Just a slave," Rusak said, waving his hand dismissively. "No one of importance. Now, why have you decided to visit?"

Dwyll cleared his throat. "As you recall, we've been working to onboard the boy we grabbed from Delphinium. I had captured the boy's sister in Devon Falls, keeping her restrained at our base at the cathedral there, but last night, the base was destroyed. The girl and other deplorables were freed or killed. Prevara was to keep watch while I was away, but obviously did not."

Rusak shook his head. "I really don't care about the spat between you two," he said impassively. "What of the weapon plans and the prototype we were working on there?"

"Prevara has a backup of the plans, but the prototype is destroyed."

Rusak hated setbacks. "That puts us at least three months behind. When you return, have the research unit double their work effort. That weapon is important to my plans for expansion into Alchemilla and Delphinium. As for the boy, I've made it clear he's to be our connection to the people of Delphinium after we've...encouraged...those in power to join us. He is important so long as he can help us."

Dwyll gave a slight bow. "Of course, Sovereign. And it would seem we have an opportunity that arose from his sister's escape. She contacted him while he was broadcasting last night, information him that her allies may know where the Lunarian Key is."

"Really?" Rusak's interest piqued.

"Even better, they told him to meet them at a specific location. I've already begun putting together an expedition. I also believe the sister has access to the Delphinium Key. If all goes accordingly, you will have two more Steradian Keys by tomorrow morning, leaving only the Alchemillan Key to obtain."

Rusak smiled. "Pull this off, Dwyll, and I'll instill you as ruler of Helenium."

Dwyll bowed graciously. "Thank you. Sovereign."

"Dwyll. Don't mess this up."

***

Ethan ran down a metal walkway high up in the cathedral, holding Summer's hand. TAKs nipped at their heels and guards shot at them as they tried finding an exit. Pulser shots whizzed by, striking a support beam holding up the walkway which snapped, lurching the platform to the side. Summer screamed as she tumbled over the railing, still gripping Ethan's hand tightly, jerking him backward. He grabbed the railing with his free hand. "Hold on!" he yelled, looking down at the floor, which seemed impossibly far away. Then Summer's hand started to slip. TAKs continued snarling at them from the platform above, and the footfalls of the guards were catching up to them.

"Don't let me go!" she yelled.

"I need you to climb up." He was struggling to hold on to both her and the railing. "I'm losing my grip. Climb!" Her hand slipped away, and she screamed, free falling into darkness. "Summer!" He reached out, but couldn't see her anymore.

"Don't worry. You'll be joining her," a guard said from above, taking aim with his pulser rifle. Ethan looked up just as the guard fired. He felt a searing pain in his chest and was knocked free of the walkway. Everything blurred, and the floor rushed towards him.

Ethan woke up startled, his vision still blurry. He found himself safe in a bunk in the Devon Falls resistance base. Pain shot through his back and he realized he was leaning up against the wall, having fallen asleep in his clothes. He felt a nudge against his shoulder and found Elise standing over him.

"Hey," she whispered. "We're all getting some breakfast before we head out. I figured I'd wake you two up so you could join us."

He looked down at Summer asleep on his other shoulder; her arm wrapped around him. He looked back at Elise, who was grinning. "We'll be there. Give me a minute to get her up."

"We'll save you two a seat. Oh, and I returned your journal and the Delphinium Key. They're at the foot of your bunk," she said, gesturing to them.

"Thanks." She waved, leaving the room. He recalled the night before. Summer had been happy to have gotten the chance to clean up, put on some clean clothes, and have her wrists checked by the medics. They had given both of them some pill called Hemofib, which they obtained on a raid of a Kriva Rasturna base a few months back. Within a couple of hours, the medication had healed his injuries from the night before.

Summer had asked him if she could just sit with him on his bunk and relax for a bit, not wanting to be alone. They must have been exhausted, as that was the last thing he recalled. Some of her hair had fallen covering her face, and he lightly brushed it back behind her ear. She stirred. "Good morning," he whispered.

Her arm squeezed around him, and her feet stretched out. She slowly opened her eyes and smiled, realizing she had fallen asleep against him. "I don't feel like moving yet."

"I'd be up for staying here a while longer, but there is that wet drool spot to consider." She quickly sat up and he smirked at her initial reaction.

Seeing the spot, she felt embarrassed. "I'm so sorry."

"Just messing with you." He stretched out his arm, moving it around to get the blood flowing.

"You'd be drooling too if you'd just spent a day chained up." She lightly smacked his chest and flinched, forgetting about her wrists; the impact still hurting regardless of the medication and thick bandages the medics had wrapped around them.

"How are your wrists doing?"

"They're still sore, but the medication healed them much quicker," she said, rubbing one gently.

"The others are meeting up for breakfast and saving us seats. Want to go see what they've got?"

"I haven't eaten in two days." She pushed herself up from the bunk. "I could stomach my brother's cooking at this point." She did her best putting her hair up in a ponytail and straitened her shirt.

Ethan grabbed the key and journal, putting them back in the hidden pocket of his vest before putting it on. They made their way down to the mess hall and were greeted by Elise, waving them over to join the group. They grabbed their food first and joined their friends. Talia had tears rolling down her cheeks from laughter; whatever the cause being infectious with everyone at the table seemingly in good spirits.

"What did we miss?" he asked.

"We've been sharing stories of our early days in the resistance and how we met Marion and Samuel. It's a good way to remember those we've lost," Fletcher said.

"Samuel didn't make it!?" Ethan asked, surprised.

"He's still recovering," Liam said, "but they had to amputate his arm. At least they got him stable by the time they released me this morning." He held up his newly cast arm. "Breaks take longer to heal, even with Hemofib."

"He'll make it," Fletcher said. "He's too stubborn to be taken out like that. It's how he deals with Marion's passing that worries me, given they were engaged."

Talia nodded. "We'll be there to help him through it. Today, though, we have something to celebrate. I'll bet you're excited to see your brother." She handed a platter of fresh biscuits to Summer. "Our comm room got word the Kriva Rasturna are putting together an expedition. Seems our plan is working."

"I'm excited, but there's so many things that can go wrong," Summer worried.

"We've been working on contingencies," Talia reassured. "For starters, we want minimal people engaging with them."

"I can't wait," Elise broke in excitedly. "I've been waiting years to find Mystell. To actually be there, walk one the same streets as Daegal, our last real Catalyst, and be one of the first to touch something from a city missing for centuries."

"You seem pretty confident about where we're headed," Ethan said.

"My family has spent decades researching likely locations where Mystell could be and, given what our research says, this is where it's all pointing."

"What if they don't bring my brother to the meeting point? Do we have some kind of backup plan to go get him?"

"Your brother is their best bet at getting the Lunarian Key," Fletcher said. "They have everything riding on bringing him. Sorry Elise, but if he's not there, then we won't be leading them to any lost cities. It will be a full stop for us finding Mystell today."

"But—" Elise started.

"No buts, Elise," Fletcher interrupted. "If they find out you're the one that can find Mystell and you're caught, it could easily mean death for the rest of us."

Talia faked clearing her throat to get the conversation back on track. "As I was saying, Fletcher and I have been working through some details. Liam, you're going to be staying here, recovering."

"After all the stories Elise has told us, I was hoping to see Mystell," he said.

Fletcher shook his head. "You're our top technology resource. If we were infiltrating a base, I'd reconsider, but there'll be nothing modern where we're going. In the meantime," he continued, "I want you checking supplies here and seeing if you can come up with a way to modify our radio equipment to match what Ethan's sister did. They'll be going home eventually, and I'd like to remain in touch with them. Summer will also need a new translator. Would you be willing to get one for her, please?"

"Fine," Liam said, defeated. He pushed away from the table, leaving the mess hall.

Talia sighed, watching him walk off. "We're also down, Marion and Samuel, on this mission, which took some reworking of the plan. Originally, we were going to have Summer and Marion be our contacts at the meeting point. Marion was going to be posing as you, Elise. Now that falls to me. Elise, we'll need you to get Fletcher and Ethan to the lost city before us. I'll be trying to lead them on the wrong path to get you more time. Any questions?" Elise shook her head. "Ok then, Summer, is there any possibility that your brother would attack us?"

"What?" she shook her head in disbelief. "Why would he attack us?"

"Well, the Kriva Rasturna has a way of getting into your head," Talia said matter-of-factly, "and I don't just mean with the scopshade. They're well versed in manipulation and from what we heard of your brother's broadcast, they've been spinning plenty of lies to him."

"Your brother will probably need some recovery of his own after we free him," Fletcher said. "To them, it's all a psychological game to gain power and they don't care what damage they cause. Hopefully, we'll get to him before he becomes another statistic."

Liam returned to the table, taking a seat next to Summer. "Here," he said, handing her the translator. "I tuned it the same as the others. You're all on the same frequency you and Ethan were on earlier. You'll be able to communicate with each other from a distance without being heard but, I'd keep communication to a minimum while you're out there. We don't know if they'll have people monitoring these frequencies or not."

"Thanks Liam." She put the translator on her ear. "For what it's worth, I wish you could come with us."

"Me too. Maybe I'll get to visit another day."

"You can count it, Liam," Fletcher said. "Now...Cormack was nice enough to lend us the tempests, saving us a two-day hike. They're going to be taking us most of the way, dropping us off about a half mile before the meeting point. That should give us plenty of time to get into position with me, Ethan, and Elise covering you two. I won't sugarcoat this. What we're doing, meeting up with the Kriva Rasturna is risky. We don't know what they're going to do or how they're going to react. If you think there's a chance of them trying to hurt you, get out of there."

"Our equipment is already packed and ready to go," Talia said. "Finish breakfast quickly, and I recommend bathroom breaks. We all meet at the tempests in twenty."

Ethan and Summer stayed to finish breakfast while the others left to get ready. After a couple minutes, a static squelch came from their translators, followed by Lilly's voice, "Ethan! You there?"

He smiled. "I'm here, Lilly. How are you holding up?"

"We're doing good. Thought I'd check in while Aiza is working on figuring out those symbols. She hasn't gotten very far with them, though. Hey, by chance, have you come across the right combination or...you know...any new animals?"

"Of course, you would ask about animals. And no, we've had a lot going on. No luck on the combination yet. We're about to head into a forested area, though. I'm sure I'll see animals there. If I have time, I'll try to sketch a couple in my journal."

"It'd be better if you just took a picture with your phone, smart guy," she teased.

"Lilly, I don't have my phone anymore. I sold it a few days ago."

"Well, what about your girlfriend's phone?"

Summer pipped up, "Hi Lilly! I don't have my phone either. I lost it in Kinsford."

There was a long silence before Ethan responded. "You forgot she could hear our conversations, didn't you?"

"Yeeaahhhh," Lilly said slowly.

Summer smiled. "It's ok, Lilly. I kind of like the title."

Both Summer and Ethan cringed as their earpieces crackled from the high-pitched squeal coming through before Lilly started speed talking. "When did this happen!? How long ago did this happen!? You better treat my brother right! Oh! Have you found your brother yet?" she asked without taking a breath.

Summer looked over at Ethan, wide eyed, who was still holding his hand over his ear. "We're about to meet up with him here soon."

"Hopefully this lost city we're headed to will have the code to get back," Ethan said; his hearing finally normalizing.

"You better get back soon. Mom and dad have NOT been doing well with you being in another dimension. Oh! And Summer, your mom has been staying with us."

"Good. That'll help her a lot."

"Hey Lilly, we have to get going," Ethan said. "Tell everyone I love and miss them."

"Can I...tell everyone that you two are a thing now?"

Ethan rolled his eyes, and Summer held back laughter. "Yes. You have our permission. Talk to ya later, sis."

"Love you! Bye!" she said before the static returned, followed by silence.

"Your sister is something else, huh?" Summer said, smiling.

"Can't argue there." He stood up. "Ready to go get your brother?"

***

Ethan felt exhilarated speeding over the Fresnel Woods in the tempest. He was enjoying the scenery of Mount Hadley with the endless forest below them.

Elise pointed forward at the canopy. "Over there, Armond!" She had to raise her voice over the wind. "See the two breaks in the canopy that look like snakes? They'll meet a few miles ahead."

"I see it," Armond said, seeing the two lines intersect in the distance. "We're not far out and I don't want them seeing us. How about landing down there?" He pointed to a clearing just big enough for both tempests to land. "That looks like a big enough spot."

"I think we're close enough. Go ahead, and take us down," Fletcher said, touching the translator in his ear. "Kaylah, we found a landing spot. Follow us in."

Armond slowed the tempest, bringing it to a stop, hovering just above the clearing. As he started their descent, tree branches swayed violently from the tempest's swirling blades. Ethan watched below as animals scattered in every direction, attempting to escape. The grass in the small clearing pushed away, and a moment later, he felt a slight bump when the tempest touched down. Armond powered down the engines, allowing the wind to subside. Everyone disembarked, grabbing a backpack of equipment and their weapons for the upcoming hike.

"Armond and Kaylah," Fletcher started, "You two stay put and hold this position until we return. It'll more than likely be tomorrow before we get back. We got here early enough that I don't think the Kriva Rasturna will spot us; especially with the thick canopy above."

Armond pulled out a pulser rifle from the tempest, powering it up, and handed it to Kaylah. "We're ready in case they show up. We'll have to be on the lookout for wildlife, too. This is a known area for wellgernots and they're super territorial. They won't like tempests being this close to their nesting sites."

"A warning shot is usually enough to drive them off. Or at least make them think twice about attacking," Kaylah said.

Ethan looked around at the small clearing they were in; the ancient forest surrounding them. Logs that had fallen over decades ago were completely covered in moss while thick, lush forest lay ahead. For the first few minutes since arriving, the only sound he could make out was the roaring river in the distance, but eventually, the wildlife sounds he'd expected returned.

"The river's not far," Fletcher said, pointing ahead. "Let's move." He pulled out his short sword, ready to hack away at any undergrowth that got in the way.

Elise felt a surge of adrenaline with the excitement of arriving, finding it difficult to contain herself. "We're finally here." She watched Fletcher hack away at some vines blocking their path. "We're going to find Mystell and be the first in the city in centuries. I can feel it."

"What landmarks are we looking for?" Talia asked.

"We'll have to follow the river until we come across a natural rock formation. Should look like an old pipe organ you'd have seen in the cathedrals before the takeover," Elise said.

"I remember those," Talia said. "So, if I see something similar, just lead them away?"

"Don't make it too obvious. I'm sure the Kriva Rasturna have done research too and will at least know to follow the river. After the pipe organ formation, there was mentioned of a sealed cave entrance nearby that's well hidden. The sound of a waterfall should be an indicator."

"Hidden entrance?" Talia questioned. "Then it should be easy enough to stall."

"Keep in mind, all our research is decades, if not centuries old," Elise said, climbing over a downed tree. "I don't know how accurate it is, but it's the best starting point we have. I just wish my mom could have joined us. She'd have been so excited."

"I'm sure she'd be proud of you, Elise," Summer said.

The sound of the rushing water grew louder the further they went. Ethan and Fletcher took turns cutting down vines and clearing the way, slicing a path around large trees and through prickly bushes. "Finally at the river," Ethan said after cutting down more branches, revealing the rushing water. A short patch of tall grass separated them from a rocky embankment just beyond.

Rustling came from the trees above, where a long-tailed lemur-like creature jumped from tree to tree. Ethan didn't recognize the species, but thought Lilly would have enjoyed seeing it. The sounds of birds chirping, frogs croaking, and other creatures filled the surrounding air. He wondered if any of them differed from those he expected back home.

"Up this way, right?" Fletcher asked, pointing upriver with his sword.

"That's right," Elise confirmed. "I'm guessing we're about a mile out from where the river forks. I'm not sure how far up from there we'll find the rock formation."

"Glad it's not mosquito season," Fletcher said, hacking down more branches.

"It's not the mosquitos I'm worried about," Elise said.

"Other than the Kriva Rasturna, what would be a problem here?" he asked.

"You remember the reports, right? I think we should keep our eyes peeled."

Talia waved her hand dismissively, following the others along the riverbank. "You're talking about the monster that shredded Kriva Rasturna guards, halting their search for the key?"

"Monster!?" Summer questioned. "No one said anything about a monster."

"It's just a story," Fletcher said. "But I spoke with a guy who overheard two survivors talking about what they saw on one of the expeditions. People don't make crap up when the person you're talking with was there too. Guy says they looked dead serious."

"I don't think it was a monster," Elise said. "I think it may have been a Guardian. While there's no mention of them in any of the research I've seen regarding Mystell, I'd rather not run into one."

"I don't know about Guardians," Ethan said, "but those TAKs could easily be mistaken for monsters when you're not used to seeing them. Maybe one escaped and started attacking them?"

"Maybe," Elise conceded, changing the subject. "If we're lucky, some of the ruins will still be above ground. Who knows how the landscape has changed over the years? We may have to keep an eye out for odd looking mounds or hills that would indicate structures underneath. The city would have been built from stone and wood, and I expect much of it to have collapsed."

"We don't have the equipment to excavate an entire city if all we find are hills," Fletcher said. "That would take years to get to the key and we don't have that kind of time."

"Before we look for hills, we should look for the hidden cave entrance," Elise said. "My grandfather's research uncovered ancient stories of an underground river and of a cave before emerging at the city's gate. It describes massive arches as you enter with sentinel towers connecting them. This allowed the Mystell military to box in any enemies, attacking them from all angels. That alone helped them stay in power for centuries."

"Why would they leave such a fortified area if they could keep people from getting the key where they were at?" Summer asked.

"My mom uncovered information about a civil war that broke out in Mystell about a year before the city was finally abandoned. That could have led to more destruction of the city than time could have ever caused, making it unlivable. If we find the entrance, we'll need to be very careful as the river could also cause a structural concern with destabilization from floods."

"So be ready to dodge falling rock...." Ethan paused, hearing humming. "Do you guys hear that?" The noise came from behind them and was getting louder. He turned, seeing the canopy of the trees above start to shake violently as the wind picked up.

"Against the trees!" Fletcher commanded. While everyone took cover, Ethan looked up as four tempests flew quickly overhead just above the treetops towards the meeting point.

"Looks like our welcoming committee is arriving," Talia said grimly.

***

Alex was in the best mood he'd been in since coming to Lunaria. He was finally going to see his sister again, getting him one step closer to returning home. He looked down at the treetops whiz by at what seemed impossible speeds. The wind blew through the craft with enough force that he may as well have been sticking his head out the door. "What did you call this thing again?" he asked.

"Tempest," Mei said, also enjoying the flight. "They're the quickest way to get around Lunaria. I got to spend a day with the

Harriers and they said these airships got their name from all the wind the twin blades generate, keeping us in the air."

"You're sure your sister said to meet her where the river forks?" Dwyll asked from just behind the pilot. He had reserved the front seats for himself so he could stretch out.

"That's right!" he said, speaking up over the sound of the rotating blades. "Summer said she'd be with some people. I don't know how many."

"No doubt she's with the dissidents," Mei said. "She could be their prisoner."

Dwyll smirked. "We have a contingent of guards ready to take them out if need be." Dwyll sat up, seeing the snaking line of the two rivers converge through the canopy ahead. "There!" he said, pointing. "That's our fork in the river. Find us a landing spot."

The pilot looked out the window. "I think I see one, sir." He banked the tempest to the right. "It'll be a bit of a walk to the meeting point, but doable."

Alex grabbed onto a handle, peering out over the trees as the tempest slowed. He occasionally saw an animal run for cover but couldn't recognize what it was, having only seen a blur. "Any animals out here that we have to worry about?"

Dwyll laughed. "It's a vast forest. Of course, there are animals you'll have to worry about. Just keep your eyes open and you'll be fine." Dwyll's response didn't calm his nerves at all as he imagined snakes, spiders, and other deadly creatures that could lurk behind a tree at any moment.

The tempest slowed and hovered over a large grassy field. Alex squinted, making out what looked to be three large white rhinos grazing near the tree line opposite them. The beasts looked up at the tempests descending and immediately took a defensive position. With the animals turning around, Alex saw they had three horns.

"You guys have dinosaurs here!?" he asked with a burst of excitement.

"Dinosaurs?" Mei asked, confused. She peered out the side at the animals across the field from them as they touched down. She rolled her eyes. "Those aren't dinosaurs. They're wellgernots."

"Yeah," Dwyll said, chuckling, "You'll still want to keep your distance from them. They don't like intruders. See how they're keeping their horns pointed at us? They're protecting something; maybe an infant." The largest wellgernot took a few steps towards them, stopping occasionally to rear its head as though challenging them.

The airship had barely touched down before guards jumped out, grabbing hiking equipment and pulser rifles. Dwyll hopped out with a rolled-up map, holding up his arm to block the gusts from the tempest. He turned around using the tempest's cabin floor as a table and unrolled the map, following the river with his finger.

Alex hadn't taken his eyes off the wellgernots. The largest of them continued to move forward, occasionally grunting. "That thing seems like it wants a fight," he said, looking at Mei. "Should we get out of here?"

"There's nowhere else for us to put the tempests down, kid," the pilot said. "We'll just have to deal with them if they start any trouble."

"Oh, for God's sake," Dwyll said, walking over to the pilot. "Give me that." He ripped the pulser rifle from his hands. "You have to make an example of one of them in order for the others to get the message." He walked towards the massive beast, agitating it. The grunts from the creature became more guttural; a warning growl for him to stop. "Come on!" he yelled in a mocking tone, waving his arms at it.

The infuriated animal charged, lowering its head to gut the intruder. As it neared, it was clear to Alex he had severely underestimated the size of it, with its hulking body being at least twice that of the rhinoceroses he'd seen at a zoo. The creature's horns were equally massive at three to four-foot-long. The ground shook harder the closer it got.

Dwyll turned the dial of the rifle to cause the most damage and took aim with it, firing a single shot at the beast. A burst of pink exploded from its chest before it shuddered, face planting into the ground and slid before rolling to a stop only a dozen feet from Dwyll. The other creatures groaned and fled into the woods. Dwyll turned with a grin, tossing the rifle back to the pilot. "Problem solved," he said with a quick bow. "Let's get organized people. We have stuff to do today."

It horrified Alex how much damage the one shot did to the creature. He got closer, seeing the lower jaw missing and where the chest would have been was a huge cavity with partially shredded organs and blood seeping out onto the grass. He cringed at the sight, heading back to where Mei stood. "Those rifles are no joke."

"Come on!" Dwyll yelled. "All of you but the pilots, get over here. I want us at the meeting point and in position before they arrive."

Alex jogged over to Dwyll. "What are the pilots going to do?"

"They'll be keeping an eye on the tempests should those creatures, or your sister's friends, get any ideas. Don't worry about them. We need to focus on getting to your sister and then finding the key."

Road Less Traveled

T alia had scouted ahead of the group, gathering intel on what would wait for them at the rendezvous. Hearing voices in the distance, she took cover behind a large tree, peering around the trunk. Six guards carrying pulser rifles stood on the opposite side of the riverbank. "Dammit," she said under her breath. More guards came into view before she noticed two teenagers sitting on a large rock among them, one being a boy with red hair. "That must be him," she whispered to herself.

She quietly stepped back, ensuring no one saw her, before bolting as fast as she could around trees and under branches. A few minutes later, she joined where the others were waiting. She slumped down next to Fletcher, catching her breath, glad she made the effort to do some reconnaissance. "We're well out numbered. There's probably a dozen guards, all armed with pulser rifles," she said.

"Did you see my brother?" Summer asked.

"I think so. He was sitting next to some girl in the middle of all the guards. What worries me is I didn't see the Czar anywhere. He's got to be with them."

"If there's that many of them, let me join the two of you," Ethan said. "If a fight breaks out, at least I can help."

"We're not abandoning them, you know," Fletcher said. "We'll be just out of sight."

"Just the same. If that Dwyll guy is with them, he'll be wondering where I am. He's seen me with Summer already. It makes more sense for me to go with Summer and Talia."

"Fine," Fletcher said, "but you're going to have to leave your key with us."

Ethan took his vest off. "I get it. They'll be searching us for weapons first thing." He pulled out the Delphinium Key and journal, handing them to Fletcher.

"You have my word you'll get these back."

"Assuming we get out of this alive," Ethan said, only half joking after what Talia reported.

Talia grabbed a small container from her pocket, removing a grey-colored contact lens. She grimaced, putting it in, and her eyes watered. She did the same for the other eye, looking miserable every second of the process, blinking repeatedly, looking like she was about to sneeze. "I don't know how Marion made that look easy, but should give some credibility for my cover." She wiped the excess tears from her eyes.

Fletcher shuddered. "You really look like a Grey with those in. I don't like it."

"It's necessary," she said, looking from Ethan to Summer. "You two ready?"

Ethan gripped the handle of his bow nervously. "As I'll ever be."

Summer stood. "Let's get him back safely."

"From here on, we split up," Fletcher said. "Elise and I will keep an eye on the three of you while making our way to Mystell. Do your best to delay them, Talia."

Elise grabbed a paper from her pack. "Talia, wait."

"We'll be ok, Elise. Don't worry."

"I know you'll be ok, but thought you should take this with you." She handed Talia the folded paper. "It's a copy of my translation matrix if you run into any written text. I don't think you'll find any, but it'll give you credibility if you're expected to decipher something."

"Won't you need it?"

"I've got it memorized, and this is just a copy. I made it for you before we left."

Talia nodded, "Thank you." She motioned for Ethan and Summer to follow her, pocketing the paper. "Keep your voices low if you have to talk. I'll let you know when we're near."

Ethan could feel his nerves getting the better of him as they made their way through the woods. It wasn't every day he willingly walked towards a group of people that would likely kill him if he looked at them wrong, but here he was. He took a couple of deep breaths, listening to the sound of the river to calm himself. He looked over at Summer, figuring he probably looked as pale as she did. Her hand trembled, gripping the handle of the sheathed sword at her hip. He reached over, taking her hand.

"We'll get through this," he whispered.

She glanced at him, smiling, and squeezed his hand. "I'll feel better when this is over."

Talia slowed, putting up her hand to quiet them. "Just up ahead," she said in a hushed tone. "Time to ready your weapons. Don't shoot unless shot at, but have them ready. Also, make as much noise as possible while we approach so we don't startle them. We don't want some trigger-happy moron killing us because they got spooked." Summer squeezed Ethan's hand one more time and let go, unsheathing her sword. Ethan readied an arrow, feeling nauseous, focusing on the sound of the rivers on either side of them.

They moved forward as loudly as possible, trying to be heard over the water, stepping on twigs, snapping them while they walked through waist high bushes and other underbrush to make their presence known. The guards on the other side of the river quickly spotted them.

"There!" yelled one of them, readying his pulser rifle. The other guards hastened to take positions, aiming their rifles. "Halt!" another guard commanded as Dwyll emerged from behind the wall of men with Alex in front of him.

Seeing Summer across the way, Alex ran forward to greet her, but Dwyll grabbed him by the back of his shirt, holding him in place.

"Wait," Dwyll said under his breath. "We don't know who that third person is. They could fire on us." Dwyll released him, stepping around him. "Well, we meet again, Summer." He raised his voice over the rushing water. "Ethan, I see you've...survived." A hint of disappointment flashed across his features. "Who's your new...friend? I think introductions are in order."

Summer glared at him. "Like when you introduced yourself with a knife to my throat?!"

Dwyll chuckled, waving his hand dismissively. "A misunderstanding, I assure you. This is a dangerous world full of dangerous people. For instance," he said with a sly grin, "I expect your friend here is with the dissenters that have been causing quite a bit of trouble for us." The guards immediately refocused their aim on Talia.

Talia remained calm and waved. "Actually, I'm an archeologist. I've been studying the legend of the Steradian Gate and the keys for years now. When you guys showed up, it proved the legend true, so I doubled my efforts in finding the Lunarian Key. I should thank you." She smiled nervously to sell the façade.

"Archeologist?" he asked, raising an eyebrow. "You'll forgive me for not taking your word. It's easy enough to validate, though. There's a shallow part of the river you can easily cross over here," he said, pointing to it. "Once across, you'll surrender your weapons and allow yourselves to be checked by the guards. You will then lead us to the Lunarian Key. Understood?"

"Why trust you? What guarantees do we have you won't just kill us?" Ethan shot back.

"My boy...you don't have a choice. Look around you. There are a dozen guards pointing their rifles at your head this very moment. You are outnumbered, four to one. You can either do as I request, or you can be killed now and we'll be done with it."

Summer sheathed her sword. "It's ok, Ethan."

He glared across the water at the guards and reluctantly lowered his bow. The three of them trudged across the freezing knee-high water. The current swept past them quickly, but the pull wasn't strong enough to make them lose their footing. As they neared the other side, a TAK pulled hard against its leash, nearly knocking over the guard holding it. Startled, Summer nearly fell backwards into the water, catching herself. The creature growled, clawing at the ground to get to them, but the guard held it back. They finished crossing, and a guard barked more orders.

"Stop right there and drop your weapons," he commanded.

Summer and Talia dropped their short swords onto the rocky riverbank with a clang. Ethan lowered the bow down, removing a dagger from his hip. Talia slowly lowered her rifle as well. A guard moved quickly to collect the weapons. Other guards roughly turned the three of them around, taking their backpacks off and throwing them to the side where another guard unzipped them, dumping the contents on the ground. Once satisfied they were no longer a threat, one of the guards tossed a backpack at Ethan.

"Repack your bags." He gave a laugh, kicking a bottle of water into the river.

Dwyll walked forward, grabbing Talia by the jaw aggressively, turning her head from side to side and looking at her eyes intently.

He spotted the translator on her ear and grabbed it, holding it out to her. "Who are you communicating with?"

She shook her head. "We have those in case we got separated. Wanted to make sure we had open communication and that none of us got lost."

"Well, you're with us now. No need for these." He threw it on the ground, smashing it with his foot. "Guards, remove their translators. We don't want any surprises. Now...Despite being one of the Cleansed, you still refused to reveal the whereabouts of the Lunarian Key. Why?"

Talia had her answer ready, knowing the question was coming. "I wanted to make sure I had it narrowed down to where the ruins of Mystell were. Wasting resources that could be better used elsewhere isn't something I would want to do. I will say, never in a million years did I think a Czar would be joining us. It's an honor to meet you." She gave a quick bow.

He looked her over, finding her striking. "Very well. Guards. You can lower your weapons, but keep an eye on our guests. We don't want them to wander."

Alex rushed forward, wrapping his arms around Summer. "I thought you were dead!"

Summer hugged him tightly. "Thank God you're ok. You wouldn't believe the crap I've had to go through to get to you."

He let go of her and laughed. "I'll bet."

"I guess introductions are in order. This is Ethan," she said, gesturing towards him. "I accidentally got him stuck in the middle of all this, but he's been by my side helping to get you back ever since."

Ethan stepped forward and shook Alex's hand. "Good to finally put a face to the name."

"Glad to hear she had some help."

Mei joined Alex, waving shyly at them, "Hi, I've heard a lot about you, Summer."

"Oh!" Alex said, "This is Mei. She's been teaching me about the world here and what she does for the Kriva Rasturna."

Dwyll rolled his eyes, "As touching as this reunion is, how far of a hike is it going to be to the ruins you said you found, Miss...?"

"Oh! Sorry, my name is Talia. And I haven't found Mystell...yet, but where I believe it to be is about an hour's hike from here. We just need to follow the river." She pointed upstream.

"Let's get a move on, then. You two!" Dwyll said, pointing at a couple of guards. "Bring up the rear and have your weapons ready should our...friends...have any tricks in mind. The rest of you follow along. You don't want to be out here by yourselves once it gets dark." He turned, putting an arm around Talia. "You, Miss Talia, are with me. Lead us to Mystell and have your name enshrined in history."

The large expedition was anything but quiet as they made their way through the underbrush of the woods following the river. Guards hacked away at branches while some of the men talked about the previous expeditions and if the rumors of a creature were true. Some made bets on who would be able to kill the beast should it attack, which had a few of them arguing back and forth.

Summer walked next to her brother, happy to have him nearby for the first time in what seemed forever, but was suspicious of Mei and the friendship Alex had with her. "So, how did the two of you meet?"

Alex started to answer when Mei put her hand on his arm to silence him. "Dwyll introduced us," she said, smiling. "Alex is very important to us, and they chose me as his mentor."

Summer looked puzzled. "Mentor of what?"

Alex broke in, "They want me to be a proselytizer."

"What exactly is a...proselytizer?" Ethan asked.

"Well, we have the honor and duty to spread the good word of the Kriva Rasturna. We want to reach as many people as we can and bring them into the fold. After all, if we're all on the same side, we won't be fighting. Peace through compliance. Right?" She grinned.

Summer didn't like what she was hearing. "What happens to the people that don't agree with your viewpoint and refuse to be converted?" she asked, wanting to hear it directly from them.

Mei suddenly looked annoyed. "Oh, you mean the dissenters? I heard you were with them for a while. We really just want what's best for the people of Lunaria. Anything else they may have told you was a complete lie."

"How about my firsthand experiences that prove you wrong?"

Alex glanced between the two, seeing the tension rising. "What about the two of you?" he quickly asked. "How did you guys meet?"

"I ran into him at the library when I was researching portals," Summer said. "Turns out he was researching too, so we started working together. After a long day, he asked me out and by the next day, we were being attacked by one of those TAKs." She pointed at the one up ahead. "It nearly killed us."

"How did you guys get here then?" he asked.

"Ethan helped get me here."

"Stop!" Dwyll said, throwing up a hand. He pushed past a guard, and stormed towards Ethan, grabbing him by the shirt. He shoved him against a tree, pulled out his dagger, and swiftly raised it to Ethan's throat.

"Hey!" Summer moved to intervene, but a guard grabbed her arm, holding her back. "Let him go!"

"Shut up, girl," Dwyll spat back at her without taking his gaze away from Ethan. "This doesn't concern you—not...anymore. So, you...you used the Delphinium Key to open the gate. Is that right?

Well...where is it? Where is the key?" he growled. Ethan stared him down defiantly, not saying anything.

Alex looked on in disbelief. "What the hell! What are you doing, Dwyll?"

"Perhaps the knife isn't necessary," Mei said quietly. "He was already searched and didn't have the key on him. The guards would have found it."

Dwyll shoved Ethan back into the tree trunk, releasing him. "Very well." He replaced the blade into its sheath. "Where!?"

Ethan straightened his shirt before answering. "I dropped it somewhere in Kinsford. No idea where it is now. It's the reason we teamed up with Talia. If we can find the key, I can get home with Summer and Alex."

"Your friend here said the dissenters in Kinsford had it. I know you were working with them at one point."

"We were with them for only a couple days and most of that, we were running for our lives from TAKs and getting shot at. We had enough and moved on, eventually meeting up with Talia, who was happy to talk about her findings to anyone interested. It was clear she was our best shot at getting home."

"How did you get the Delphinium Key in the first place? Jerran has had it for years."

"You knew my uncle?" Ethan asked, surprised.

"Knew...your uncle?" Dwyll repeated, the realization causing a smile to form. "That fool finally died?!" He let out a laugh. "And your uncle, no less?! HA! That jackass deserved whatever fate he got. Constantly a pain in my ass. Prevara had been tasked with bringing him to Rusak to answer for his crimes months ago. It took weeks of failure for her to at least came back with this kid." He jabbed a finger at Alex.

"Crimes?" Ethan asked, confused. "He was no criminal."

Dwyll smirked, "If you're against us, you are...a criminal. Listen close because I'm only going to say this once. If you follow in your uncle's footsteps, I'll kill you myself. But if you're a good boy and do as you're told, maybe you can go home with your friends after we find the key." Ethan looked at him with disdain, making Dwyll chuckle. "Glare at me all you want, boy. It won't help you. Guards, release her. Let's get back on track, hmm?"

Summer pulled her arm free from the guard's grip. "Jerk," she muttered under her breath.

Shock still lingered in Alex's eyes. "I...I'm sorry. I've never seen him act like that before. He's always seemed nice to me."

She shot him a look as the group began moving again. "Nice? He had a knife at my throat. He beat me and had me chained up. It was Ethan that helped me get away."

"Mei, why the hell would he do that to my sister?" he asked angrily.

Mei looked at him flatly. "His actions are for the greater good of all the dimensions. He could have done worse. If one or two people die to benefit everyone else, it's an honorable death, right?"

"It's honorable and brave if people make the choice to sacrifice themselves to save others," Ethan said. "If someone is killed against their will, being told they're a sacrifice...it's called murder. There's a difference."

Mei didn't like his tone. "I don't think we're going to see eye to eye on this right now, but you'll eventually see it our way. Everyone does."

"Obviously not or there wouldn't be a resistance," Summer said. Mei ignored her, making it clear she wasn't going to engage in any further debate.

The next half hour was spent in silence, with most in the group lost in their thoughts or focused on getting around obstacles. They had reached the foot of Mount Hadley, with the landscape sloping upwards. The river they followed cut through the land, creating a deep trench that eventually disappeared into a shallow cave. A rock wall stood before them, with the waters erupting from the cave's opening. There was no way to enter from this point, with the force of the water powerful enough to wash away anyone foolish enough to attempt entering.

"Does that cliff face look like an old pipe organ to you?" Ethan asked Summer in a whisper. She nodded in agreement.

"Where do we go from here?" Dwyll asked. "It's not looking like my men can make it through that hole. They'd drown before making it safe for us to enter."

"I was expecting this," Talia said. "We go up and around from here." She climbed up a short rocky ledge, getting back onto grass and headed towards a deeper wooded area. She led the group up the mountain, away from the river, hoping she could get them away from the landmark and any hidden entrances. The further they got from the rushing water, the easier it was to hear the noises of wildlife. They continued through the brush, weaving around trees for some time before a fog rolled in. Talia slowed a moment, noticing the sounds of the animals and insects had disappeared. The guards suddenly became nervous, readying their weapons. Then the TAK growled, staring into the fog, but the men saw nothing.

"Heads on a swivel, men," the captain said. "Call it out if you see something."

"What's going on?" Alex asked.

"We're entering the hunting grounds of a problem," Dwyll said. "A couple of years ago we were searching these woods for the key, but had to stop because our men kept getting killed."

"The creature is a myth," Talia said flatly. "No one has documented anything on it."

"Only two people from our first expedition made it out alive. I think they'd disagree with you." Dwyll smirked.

"What does it look like, then?" Ethan asked.

"Those that survived simply ran. They didn't stop to study the thing. My guess is if we run into it, we'll know."

The fog became thicker as they moved forward. Ethan saw a massive object ahead of them but couldn't make it out until they got closer, finding it was the side of the mountain they'd been walking around. Scraggly branches from dead bushes lined the wall, and they could hear the faint sound of a small waterfall from within.

"I'm not sure we're in the right spot," Talia said, looking nervous. "I think maybe further into the woods is—"

"No," Dwyll said, cutting her off. "We're close. Guards, we need to get to wherever that waterfall is. Make us a path." Three guards unsheathed their short swords, hacking away at the branches. Dwyll glared at Talia. "I recall from reading the legend of Mystell that there's a hidden cave entrance near an underground river. I would have expected you to know that."

"I expected a large waterfall back at the river," she said.

"The one we're hearing probably feeds into it," Dwyll said, just as a clang sounded.

"Over this way! I see something," a guard said.

Dwyll smiled. "Seems like we're here."

The guards ripped away branches and thick moss, uncovering ancient text etched into the stone. A guard wiped his hand across the lettering, dusting away the dirt. "Czar! There's something written here."

Dwyll joined him, looking over the text, and Talia swore under her breath, having failed to divert them. Dwyll waved her forward. "Talia, you're an archeologist. Translate this."

Talia stepped forward, pulling the paper from her pocket. She unfolded it, looking at the etched symbols in the stone and back down to the paper. She breathed a sigh of relief, finding the text on the paper matched what was written in front of her. "I think I should be able to." She wiped away more dirt from the etching and started translating. After a couple of minutes, she could make sense of it. "It reads like a warning. Says it's forbidden to journey beyond this point and to enter is considered trespassing. It goes on to warn about guardians that are watching us and will determine our fates."

The TAK continued to growl at something in the fog, and the guards kept their rifles ready should anything move. "The oldest no trespassing sign I think I've ever heard of," Dwyll said, unamused. "Guardians...Of all the stupid, superstitious crap. Even if true, their guardians will have been long dead." He looked along the wall, seeing a few cracks, but nothing looking like an entrance. "What else does it say? There must be something about how to enter."

Talia shook her head. "That's everything written here. It doesn't mention the entrance."

Dwyll snatched a pulser rifle from a nearby guard, causing the man to stumble, not expecting it. He brought the rifle up, pointing it at Summer. "I'm so sick of these games. Get me inside or I kill your friends." Alex ran forward to stop him, but a guard punched him in the gut, dropping him to his knees.

Ethan held his hands up, stepping in front of her. "I might be able to get us inside. There's no need for threats. Right now, we're all on the same side. We need the key too, remember?" Alex regained his composure, still holding his stomach.

Dwyll was tempted to pull the trigger and just end the conversation, but couldn't chance killing an asset that could deliver him the key. He lowered the rifle. "You have ten minutes. Try anything, and I'll kill her in front of you."

Ethan stepped forward, examining the glyphs etched on the mountain first using the translation sheet. Satisfied that Talia correctly translated the text, he moved along the wall, running his hand across cracks, trying to find a pattern. To his left, at the very edge of what remained after guards had revealed the text, an etched line was barely visible, peeking out from under the moss. He tore down more branches and clumps of moss, fully unveiling what laid hidden behind. He took a step back to examine the large semi-three-dimensional carving displaying the Lunarian emblem of the wolf-like Guardian. It looked nearly identical to the one on his key, but the detail was far more intricate with the layering of fur and texturing.

"That's stunning," Summer said, stepping forward. "Must have taken ages to complete."

"Yes, truly a piece of art, but this isn't getting us inside," Dwyll said. "Clock is ticking."

Ethan looked over at Talia, who looked awestruck. "Talia, can you read me the passage over there again? Needing word for word on the part about the Guardians."

"Uh..." she shook her head, getting in front of the passage and bringing up Elise's paper to translate. "The Guardians...protect Mystell...now and forever. They will pass...judgement...upon all who enter. They are watching." She looked over at Ethan. "That's where it ends."

Ethan paced, thinking to himself. There was something off about the carving, but he couldn't quite place it. He thought back to all the times he had seen the emblem before and stopped. On all the other renditions of the Guardian, even on his key, its eye was closed. He looked up at the carving, finding the eye was open.

"Your time is almost up," Dwyll pressed.

Ethan stepped forward, running his hand over the eye, trying to find any clue, and while incredibly detailed, there was no indication the eye was anything more than a part of the carving. Placing his thumb over the Guardian's iris, he pressed it inward, moving it back an inch, and a noise came from behind the wall. Suddenly, a portion of wall between the carving and the etched text crumbled, with rock splashing into the shallow water, revealing a cave.

"Excellent," Dwyll said, walking in front of the entrance. "Seems you're just as capable as our archeologist friend here." He put his arm around Talia, escorting her into the cave with a couple of guards following.

Ethan fell back to Summer and nudged her, getting her attention. "Stay close. We don't know what we're going to run into." She took his arm, following him in.

The entrance of the cave sloped downward, and daylight beamed in where the waterfall had eroded the ceiling. The floor had long been flooded, making a knee-high pond with water escaping into a dark void at the back wall. To their left was a set of stairs carved into the rock with the bottom stair submerged.

Dwyll and Talia had already crossed the shallow water, starting up the stairs by the time Ethan stepped in with Summer, bypassing some of the stone that had collapsed in. He sloshed through the water, nearly slipping on the first step covered in a slick moss. Once on solid rock, he helped Summer skip the mossy step and followed her up the stairs. When they reached the top, the cave opened to a narrow canyon and just ahead of them on the ground, laying on top of rubble, was a thick iron gate that used to block off the cave.

Fifty feet ahead of Ethan stood a massive five story medieval stone fortification, blocking entry into the city. Two rounded towers stretched to the top, connected by a wall with archery slits on each floor and centered at the bottom, an arched two story tall stone entryway; its gate ripped off the hinges. The builders had cleverly used the interior of the mountain to not only hide the city entrance, but to funnel any intruders, extending fortified stone walls from the towers out to either side of the passage.

From where he stood, it looked as though the canyon widened significantly beyond the wall as he could make out tree tops. They made their way forward, seeing nature had reclaimed most of the entrance with much of it covered in moss. At the base of the left wall, a tree had grown, pushing some of the stone bricks inward. Foliage grew around and from the mortar of bricks forming the towers.

He couldn't believe they were standing at the entrance of a once hidden city. Excitement bubbled up within him at the possibilities of what they would see and the history that had taken place in this very spot. Even more exciting was the prospect of possibly finding the combination to get back home. He looked over at Summer, expecting to share in the excitement, only to see a haunted look in her eyes. His smile faded when he followed her gaze, finding the long dead bodies of dozens scattered about; arrows and swords still sticking out from their skeletal remains.

"What happened here?" he asked.

MYSTELL

Ethan sidestepped around a skeleton which still held a rusted sword and had three arrows sticking out from its ribcage. He moved onto the large iron gate that once protected the only way into the city, following the expedition through the stone archway. Remnants of a siege that had taken place centuries earlier greeted them with skeletal remains either leaning against the walls or crumpled on the floor. The wind blowing through the doorways and archer slots was haunting as they crossed the room towards the last gate, which looked to have been bent from an explosion; the brick holding its upper hinge missing with some of the wall toppled. No one spoke, taking in the chaos frozen in time.

Beyond the wall, the settlement didn't look much better. Dozens of remains littered the area leading up to a large stone fountain, its centerpiece having long since toppled over. Trees had reclaimed the plaza and concourse, creating a canopy that camouflaged the city from anyone that would have spotted it from an airship. Beams of sunlight occasionally burst through, burning away the lingering fog in spots.

Segments of cobblestone popped out between the moss and underbrush, giving a glimpse of what the city looked like in its prime. Sidestepping another skeletal figure heaped on the ground, it was clear this battle was one of the last moments of Mystell's history.

The main road stretched beyond the fountain, with buildings lined up on either side of the canyon in various states of ruin. Oddly, the architecture of most of them looked more modern than the stone entryway they'd just passed through. A building to their right had a collapsed roof with a tree growing up from the debris. Other buildings had vines growing up their sides, with greenery growing out from the walls. Ethan couldn't believe most of the buildings still stood after all this time.

"Spread out and find me the Lunarian Key," Dwyll said. "Stay in groups of three." Guards grouped up, splitting off to explore the ruins as he glared at Ethan and Summer. "I trust you'll be looking for the key as well if you ever want to get home. But should you get any ideas..." He shoved a pulser rifle into Mei's hands. "You will join them. If they try anything, shoot the boy. Are we clear?"

Mei nodded nervously, feeling unsure about the possibility of having to kill someone. She'd never had to do the dirty work before. "I'll yell out for help, too."

"Alex, you'll be joining me," Dwyll said with a smile. "We can't have you and your sister running off before we find the key, now, can we?"

His shoulders slumped, and he shoved his hands in his pockets. "Fine."

"Talia, you're also with me." Dwyll put his arm around her again, giving her the creeps, and led the two down the road. "Let's explore further up the street and see what we can find, hmm?"

Ethan pointed to a building on their left. "We'll start there. It looks mostly intact. Hoping it won't collapse on us."

The captain of the guard walked up to him, not looking amused. "The two of you checking the building closest to the exit with this...kid...watching you? I don't think so."

"I'm nearly an adult and have more sway than you'll ever have," Mei said pompously, continuing to fumble with the rifle.

"I'm going to be keeping an eye on the two of you," the guard asserted. He stepped back, seeing Mei's rifle swing up, nearly catching him under the chin. He grabbed the barrel roughly, pointing it to the ground. "I'm going to keep my eye on you as well. Keep that damn thing pointed at the ground unless you intend to shoot someone. We don't need any accidental casualties today. Now come on. We have a lot of ground to cover, and I don't like the idea of having to babysit some kid that's never held a rifle before."

Mei glared, walking toward the building in a huff. Once she was out of earshot, Ethan lowered his voice, "Your eyes. You're not one of them?"

"A Cleansed?" he asked, looking around him. He spoke in a hushed voice, "No. They think I'm a true believer."

"Think?" Summer asked.

He let out a sigh. "I'm only telling you this because I know you're not with them, but if you repeat what I'm about to say, I'll deny it and it won't end well for you." He took a deep breath. "I've seen what the Kriva Rasturna are and what they do to those who don't march in lockstep. Fearing for my job, I played along when they took over a few years back, knowing I could do more damage trying to stop them from within. Name's Cooper." He nodded towards the building. "Let's go or she'll get suspicious."

The three of them walked towards a gaping hole in the building's side created by a tree that had grown through it. "Must have been difficult to keep it up," Ethan said.

"There have been some rough times, and close calls, but I'm hoping we can keep this key out of the wrong hands. I want to see an end to this. I want Maraldi and all of Lunaria free again."

Ethan ducked under a branch to enter the building and found himself in what used to be a tavern. Just ahead were the remains of a portion of the upper floor that had collapsed. Wooden tables and chairs had been knocked over, scattered about with a shattered glass chandelier laying in the middle of the room. To their right, a staircase led up to the second floor that had been mostly shielded from the elements, being further away from any damaged walls.

"I wonder if this used to be an old inn?" Summer asked. "There might be something upstairs. I'm going to check it out."

"I'm not sure I'd trust those stairs," Ethan said.

Cooper surveyed them, not seeing any discernable damage. "I wouldn't make it, but you girls might be light enough if you go one at a time. Just be careful. I don't want this place crashing down on us."

Summer headed over to the base of the staircase; glass cracking with each step from the remains of the chandelier. "Are you coming Mei?"

"Yeah, I guess." She joined Summer at the foot of the stairs. "You, first."

The staircase looked to be in good condition for its age. The supports were thick, still looking sturdy, holding up the ornate wooden railing. Summer put her hand on the spherical finial for balance, stepping onto the bottom step. She bounced on the balls of her feet, testing if it would hold her weight. It creaked, but held and she moved onto the next. It was slow moving as she made her way up, testing each step to ensure she wouldn't fall through, eventually reaching the top, relieved.

Straight ahead, a large broken window gave her an incredible view of the city and the greenery taking it over. Debris from the roof lay on the floor in front of her with a skylight of damaged wood taking its place. The mezzanine extended to her left, stretching into a hallway that led to a handful of rooms. A tree branch growing through another window partially blocked the hall. She looked over the railing at Ethan and Cooper, investigating what was left of the bar below. "I made it up," she announced. "I'll let you know if I find anything."

"Be careful," Ethan said. "Feels like this place could collapse at any moment."

Summer looked back at Mei, seeing she was already halfway up. She slowly moved towards the hall, still unsure if the floor would hold her weight, the wood creaking beneath her feet with each step. The tree limb took up half the width of the hall and small dirt tracks remained from tiny animals that had used it as a way in.

She neared where the first room would have been, finding only half of a door frame. The rest of the wall leading to the mezzanine had collapsed onto the bar below. Daylight poured in through a hole in the ceiling created by centuries of rain.

Mei had finally reached the top, not liking the sound the wood made beneath her feet. "I'm going to stay here while you search. I don't feel like dying today."

Summer waved an acknowledgement, continuing to the second door, which was partially open. She pushed against it, hearing it creak before the snapping of wood. The door ripped off the hinges, falling to the main floor below with a crash, Cooper dodging out of the way at the last second.

"Hey! Watch it! We're still down here!"

"Sorry!" she yelled down from above. She headed towards the large tree branch, having to push it aside to get past. Glass from the window crunched under her feet as she moved towards another doorway.

Inside the room, she found the door had already ripped away, laying on the floor. The room was sparsely furnished with a small bed in the corner; the floor beneath it sagging. She tested her weight, taking a step in and found a short three tier shelf directly to her left, and gasped, stepping back. Sitting on the floor, leaning against the shelf, were the skeletal remains of a woman wearing a tattered dress that still hung off the bones. The dress had a large stain of dried blood with a rip at the rib cage. The arms were crossed across her lap, holding a book. Summer didn't like the idea of taking something from the dead, but her interest was piqued, wondering what was important enough for this woman to hold on to when she'd died.

She gently picked up the book, dusting off the cover, finding it strange that there was no title on the front, and checked the spine. "Mystell, 1427," she read out loud.

"Are you still alive!?" Mei yelled from the top of the stairs.

Summer didn't have time to read it now. She crouched, putting the book in her pack, knowing she'd regret it if she left it behind. "Sorry," she whispered, looking back at the remains before standing up and peering out the door. "I found a skeleton." The wind outside had picked up, causing the entire building to creak. It was time to leave.

She headed back towards Mei, making it past the tree limb, when she heard the distinct sound of claws on wood coming from behind. She spun around, yelping in surprise, when a small animal similar to a raccoon jumped to the tree limb and scampered out the window.

"What was that!?" Mei asked.

Summer turned, continuing towards the stairs while trying to calm herself. "It was some kind of animal. Scared the hell out of me." The wind continued pressing against the structure, making the walls creak and she could feel the building sway ever so slightly.

Mei took a couple of steps towards Summer. "All you found was a skeleton an—" the floor suddenly gave out from under her. She screamed, dropping her rifle as she fell, barely grabbing the edge of the flooring and feeling jagged wood cut into her. Planks of the stairwell whined and cracked, with the topmost stairs clattering to the floor below.

Summer moved quickly, lunging for her, and grabbed her by the wrist before her fingers gave out. "I've got you!"

Ethan and Cooper rushed to the commotion, seeing Mei's legs dangling above. "Oh hell! Place is coming apart!" Cooper said. "I need you to swing over to me. I'll catch you."

"I don't think that's going to work!" Mei yelled, panicked.

Cooper got as close as he could, holding out his arms. "Just count to three. Then drop down to me. Nice and easy."

Summer looked down at her. "You ready?" She nodded, regardless of the knot in her stomach. Summer swung her gaining momentum and counted out loud, "One...Two...Three..." With the third swing, Summer released her and she cleared the jagged wood below, landing in Cooper's arms. Mei's arms suffered cuts and started bleeding from the splintered wood.

Looking at Ethan, Cooper pointed up to Summer. "You get her while I get this one patched up."

"I don't think the stairs would hold if I jumped to them," Summer said, worried.

"Well, how much do you weigh?" Ethan asked, smirking.

She glared at him. "You're hilarious."

Ethan saw what remained of the mezzanine and upper staircase, not liking their options. "I think our best bet is if you take a seat and then hop down to me."

"You sure I'm not too heavy for you?" She took a seat, having second thoughts when she looked down, but knew she didn't have much choice.

"I deserve that," he said, still smiling. "Ready?" She pushed off, landing in his arms, knocking him over. He grunted, hitting the floor, but managed to break her fall. "You were supposed to give me a warning."

"Maybe you should have braced better." She looked pleased with herself, getting up.

"Paybacks for the comment, huh?" He stood up, brushing himself off.

"I guess you'll never know."

Yelling came from outside. Ethan hurried to the entry with Cooper, peering out before quickly moving back into the room. Cooper readied his pulser rifle.

"What's going on?" Summer asked.

Ethan put his finger up to his lips. "We're not alone," he whispered as a guttural growl sounded. Everyone froze in place, not able to recognize what kind of animal it came from. Screams and pulser rifle shots sounded from outside near the ancient fountain.

Ethan checked again, seeing something move so fast, he couldn't quite place what it was. Then he spotted the shredded remains of the TAK on the ground. He leaned back inside, pressing up against the wall. "We could really use our weapons right about now."

Cooper peered over his shoulder at a massive fur covered creature lunging for his men. "You three head up the street away from here. Run!" He jumped through the opening in the building's side, firing at the creature. More guards joined in the fray against the beast trying to subdue it, but it was so large and so quick that it seemed unfazed by their attempts.

"Come on," Ethan said, grabbing Summer's hand. They exited the building, running up the street, away from the commotion. As they ran, they passed decorative stone statues and intricate architecture, but they didn't have the luxury of time to look at them. They dodged trees growing in the middle of the cobblestone road and hopped over moss covered debris. Ethan looked back to see if they were being followed, watching Mei struggle to keep up. He tripped over a loose stone and slammed into the wooden handle of an old cart, snapping it off and knocking the wind out of himself. He slowed, but pushed through the pain with the sounds of pulser rifles fading in the distance.

Up ahead, Ethan spotted Dwyll with Alex, Talia, and two guards at the front of a large four-story stone building that looked like it could have been a church. Dwyll pushed open the massive door with Alex's help and the two guards readied their rifles, seeing the three of them rushing forward.

Mei waved her hand forward at the guards. "It's coming! Move!"

"What's going on?!" one guard demanded as the three of them arrived.

"Some kind of animal!" Mei yelled half hysterical, trying to catch her breath.

Ethan tried explaining, but was still breathing too heavily to make sense. "There's a creature...at least two to three times...back at the entrance." He pointed. "It's attacking your men. Cooper went to help, but I don't know what happened after."

"Everybody inside!" Cooper yelled from down the road. A group of guards ran towards the church, following him. Cooper and a couple of others occasionally turned to fire their rifles behind them as they ran.

Dwyll was already inside before the others could react. Two guards stayed out front with their weapons ready to give covering fire. Ethan could hear more shots and the sound of panicked footsteps rushing towards the doors, getting both himself and Summer out of the way as the group of guards came charging in.

More shots sounded and Cooper appeared, backing inside, continuing to fire. "Close the door!" The group of guards pushed against the heavy door with the hinges squealing in protest before it shut with a thud. The creature slammed against it with enough force to knock one of them backward, briefly opening the door before the guards slammed it shut again, holding it in place. Its growl morphed into the sound of a woman screaming, and then there was silence.

"What the hell is going on!?" Dwyll asked.

Cooper came forward, holding his side where blood was seeping out. "Seems the Guardians are real and they're still here. Might even be the same creature from the earlier expeditions, sir. Whatever the hell it was, it was strong enough to rip the TAK in half and drag Braden off. We tried to kill it, but it's too damn fast. None of us got a shot on it." Another shove came at the door, followed by clawing, and another slam. The guards strained to hold their ground.

"You're wounded," Ethan said. "Is there a med kit?"

Cooper looked down, removing his hand. "Yeah, got me pretty good."

"Find something to bar the doors," Dwyll said. "I'm not letting some animal take this key away from me. You and your men are to hold position and keep this building secure. Understood?"

Cooper nodded. "Yes, Sir."

"Good, the rest of you, fan out. The key is a top priority. It must be here. Talia and Alex, you're sticking with me while we search down here. Mei, you and your new friends go look upstairs."

"Need...to catch my breath." Mei took a seat on the curved staircase, still wheezing while she checked her arms.

"Can't I search with my sister?" Alex asked. "We won't leave."

"No!" Dwyll shot back. "You're going to stick with me until we have what we came here for. We don't need your sister thinking of taking off with you, do we?" He looked over at Ethan and Summer. "And if the two of you think of leaving, just remember what's waiting for you should you try to run." The creature slammed against the door again.

Ethan glared for a moment before taking the room in. His eyes widened in awe at the entryway. The ancient stonework held up, looking nearly untouched with the detail work still intact. Large, curved staircases on either side of the room led up to a loft, under which was a fifteen-foot-tall hallway, adorned with statues of people long forgotten, extended straight back from them.

Through the layers of dust and dirt, they could make out the artistic tile work under their feet. Ethan took a step back, examining it and found it displayed a large eight directional compass with more cryptic writing above the three northern most points. The different emblems of the dimensions displayed matching the placement on his key. "They don't do anything small around here." He scraped away some of the dust with his foot.

"I can't believe how well preserved this building is compared to the others," Summer said. "The one we explored was barely holding together."

"This place can be destroyed for all I care, so long as we find the key," Dwyll sneered, walking up to one of the statues.

Talia moved down the hall, examining the marble effigies. "I think it's safe to say we're in the right place." Five of the eight statues depicted figures holding Steradian Keys. One held a book with a quill looking ready to write, one had a sword at the ready, and the last was wearing a cloak holding a scepter.

Dwyll put a hand on one of the statue's arms. "I bet all the keys were in this building at one point. Now, we just need to find where they hid the Lunarian Key." Bypassing a door on his left, he walked to the end of the short hallway to a smaller set of double doors. He tried opening both, but they refused to budge. Frustrated, he raised his pulser rifle, firing at the iron handle on the door. The handle blew off, flying inside the room beyond, sliding across the floor. The sound caught the attention of a couple of guards, who peered around the corner to see what was going on, but seeing no struggle, they went back to securing the area.

Dwyll pushed against the heavy door, the hinges creaking under the weight. It swung open, revealing a large wooden table with another dozen skeletal remains littered around it. Broken windows lined the right side of the room, allowing daylight to pour in. "It would seem the war didn't stay at the front gates." He smiled and headed inside.

The guards had secured the front doors of the church with those that had been holding the door shut, slumping over, exhausted. The creature slammed against the doors a couple more times, letting out another shrill cry.

Cooper winced, holding his side, still bleeding. "All of you, listen up. This building needs to remain secure. Windows on either side of this lobby need to be monitored at all times." He pointed to a door to their right. "You four, go check the door over there. It might lead us to the key. Keep your weapons at the ready." The group of men nodded, following out the orders. Cooper could feel himself getting weaker. He walked near one of the staircases and leaned against it, sliding to the floor. He sat, bringing his hand away to inspect the wound.

"You're not looking so good," Ethan said, kneeling beside him.

"There has to be some kind of medical kit," Summer said, looking worried. "What about that pill you guys have?"

Cooper chuckled. "Yeah, Braden was our medic. All the supplies are scattered around his body on the other end of the town. I'm not worth sending more men to die." He flinched, putting pressure back on the wound, and looked around, ensuring his men weren't nearby. "Look, you may need someone on the inside. Locate Remage in Heraldrin. Your brother trained with him recently and will know where to find him. He's skilled and will help."

"Just keep pressure on your wound until we figure out a way to get those supplies," Ethan said, trying to get his spirits up.

Cooper kept his voice low. "You two have a key to find. I won't be able to help you in this condition and the rest of this expedition are all Greys. Make sure they don't get their hands on that key."

"We'll check on you in a bit," Summer said.

"Go on. I'll deal with this."

Ethan stood, realizing there was nothing he could do for him. They headed up the stairs, taking in the view of the tall lobby. Intricate stained glass windows adorned the upper walls of the open room, with many having broken over time, leaving only a handful intact. Centuries of rain pouring in through them had destroyed the once beautiful red carpet draped over the stairs, now covered in moss and mold, turning portions a sickly greenish brown.

When they reached the top, they found the entire back wall and much of the sides lined with massive bookshelves. One of them had fallen over some time ago, its books scattered all around. Others had shelves that had given way. Bits of stained glass from the shattered windows speckled the floor and the smell of mildew hung in the air. The bookshelves at the center of the back wall held up; having been more protected from the elements.

The left most corner had two decorative couches that had molded, losing their appeal. Between them sat a coffee table with tipped over candlesticks laying on top covered in a thick layer of dust and webs. Near the opposite corner were two plush chairs in a similar state, with a large floor standing globe against the wall. Two sconces hung just above the globe, still holding candles. Mei was crouched next to a pile of books laying in a heap on the ground. She stood flipping through one of them.

"Have you found anything?" Summer asked.

Mei shook her head, tossing the book on the floor. "Nothing yet. Just some smelly old books and broken glass."

Ethan made his way towards the globe, stopping when the tiling on the floor caught his attention. It was another compass design, looking to be a duplicate of the one in the lobby below. He looked over the railing, noticing the northern point of the two were pointing at each other, which he found odd, wondering if it was intentional.

He continued across the loft, reaching the globe, and wiped a streak through the thick layer of dust with his hand, showing the dark red stained wood of the globe's mounting still had a sheen. He stepped back, examining it. The north pole was pointed straight up instead of at an angle, as he would have expected. The globe's four legs connected to each other near the floor, reaching up at the equator to a four-inch-wide horizon band encircling it. A wooden meridian divided the globe into two vertical hemispheres, with a thick support beam underneath.

He attempted to spin the globe, discovering it barely moved. Wiping away more of the dust, he found he didn't recognize any of the land masses portrayed. The artwork was intricate, displaying not only the land but also drawings of ships, potential trade routes and even an occasional sea beast for good measure. "This looks a lot different from the Earth we're from. The shapes of the continents are all wrong."

Mei walked over, glancing at the globe, and shrugged. "It looks right to me."

"Here's a cartouche," he said, pointing to a label on the globe. "Behaim, 1485."

"That's nearly six hundred years ago," Mei said with a bit of shock. "How old is this place and how is any of this still standing?"

"At least six hundred years old," he said, watching her roll her eyes at him and walk away. He turned his attention back to the globe, finding a legend printed just below the cartouche. He looked at the markings, trying to find them somewhere on the globe, but couldn't find any of them, and wished he had his journal to sketch them.

Summer studied the bookshelves, finding one had a bronze label that had turned green with patina. She could still make out what it said, reading it aloud. "Mystell Historical Record, 1428 - ." The books lining the shelf all had their spines labeled, the first starting with that year. Summer hid her excitement, remembering the book she'd picked up earlier. She began to take off her backpack when she heard footsteps coming up the stairs.

"What have you guys found?" asked one of guards, sounding annoyed. He walked over to the fallen bookshelf under a window and kicked an old book. He seemed to get some form of satisfaction, watching it slide across the floor, pages shredding with a couple ripping from the binding.

"Nothing looks important up here," Mei said. "Some kind of old library for whoever lived here."

"Maybe you three just need some encouragement." He lifted his pulser rifle, pointing it from Summer to Ethan and then to Mei.

"What the hell are you doing!?" Mei asked. "I'm a proselytizer—I outrank you, and we need these two to help us find the key!"

"I'm thinking our best bet out of here is to toss one of you to the beast so the rest of us can make a run for it. Better one of you than me."

"Hey," Ethan said, staying calm, "Remember, we're all on the same side right now. We all want to find the key. The more eyes, the better in helping to find it. Right?"

"Shut up!" the guard yelled. "I just lost my friend out there to something that shouldn't exist and I'm not about to join him. So who's it going to be?" He continued to point the rifle between the three of them, stopping at Summer.

"Hey!" Ethan said. "I'm sorry about your friend, but we didn't have anything to do with it. Don't point your rifle at her."

The guard slowly took aim at Ethan again. "Ah...a volun—" the guard grunted, collapsing under the weight of someone dropping from above.

Ethan barely had time to register what had happened before he saw Fletcher push himself off the man and grab the pulser rifle.

A sly grin plastered on Fletcher's face quickly faded and he took aim at Mei. "Who is she?"

"Hey!" yelled a guard from below. "What was that?"

Fletcher glared at her. "If you give us away, it'll be the last mistake you make."

Mei considered her options a moment and walked to the railing overlooking the lobby. "One of the old bookshelves gave way, dropping a bunch of books."

"Well, keep it down!" the guard said, getting back to his search of the main floor.

Mei returned to the group, raising her hands. "As I just said, I'm a proselytizer with the Kriva Rasturna."

"Hold on," Ethan said. "She's helping us find the key. And is a friend of Summer's brother."

"We can't trust her. You know she'll stab us in the back the second she has an opportunity."

"For now, we have to trust her and hope for the best."

Fletcher lowered his rifle. "Fine, but if she steps out of line, there will be no second chances."

Mei lowered her hands. "I won't make trouble."

Elise peered inside from the window above while Fletcher made sure the guard was still unconscious. Feeling confident he wouldn't be waking up anytime soon, he motioned for her to join him. She quickly and quietly made her way in, dropping from the window to a bookshelf, using the shelves like a ladder.

Summer walked over, giving her a hug. "How did the two of you get past that thing outside? We saw it rip a guard to shreds."

"That's how we got past it," Fletcher said. "He was busy snacking on one of these guys, giving us the opportunity to slip past it from the other side of the road. Then we lucked out with a good climbing tree growing outside this wall." He pointed his thumb towards where Elise had come in. "Had plenty of branches and we climbed to the window before it spotted us."

"Who exactly are you people?" Mei asked.

"We're here to help them," Fletcher said with a nod to Ethan. "That's all you need to know for now." He looked over at Ethan. "I'm sure Elise is already taking everything in, but what have you two found?"

"I've been checking out the globe over there," Ethan said. "It has some markings in the legend that I'm not seeing on it. Do you still have my journal?"

Fletcher pulled off his pack. "Yeah." He opened the pack and pulled the journal and a pencil out, handing them to Ethan.

"Appreciate it. Second thing is this compass in the tile work. There's one down in the lobby area too, but they're not pointing in the same direction. Not sure what to make of that, but my dad used to tell me stories of old places like this that have my curiosity piqued."

"This seems to be the town's library and I think I found their historical records," Summer said, walking to the shelf. She grabbed the first book from the shelf, handing it to Elise. "The first one here says 1428, but when we were checking the building near the fountain, I found another." She knelt, pulling off her backpack, and pulled the book out. She looked at the spine again, seeing *Mystell, 1427* written. "A woman had been holding it as she died. It must have been important."

"So you did find something," Mei said.

Ignoring her, Summer watched Elise flip through the book carefully, reading ledgers and other documentation from the early days of Mystell. She opened the one she'd found and gasped. "It's hollow," she said.

"The book?" Elise asked, looking up.

"Yeah, there's a pouch sewn to the back." She quickly untied the string securing the top and reached inside. Something cold and metallic greeted her before she pulled out a bronze piece. "It looks like a chess piece—maybe a bishop?"

"Can I see it?" Elise asked. Summer handed it to her, and Elise held it up, examining it in her hand. It was three inches tall with a small sphere at the top and the body widening gradually towards the base. There were no apparent markings, but had a twisted piece of metal protruding from the bottom. Elise shook her head, not sure what to make of it.

After finishing copying the legend, Ethan joined the others to see what they had found. He smiled, looking at the piece as an idea came to him. "That looks like a key to me, and I think I know where it goes." He motioned for the others to join him, hurrying back to the globe. Summer and Elise joined him, looking intently at the globe's intricate design. He pointed to the north axis where a keyhole was located; the shape looking identical to that of the metal sticking out from the piece Elise held.

She excitedly stepped forward, examining the lock, and slid the key into place. She slowly twisted it counterclockwise, and a click sounded from within the globe, with a second click coming from behind them where Fletcher and Mei stood. Feeling something release under their feet, they quickly moved off the compass embedded in the floor.

Summer exhaled, realizing she'd been holding her breath, waiting for the tile work to open. "I'm not the only one that heard that, right?"

Fletcher shook his head. "No, something moved under us."

"Now what?" Mei asked, puzzled.

Elise shrugged. "Maybe the mechanism corroded over time?"

Ethan put both hands on the globe and rotated it. There was a good amount of resistance, but it didn't stop as it had before. A low rumble came from under the tile as the compass rotated with the globe. "Globes spin," he said, grinning, continuing to rotate it a full one hundred eighty degrees, matching its north point to the compass at the entry. The rotated compass sank into place with a loud thud, followed by a click behind a centered bookshelf that began to creek, slowly swinging open to reveal a hidden passage.

"I think we've found our way forward," Elise said, smiling.

"Hey!" yelled a guard from the lobby below. "What's going on up there!?" Not waiting for an answer, a group of guards ran up the stairs to investigate the noise, only to find one of their men unconscious and two people they didn't recognize.

"What do we have going on here?" the guard asked, raising his pulser rifle.

Ethan rushed forward, kicking the guard square in the chest. Not ready for the impact, the guard flailed, trying to grab hold of something to stabilize himself, pulling the trigger before crashing backward into another guard behind him. The pulser shot flew past Ethan's head, hitting stonework near the ceiling; bits of stone crumbled to the floor.

"Go!" Fletcher yelled, pointing to the passageway. "We'll hold them off!"

Ethan blocked an incoming punch to the face but didn't react in time to stop the blow to his stomach. He staggered backward a couple of paces, trying to regain his breath, but the guard moved forward, intending to strike him, when a flash of movement caused the guard to crumple backwards. Ethan looked up at Summer, holding a large candlestick.

He grinned, turning to see Fletcher get hit hard in the face, knocking him backwards. Ethan started for the attacker but paused, seeing Elise already throwing a flurry of punches and kicks at him. Ethan almost laughed at the sight when he heard running behind him. He turned to watch a guard smack Summer across the face with the stock of his rifle. She fell backwards to the ground, not moving.

Ethan charged, punching the guard as hard as he could in the gut. The guard dropped the rifle but reacted quickly, bringing his forearm up under Ethan's jaw. He stepped backwards, tasting blood, and rushed the guard again, knocking him backwards into the wall. He balled his fists up, striking the guard in the face repeatedly, but his opponent seemed unharmed, grabbing Ethan by the throat and hoisting him off the ground towards the railing overlooking the floor below.

Ethan gritted his teeth when the railing hit his legs, flipping him over. He reached out instinctively, grabbing one of the rungs, feeling as though he'd nearly dislocated his arm in the process. He reached up, grabbing another rung to pull himself up, only to find the guard looking over the railing at him with a dark smile. The guard put his boot on Ethan's fingers, applying pressure slowly. Ethan grunted with the pressure and pain gradually increasing. Relief came a moment later when the guard flipped over the railing, landing below with a sickening crack. He looked down, trying to see what happened to him when he heard Summer.

"He's still hanging on! Help me!" she said. Ethan fixed his grip on the railing as Fletcher came running up to help. It felt awkward as they pulled him up and over to safety, but was happy to be back on solid ground. He took a moment to catch his breath and looked around at the guards they had taken care of. He stood up after regaining some strength, seeing blood run down Summer's forehead from where she had been struck.

"Are you ok?" he asked.

She felt the small gash on her forehead and made a face. "I'll be alright."

A guard moved weakly, getting Ethan's attention. "Let's get out of here while we have a chance. I'm not ready for round two just yet."

"Agreed," Fletcher said. "Let's go."

"You guys get to the passage. I'll grab the key from the globe so they can't follow us," Ethan said, jogging over to it. Once everyone had safely made it in, he twisted the key back to starting and pulled it out. The compass on the floor and the globe rotated back to their original positions, slowly closing the bookshelf. He ran for the opening, jumping over the body of a guard, and barely made it before hearing the thud of the door shut tight behind him.

The Ruins

Dwyll stepped over the crumpled remains of the deceased, reaching the opposite end of a large table at the center of the room. Against the back wall stood a three-foot replica of the Lunarian Key carved from marble, with oil paintings hanging on either side of it. One displayed the light dome the Steradian Gate activates with onlookers standing back in shock. He walked to the other, which had been ripped; the top folded over, blocking the artwork. He lifted the torn flap, revealing artwork of a marble stand holding the five Steradian Keys in a circle.

"Interesting," he said, dropping the flap.

Talia took in the room, unnerved at the skeletons wearing moth eaten, dusty garb and still seated at the table as though waiting for a meeting to begin. A couple had slumped over their chairs or lay on the table with no signs of how they perished. A tattered tapestry hung in front of the windows with another set of remains laying under it. Shattered glass crunched underfoot as she approached the skeleton, kneeling and recognizing the marking on the sleeve of the tunic as nobility. "I think whatever happened with Mystell, it started here." A guard grabbed the hilt of a sword sticking out of a skeletal ribcage, pulling it free. "Let's show some respect, please."

"Oh, shut up. He doesn't care," the guard said, swinging the sword a couple times, getting a feel for it. "Hard to believe this was the best they had back then." He tossed it aside; the sword clanging against the stonework producing a jarring interruption to the quiet.

"Don't...do that again," Dwyll snapped.

"Sorry, sir," the guard said meekly.

"Anything interesting?" Alex asked, joining Talia.

She stood up, shaking her head. "I can't be sure, but I think these people might have been part of the Mystell government." She looked around the chaotic scene of the room. "From the looks of it, they all killed each other, but it's not clear why." She leaned closer to Alex and lowered her voice to a whisper. "I hope you see Dwyll for who he really is."

Alex sighed. "I'm starting too." From his peripheral vision, a blur caught his attention as it shot by the windows through the undergrowth outside. "Did you see that?"

She put her hand on Alex's arm. "Yeah..." The two backed away from the windows when a guard took notice of them.

"What are you two on about?"

"I think it's back," Alex said in a low voice.

The guard scoffed, walking towards the windows, flinging the tapestry out of his way. Centuries old dust flew everywhere, and he waved his hand to clear the air, looking across the overgrown ruins. There was no movement other than a small waterfall in the distance feeding a creek. "There's noth—" glass shattered and wood splintered as massive jaws smashed through the frame, snapping around the man's body. He screamed, yanked back through the window, breaking away more of the fragile structure. Talia shrieked, jumping backwards, knocking a chair against the table.

"It would seem we're not safe in this room," Dwyll said impassively. "I think we've looked here long enough. Let's go check what the others have found." Alex and Talia rushed for the door, happy to be rid of the death-filled room.

Alex didn't get more than a couple of steps down the hall when he saw a guard kneeling next to the body of another. "What happened?" he asked, wondering if the creature had gotten in.

Dwyll stepped forward, shoving Alex aside. He plodded down the hall past the statues. "Where's your captain?"

The guard stood up, pointing to Cooper, who lay slumped over against the staircase. "He didn't make it, sir. Bled out."

"You were supposed to secure this lobby."

"We just got back from checking the hall over there," he said, pointing. "Found them like this when we returned—neck broken. Don't even know what would have done this to him."

"Have you checked on the others upstairs?" Dwyll asked condescendingly.

"Not yet." The guard looked at the others. "You two, with me." They bolted up the stairs, readying their weapons. Dwyll followed, hearing the guard yell out. "Man down!"

Dwyll reached the top finding three guards laying across the floor. One of the guards stood, having checked on one of his fallen comrades. "He's breathing, sir. No sign of the others."

Dwyll looked across the loft. A banner hung lopsided near one of the broken windows swaying in the wind. "Where did they go?"

***

Fletcher was thankful to find two torches waiting for them on the other side of the bookshelf. He lit each of them with matches he'd brought, handing one to Elise to take the lead. She held her torch ahead while the group followed her through the hallway, veering to the right. Bugs scattered along the wall, escaping the light as they grew near. The hall eventually led them to a spiral stairwell made of stone, and they began their descent. The surrounding air became more stale the further down they went, with the torches flickering momentarily before flaring back up.

Summer had a shiver roll down her spine, ducking under a large spiderweb. "Of course, there had to be spiders." One arachnid was big enough to fit in her palm, crawling across the webbing quicker than she liked.

"We must be at least fifty feet down by now," Ethan said.

"I just hope Alex will be ok. I don't enjoy leaving him back there," Summer said.

"Talia will keep him safe," Fletcher said. "She's resourceful."

Mei shot Fletcher a look. "Talia's with you? Let me guess, she's not the archeologist she claims to be?"

"Nope. That's me," Elise said with a wave. "I gave her an idea of where to look and am happy to see my research was right. Did you see that incredible stone carving of the Guardian back at the entrance!? Absolutely amazing!"

Mei didn't care about some old art, angry they hadn't been up front. "Why the secrecy? Why not just come forward and help with the search? The fight back there didn't have to happen."

"We'd probably be dead by now if we'd have done that," Fletcher said. "Your precious Kriva Rasturna doesn't like anyone they can't control and will happily destroy anyone who doesn't fall in line with their beliefs."

Mei shook her head. "That's not true at all. You're being ignorant and don't know what you're talking about."

"Sure, whatever," Fletcher said flatly. "This argument isn't worth having given that you're a Grey. Do you even remember being injected with scopshade? It makes you easier to manipulate, forcing you into believing anything they tell you."

Elise's torch flared for a second, and daylight appeared around the corner. "Hey! We've reached the bottom. There's light up ahead." She ran forward, having to stop herself from falling into a wide chasm; gravel fell over the ledge from her skidding. She checked her surroundings, finding a natural stone bridge, and looked over the side, not able to make out where the bottom was. The light from her torch flickered against the walls and she looked up at stalactites hanging above. The sound of rushing water came from a continuation of the tunnel on the other side of the gap and daylight struck the cave wall where the tunnel curved ahead.

Summer made a face when the musty smell hit her. Covering the ground were small mounds of something greyish-white, which she expected was the source. "What's all over the ground?"

"Best guess is it's a fungus growing on top of bat guano," Elise said. "You're going to want to take it slow as we cross the bridge. It may be slick." She slowly tested her weight on the two-foot-wide stone bridge, thankful it was holding. Each step she tested the surface, ensuring her foot wouldn't slip, letting out a sigh of relief when she made it across. "One at a time. We don't want to chance a collapse."

Summer and Mei had crossed without issue, but Fletcher had slipped, barely regaining his balance. Ethan was the last to cross, looking down at the slide mark left by Fletcher halfway across the bridge. Not wanting to slip as well, he stepped to the side of it on a mound of guano and cringed, feeling it ooze out from under his shoe before realizing his foot went further down than he expected. He heard a click followed by a noise he couldn't quite place from off to his right. A blur came from the shadows swinging towards him.

He stepped back, his eyes widening as a spiked club the size of a man flew past him, only an inch from his face.

"Ethan! Behind you!" Summer yelled as another swung towards him from the left. He moved forward, hearing the rope holding the second club snap. It crashed into the stone bridge directly behind him, sending chunks of rock in every direction. He stepped back again, dodging the first club swinging back while the other crashed into the ground, deep in the chasm below.

"Run!" Elise yelled.

The bridge cracked at the point of impact, and a chunk broke off, falling into the darkness. Ethan took a couple of running steps, his foot slipping when he leapt as the club came back again, barely missing him as it swung by. Fletcher reached out, grabbing his arm just as he landed on the end of the bridge. More guano made sticking the landing impossible, and he slipped off the side, slamming hard into the rock face. With the wind knocked out of him, his grip around Fletcher's wrist was getting weaker.

"I got ya," Fletcher said, pulling him up. Once again on stable ground, he rolled to his side, catching his breath.

"Are you hurt!?" Summer asked. He shook his head, not yet able to speak. He pushed himself up, sitting for a moment.

"I don't remember you saying anything about traps, Elise," Fletcher said, looking into the chasm.

"How was I supposed to know any traps left behind would still work? It's literally been hundreds of years."

"I'm ok," Ethan said, getting to his feet. "Just wasn't expecting that." He looked back at the club, still swaying slightly. He reached back, feeling cool air, and found a hole where one of the club's spikes ripped his shirt. "That was closer than I thought."

Mei looked at the daylight coming from the bend in the tunnel ahead. "This way has to be nicer than in here with all the bat poop."

They followed her through the tunnel to an opening, cherishing the fresh air. When they emerged, they found themselves in a far larger cavern. Daylight peered through a massive aperture sixty feet above them, reflecting off an underground river cutting through the landscape before them. Vines and roots coiled downwards from above, with foliage lining the cavern walls. The ground was equally impressive, being covered with grass, underbrush, flowers, and trees nearly tall enough to touch the cavern ceiling. On the other side of the river, a small inlet had formed, overtaking a portion of an old stone church damaged from time. A flock of birds took off from the rooftop, flying towards the aperture and sunlight reflected off arched stained-glass windows at the church's front.

"I really wish I had my camera," Summer said. "This is beautiful."

"That's an understatement," Elise agreed. Ahead of her were thousands of purple flowers mixed in with grass, ferns, and other underbrush. She knelt next to a grouping of them, examining them, careful not to bother the bees collecting the pollen. "Purple daisies with a teal center disc. I don't think I've ever seen daisies like these before." She leaned forward, smelling one of them. "Smells like lavender."

Mei walked past her, looking at the flowers. "They are pretty. I don't think I've seen this many flowers in one place before. Of course, living in a city, there isn't as much nature around." Her foot caught the edge of a root sticking up from the ground and with a shrill yell, she fell forward into a bed of the flowers, a teal cloud of pollen flying up around her.

Elise laughed, but thought it best to still check on her. "Are you ok?"

Mei rolled to her back slowly and pushed herself up. "Yeah, I—" Her arm suddenly jerked out from under her, and she began to convulse. The others quickly surrounded her, wondering what was going on.

Summer knelt next to her. "Give her some space, guys. I've seen a few seizures before." Elise crouched next to Mei, putting a hand on her shoulder. "Don't hold her down," Summer said. "When she comes out of it, we'll need to turn her to her side and check to see if she's vomited." The convulsions slowed.

"Look at her eyes," Elise said, pointing. "Weren't they solid grey before? They're...turning purple."

Fletcher moved forward, examining her eyes. By the time she could blink, coming out of the seizure, the grey was almost completely gone; replaced by the natural purple color of someone from Lunaria. Mei blinked a couple more times and her breathing slowed. She sat up, looking around at the others. "What...what happened?"

"Are you feeling, ok?" Summer asked. "You took a spill and then went into a seizure."

Mei shook her head. "I've never had seizures before."

"I wonder..." Fletcher said to himself before addressing her. "Mei, what are feelings on the Kriva Rasturna?"

Rage flashed across her features. "Those bastards turned my parents on me! They had them hold me down and inject me with something! It was terrifying! How do you think I feel about them!?" Her anger suddenly turned into a stunned silence. "Did I...just say that out loud?"

Fletcher smiled. "Yeah, you did." He held out his hand to help her up.

Mei got to her feet, looking at the others. "I hate the Kriva Rasturna!" she said out loud, testing her ability to speak freely. The moment sunk in, she smiled and began to tear up. "I...can say what I'm thinking...and do what I want. I'm...I'm free of them!" She stopped short, remembering everything she had said and done in the name of the Kriva Rasturna. "Oh, my God. What have I done?" She crumbled back down to the ground, hugged her knees, and started to cry. "I helped them. The crap I preached and went along with, knowing it was wrong, but I couldn't control myself. I helped them to turn so many people against their families. I'm...I'm horrible."

Elise took a seat next to her, putting her arm around her. "It's going to take time to forgive yourself and heal now that you're you again." They looked out over the river for a moment. "You're not alone in this, though. People will know you weren't thinking right and I think you'll find most are forgiving. We're here for you if you need someone to talk to. We all are."

Mei reached over, hugging her. "Thank you." She looked up at Summer. "I'm sorry for trying to get Alex to join the Kriva Rasturna. I really am."

Summer helped her to her feet. "Like Elise said, you weren't yourself."

Mei gave her a quick hug. "Where did you learn about seizures?"

"My adoptive mom is a nurse and a couple times at church someone would have an episode and she always stepped in to help. I guess I picked up a few things."

Fletcher looked out over the cavern floor at the thousands of flowers. "Once we have the Lunarian Key, we'll need to figure out a way to get these back to Devon Falls and to the masses. They're obviously some kind of natural antidote to scopshade. We can finally get people back into their right minds."

Ethan looked over at the river where a bridge once allowing passage across lay in ruins. Large moss-covered stones from its remains breached the water, causing ripples as the current swept by. Just on the other side, he could see the remnants of a brick walkway protruding from the water, leading up to a set of solid looking doors at the front of the dilapidated building. "Getting across won't be easy," Ethan said, pointing. "I don't suppose someone brought a chainsaw to cut down one of these trees?"

Fletcher looked over at what remained of the bridge. "That makes things a bit more difficult." He took a knee, bringing his backpack down, and pulled a large coil of rope out. "No chainsaw, but we should be able to use this with an anchor point to help us across."

"Here," Ethan said, holding his hand out for the rope. "I'll get this tied around that tree. It should hold our weight if we slip into the water."

Fletcher nodded. "Why don't you take this back as well?" He pulled out the Delphinium Key, handing it to Ethan with the rope.

"Appreciate it." He put the key in his jacket pocket, still keeping it hidden from Mei, not yet ready to trust that information with her.

"Can you get across?" Fletcher asked.

Ethan looked at the stones in the water, and how fast the current moved. He tied the rope to a thick tree trunk, pulling hard to tighten it. "We'll see what happens."

"Be careful. We don't want to fish you out, but it would be funny." Summer grinned at the thought.

He let out a sarcastic laugh, tying the other end of the rope around his waist. He loosely held the coil in his hand, letting the rope easily slide out as he made his way to the riverbank. "The first jump is always the hardest, right?" he said under his breath. He could make out a stone just under the surface of the water covered in moss and it was close enough he wouldn't have to jump. He carefully stepped over to the submerged stone. The cold water enveloping his feet sent a shiver through his body.

Most of the rocks ahead appeared to be above water and not nearly as mossy as the one he was standing on. Using the mossy stone's edge as leverage, he leapt to the next stone, landing on a dry spot. He continued carefully, making quick work crossing the rest of the way, but nearly slid off the final submerged stone. Had it been any smaller, he wouldn't have regained his balance. He hopped over to the remains of a brick path, securing the rope around what was left of the bridge's support structure and swung the rope around a second post a couple of extra times, holding it tight. "You should be good to go! Just keep hold of the rope as you cross and watch out for the submerged stones. They're a little slick!"

The group crossed one at a time. Summer quickly crossed without issue, whereas Fletcher and Mei nearly fell in at different spots, having to regain their balance using the rope. When Elise began crossing, a thunderous explosion sounded, ripping her attention away. She lost her footing, slipping off the rock and submerged her legs into the frigid water. The ground reverberated and dust blew into the cavern from where they had entered. Elise dangled from the rope, clenching it tightly with both hands.

Ethan looked up, hearing a loud crack as a massive stalactite broke free from the shockwave. "Look out!" he yelled, seeing it hurtle towards them. No one had time to react as it smashed directly into the entrance of the ruins. Bits of rock, splintered wood, and brick flew in every direction. The group did their best to shield their faces from the debris and dust filled the air. After a minute, the thunderous noise subsided, and the dust settled. Coughing echoed in the cavern, with most in the group swatting the air to help clear it. Elise had managed to regain her footing, but was still hanging onto the rope at an awkward angle. She wiped the dust from her eyes with her sleeve and continued across.

"Is everyone...ok!?" Summer asked between coughs.

Fletcher looked at the others. "I think we're good. Just a few scratches."

"What happened?" Mei asked.

"I'd bet that's your old friends blowing a hole to come after us," Fletcher said. "I doubt we have much time." His jaw dropped when he looked over at what remained of the main doors. Almost nothing was intact; replaced by a pile of rubble. "We can't go in that way anymore. Need to find a new way in. Ethan, you mind checking over that way? I'll help Elise finish up."

"On it," he said, looking down the river and finding a small inlet where it touched the front wall of the ruins. "Want to join me, Summer?"

She finished brushing the dust off herself. "Sure. I just hope nothing else falls on us."

They followed the stretch of grass between the river and the front of the ruins for a bit before Ethan picked one of the flowers growing through the bricks, and handed it to her. "It's been a long few days. How are you holding up?"

She looked down at the flower, twirling it between her fingers. "I'll be better once we get my brother and get out of here. I don't want to think about what Dwyll will do to him if he suddenly snaps again."

"Yeah, he's not very stable, is he?" Ethan chuckled. She shot him a look disapproving the humor, making him clear his throat to play off the laugh. "I believe we're going to find what we're looking for in here. Then we'll grab your brother and get back to—" he stopped mid-sentence and sighed, slowing to stop.

"What? We need to stick to the plan. We all need to get home and away from them."

He looked into her eyes. "There won't be any escape from these guys. Their plans—they don't stop here. Eventually, they'll make their way to us and do the same thing they've done here. Then they'll be even more powerful."

"The resistance might win," she said, feeling her response was hollow.

"Let's say they win...in time. We find the combination to get home, we go grab your brother, get back home and hide out for a while. Can we live knowing we could have helped stop them but did nothing?" He shook his head. "I don't know about you, but I don't think I can. We might be the difference between one of our friends surviving or not until the Kriva Rasturna can be defeated. We've seen what they do to people. My parents always said I should do what's right, stand by my convictions, and have integrity. Right now, that means standing with Fletcher, Talia and the rest."

She looked down at the water, watching it flow. "You're right." She fixed her gaze back on him. "Honestly, I've been thinking the same thing. I hate we were dragged into this, but we have to help stop what's happening. We don't have a choice anymore."

"Not if we want any semblance of freedom, anyway. First things first. Let's find the Lunarian Key and get your brother back. Agreed?" He smiled at her.

She nodded, smiling back. "Agreed."

He looked over at the inlet, watching water flowing under the brick and into the building. As they neared, he crouched, looking below the surface. The ground had washed away, and part of the wall was missing, allowing the waters to flood a basement area. "I think we may have our way in. That hole should be big enough to fit through. I'm going to go check it out."

"That doesn't seem like a smart idea. This place is literally falling apart."

"We need a way in." He shrugged. "I'll be quick."

She hugged him. "I'm only giving you five minutes before I have Fletcher jump in after you." She let go of him and stepped back, not wanting to get wet.

Ethan jumped into the water, immediately regretting it as the cold bit at him from all sides. He ducked under the surface, grabbing at the bricks in the wall to help pull himself through the opening.

The basement was completely submerged, and from the looks of it, had been used for storage. Below him were the remnants of barrels sticking out from a mound of dirt and brick that had collapsed years before. At the opposite wall ahead of him, he could make out a stairway leading up to the left, most of the wooden boards looking severely degraded. To his right was sediment and new debris from the floor above, where the stalactite had crashed down.

He swam over to an opening in the floor above, created by the collision, and surfaced, finding the support beams still holding up a majority of the main floor. He grabbed the ledge, pulling himself out of the water and took a seat, testing the area to ensure it would hold his weight. The air was stale, and the sound of debris crumbling down occasionally caused an eerie echo. The only light in the room came from a couple of broken windows above, making it difficult to see much around him.

Muffled shouts came from outside, and he heard something hit the outer wall. "Crap," he said, dropping back into the water and swam to the exit. When he surfaced, he heard pulser shots being fired, hitting the outer wall of the ruins. He wiped the water from his face, finding Summer and Elise taking cover behind a thick tree trunk. Fletcher and Mei were near a boulder, with Fletcher returning fire towards Kriva Rasturna guards across the river.

Ethan got out of the water and ran towards Summer, diving as a pulser shot whizzed by his head, barely missing him. "I can't leave you two alone for five minutes."

Summer smacked him lightly on the shoulder. "This isn't funny." Elise fired a shot from her pulser rifle to keep the guards at bay.

"Enough!" Dwyll yelled. "Hold your fire!" The pulser shots ceased and Dwyll emerged from behind a tree holding a rifle at Alex's head. "Let's move this stalemate along, shall we?" A guard walked Talia out from behind another large tree, holding a rifle at her back. "Your ruse only lasted so long. We discovered your archeologist friend here isn't much of one and is working with you."

Ethan peered from behind the tree to get a better view, but before he could react, Summer was already walking out from behind the tree with her hands up.

"Let my brother go," she demanded. "We just want my brother." Ethan came out from behind the tree, joining her, still sopping wet.

Dwyll shook his head, letting out a single laugh. "Had a spill, did we? Where's the rest of your friends?" He looked back and forth along the other side of the riverbank, not seeing anyone move. "Yes," he raised his voice an octave, rolling his eyes. "This is the part where you drop your weapons and come out. I can kill them both right now if you'd rather?" Fletcher and Elise tossed their weapons aside and joined the others, with Mei joining as well.

"He was helping you," Mei said, gesturing towards Alex. "It doesn't matter though, does it? No one means anything to you unless they help you control others."

Dwyll peered from around Alex, raising an eyebrow. "How has the scopshade worn off?" he questioned under his breath.

"That's right!" Mei said angrily. "I'm myself again, you bastards! I know what you stand for."

"Interesting," Dwyll said. "No matter," he shrugged, taking aim at Mei.

"No!" Alex yelled, pushing the rifle away as Dwyll fired. The shot went wide, blowing a hole near the top of the ruins. Dwyll backhanded him, dropping him to the ground.

"Never get in my way, boy," Dwyll spat. Summer stepped forward, stopping short when Dwyll pointed the rifle at her brother. "I can still kill him. Any of you make a move for your weapons and I'll kill them both." He roughly picked Alex up, shoving him towards a guard. "If they try anything, you know what to do." The guard nodded, digging his rifle into Alex's back.

Dwyll jumped to the first stone, grabbing hold of the rope to cross. Deciding his next leap, he swiveled, hearing a growl behind him. A massive wolf-like creature stood, emerging from a grouping of large bushes near the water. Its elongated snout, stained with blood, displayed sharp teeth; its long, pointed ears lying flat against its head. It was as tall as an adult human covered in a short, faded blue fur. Spikes protruded in a single row along its spine, making the already intimidating animal even more so, its tail dragging lightly along the ground. Then it crouched, poised to attack.

The guards backed away when the creature snarled, still fixated on Dwyll. Then a second growl came from behind the guards. They quickly turned, seeing a second creature with dark grey fur. It stalked towards them, heading directly for Alex. Summer looked on horrified, knowing there was nothing she could do to help him.

"Shoot them, you fools!" Dwyll commanded. The guards immediately open fired just as the creature close to Dwyll lunged. He took a step back to evade, only to lose his footing and fall into the water. Ethan watched him come up for air while being swept downstream.

Talia grabbed Alex by the shoulder, pointing to the remains of the bridge, and shoved him towards it. "Go!" she yelled. The grey creature behind them grabbed a guard in its jaws, shaking him violently back and forth. The man screamed in agony as both she and Alex ran for the bridge; pulser shots sounding behind them. The second creature leapt at a nearby guard, slashing him across the chest and knocking him backwards into a tree hard.

Alex made a running jump to the first dry rock sticking out of the water, making quick work crossing the makeshift bridge, holding onto the rope with Talia close behind. Ethan and Fletcher waited at the other end of the crossing, ready to help them make the final leap.

"Hurry!" Fletcher yelled, watching the chaos unfold on the other side coupled with the sounds of screams, snarls, and pulser shots being fired. He jumped onto the closest stone, not willing to wait any longer. "Come on!" he encouraged. He grabbed Alex's arm, practically tossing the teenager over to Ethan. Talia jumped to him next, losing her footing, but Fletcher grabbed her arm, pulling her back up before looking across the way again. The grey creature appeared dead, laying on its side, while the remaining guards continued their assault on the other.

Ethan yelled to the others, pointing towards Summer and the inlet. "I found a way in. She knows where it is! Go!" Alex grabbed Mei's hand, running with her to where Summer was waving them over. Once everyone caught up, Ethan pointed to the hole in the wall just beneath the surface. "You'll have to hold your breath for maybe twenty seconds before you get to an opening in the main floor. You'll be able to surface there. It's off to the right. Go. Go!" he yelled, hearing another scream in the distance. He turned in time to see a guard getting mauled by the beast.

One by one, the group dove into the water, the sound catching the creature's attention. It quickly advanced, leaping nearly halfway across the river, landing on a partially submerged stone before effortlessly jumping to the opposite riverbank near where Elise had just dove in, cutting off Summer and Ethan from escape. The two slowly backed away, and the creature gave a guttural growl, getting in front of them, forcing them against the wall.

Its jaws came within inches of Summer's face. She clenched her eyes shut, turning her head away. Ethan inched towards her, putting his arm in between her and the beast, getting its attention. The creature stopped snarling and took a step back as though judging them. Then a pulser shot ricocheted off the wall nearby. The creature backed up, confused for a second, when another shot flew by, impacting the ruins. Its features became menacing again, and it turned seeing a wounded guard firing at it. It howled in rage, sprinting towards the bridge and leapt onto it.

Ethan grabbed Summer's arm. "Now's our chance. Go!"

Summer entered the waste high water hearing a scream from the other side of the river. She took a deep breath and ducked her head under. The cold bit at her, making her shiver and clench her fists. She forced her eyes open and swam forward into the darkness.

ONCE HIDDEN

As Summer swam through the dark, flooded basement, all sound was muted aside from the water swirling around her. Following Ethan's instruction, she found the opening in the floor just ahead, eventually surfacing. She reached up, grabbing the ledge, and felt someone grab her wrist, pulling her from the water. She got to her feet, immediately getting goosebumps from the cool air. Fletcher pointed over to Alex, who was shivering ahead of her, and she wrapped her arms around him. "I thought he was going to kill you."

"Glad...he didn't." The words coming out jittery.

"I thought Ethan was with you," Fletcher said.

She looked back into the water. "He was right behind me."

"We have definitive proof the Guardians are real," Elise said, wrapping her arms around herself for warmth. "Those creatures match the descriptions identically. They're no longer a myth." She looked over at Summer. "How did you guys get past it?"

"I thought it was going to kill us, but it stopped and went after a guard instead."

"There!" Mei said, pointing in the water, seeing movement.

Ethan surfaced, gasping for breath, and waded over to Fletcher, offering a hand up.

"What took you so long?" Summer asked.

"I was trying to see what happened to Dwyll. I couldn't find him, but saw that wolf-thing heading back to the bridge. That cut my search short."

"Can it get in here?" Elise asked, looking up at the windows.

Ethan stood; the drops of water dripping off him reverberated through the dark room when they hit the floor. "The hole seemed too small for something that size, but who knows?" He looked over, finding a torch mounted on the wall. "Hey Fletcher. You still have those matches on you?"

"Yeah," he said, pulling them out of his pocket, "but I'm not sure if they'll still work after that swim." He handed them to Ethan, who took a match out, striking it without success; the tip snapping off. He pulled out another, striking it while using his finger as support, watching it flicker a bit before coming to life. Not wanting to chance it going out on him, he quickly lit the torch, enveloping the room in a dim glow. He grabbed it from the wall, looking around to get a better sense of their surroundings.

A decorative couch across from them was missing two of its legs, tilting over. Next to it was a coffee table with a fireplace a few feet beyond and on the opposite wall, a second torch was waiting to be lit. He walked over, holding his torch up, lighting the other.

Elise's jaw dropped. "I think we're in the right place." Lunarian banners hung from the two-story ceiling, completely intact. The fireplace was intricate, embedded into the wall with a landscape painting hanging above it. The coffee table was covered in a thick layer of dust and cobwebs, with a matching wood trim to the broken couch and a set of standing chairs. A set of double doors was set opposite the fireplace near a collapsed portion of the wall where the stalactite had smashed through.

Ethan moved toward the double doors, seeing one of them ajar. Grabbing the handle, he pulled hard, but the doors were so heavy it wouldn't budge. "Here," he said, motioning for Elise to take the torch. Sticking his fingers through the thin opening, he used both hands to pry the door open. The hinges squealed in protest, making him stop once the door was open enough for them to fit through. He looked at the rusted hinges. "I think that's good enough. Don't want the door to snap off."

Elise stepped out into a large twenty-foot-wide entry way. To her right, only a pile of rubble and splintered wood remained of the massive double doors that once stood. Light came in from a hole, four stories up, leading down to where the stalactite had torn through the front of the building. Debris littered the floor and dust still hung in the air. From either wall, large, serrated blades attached to thick spears jutted out, most being snapped off. "It's a good thing we didn't come in that way. Looks like another trap was waiting for anyone that entered."

"That's a good sign the key might still be here," Ethan said.

To their left, the entryway extended another sixty feet, where two more decorative wooden doors waited with the Lunarian emblem etched into them. Tattered banners displaying the emblems of each dimension hung from the vaulted arched ceiling, and paintings lined the walls with an occasional bench or statue decorating the hall. The others had joined her, equally impressed by its size.

"At least this area is well lit," Talia said, holding her torch.

"Hey!" Alex said, heading towards one of the statues. "I recognize this guy from the mansion up top. In fact..." He looked from one to the next. "I think I've seen all of them before. Who were these guys?"

Elise started examining the first effigy. "I believe these are the founders of Mystell." She leaned in to get a closer look at an emblem on the statue's collar. "Yeah," she said, smiling, quickly moving to the next and examining the emblem on it as well. "The legend was true. These are the founders of all the Mystells."

"All the Mystells?" Summer asked. "As in plural?"

Elise nodded. "My grandfather discovered writings explaining there are sister cities in every dimension. I don't know if they were all called Mystell, but they're similar to what the Kriva Rasturna have been doing; building a home base in the same spot in each dimension. I believe each of these statues represents a founder of a Mystell from their dimension." She pointed from one statue to the next. "You see how they're each holding Steradian Keys? This one here, it's the Delphinium Key. The very same that Ethan has." She walked down the hall, inspecting each of the statues and the keys they held before stopping. "This one here—I think it's the Lunarian Key," she said, almost giddy. "The same one Daegal held as our last Catalyst. He must have walked down this very hall!"

"How old are these keys again?" Ethan asked.

Elise shook her head. "Older than this place. It's been suggested the keys are millennia old. No one seems to know where they came from, who made them, or even how they work. That's just a few of the mysteries that piqued my interest in them."

Fletcher was already pushing against a large door at the end of the hall. "They don't make 'em like this anymore. Need some help, Ethan." Ethan joined him, helping to push against the massive door, and it finally moved. The wall cracked near the hinge and the door fell forward, ripping bricks away from the once secure frame.

"Watch it!" Ethan yelled, seeing Fletcher fall forward, having been using all his strength to push against it. The door smashed down with a deafening boom, and the connecting wall crumbled, partially collapsing and causing dust to fly out into the hallway, making everyone have another coughing fit.

Talia rushed forward, having lost sight of him, waving dust from the air. "Fletcher!"

The echo from the collapse finally subsided, with chunks of crumbling brick still falling from the wall occasionally. From within the room, they could hear Fletcher cough and a moment later, they saw him hunched over, using his knee to prop himself up while he waved away the dust with his free hand.

"You good!?" Ethan asked.

"I'm good. Just...needed to take a moment after that."

With the dust settling, Elise and Talia moved into the room, holding up their torches. The others followed, and the sound of their footfalls echoed off the walls. Ethan looked up to find a chandelier hanging centered between two columns. "This place is massive." He squinted, trying to make out more detail, seeing that the chandelier looked to be attached to one of the columns. "Can I have one of the torches, please?" Talia handed hers over and he took it, holding it up higher to get a better look, but the light still didn't reach where he needed it to.

He noticed the pillar had a torch mounted to the side and went to light it. When he neared, he found the torch far more decorative than his, with a matching decorative trough made of marble spiraling around the pillar going up into the darkness. He lit the torch, and the fire came to life, spreading to the trough and racing up the spiral, eventually reaching the chandelier hanging above. The group watched, amazed as bowls on the chandelier lit sequentially, lighting the room enough that they could make out another set of pillars and chandelier a few feet ahead.

"I've got this one," Elise said.

Talia looked up at their new light source, amazed at its size. "Imagine having to refill those. What a pain."

The decorative chandelier had also caught Summer's attention as she walked further into the room, tripping over something, catching herself and hearing a noise she couldn't place. She looked back, annoyed that she hadn't been paying attention to where she was going, and let out a shriek, jumping back a step.

"What is it?" Alex asked before seeing the culprit. "Oh..." More skeletal remains lay on the ground where she had tripped with a sword sticking out of its chest. She had knocked it over, separating the skull from the body.

The room brightened as the second chandelier roared to life, revealing they were in a circular meeting chamber. The floor was raised where a curved table with five chairs was positioned along the far side perimeter facing the entrance; a large floor standing globe stood just to the right of it. On the opposite side of the circular parameter, closest to them, stood a slightly angled four-foot-tall marble circular sculpture.

Summer looked around the room at the various remains littering the floor. "I wish we knew why so many died here."

Fletcher shook his head. "Could have been anything. Most likely was a fight over ideology. Good and evil take on different faces and names through time, but it seems humanity is always fighting that same battle over and over."

"Like the fight against the Kriva Rasturna?" Summer pointed out.

"Exactly," Fletcher said, looking around the room. "Everyone spread out and look for the key. It has to be here somewhere."

Ethan approached the sculpture, admiring the design. It was a precise replica of one of the keys, only instead of the emblems for the dimensions, five indents were laid out in a semi-circle, each about a half inch deep with what looked like raised pressure switches. At the center of the sculpture were a row of seven symbols he recognized from the outer ring of his key. Each was imprinted on the edge of discs that looked to rotate on a dial like a combination lock. He tried to move one of them, but it didn't budge.

Looking closer at one of the indented areas, it looked to be the same size as his key. He quickly took off his vest, grabbing the key and placed it into one of the indents with the stone facing up. It fit almost perfectly, sliding into place, followed by a click from inside the sculpture. The symbols at the center rotated and bits of dirt and dust moved for the first time in centuries, sliding down the angled surface before the symbols came to a stop, displaying a combination he didn't recognize. He pulled the key away, hearing another click, and the symbols rotated again, stopping at their original positions. He placed the key into a different indent, watching as a new set of symbols appeared.

"Summer!" he said excitedly. "I think I may have found our way home!" She came running, meeting up with him just as the symbols reverted to their original placements again.

"This shows us the combination we need to get back?" she asked.

"Combinations anyway. The only problem we have now is this isn't telling me which combination goes to which dimension. My key fits into all the indents." He took out his journal and quickly sketched the sculpture's layout, drawing lines from where each indent was to label the different combinations produced. He placed his key into the first indent and started writing.

"Any luck?" Fletcher asked. "It was supposed to be in these ruins. Right?"

"Nothing yet," Elise said, "but it's here somewhere. At least...it must have been here at some point. We have to keep looking. Maybe there's a clue of where it might be." She hopped up on the raised platform next to the globe and looked at the chairs behind the massive desk. A slack-jawed skeleton lay back in the center chair with its remaining clothing hanging off the bones like tattered sheets. On the table in front of the figure was an open book with a quill laying next to it. "Maybe seating for Catalysts? Some kind of 'Steradian Gate Committee'?" she said to herself.

She looked over at Talia standing near the back wall, which had a large decorative fireplace embedded with bookshelves full of dusty manuscripts framing it. Then she looked back towards Ethan and Summer across the circular meeting area, getting a feel for the space, and trying to imagine what it was like to be seated here as a Catalyst so long ago. She blinked, cocking her head to the side in curiosity, almost making out words in the book beneath layers of dust. She leaned in closer, blowing off the top layer; a thick cloud flying into the air. She scanned the page and excitedly grabbed the book, flipping back a page. "Guys! I think I've found a written log about what happened here—what happened to Mystell!" She stayed standing, reading the details.

"Are you going to tell us what it says...or do we need to guess?" Talia asked.

Elise leaned against the desk, sitting on the edge. "Oh! Yeah. Yeah." She found the start of the entry and began to read aloud. "We succeeded. Succeeded in saving Lunaria from an unspeakable evil spreading like wildfire, but I fear the cost was too great. Mystell and its people have fallen victim to its destructive force; caused by a recurring nightmare that plays across history. The warning signs were there, as they always are, but were ignored until it was too late. The mind virus quickly spread, enjoying the destruction of families and the othering of friends."

Fletcher looked over from a bookshelf. "That's sounding all too familiar."

Elise nodded in agreement, continuing. "Lines were drawn and factions created. Dozens were slaughtered in battle before we found the true culprit. Myself and the other four Key Holders banished the source, however temporary, but the damage has been done with minds destroyed. Last night, those of us that remained made a pact to hide the keys in the hopes of averting this evil in the future. Before the other Key Holders left, we summoned the Guardians who were good enough to hear our plea and accept the immense responsibility of being the sentinels of Mystell."

"What source is he talking about?" Ethan asked.

"I'm not sure, but there's more in the log," Elise said, turning back to the book, continuing. "Alone, I hid the Lunarian Key, fearful the turned would enter these halls at any moment as they had previously, regardless of the main access to these hallowed grounds being destroyed. This morning, I gave my beloved Magge the way to access the key and sent her through the secret access to take it far away from here. I can only hope she made it out of Mystell unscathed. After she left, I activated all manner of traps to prevent the key being found and now here I am, alone, the only one with the knowledge that must never get out. To ensure the secret is kept, I've taken poison. One more death to save millions. Final farewell, Daegal."

"Then I must have found...Magge," Summer said. "Putting a name to a corpse is a bit...sobering."

Elise looked down at the ground, finding a small glass vial covered in dust, and back to the skeleton. "Daegal...the last true Catalyst of Lunaria. He sacrificed everything to save generations from evil." She stood up, placing the book back on the table. "We have to find the key and continue his work—keeping it away from evil. It should still be here somewhere. Keep looking."

Mei walked with Alex along the parameter looking for anything out of the ordinary. She looked over at him, not sure where to begin. "Hey, I uh...I wanted to say I'm sorry. A lot of the stuff I was saying was—"

"A bit crazy?" he said, finishing her sentence.

"Yeah...I'm back to being me, though. The flowers out there...they cured me. I can think like myself again."

He looked into her purple eyes, smiling. "Glad to hear it."

"So...are we still friends?"

"Of course. By the way, the purple suits you. You're actually pretty cute."

She blushed, looking away. "Let's go check over this way."

Ethan had finished jotting down the last of the five combinations, including the default combination for good measure. He looked up, seeing Elise near the globe. "Hey Elise. That globe looks identical to the one from the mansion. Have you checked it out yet?"

"I was thinking the same thing. Just started looking at it."

Ethan and Summer joined her. He crouched next to it, looking at the artwork. A couple dozen markings in different colors displayed across the map. He tried spinning the globe, finding that unlike the other, this one freely spun with no intervention needed. He stopped it, looking closely at the land masses, still not recognizing any of the continents but seeing markings. "Hey, these weren't on the other globe. Where are we at on here?"

Elise slowly spun the globe back around, pointing at are large continent just north of the equator. "We're here on the Eratoshen continent."

Ethan found five of the markings spread across the continent in an oval. "Do the locations of these markings mean anything to you?"

She shook her head. "No major cities. Maraldi wasn't even founded yet. This would have been all forest back then."

He studied the markings a moment before shrugging. "They're just different colors; purple, blue, green, grey and orange."

"Aren't those the colors that represent the different dimensions?" Summer asked.

Ethan flipped through the pages of his journal, eventually coming to a stop, pointing to one of the pages. "Here's the set of symbols we used to get here to Lunaria." He kept his finger on the page as a bookmark flipping back to where he had just copied down the different symbol combinations. He flipped back and forth a couple times, comparing combinations before looking back at the globe. The placement of the purple marking is in line with where the Lunarian combination was produced on the sculpture. They were a match. He scribbled an abbreviation for the name of each dimension next to its corresponding color on the map.

"Summer...I think we did it. We can go home." She wrapped her arms around him, squeezing him tightly, making him nearly drop the journal in surprise. He looked into her eyes and leaned in.

"Alright, you two. Enough of that," Alex said, walking by with Mei.

Summer shot him a look, unamused. "Leave it to you to kill the mood."

"Hey, gotta keep you on your toes, sis." He laughed, meeting up with Talia and Fletcher at the far wall, who were still searching the fireplace and surrounding bookshelves. "Anything interesting over here?"

Fletcher was becoming frustrated. "Was hoping to find some kind of hidden passage, but so far nothing." He pressed his hand against another brick. It was sturdy, with no sign it had ever moved. "Damn."

Talia pulled another book, hoping to trigger a mechanism. "I'm not doing much better over here. Just a lot of logs of which dimensions people went to and what they found. Travel looked very controlled. Then over here," she said, walking over to a charred bookshelf, "it looks like someone was trying to destroy these records for some reason." Books and scrolls were partially burned to ash. Skeletal remains leaned up against the shelf with a sword in their back, the bones looking burned as well. "It's possible whatever they were trying to destroy might have been the start of their civil war."

Mei joined Talia, pulling a book from the shelf, the bottom corner of the spine crumbling away. "Would there be anything in these books that could point us in the right direction?" She opened it and bits of the brittle pages snapped off, falling to her feet.

"It's possible, but there's so much damage here that the information we're looking for may have been destroyed during the conflict."

Fletcher looked over his shoulder, hearing Elise's excited squeals. "Let's go see what the others are up to. Maybe they're having better luck." As they walked up, Elise and Ethan were hunched over the globe, pointing at it. "What did you guys find?"

"We found the combination to get home," Summer said excitedly.

"We also just found other markings on this globe that have nothing to do with the combination sets," Elise said, clearly focused. "The meridian of this globe is metal instead of wood, like the one at the mansion. It's also wider, being a couple of inches thick, having holes lined up to the top so you can see the artwork beneath. When we spin it, different markings line up with the slots at different times and sometimes...the same slot will have different markings show up." She slowly spun the globe, trying to make sense of it. "There has to be something to it."

Ethan had his journal out, examining some of his earlier sketches. "I had seen these markings on the legend of the other globe but didn't see them anywhere else on it, so I sketched them just in case." He shrugged. "Maybe try spinning them in order from top to bottom?"

Elise took his advice, spinning the globe until the first marking Ethan had sketched lined up in the first slot. Nothing seemed to happen. She looked closer at the meridian, following it to the top and found another keyhole. "Ethan! Do you still have that key!?" she asked excitedly.

"Yeah, of course." He pulled it from his pocket, handing it to her.

"Thanks," she said, examining it. She placed the key in the top, turning it and heard a click come from within the globe. Everyone started looking around the room for any movement or anything different, but nothing seemed to happen. "Hmm...It must have done something." She stepped down from the platform to study the circular flooring.

"Did it unlock anything?" Summer asked.

"Nothing over here," Alex said, looking towards the fireplace.

"Last time, we had to spin the globe to turn that compass mechanism," Ethan said. He spun the globe again, only to find the sections between latitude lines now rotated independently of each other. "That's new." He looked down at his journal again, moving the top section until the marking that matched the first in his sketch lined up with the topmost hole in the meridian. He moved on to the rest of the markings, aligning them in the order he had copied. As the final marking lined up, a click sounded, followed by a low rumble coming from the sculpture where he had gotten the combinations.

Both he and Elise looked over, watching the top of the sculpture lift from the base. She jogged over to it and gasped. A once hidden compartment had risen out of the base of the sculpture and embedded within it was the Lunarian Steradian Key. The look on her face had the others running to join her. The dark purple stone embedded in the center of the key almost looked to be glowing. "It's beautiful," she said.

Talia wrapped her arms around Elise. "You found it! You found the key, Elise!"

"Congrats Elise!" Fletcher said, beaming. "I know how much this means to you."

"I...I found it. I found it!" She repeated the words with a look of pure joy. She slowly reached for the key, picking it up with reverence, admiring the craftsmanship as she turned it in her hand.

Ethan looked at where the key had been, finding another pressure switch still pushed in. Unlike the other switches, this one looked to be made of obsidian. A silver symbol he didn't recognize was etched at its center, and it looked as though it had stuck in place. He wondered if anything would happen if he got it unstuck and went to press it when a bright purple flash came from the Lunarian Key.

Elise's eyes rolled back, and she collapsed. Fletcher caught her, but the key hit the ground, echoing in the chamber. Everyone backed up, giving them space.

"What just happened?" Summer asked. "Is she ok?"

Fletcher laid her down and checked her breathing. "She's alive."

Talia knelt next to them. "We need answers, but she'd normally be the one to give them."

Ethan picked up the Lunarian Key. "I passed out when I first held the Delphinium Key." He compared the two keys in his hands. "Back at the archive, I read there are very few that can use these from each dimension—"

Talia interrupted, "A Catalyst. We know. Only two or three per dimension at a time."

"Wait," Fletcher said, "are you saying..."

"Yeah, I think Elise is a Catalyst for Lunaria and if I'm right, she'll come too in a few minutes. She probably didn't even know."

"Interesting," came a voice from behind them. The group turned to see Dwyll aiming a pulser rifle directly at them. "Congratulations on finding both the key and the Lunarian Catalyst. On behalf of Sovereign Rusak and the Kriva Rasturna, I thank you for your diligent work."

Ethan started towards him angrily. "You son of—"

"Ah!" Dwyll said, aiming the rifle at him, halting his approach. "My guards may be gone, but I still have my rifle. Don't think I won't use it." Ethan stepped back, glaring at him. "Good to see that you understand. Oh! And you have the Delphinium Key as well? That saves me time. Now...put both the keys on the ground next to your friend and back away." Ethan hesitated, slowly putting them on the ground as Fletcher picked up Elise and they stepped back with the rest of the group. "I didn't say you could take your friend," Dwyll snarled, lowering the rifle slightly. "Put her back down and leave her with the keys. I won't ask again."

"Elise isn't going anywhere with you," Talia yelled, nearly shaking with rage.

"That's not for you to decide, girl. I take what I want for the Kriva Rasturna and, frankly, I grow tired of you all." He raised the rifle again, taking aim.

"Stop it, Dwyll!" Mei said, stepping forward. "You got your damn keys, but you're not taking any of them. No one belongs to you or the Kriva Rasturna!"

He lowered the rifle, perplexed at the change in her. "No one belongs to..." he started. "You foolish girl. We gave you everything and you throw it away so easily." He sighed. "So be it." He took aim and fired, the shot hitting her in the torso. She flew backwards into Alex, knocking him over before tumbling across the floor, sliding to a stop behind him.

"Scatter!" Fletcher yelled.

Dwyll repeatedly fired at them, missing them by inches as they ran for cover. A sense of glee enveloped him, laughing as splintered wood and other debris flew into the air with each shot. He moved forward with a wicked grin, ready to kill anything that showed itself. "Such sport! Yes!" He stepped forward, continuing to fire at the desks and pillars his enemies hid behind. He paused, picking up the keys, and saw Talia's head peek around a pillar. He let off a couple shots, barely missing her.

Summer crouched behind a desk with Ethan, flinching whenever a pulser shot destroyed more of the desk they were behind. "We need to get out of here."

Ethan looked around, finding a sword sticking out of a skeleton near a pillar to his left. "Over there." He pointed to it. "Can you distract him? You know, without getting killed."

"Uh, maybe? What are you going to do?"

"Trust me." He looked around the desk at Dwyll, who turned, firing towards a pillar on the other side of the room. "Now or never, I guess." He got up, bolting from behind the desk.

Dwyll saw the movement from the corner of his eye, turning to fire on him. "Where do you think you're going!?"

Ethan sprinted as quickly as he could, hearing the shots whiz by him, slamming into the stone wall. He dove, feeling a shot go by just under his chest before he landed, rolling behind the pillar. He quickly backed up to it, orienting himself so Dwyll wouldn't be able to see him. "Sorry," he mouthed, pulling the sword out of the ribcage.

"Come on!" Dwyll yelled, "It'll only hurt for a moment. Better to have it over with than worry about what it'll feel like when I kill you with my sword."

"Stop this Dwyll! Let us go!" Alex pleaded.

"You're right, Alex. Fine," Dwyll said, trying to sound apologetic. "Come on out and we'll talk."

Alex started to put his head up when Talia grabbed his arm, pulling him down hard. Another pulser shot flew right where his head had been, causing more wooden shrapnel. "I need to go check on Mei!" Alex yelled.

"She's dead, kid," Dwyll said, turning to fire at the voice. "There's no rescuing her now, but don't worry. You'll be sharing her fate soon."

Summer had to get his attention, but her options were limited, deciding to talk. "She was with the Kriva Rasturna for years—one of you and you killed her."

"You turned her against us!" Dwyll sneered. "She wasn't one of us any longer! She was a traitor!" He continued to fire in the direction the voices came, not seeing Ethan coming up from the side until the last second. Dwyll turned, holding the rifle up, deflecting the sword coming down at him. Ethan's sword glanced off the barrel, sliding down until it struck Dwyll's hand. Dwyll yelled out, dropping his weapon and stepped backwards, watching the blood drip from his knuckles. "So, you want to play?" he said behind gritted teeth. "I will enjoy watching you squirm."

Dwyll unsheathed his sword, getting into a stance. He lunged forward, but Ethan managed to block; the sound of the swords striking reverberated throughout the room. Dwyll attacked again, bringing the blade down at Ethan's head, but he moved out of the way, feeling the breeze of the sword fly down, nearly striking the stone floor. He returned attack swinging his sword at Dwyll's side, but another clang greeted him as his attack was effortlessly blocked. Ethan moved to strike again, only to be met with a foot to the chest; Dwyll kicking him backwards forcefully. He stumbled a moment, regaining his footing.

"Pathetic," Dwyll mocked. "You're unpracticed and no match for me." He swung his blade at Ethan, swinging wide as Fletcher body checked him, knocking him to the ground.

"You didn't think he was alone, did you?" Fletcher said, reaching for Dwyll's sword. Quick to recover, Dwyll kicked him in the knee, making Fletcher drop, cradling his leg. Dwyll picked up his sword and lunged at Fletcher. Ethan intervened, grabbing his arm, but Dwyll wrenched his arm free, smashing Ethan in the face with the pommel of his sword's hilt, forcing him to stumble backwards, holding his face.

Talia sucker punched Dwyll when he turned to re-engage Fletcher, but it barely fazed him. He grabbed her by the throat and ran his blade through her abdomen. She screamed at the searing pain and he smiled. He pulled the sword out and kicked her to the floor with enough time to block Fletcher's incoming punch. Fletcher swung again, only to get deflected and the full force of Dwyll's elbow to the face a second later.

Summer brought the remnants of a chair leg down hard, hitting Dwyll in the shoulder. The wood cracked, making him grimace. Annoyed, he moved to swing his sword at her but stopped, seeing movement to his side. He stepped back just in time to see Ethan's blade swing down where his face would have been and kicked Ethan in the stomach, forcing him backwards again. "Almost isn't good enough, boy."

"I'm betting you're your biggest fan," Ethan said, swinging his blade again. Dwyll blocked with ease and lunged, anticipating how Ethan would block, letting the impact of the blades start his momentum for a turn. He swung his sword in a three-sixty. The move barely registering in Ethan's mind as he began bringing his sword up to block. Dwyll's blade came full force towards his shoulder and the two blades struck in a deafening clang. While the strike was successfully blocked, the force of the incoming blade was too much for the aged steel. Ethan's sword shattered, sending pieces of the blade across the floor, clattering into a nearby pillar.

Ethan looked at the broken weapon, not sure what to do next, when Dwyll grabbed him by the shirt, smashing the hilt of the sword into his face again, shoving him backwards into the sculpture that once held the Lunarian Key. He held his nose, trying to stop the blood from gushing.

Fletcher punched Dwyll in the side, enraging him as he blocked another incoming punch, kicking Fletcher in the stomach and immediately kneeing him in the face. He grabbed the back of Fletcher's head, kicking out his leg from under him, and forced his face into the stone flooring, hard. From the corner of his eye, he saw Summer swinging her makeshift club and blocked it with his sword. He brought his other hand up in a palm strike to her mid-section with enough force to lift her off the ground, sending her backwards, tumbling.

Ethan stood, seeing Alex tending to Talia. Fletcher was unconscious, and Summer was hurting, trying to get off the ground with the wind knocked out of her. Dwyll returned his attention to Ethan with a malevolent grin.

"It's the end, boy." Dwyll swung his sword down at him again.

Ethan instinctively held up what was left of his weapon, blocking the attack with the hand guard and the three inches of blade left. Dwyll yelled angrily, striking again and again, forcing Ethan down with each blow as he continued to block, but the remains of his sword held up. He was tired, and his hands ached with each strike from the reverberation and impact.

Dwyll smiled, seeing his enemy grow tired, unable to go any lower as the boy was now sitting against the sculpture. He moved forward, swinging his sword with all his strength at Ethan's neck, knowing he wouldn't have the strength to block him again. As the blade swung, Ethan rolled out of the way and it struck the sculpture, embedding right where the key lay hidden for centuries.

Near his blade's edge, an obsidian pressure switch caught Dwyll's attention as it came loose. Gas burst from the sculpture into his face. "What the hell—" he said, stumbling backwards. Ethan backed away quickly, pulling Fletcher with him to keep their distance.

Dwyll dropped his sword, coughing uncontrollably. The gas was quick to dissipate, but the damage had been done. His coughing worsened and bits of blood erupted with each convulsion. His throat dried, and his eyes watered just as a burning sensation on his hands and face intensified. He brought his hands up, seeing massive blisters forming, and dropped to his knee. The burning continued to worsen, and he tried to catch his breath, but his lungs felt on fire and his breathing became raspy. He shakily moved his hand up to touch his face, feeling the blistering had spread. His vision darkened, and a panic rose within him. He screamed, but no sound escaped. He fell to his side in agony and darkness and began vomiting blood.

"What just happened?" Ethan said, still backing away. "Stay back everyone!"

The others looked on, seeing Dwyll convulsing. "What the—" Fletcher said, having regained consciousness. Dwyll looked to be screaming, blood pooling under him as he became unrecognizable from the blistering. Fletcher sat up and watched the writhing figure in disgust while Dwyll slowly stopped moving; a shallow pool of fluids still forming around his body.

Decisions

More than an hour had passed since Dwyll's grizzly end and the fuel for the chandeliers was running out, dimming the lighting of the room. Fletcher had used his shirt to bandage Talia's wound, glad that Dwyll's attack caught her at the side, missing vital organs.

With the Steradian Keys being so close to the sculpture, everyone wanted to give more time before going anywhere near it. Eventually, Fletcher poured water over them, wanting to ensure whatever happened to Dwyll wouldn't happen to anyone picking them up, letting them dry before deeming them safe enough to handle.

Ethan had examined the pressure switch that released the gas, finding a symbol neither he nor any of the others recognized. Considering the symbol to be a warning, he sketched it in his journal, hoping to avoid any future traps. He got up, joining Summer, who was crouched next to Alex, mourning the loss of Mei. "How's he holding up?"

Alex looked up with watery eyes, wiping away the tears. Summer put her hand on his back. "It's going to take time," she said.

Talia sat next to Elise, who still lay unconscious, using Ethan's vest as a pillow. She began to move, stretching, and slowly opened her eyes, grimacing from a newfound headache. "Elise! Thank God," Talia said. The others quickly gathered around.

She sat up, holding her head. "Did I get hit with something?"

"Not exactly," Ethan said, "but you've missed out on quite a bit. For starters, the Lunarian Key was booby-trapped. If the pressure switch hadn't malfunctioned when you picked up the key, we'd look like Dwyll over there." He pointed, and she shuddered at the sight of the remains.

"How long was I out?"

"About an hour or so," Summer said.

Ethan looked up at the chandelier as the light flickered. "If you feel you're good to move, we should get out of here before we run out of light." He held out his hand and helped her up. Summer reached over, hugging her.

Fletcher was the last to join them, having been going over what was left of the manuscripts at the bookshelf. "Glad to see you're finally up. I've been ready to get out of here for a while."

"What happened to you?" Elise asked, pointing to Talia's wound.

Talia looked down, gingerly touching the bandage through the hole in her shirt. "Dwyll got a lucky strike in with his sword. Fletcher got me fixed me up."

"That looks bad. Are you ok?"

"It hurts like hell, but the bandage should hold me over till I can get some Hemofib back at base."

Elise tried to remember the chain of events before the darkness. "I've never passed out before."

Fletcher handed her the Lunarian Key. "Ethan has a theory on that."

Ethan grinned. "Theory is simple. I'm betting you're a Lunarian Catalyst. Back when I first came in contact with the Delphinium Key, I passed out too. Of course, it's just a working theory."

She looked down at her Steradian Key, smiling, touching the stone at the center. "I didn't dream that we found it?"

"Let's get out of here," Talia said. "You'll be able to see it better in the daylight."

"We need to give Mei a proper burial," Alex said. "We can't just leave her here."

"What?" Elise said, seeing Mei's body across the room. "What happened?!"

"Dwyll killed her..." Alex said, tearing up again. Summer wrapped her arms around him.

"At least she died as herself," Elise said. "Not some puppet of the Kriva Rasturna."

Talia looked over at Mei's body and back to Alex. "We still have some time."

Fletcher shook his head. "We don't have the equipment to dig a grave."

"We can think of something," Elise said.

"I'll carry her," Alex said, walking over to where she lay.

"How are we supposed to get out of here?" Summer asked. "We still have the Guardian to worry about. Right?"

Fletcher picked up the pulser rifle Dwyll had dropped, checking to see if it would work. "Yeah. Forgot about that. We'll have to take it out if it attacks us."

As they started for the doors, Ethan looked down at Dwyll's remains. Most of the flesh on his face and neck had been eaten away. His hands were nearly all bone as well. A pool of bodily fluids outlined the body. The sight, coupled with the smell, nearly made him lose his lunch. He moved on, happy to be rid of the man. Upon entering the hall, they were greeted with fresh air coming in through the half-destroyed roof. Debris, once blocking the main entry, had shifted, creating a large enough hole for them to pass.

Fletcher cautiously moved through the opening, looking for any sign of movement, but there was none. Peering out further, he caught sight of some bluish fur a few dozen feet away and took aim. He lowered the rifle, realizing the creature had already been killed; a gaping hole replaced its chest. Still wanting to be cautious, he slowly moved out into the open. The body of the second Guardian lay motionless near a couple of dead guards on the other side of the river. He scanned the area again and motioned the others to join him. "Both of the Guardians are dead. We should be good from here."

The group emerged from the debris. Summer was happy to breathe the fresh air after the stuffiness of the ruins and Dwyll's remains. She walked up to Ethan, taking his arm, and looked out over the thousands of flowers growing in front of them. The sound of the river flowing gave her a sense of calm. "It's really an amazing place, isn't it?"

"Yeah," he agreed, smiling.

Alex walked by them carrying Mei, placing her gently in the grass. "Where should we bury her? It can't be too close to the water. I don't want her getting flooded."

"Well," Talia said, "She showed us these flowers can reverse the effects of scopshade."

"That's right," Summer said. "I'm sure she'd approve of being laid to rest surrounded by the same flowers that cured her."

"The question remains, how do we cure everyone else?" Talia asked.

Ethan glanced toward the river. "I might have an idea. Where does the river lead?"

Fletcher shrugged. "If I had to guess, I'd say this probably feeds into the Bonitatis and Veris Rivers, being a main water supply for Maraldi leading all the way down to the farmlands. Might even go as far west as Mincer. No way to know for sure without a map."

"I think I know where you're going with this," Elise said enthusiastically. "The problem is we don't know how much of the pollen it takes to cure someone and no matter how many flowers we put in, the dose would be so diluted that it probably wouldn't be enough." She started picking flowers, putting them into her satchel. "I know of a couple resources we have in the resistance that have a background in chemistry and botany. They might be able to figure out a way to mass distribute the cure."

"There's thousands of flowers here," Ethan said. "Would it be worth our time to try putting a few hundred into the water?"

"I think it's worth a shot," Talia said, groaning when bending over to pick one. "I'm not going to be much help here, but millions of people need this antidote. All we can do is hope the pollen is potent enough."

Fletcher looked out over the field. "Everyone, start picking flowers and toss them into the river. If we can snap people out of Kriva Rasturna control, we may be able to boost recruitment. This could be a turning point for us."

Summer put an arm around Alex. "Let's go pick a spot for her. We can clear an area and have her buried so she can be at peace." The two of them walked down the way in search of an appropriate resting spot for their friend while the others started picking large handfuls of flowers. Over the next few minutes, it felt like they had tossed more than a thousand of the flowers into the river. Ethan looked around, seeing they had barely made a dent in the numbers growing in the cavern.

"That should do for now," Fletcher said. "We'll know in the next day or two if there was any effect. If not, hopefully our team in Devon Falls will be able to help, as Elise suggested."

"We found a spot for Mei and got it cleared," Alex said, joining them. "I'll need some help digging."

Ethan and Fletcher joined him, grabbing thin stones from the river to help. They dug in silence until making a hole deep enough to cover her and gently placed her body in its final resting spot. Once buried, Alex created a stack of stones at the head and placed a couple of flowers on top.

Summer gave him a hug. "It's a beautiful spot." Surrounded by the flowers, the grave overlooked the river.

The sky had started changing color, and the light faded. "I hate to say it," Fletcher said, "but it's time for us to move on. We'll make our way back up to the mansion and setup camp there for the night. We'll meet up with Armond and Kaylah in the morning. They were prepared to stick around."

They helped each other across the river, making it to the cavern entrance before darkness fully took hold. Fletcher relit the torches handing one to Summer, lighting up the chasm they had crossed earlier. They found the remaining spiked club had been cut down, presumably, by Dwyll when they came through. The stone bridge looked to be intact regardless of the chunk taken out by one of the spiked clubs. "If the Kriva Rasturna could cross, we'll be fine," Fletcher said, taking the lead.

New debris greeted them when they reached the bottom of the spiral staircase. The further they ascended, the more debris littered the stairwell as evidence of the explosives Dwyll and his men used to gain entry. The damage only got worse, nearing the top, with the walls and stairs scorched from the blast. Bits of singed parchment lay scattered amongst the rock and bits of marble. At the passage entrance, barely anything remained of the sliding bookshelf once concealing the entrance and the marble flooring was cracked with a layer of ash from the priceless documents burning up.

Fletcher shook his head. "I guess we're the last ones to discover the passage the way it was intended. I wouldn't have thought they'd have brought that much explosives."

"I can't believe they destroyed this archeological treasure," Elise said angrily.

Talia pointed to the shelves outside of the blast radius. "At least some of it can be salvaged. We'll have you lead a team later to learn more about this place."

Elise felt a little consoled by the prospect. "That'll give me something to look forward to, anyway."

"Let's see what we can do about getting a fire started," Fletcher said, looking around.

"We'll need someone to go out and get some firewood," Talia said.

"I'm not going out there alone," Alex blurted out. "What if there's another of those things?"

"Don't worry about it Alex, I'll handle it," Ethan said.

"I'll come with," Summer said. "You might need an extra pair of hands." She followed him down the stairs and helped unbar the doors. He pulled one of them open just enough for them to squeeze through and they exited into a courtyard finding moonlight beaming through openings of the canopy, sporadically illuminating parts of the city. The sounds of a creek with crickets and frogs in the distance were calming after the harrowing day. She took his hand, squeezing it. "What's on your mind?"

"Quite a bit." He led her towards a tree to their right hoping to find some dried wood. "I'm trying to figure out how we survived all of that while mentally going over our next steps."

"Next steps for what?"

"You're still ok joining up with Fletcher and Talia and fighting back against the Kriva Rasturna, right?"

She nodded. "I haven't changed my mind." She looked out over the city, watching fireflies hover over the shallow creek and then back at him. "I was..." she stopped and looked down at the ground, trying to figure out the best way to ask.

"It won't be easy, but I'm sure we'll stop them, if that's what you're worried about."

"Oh, uh... No, that's not it. I..." she sighed, deciding to just get it out in the open. "After I lost my parents in Alchemilla and then my adoptive father and even Alex over the last month, I...I'm just not wanting to lose anyone else. Especially you."

He took her hand. "I'm not going anywhere." He smiled, looked into her eyes, brushing a strand of her hair behind her ear, and leaned in, wrapping his arms around her. She squeezed him back, and he felt her smile as they kissed under the moonlight.

She couldn't stop smiling, keeping her arms around him and leaned her head on his shoulder. "I was hoping you'd make a move back when you got me out of those chains. Took you long enough."

"Hope it was worth the wait."

She stepped back, still smiling, "It was."

"Now, what were we out here for again?" he asked, having completely forgot.

"Firewood. We should probably get it before they worry."

"Yeah. Don't want Elise thinking a Guardian got us." He looked around, picking up dried sticks of varying sizes, and they headed back in. He leaned against the door, shutting it again, and looked over at the staircase, suddenly saddened. Ahead of them was Cooper's body, covered by a blanket. "He didn't make it."

"He was a good man." She looked over at Ethan. "He had said something about someone we needed to contact. The name started with an R, but I can't remember."

"I remember him saying your brother would know. Let's go ask him."

When they got to the top of the stairs, Fletcher greeted them. "Good timing. Go ahead and put the wood here on the compass. Should keep the fire away from anything else that can burn." Ethan dumped the sticks and started sorting them quickly.

Summer walked over to Alex. "Hey, who did you train with? Cooper was telling me and Ethan about someone we needed to talk to that worked in the resistance."

"Remage is the only one that trained me. He even gave me these." He pointed to his sai proudly.

"That's it. Remage." She looked at the weapons and raised her eyebrow. "Not sure mom would approve of you having those."

"We've been working with Remage for about a year now," Talia said. "He's been giving us intel on what Rusak and the Czars have been pushing and whatever plans they let him in on."

"Why didn't he tell me he was working with you?" Alex asked.

"He probably couldn't chance you telling Dwyll," Fletcher said.

"He was one of the only people making sense in Heraldrin," Alex said before shaking his head in realization. "We need to get him out of there. They would kill him if they knew."

"Hate to say it, but we need him where he is for now," Fletcher said. "Of course, that's not my call."

"Besides, I think it's about time we got home," Ethan said, looking at Alex and then Summer.

Fletcher smirked. "I almost forgot you're not from here." He reached over, patting Ethan on the shoulder. "You did more than you said you would. I don't know if you'll ever understand how big of a help the two of you were."

Elise hugged Summer with Talia, grabbing the two of them from the side for a group hug. They all started to tear up; Talia partially from her wound.

"This isn't goodbye," Ethan said. "Summer and I talked it over."

"What exactly are you saying?" Talia asked.

"We're in this fight with you," Summer said.

Elise squealed with excitement, hugging her even tighter. Fletcher had an enormous grin and let out a laugh, smacking Ethan on the shoulder again. Ethan chuckled, rubbing the impacted area. "Welcome to the resistance!" Fletcher said excitedly. "What made you decide to stay? You could be done with all this."

Ethan looked at each of them. "My dad told me you when you see something wrong, you can either try to avoid conflict and probably still be affected by it eventually, or you can stand up for what you believe in, face the danger, and hopefully make the world better. We all know they won't stop here in Lunaria. Sure, we could leave you guys to fend for yourselves, but leaving a friend in that kind of situation isn't an option. Not for me."

"Good man," Fletcher said.

"Plus, I was going to be devastated having to say goodbye to you guys," Summer said.

"You're officially part of the team now," Talia said, smiling. "Hopefully, we'll have some good news for you by the time you return."

Elise pulled a handful of flowers from her satchel, handing them to Summer. "Take these with you. Maybe you know someone that can research the pollen quicker than we can."

She nodded. "I'll do some research when I get back."

Ethan looked over the railing at the entryway. "Maybe we should be on the first floor while doing this. I don't like the idea of falling on my face when we get back."

"I'm not carrying either of you home if you break a leg," Alex said, feeling his mood improve. He headed down the stairs. Ethan shook hands with Fletcher while Summer gave a final hug goodbye before following Alex down. They walked to the center of the embedded compass in the tile at the entrance. Fletcher, Talia, and Elise leaned against the railing above to see their friends off.

Ethan knelt, pulling out his journal, and flipped to the page with the sketched combinations. "Can you hold this for me, please?" He handed the journal to Summer, and she held it up for him. He looked between Summer and Alex, seeing their looks of apprehension. "This should be enough space. You guys ready?" They nodded, and he looked up at the balcony at his friends; Elise waving dramatically, making Talia and Fletcher laugh.

Ethan looked down at the key, twisting the outer circle back and forth, stopping at each of the seven glyphs listed. A chime sounded with the Delphinium emblem lighting up at the northern point of the compass on his key. He pressed his thumb to the centered stone. The etched glass underneath lit up and a second chime sounded as a glowing blue dot appeared in front of them, drawing a circle around them that pulsed as an illuminated emblem appeared on the floor ahead of them. The glow continued to intensify until light erupted from the circle, creating a transparent dome of light around them. Wind swirled, forming a funnel that pressed against the dome, spiraling ever faster until it stretched out towards them. Ethan reached out and took Summer's hand. He saw her smile before they were lifted off the ground and a flash of light enveloped them.

***

Aiza slammed her hand on the table. "This is so frustrating! I've gone over everything! It should work! We had it working." She wiped away a tear.

Ellena sat next to her. "You were able to do what no one else has ever done. You'll get it working again. There has to be a reason we haven't been able to reach him."

"That's what I'm worried about, mom. What if it is working? What if something happened to him? What if he's dead?"

Mason sat up from across from her. "We can't start thinking like that. He's a smart kid. He can get through this."

Lilly sighed. "I don't know how many hundreds of searches I've combed through looking for anything that has to do with symbols and dimensions. Nothing has been matching."

Aiza shook her head. "I researched multiple archeological studies around ancient Phoenician, and nothing there either." She looked at the table, tearing up again. "He was counting on us, and we let him down."

"Enough!" Mason said. "You need to stop putting yourselves down. I'm proud of both of you for everything you've done. You know this isn't over yet." He sighed, looking up at the clock. It was nearing ten in the evening. "It's getting late. Let's...Let's stop for the night."

Marie walked in from the living room, leaning up against the wall. "Your father's right. We can't give up. Summer and Alex are all I have left after my husband passed away. They're my kids, just like Ethan is your brother. You can't give up on family."

"We're not giving up," Aiza said angrily. "It's just—"

"We understand," Ellena said. "Your father's right on needing to call it a night, though."

"We'll go back to your lab in the morning, Aiza," Mason said. "The only thing we can do is continue trying to reach out to him and hope we're able to make contact again."

Ellena took a deep breath, pushing her chair away from the table and headed into the living room. She grabbed her crochet project from the couch and sat to take her mind off the situation.

Marie sat next to her. "I wanted to thank you again for inviting me over the last few days and keeping me in the loop. It would have been so hard to be alone during all of this, not having any idea what was going on."

"Of course. I'm just glad Summer left your phone number for us." A knock came from the door. "Who would that be at this hour?" She put her project down and headed to the door, turning on the porch light. She opened it and let out an uncontrolled shriek of happiness.

Mason came running from the kitchen. "What's—" He stopped short, seeing Ellena hugging Ethan. Summer stepped forward, wrapping her arms around Marie in a teary reunion while a boy Mason didn't recognize stood at the doorway looking awkward.

Both Aiza and Lilly walked into the room, seeing what caused the commotion, and rushed forward, nearly knocking Ethan and their mom over, hugging them tightly.

Epilogue

It had been an odd few days for Cassie. Her week had started out normal enough, going about her daily chores at her apartment in Devon Falls when she had collapsed in a fit after taking a break and getting some water. She hadn't been the first either, with others around town having similar reactions after consuming water from the fresh spring.

When she came around, her head felt clear for the first time in years. She recalled being in an angry haze, going around with a group of girls bullying others, which made her feel sick to her stomach. She got herself up from the floor and headed to the bathroom sink, splashing water on her face, only to find her eyes had returned to their original purple color when she looked up at the mirror.

That afternoon, the girls she used to hang around came to her apartment wondering why she hadn't joined them for their rounds at the market. They had barely gotten the question out when they noticed her eyes, calling her all sorts of horrendous insults, and angrily walked off, leaving her behind. She closed her door, happy to no longer be a part of such a toxic group. Still, after what they'd just called her and knowing how they acted, she didn't feel comfortable that they knew where she lived, feeling as though they would come after her.

The next day, she'd gotten a letter in the mail informing her of her father's passing in Brexel. She hadn't seen him in years, but knowing she'd never gotten the chance to apologize for the terrible things she'd called him tore at her. Regardless of their argument, he had left her his home and his shop in the will. She took it as a sign, packing up her things, and moved.

She'd been in Brexel now for the last couple days, getting accustomed to her new surroundings. She'd met up with one of her father's friends who'd provided her the key to his home and shop. He gave her a brief idea of what occurred, saying he'd looked after things in the following days, cleaning everything as best he could. She thanked him before heading to her new home and started rummaging through her father's old belongings. It was a nice enough place, but older and simpler than she was used to.

During her search of the home, she came across a box of letters addressed to her Devon Falls apartment tucked behind some books. She looked through the box, finding he had written to her every week since their argument. A wave of guilt washed over her, and she didn't blame him for never sending them. Given her previous state, she'd have probably ignored them or even thrown them away. Now, though, she considered them a treasure trove, allowing her to know what her father had been up to the last couple of years.

She grabbed the box of letters, deciding to take them with her while she checked out the shop. It was a short walk, and she tried introducing herself to everyone she met along the way, showing herself to be friendly. Most were happy to see her, giving their condolences and sharing a time when her father made them laugh or did something kind for them. A couple of people along the way had ignored her introduction, trying to preach about the good the Kriva Rasturna does. She wasn't surprised to see their eyes were grey, and it saddened her their reach stretched this far from the city. She kept her opinions on the subject to herself, not wanting to start an upset.

When she had finally reached the shop, she unlocked the door, entered, and heard the chime of a bell. The air was musty with the shop having been closed for so long, but everything looked to be in its place. Heading further in, she passed the clothing racks and took everything in. She moved to the back room, finding boxes piled up, a heavy smell of cleaner hitting her. A reddish blotch stained the wood floor, and she left the room, taking a seat behind the counter. She started to tear up, knowing that was where her father had been brutally murdered.

She opened the box of letters and began to read them, needing to take her mind off the matter and focus on his life instead. The letters didn't disappoint. She discovered he had joined up the resistance, fighting against the Kriva Rasturna in the hopes of one day being able to cure her of something called scopshade. She guessed that was what made her angry all the time, but had never heard the term before.

Over the next hour, she continued going over the letters, coming across one dated only a week prior. It outlined how he met two people from Delphinium and how he had saved them from a czar before they headed off to meet up with the Kinsford resistance cell.

The bell chimed, and someone entered the shop, startling her. A man in a brown trench coat walked in, having short grey hair and a five o'clock shadow. "Can I help you?"

The man walked up to the counter, appearing to be in a cheerful mood. "Hello young lady. I was hoping to find TerRan. Glad to see he finally took my advice and got himself some help with the shop. Do you know where he is?"

She looked down at the counter. "I'm his daughter, Cassie. I'm afraid he passed away last week."

"Oh no. What happened? I've been out of town for a while."

"Murdered."

"Oh...I'm sorry to hear that. Is there anything I can do?"

"No. I'm still wrapping my head around everything, having just moved here from Devon Falls. I don't even know how to run a shop."

"I've been hearing interesting things coming from there. I got word just the other day the resistance had some help from people coming from Delphinium of all places. By chance, did your father mention anything about them to you before he passed?"

"I don't want any trouble," she said.

He leaned in, opening his eyes wider. "Go ahead and check. I'm not a Grey."

She squinted in the bad lighting, making out his blue eyes past his bushy eyebrows before feeling comfortable enough. "Look, I don't know you..."

"I'm not going to hurt you. I've been a friend of your father's for years now. See over there," he said, pointing to a photo hanging on the wall. "That's the two of us at the town festival last year."

She looked over, picking up the frame from the wall, and studied it a moment, looking back at the man. "You really knew him, huh?" The man nodded, and she let out a sigh. "I was just reading a letter he had written me. He helped a couple of people from Delphinium get to Kinsford. Even saved them from a czar."

"He was a good man," he said, looking at the trinkets on a shelf behind her. "Excuse me, but can I see one of the items from the shelf behind you? It's a black, flat object that looks to be made of glass."

"I'm not open to sell anything just yet."

"I'll make it worth your time," he said, putting a bag of coin on the counter. "It'd mean a lot to me just to look at it for a minute."

She shrugged, turning to look at the trinkets. "It's smaller than I expected," she said, picking it up and studying it. She handed it over. "I've never seen anything like that before. Not even over in Devon Falls. Any idea what it is?"

"I have a good idea," he said, finding the power button on the side and holding it down. A logo popped up on the phone's screen while it loaded, displaying a low battery warning. A home screen finally came up with the photo of a dog set as the wallpaper. He smiled, recognizing the animal, and navigated to the gallery.

"How do you know how to use that thing?" she asked. "Who are you?"

He pulled up the most recent photo, seeing a selfie of a boy and girl with Brexel behind them in the distance. "Excuse my manners. My name's Jerran Burke." He flipped the phone around, showing her the photo. "And this is my nephew, Ethan."

Thanks for reading.

Please consider leaving an honest
review on Amazon, Goodreads,
and/or your favorite site.

Check https://www.thesteradiangate.com
to stay up to date on The Steradian Gate series.

Ethan and Summer's adventure has only just begun!

Abandoned settlements, submerged
laboratories, and long sunken shipwrecks
await in book 2, Contagion.

Acknowledgements

I first want to thank my wife and children for being patient with me during the process of creating The Steradian Gate. I am a truly lucky man to have met such an incredible woman as my wife. While they already know, they are the inspiration of the Burke family within the series; each character reflecting parts or most of their real-life counterpart's personalities.

I next want to thank extended family and friends who, without them, I may have never become an author at all. It's interesting to look back on one's life, reflecting on how large an impact someone can have on you and the course you took to get where you're at.

Then there are those that may not know they were an inspiration at all. They are the writers and creators of the past and present that ignited my imagination and sense of adventure. They are also the point of the spear in creating new content and culture—culture that's badly needing to be brought back for the future of humanity to prosper.

Last but not least, I want to thank you for reading this novel. I genuinely enjoyed writing it and I hope you have enjoyed reading it and will continue to find enjoyment in the series as each new book is released.

About the Author

Nathaniel Blevens is a husband and father that writes gripping and suspenseful science fiction adventure based on family, friendship, and freedom. He has long had a sense of adventure stemming from growing up in the Pacific Northwest. Now he strives to bring that sense of adventure into his books while teaching life lessons to the next generation.

Outside of writing, he spends most of his time with his family, going on hikes and introducing his kids to various pop culture from the 80s and 90s. He cracks dad jokes regularly, enjoying his family's eye rolls and sighs.

He's always had a creative side, having a project in the works continuously. From creating intricate displays, to board games, retro video game art and now storytelling, he's always creating something.